Kemitt Mirrors

Feat. Visions "Got a Story to Tell"

Written By: Derrik "Twin" Strother

The Sub title Feat. Visions "Got A Story to Tell"

ISBN: 978-1-09834-509-9 (softcover)
ISBN: 978-1-09834-510-5 (eBook)

Kemitt Mirrors vol.1

Feat. Visions "Got a Story to Tell"

CONTENTS

Kemitt Mirrors. Intro / chapter 1

Buck shots cut through the dark fog night, followed by loud chattering of men ("over here, I see'em). While three shadowy figures run through the heavily wooded area and high grass only spots of moonlight threw the branches illuminates a shady path to follow.

(Boom, Boom) "Surrender or die". The loud chatter is starting to get closer; the words are getting clearer the whistles of bullets are now knocking bark and moss off the giant trees.

Rain begins to come down with no warning making the soil like quicksand slowing the three asclients down.

Up ahead there looks to be an shallow pond they must get across. They break for it (more bullets fly pass), they make to the edge of the pond when "Aww" one is shot (in the leg) they pull'em towards the water, one of the men giving chase has caught up , catches the wounded person leg as they're getting help from the other two into the pond, they have an quick struggle (Pow) A gunshot goes off, the other men catch up with their partner to see his pistol by his side an hatchet cut in his wrist and a dagger knife in his shoulder, but no sign of the three figures.

1

Living life: The introduction of Alonzo & Terry

Present time: (2022) (Goodie Mob, song: Black Ice playing in the background)

Alarm goes off (err err err err). Alonzo slams his hand on the clock, "Damn" runs to the bathroom, takes a quick shower hurries and gets dressed. He maneuvers his way around empty liquor bottles full ashtrays and other trash from partying the night before. Running out the front door, Terry's already waiting at the car smoking a joint.

Terry: "Well it about damn time" he says jokingly in his best red neck country voice.

Alonzo: "Whatever man Aey , don't smoke that shit in the car!"

Terry: "What?"

Alonzo: "Not today bra" he says as he gets into the car, looks at Terry taking hard pulls from the joint..."Hurry up man!"

Terry: "Oh now you want to rush me after 20mins of yo ass being late." (flicks the joint before getting into the car)

Alonzo: "Fool you kept me up all night, inviting everybody and they mamma over…smoked ALL the weed up... I don't know how you do it."

Terry: "NO...I don't know how youuu do it" Starts laughing hard doing a funny version of the Harlem shake dance.

Alonzo: (Driving looking at Terry funny) "What the hell wrong wit yo body functions!"

Terry : (Dancing in the passenger seat) "You ever see a Mississippi nigga do the Harlem shake "(Flash back of last night party Alonzo singing special delivery song by G-dep on the karaoke machine drunk as hell) Terry start to watch it on his phone.

Terry : "Im sending this to auntie right now!"

Alonzo tries to smack the phone out Terry hands but can't get it, "Well send the part you was doing the butterfly to Whoop There It Is then muthafuka."

Terry: “Where you get the jersey and the sweat bands from doe! “

Alonzo pulls into the neighborhood gas station where a lot of the hustlers’ hangout at.

Alonzo: “Ighit bra you got 10 on the tank.” (Alonzo holds his hand out)

Terry: “I ain’t even got it my boy, (pulls out a big stack of money) I got 5 on the tank and two Arizona’s.”

Alonzo: “Nigga” looks at Terry crazy.

Terry: “What, this my half of the re-up, you always talkin bout movin up , lets move up nigga...consistancy! “

Alonzo: Snatches the money as he gets out the car “Yeah you real consistant... an consistent disappointment.”

Terry: “Yo I aint gone take your verbal abuse!”

Alonzo: “Whatever maine just put 15 in the tank” as he walks into the gas station.

Terry: “Fool I aint the butler” as he steps out to pump the gas.

Alonzo walks to the back of the store grabbed two drinks, then goes to the cashier.

Pop the Cashier : “Lonzo what’s up buddy..you still in school” He saids with a smile.

Alonzo: “Yeah man you ask me damn near everyday shit aint change that quick!”

Pop the Cashier: “It’s been almost 10 years right; you must be studying Bull-shit-tography!”

Alonzo: “I’m studying to be Muhammed-Jesus, remind me to put my sandal up yo ass after spring break muthafuka , can I get my change!”

Pop the cashier : “I know business accounting right.”

Alonzo: “That’s right.”

Pop Cashier : “When you finish you can help me expand my business..Aey!”

Alonzo:” Hey maybe” (he gets his bag off the counter) “Later bro!”

While Alonzo was in the store, Terry was outside pumping the gas when someone sneaks up behind him. “Yeah nigga you know what time it is, run dem slim jim.”

Terry: “Fool if you don’t get you stubby as finger off my hip nigga.”

Will : “See nigga you slippin out here!”

Terry: "Fool I seen you pull up in dat fine thang (walks up to the new Lincoln Continitel with 24inch Savini wheels)

Alonzo: Walking up to the car sees Terry and Will talking, "look at the muthfukin wheels" (greets Will with an handshake) "You just pullin tricks out the hat on niggas huh, when you get this?"

Will: "I had it for couple days just got it out the shop, had to get it ready for the summa, ya dig...Oh yeah (hands Alonzo$100 dollars) here what I owe you from last night… boy Lonzo you a fool where you get all those sweat bands from(Terry laughin "I told you") All these years I never saw you touch a ball!"

Alonzo: "So we just gone ignore the fact THIS NIGGA HERE was doin the butterfly & the tootsie roll last night!"

Will: "But he had the girls doing it to, you was up there lookin like R.Kelley done had a seizure."

(Terry imitating Alonzo's Harlem shake "fiesta fiesta")

Alonzo: "Bra fuck yawl and dat karaoke machine!"

Terry : "Nigga you bought it!" (Laughin)

Alonzo: "Whatevea man we gotta roll, we on for later on bra."

Will: "Fa show hit me in a couple hours!"

Alonzo, Terry jump in the car and heads out.

Kemitt Mirrors

[If it ain't one thing it's another]

Terry: "Aey man as soon school over, I'm ready to get our business started."

Alonzo: "Yea I can hear yo mamma now... y'all went to school to sell weed, yall niggas could of stayed in Atlanta for all that foolishness.

Terry: "Yea but are strains go be the shit... send a nigga to the moon!"

Alonzo: "Man, are mission is to help naturally heal people."

Terry: "Yeah dat too" they both laugh.

Alonzo: (phone vibrating) "Amen to dat "... (checks his phone message)

Alonzo plays the voice message on loudspeaker. "Hi, this message is for Alonzo Stuart, Pennsylvania Community TECH COLLEGE IS OWED 11,970 DOLLARS BEFORE NEXT Semester or you will have to forfeit your graduation credits until payment of funds is credited to your account with us. Please come to the school administration office asap Thank you have a bless day."

Alonzo: "Ain't this a bitch!!"

Terry: "12,000 goddamn fool how you owe dat much?"

Alonzo: "I didn't have a big cousin to tell me don't use student loans to live on ...but 11000?"

Terry: "Nine hundred and Seventy... just round dat to 12."

Alonzo: "Man this ain't funny."

Terry: (Mumbling under his breath) "Well shit nigga you been here since I graduated high school, I mean dat about right."

Alonzo: "Man get out!"

Terry: "What?"

Alonzo: "Gone get I gotta go."

Terry: "Go where ain't you going to the office?"

Alonzo: "I was for the 4200, ain't got 11,000 I gotta go see if I can get an advance on my check at the job."

Terry: "If you need some money, I got you."

Alonzo: "Naw I got it man, gone get."

Terry: "You can't kick me out the car I'm already getting out!" (He gets out arguing) "Well you gone pick me up right."

Alonzo: "I'll be back at 3oclock." (Alonzo says as he starts to back out the parking space & pulls off pilling rubber)

Terry: "I'm out at 2 (he shouts back)..Man he trippin. "

(Watching Alonzo race through the parking lot running the security guard golf cart off into the grass hitting the water fountain) "This nigga crazy" then ducts off into the building.

[Terry goes to class]

Terry enters his classroom and heads right to his seat, when he hears a loud whisper "Yo T , T wudup" . Terry acknowledge it's his friend Jay calling him. Jay slides into the seat next to Terry.

Terry: "Wudup Jay what's happin wit cha."

Jay: "Aey remember the professor we had for a couple weeks last semester."

Terry: "Yeah..I remember she talked about plants is life and how to make cures and thangs that shit was cold."

Jay: "Yeah well I saw her in the hallway earlier. "

Terry : "Oh she back huh."

Jay: "I hope so, she was on some uplifting the hood shit fo real tho" they both laugh in agreement.

Terry : "Hell yeah me and Lonzo peep dat shit too."

Jay: "Where dat fool at?"

Terry: "He had to take care of some business. "

In the mix of them talking the professor Ms. Ross walks in the classroom.

Ms. Ross presence automatically commands attention. Her dark tone was flawless with her braided silk hair, golden brown eyes, juicy full lips and if you stare too long...(You can fall into an ... Trance)

(Boom) Ms. Ross drops her books on her desk, the sound echoes through the classroom, knocking the students out of their curiosity trance.

Ms. Ross: "Hello class if you remember me, I'm professor Ms. Ross" ("Ms. Ross",Terry & Jay say it at the same time under their breath). Last time I was here we talked about how soil breads living breathing organisms in plants as well as other things. With plants you have the best herbs and spices, to growing the best fruit and vegetables, even healing wounds, to making clothes and everything else in between."

Terry: "The finest cheiba" (the class laughs)

Ms.Ross: (Ms.Ross looks right at Terry) Yes Mr. Davenport Tetrahydrocannabinol can also be found in certain plants. "

(Terry looks surprised that she remembers his name)

Ms.Ross: "So I have all these books of knowledge and opinions, but having the experience is the lesson & the first lesson is respect the soil, the land, the earth in return you'll receive the greatest gifts from the seed."

Ms. Ross continue to teach the class, while just outside the city Alonzo pulls up to a farm where he works.

[Alonzo day off]

Alonzo walks pass the horse stables to the main building (barn) where they conduct the retail business, of selling fresh fruits and vegetables as well as merchandise.

Cassandra is working the front.

Alonzo: "Hey Sandra is Rico here?"

Cassandra: "Yeah he should be out in the fields, what's wrong everything okay?"

Alonzo: "Yeah I just ran into a little snag at school just seeing if he can help me out." (Alonzo starts heading toward the fields) "You know if it isn't one thing it's another."

Cassandra: "I know child, hope it works out for you."

He walks through the field greeting his coworkers, then finally sees Rico riding the 4-wheeler hauling fresh food.

Alonzo: "Yo Rico what's up!" (Rico stops to talk to Alonzo)

Rico: "Lonzo, hey you work today?"

Alonzo: No, I'm off today, but I can use your help."

Rico: "Ok well walk and talk, matter fact gone head and grab some of that corn for me."

Alonzo helps unload the wagon, putting the produce on a table in the green house.

Alonzo: "Yeah well you know I'm supposed to be graduating this year."

Rico: "Supposed to be?"

Alonzo: "Well the school saying I need to settle a certain amount of debt to continue the next semester, my last semester."

Rico: "How much to continue? "

Alonzo: "11,970 to clear the debt (Rico pauses for an second) but all I need is about half, I got some money saved up.

Rico: "So what are you asking me?"

Alonzo: "If i can get an advance on my check. "

Rico: "An advance...??(sees the truthiness Alonzo face) "Ok I can help you out but how much you need "

Alonzo:"6,970?" (Rico looks at him crazy) "2,970!"

Rico: "That's a lot of free over time."

Alonzo : You got It."

Rico: "Okay, stop by my house around 7oclock, I got you. "

Alonzo: "Thanks man, you don't know how much u saved me!"

Rico: "I haven't saved nothing you got to work it off!"

Alonzo: "I know, I know but thanks."(Alonzo takes a pause sniffing the air...) "Em I trippin...why I smell weed." (smells himself)

Rico: "Oh Yeah thanks to you always talking about the cannabis business, we're exploring that step, extracting the CBD into drinks, like our lemonade.°'

Alonzo: "Aww man I got to be apart of that."

Rico: "Of course but in due time, this is still a sensitive thing but will help us a lot in revenue, you know you're not the only one having problems. "

Alonzo : "The farm got money problems?"

Rico: "We didn't but they keep upping taxes on us fining us for stupid things, they want us to sell I said no so they're finding ways to take!"

Alonzo: "Who's they?"

Rico : "*Blank* faces with strong political ties!"

Alonzo: "Damn!"

Rico: "But don't worry about it, it'll work out."

Alonzo: "Man I hope so, I do like my job... but hey I gotta cut out and pick T up from school, I'll holla at you later."

Rico: "Alright later."

[Yola has a bone to pick]

Class for Terry has ended, him and his classmate Jay walks into the cafeteria for lunch, they find a clear table to eat while jokingly discussing the prior classroom conversations with their New professor Ms. Ross.

Terry: "Yo at least class wasn't boring, it was like she really knows what she takin bout, reminded me how Lonzo talked me into taken this class in the first place".

JAY: "$80 dollars for this book I need my money back!"

Terry: "You ain't lying bout dat, shit she was saying got me looking at thangs a whole different way...especially what we (him and Alonzo) trying to do."

"I hope you ain't telling this nigga none of yo business ". The fellas turn to see Yolanda approaching their table from across the room.

Jay: "Who you talkin too" he said with convention.

Yolanda: "To the nigga who responded, you know what you did!"

Terry looking at both of them confused and intrigued where this conversation is going.

Jay: "What I do Yola (her nickname)?" He says in a smartallic way.

Yolanda: "Because of you my cousin hooked up wit yo crazy ass sister that got him locked up. "

Jay: "Locked up…how?"

Yolanda: "He was over her house she start trippin over his phone, they get into it, while he's getting into his car to leave the boys (police) show up pulls him out the car search the car find 8pounds of weed and a gun in the car!"

Jay: "How is that my fault!"

Terry just sitting there thinking to himself putting 2 and 2 together, when all of a sudden Yolanda gets louder and even more upset.

Yolanda : (talking fast)"Because you was running yo mouth about what he be doing at the club and his business in the street ,when he was helping yo business wit that dumb ass (car shop) body shop and I know that Jenny bitch crazy because I work wit the bitch and when I see her Ima dust her muthafukin ass!"

JAY: Jay starts getting heated, stands up "First of all you ain't gone touch none mine family ".

Terry breaks up their argument.

Terry: "Wait,wait hold up both yawl trippin now calm down "...Terry now tries to get some answers..."So hold up ...Jay weren't you and Will doing the car thang?"

Jay: "Yeah that's my boy I don't know what she talkin bout!"

Yolanda:" You know what I'm talking bout."

Terry: "So the homie Will your cousin?"

Yolanda: "Yeah and they only been hanging for a couple of months, so don't be trying to act like yawl supertight like that."

Terry: "Alright but I just seen this nigga earlier today."

Yolanda: "This just happened about an hour ago (pulls out her phone) look text from my mama (she starts reading the text) hurry up and get home we gotta bail William out of jail, and when I see that bitch jenny Ima dust her muthafukin ass I never like that bitch anyway."

Terry : "Damn yo mamma talk like that" but quickly thinks about his business with Will and knows he got to call Alonzo to figure out an solution to a problem they now have with Will getting locked up. "Look here y'all both black so ahhhhhh be proud, I gotta go."

Yolanda and Jay are both briefly confused by Terry's un usefulness advice and departure but get right back to arguing.

Terry slams through the backdoor to the parking lot, calling Alonzo.

Alonzo: "Yo" answers the phone.

Terry: "Say bra we got a problem. "

Alonzo: "What's up?"

Terry: "Where you at" looking around the parking lot.

Alonzo: "Pulling up right now. "

Alonzo pulls into the parking lot, Terry jumps into the car.

Alonzo: "Got damn nigga you gone wait for me to stop the car first."

Terry: "Man Will just got locked bra."

Alonzo: "Okay but why you jumpin in the car like a damn crack head, sweatin an shit."

Terry: "Man the nigga got busted wit the shit we was getting from him tonight, man what we gone do?"

Alonzo: "Oh now it's time to panic you was laughing at me earlier, relax fool... how you know he locked up?"

Terry:" His cousin Yela, Yolanda some shit... was just in there arguing wit Jay about it."

Alonzo: "Oh Yola yeahhh... she thick ass hell, damn that is Will cousin I forgot bout that, but what Jay got to do wit it?"

Terry: "Man whole bunch of circles of nothing, bottom line is I already gave him my half at the gas station. "

Alonzo: “Nigga why, obviously you don’t know how drug deals go I got the money you got the product then switch nigga.”

Terry: “I know man I was just excited getting that grade of weed for that price I wanted to show we was serious plus I know Will good for it but got damn that all I got.”

Alonzo: “All you got? So what about before you said you’ll lend me the money for school. “

Terry: “After this weekend I would’ve had it...fuck!”

The security guard patrolling the lot sees Alonzo car and starts to head their way.

Alonzo: laughs “All shit time to go, don’t worry bout it we’ll find something.”

Alonzo plays chicken with the security guard golf cart, the security guard swerves at the last second running into a parked car .

Car alarm going off ,the security guard tuck and rolls out the cart pulls out the flashlight like a gun yells “stop your vehicle “then flashes the light like he’s pulling the trigger only to see Alonzo speeding out the lot.

[Somethin got da shake]

Terry: “Man what is it with you and the security dude?”

Alonzo: “Man I was downtown paying a ticket, his punk ass gave me a parking ticket, when I was right about to leave.”

Terry: laughs “He a parking meter maid too!” (laughing)

Alonzo:” Hell yeah fuck dude man!”

Terry:” Well he got yo plates it’s only a matter of time before he finds you and beat yo ass! “

Alonzo: “Ain’t nobody worried bout dude!”

Alonzo drives around the neighborhood where Will’s girlfriend Jenny supposed to live.

Terry: “So what’s the plan?”

Alonzo: “What plan?”

Terry: “Man you telling me to relax like you got something up yo sleeve, nigaa pull a handkerchief or something!”

Alonzo :”Damn look!” Alonzo pulls the car over.

Terry: "Oh that's his whip!"

They see a police car in front of Will's new car. A tow truck comes and gets his car out the driveway, because the car was in park they see the tow truck driver drag the car out the driveway brand new rims and paint being smutted through poodles of mud and gravel without any care.

Alonzo & Terry looking in devastation.

Terry: "N0000!"

Alonzo: "This is a crime in its self, I wanta press charges fo this shit here!"

Terry: "Look what they do to an fine automobile."

The tow truck man straightens up gets out jam the gear shift in neutral and get the car all the way up then, drives away with the police following.

Terry: "Damn I think I'm bout to shed a tear for that shit fuck!"

Alonzo: "Let's get to the crib , its been a long ass day."

The boys arrive at the house to see a note on the door, Alonzo rips it off the door goes inside.

Alonzo: Reads the letter "Electric will be shut off $600 dollars due by Monday."

Terry: "Got damn can a nigga get a break" goes to the fridge "you want a brew."

Alonzo : "Naw I need something stronger than that."

Terry pours both of them a shot of liquor. Alonzo sits on the couch turns on the TV the local news pops on the screen.

News reporter: "P.P.D makes an arrest this afternoon taking 4pounds of marijuana and an automatic weapon off the streets (shows Will mug shot, both shaking their head at the news) in the local area.. more on that tonight for news @11 for weather what do we have Tim. "

"Tonight its going to be clear sky's but look for full moon"....(The news continues in the background)

Alonzo: "Yeah right 4pounds" phone alert goes off, he looks at a text.

Alonzo: "Yes finally some good news, Rico said he be home in 20mins. Ima take a quick shower."

Terry: "Yea nigga you smell like you been in a barn!"

Alonzo: "Why you playin you gone be up there wit me fool (Throws the Electric bill at him) it's was all good just an hour go!"(sings the Jayz, too short song)

Terry: "Yeah whatever man."

Alonzo: "You know Rico been talking expanding to cbd "as he walks to back getting ready for his shower.

Terry: "Hemp nigga, (laughs) I can't see this nigga growing nothing illegal he straight square space nigga I WANT GAS fuck all that!"

Alonzo: shouts from the back "Cause you ignorant!!"

Terry: "Whatever nigga it must been yo idea huh, but fo real I'm wit it!" Terry thinking out loud "shit I'm broke as shit no assets nothing... lint to got damn pocket, I was just rich 7 hours ago 2,000 dollars thought I was the man got damn.

[Convo with Rico Mo]

Alonzo and Terry pull up to Rico house, they see his truck in the driveway.

Alonzo: "Alright man look don't say no dumb shit when we get there, I'm already asking too much besides trying to get you a job with it. "

Terry: "I am not gone speak less spoken too I know this nigga don't like me."

Alonzo: "He like you; he thinks you talk without thinking. "

They walk up to the front door (ring doorbell)

Terry: "Aey that's what I do I speak my minndd…oh this nigga gotta working doorbell so he think he better than everybody, he say something to me wrong I'm Going Ape Shit u heard me bra Ape.. "

The door opens and Rico 6 foot 4 shadowy frame fills the screen door, the door opens.

Terry: "What's up big dog , love the door ain't no squeaking or nothing, what you put dw 40 (oil) on the corners what's the secret bra!"

Rico jesters to come inside.

Alonzo slaps Terry in back of the head.

Alonzo: "Bra shut up" as they walk inside Rico's house.

Alonzo and Terry find an seat on the couch, Rico goes to the kitchen finishing up the homemade lemonade he was making.

Terry: "Love what you done wit the place, I remember when I first moved here (to town) this was a straight crank house them niggas was getting it fo real boyyy... "Alonzo give an quick elbow to Terry ribs.

Alonzo: Whispers "Shut up" Terry nods ok.

Rico runs the blender while dropping ingredients into the mix, at the same time giving a look at Terry like he could RIP his head off at any second. About 10 seconds go by and the blender stops. An awkward moment is in the air.

Rico (MO): "Lonzo you want a drink, fresh lemonade here!"

Alonzo: "Lemon's from your garden, yeah fo sho appreciate it big bro."

Terry: Whispering "Big bro, nigga you fool!" Terry saids with a smurk.

Rico hears Terry whispering something to Alonzo, most likely talking about him.

Rico (mo): "Would you like a drink (Terry)."

Terry: "Oh yeah big bro fa sho let me get a shot of that vodka wit it big homie appreciate that holmes!"

Rico (mo): Looks at the big bottle Terry must be referring to "Oh no that's just water, alkaline water."

Terry: "Aww okay I thought it was just cheap liquor but I wasn't judging yo get down tho but that's gravy just hit me wit a shot of whiskey or brandy or somethin ya dig!"

Rico (mo): "I don't drink I don't have any liquor here."

Terry: Turns to Alonzo "See I don't know why you always gasin Jones up, what kind of a grown man don't have liquor in the cabinet, yo mamma is an recovering alcoholic and she still got a stash for guest!"

Alonzo" Mannn... shut.. up!"

Rico comes over with the drinks on a tray.

Terry:" This nigga got an tray...ha.."

Rico hears another one of Terry's comments but pays it no mind. He puts the tray down on the table the boys grab their glasses.

Terry: "So Rico where you from!" Cross his leg while he drinks like he's really interested in Rico's answer.

Alonzo intercepts the question while hitting Terry for the 4th time.

Alonzo: "Once again man, thanks for this advance it's a crucial time for me."

Rico: "Now don't expect this all the time" points to the envelope on the table"

Alonzo grabs the envelope and puts in his pocket, (not even looking at it) [shows his trust of Rico]

Alonzo: "Thank you!"

Terry: "Hey Alonzo said you guys are looking into cbd oils and things "Terry saids in his sarcastic professional voice.

Alonzo looking at Terry like not now.

Terry:"So is Alonzo going to be ahead of that department I mean it was his idea to push that line. "

Rico (Mo): "Actually yes, I was thinking the same thing (Terry smiles at Alonzo) but right now there's an group that wants the land and they're not taking no for an answer, we are day to day with this" gets up shows grabs an letter off the kitchen table , gives it to Alonzo.

Alonzo reads the letter and notice a crazy emblem of a dragon with curly horns in a circle stamped at the bottom.

Alonzo: "So basically this is a threat "passes the letter to Terry .

Rico: "Definitely making their point!"

Terry:" Why don't yall just sale, I'm sure they offered something nice?"

Rico (mo): "Then what , the people here relies on our fresh produce, you know how much they charge for what they call whole foods, our food is pure from noncontaminated soil, our food is for the health and soul not this cancerous contaminated clone catastrophe of bull there giving the public! "

Terry:" Whoa brother man...that was a lot."

Alonzo: "So I'm out of a job soon?"

Terry: "Oh is that what he was saying "he says in a trembling voice.

Rico:" As of right now no, but I don't know the outcome of this ...these aren't just investors this is a more powerful group!"

Terry: "Damn nigga I'm fired before even hired."

Alonzo: "I know it's a lot, but I was going to ask if Terry could come on to the job but..."

Rico: looks at Terry, takes a deep breath..." Terry your welcome to come aboard but I don't know for how long and at this point not at the same wages I pay Alonzo."

Terry:"Well how much this nigga make, he been holding out or somethin what's really going on?"

Alonzo interrupts again while putting the letter on the kitchen counter.

Alonzo: "Hey Rico thanks once again but we gone head out but thanks." He finishes his drink grabs an couple bottles of Rico's Lemonade drinks out the fridge and start slightly pushing Terry towards the door.

Rico: “Ok see you Monday.”

Alonzo: “Okay peace bro!” They get out the door onto the porch.

Terry: “Ok man damn get yo hands off me shit I get it he your hero...now let’s go home and try to find some weed between the couch cushions cuz we both broke ass hell”

Alonzo: “Shut up and get in the damn car!” Alonzo finally gets Terry in the car and they head home.

(Master Minds??)

The boys get back to the house, Terry crash on the couch and Alonzo falls back into his recliner chair. Alonzo reaches in his pocket, pulls out the envelope and opens it.

Alonzo:”Yeah man Rico came through, now how we going to pay the rest of the bills?”

Terry: “Rob a bank, shhitt take care all our problems. “

Alonzo: “Come on bra fo real, something gotta shake.”

Terry:” look we cash that check tomorrow and go see yo boy Streez I know he look out.”

Alonzo:” Streez been chilling, I ain’t bothering him.”

Terry: “Well I don’t know, I guess I’ll just be seeing you at the job Monday, (starts to rambling, Alonzo reclines in his chair trying to think)should’ve used those seeds to grow my own damn plant , I mean it would’ve been reggie but fuck it all profit.”

Alonzo raises up fast out the recliner slamming the foot stool down.

Alonzo: “Bro you right , that’s it!!!”

Terry:Surprised Alonzo just got up that quick” Nigga what?”

Alonzo:” All profit....we go down to the field and get the fresh buds.”

Terry: “So yall are growing up there, you sneaky someofabitch you been holding out...(Alonzo now pacing back and forth...Terry can tell Alonzo is planning in his head) what about Rico though?”

Alonzo: Stops pacing “What?...Damn you right he did just look out.”

Terry: “But they might be closing soon right?”

Alonzo shaking his head agreeing.

Terry:"That mean they gone burn all that shit (Terry egging Alonzo on now) hell we might be saving people from going to jail…shit fo real."

Alonzo goes to his bedroom comes back out in all black clothes mask cheap night vision googles book bag in less than one minute .

Terry: "Well goddamn fool what you been doing in yo spare time."

Alonzo heads for the back door "let's go. "

Terry: "Well let me change nigga damn!"

Terry finally jumps in the car all black wit swim goggles on, Alonzo already been waiting.

Alonzo: "What the helll..you got on … Swim goggles!?"

Terry:"You got goggles, where you get yo goggles from?"

Alonzo: "Don't worry about where I get my shit from." (Starts the car)

Terry:"There you go wit that secret squirrel shit... I saw that shit at Target (Retail Store) in the kids section. "

Alonzo: "If you know so much shut the hellup! "

Terry:"This nigga got spy tech glasses"(laughs).

Alonzo pulls off headed towards the farm.

(The car ride)

Terry: "So what exactly is the plan again?"

Alonzo:" Why gettin nervous, better say something now another 5 minutes its point of no return."

Terry: "Naw I'm cool I just don't want to go up here for nothing."

Alonzo Doesn't say anything stays concentrating on driving.

Alonzo :"Umhmm"

Terry: "So what makes you so sure this is worth doing. "

Alonzo: "The tea."

Terry: "The tea?...You ain't gotta get sassy but yeah nigga spill it ...what's up."

Alonzo: "No fool the tea we brought home earlier. "

Terry: "From Rico's crib?"

Alonzo: "Yea, you ain't notice the feeling like you was a little buzzed or..."

Terry: "High yeah but I smoked earlier so I didn't think nothing of it, but dat had a hint of watermelon in it.. that shit was bangin."

Alonzo:" Exactly!!"

Terry: "What the watermelon?"

Alonzo: "Yup."

Terry: "Fool you want to go up there & steal some watermelons?!!"

Alonzo: "No you smart muthafuka we gone get the weed growing in and around the watermelon patch"

Terry: "Okay okay...Ah so what's the plan Mc Guyver. "(looking at the tools in Alonzo half open bag)

Alonzo: "The plan?? (concentrating on driving)

Terry: "The Plane boss the plane (in Tatu voice) yeah man, you gave me your hypothesis what's the plan?"

Alonzo:"Ahh the plan... is to get the buds off the plants."

Terry:"Sooo we gone carefully pull buds off a plant in the dark, that we have to find first?"

Alonzo points to his night goggles he has hanging around his neck.

Alonzo: "Yup."

Terry: "Nigga I ain't got no night goggles! "

Alonzo: "Okay then we get in there find the plants pull'em out toss them in the trunk and get out...is that simple enough. "

Terry takes a deep sigh.

Terry: "This nigga ain't got no plan"(he says thinking out loud)

Alonzo: "A man you were the one egging me on, (starts imitating Terry) they gone burn it all anyways, we saving lives."

Terry: "First of all I said saving people from jail, second of all what if everything already gone?"

Alonzo: "There he go coppin duces "he sings in a lazy opera voice.

Terry: "Man fo real worst-case scenario then what "?

Alonzo: "First of all (mocking Terry).. if everything was gone they wouldn't be in a community meeting tonight about the land anddda worst case...(starts talking fast)we grab the soil and bring it back" Alonzo sips his cup out the cup holder.

Terry:"Dirt!! We goin up here for dirt!! I knew this was some bullshit."

Alonzo: “You want to get out the car Tray get out the car!”

Terry:”I ain’t hear nothing bout no damn town meeting. “

Alonzo:”Cause you listen you don’t read between the lines”. Takes another sip out the cup.

Terry: “Man what?...What you sipping on man” grabs the cup.

Alonzo:”Aey man don’t be grabbing my shi...”

Terry cracks the lid and smells the inside of the cup

Terry:”Nigga no wonder you been talking high you been drinking Rico tea the whole time.”

Alonzo: “Rico tea (laughs) nigga you stuuppid.”

Terry: Takes a sip “So ya’ll been skeemin the whole time...Hemp tea lemonade my ass...”

Alonzo:”No man the hemp tea is real...Remember the food drive we did a couple months back.”

Terry:” Yea I remember I don’t need the back story… “

Alonzo:”So that’s when we came up with using the cbd with the natural drinks we already have right “

Terry:”Huh..Ok.”

Alonzo: “So the next day he had me drop off some soil at his crib but it wasn’t the soil we have packaged up for sell, so when I put the bags in his shed, where I saw he must of start experimenting with the hemp but earlier today helping him unload the trailer, he had two big bags ,we in the green house talking when he gives me the ok for the drinks with cbd, but the black bag he put in the corner had weed In it , I saw it on my way out but I didn’t ask about it I figure he’ll fill me in on that later ,but when we got to his house we end up talking about possibly losing the land and you working there but when we left like usual I grab a couple bottles of the drinks but this time I grab the yellow bottle cause I figure it’s the new batch he just made.

Terry:”To be buzzin you show seem focused… when did you realize it was drank with the weed in it?”

Alonzo: “When we got in the house I know I haven’t smoked all day but felt high but an cool calm high so when the news came on, it was like voice in my head saying go to the farm.”

Terry:”Yeah me!”

Alonzo:”Besides you.”

Terry:”Dirt we going up here for dirt I knew this was some bullshit. “

[The Time lapse]

Once they make it up to the farm Alonzo takes the back way to the farm on a dark windy (paved)road, on the left side heavy wooden area on the right side you can see the crops and the barn in a distance. Alonzo pulls the car over and cuts the lights off.

Alonzo: "Alright look we going up on the left side of the field, it should be some plants on that side." Alonzo says while putting on his gloves.

Terry grabbing the trash bags.

Terry: "Why we way down here? I thought we was gone get in and get out?"

Alonzo: We gotta keep the car out of site man let's go!"

They stay low moving through the corn fields. Terry lacking behind, keep tripping and getting hit by crop leaves in the face.

Alonzo:(Whispers) "Come on fool!"

Terry : "This dumb ass plan, I don't know why I even listen to yo ass, I could've been chillin at home watching a movie, but naw I'm out here in the boonies wit yo dumb ass..."

Alonzo suddenly stops.

Alonzo: "Right here."

Terry takes out his flashlight shines the light on the plants, he sees they have buds on them.

Terry: "I knew you know what you were doing man you always were a gifted child, I remember when we were kids..."

Alonzo: "Would you shut up and start cuttin!"

Terry: "OH yeah right. "

The boys continue to cut the plants and put them into bags, when all of a sudden, Terry stops Alonzo cutting.

Terry: "Shush"

Alonzo stops looks around.

Alonzo: "What?"

Terry: "You hear that"?

Alonzo looks around "No... man come on."

As soon as he says that he sees a light shine from the distance. They both get on the ground, they see three flashlights making their way through the fields.

Terry:"Aey we gotta bounce."

Alonzo: "Stay down they don't see us."

They hear talking in the distance, but it seems safer to stay hidden. Then two more flashlights show up, now you can hear barking and growling, getting closer, a man yells "Go get'em boys". The dogs moving fast through the fields right towards Alonzo and Terry.

Alonzo and Terry look at each other "Shit" grab the bags and start running, the lights are now flashing in their direction and the dogs are on their trail. They make their way out of the field back to the road.

Alonzo: "Damn the car down there "he says to Terry.

If they run towards the car the dogs and the men chasing them could cut them off and possibly be caught.

Terry:"Go, Go,Go" Terry points straight ahead into the woods.

They cross over the road into the woods, they hide behind a big tree.

Terry: "We gotta stash the weed the dogs can sense that shit!"

Alonzo: Agrees points to a ditch nearby "over there!"

They get to the ditch digg a shallow hole puts the bags in, they mark the whole (Dogs barking) then they run a little further into the woods crossing over a creek. When all of a sudden (They here boom sound) Thunder and lightning rainstorm out of nowhere. They try to take cover under some trees and look out for the dogs.

They look around the moonlight illuminates the wooded area.

Alonzo looks around

Terry: "I don't see nothing. "

Alonzo: "Maybe they stopped because of the storm "as soon as he says that the rain just stopped. No sound of any dogs or men chasing them.

Terry: "I think there gone"?

Alonzo: "Yeah I think so, we gotta get back to the road and get to the car".

They start to make their way back through the woods, Terry pulls out his flashlight out.

Terry:"Yo the ditch should be this way, we can get the plants", then he shines the light on Alonzo and what looks like small crystals on his shoes and bottom of his pants "Nigga you got glitter on yo pants".

Alonzo looks down then looks at Terry.

Alonzo: "I don't know but it's on your shirt too (Alonzo smells his hands) smells like weed...HTU".

Terry:"Htu?" Smells his shirt.

Both: "Watermelon weed"!

Terry shines the light on the ground and see crystals in form of a path.

Terry: "It's going both ways...should we follow it"?

Alonzo: "Let's get back to the car first"!

As they walk back towards the direction of the car, they see the path widened out.

Terry: What if this is the soil, man you might be right this gotta be the jackpot "!

Alonzo stops looks around.

Alonzo: "Where's the ditch it was right here damn ...I think we lost, but we can't be the road right there."? (The road is now dirt/gravel road)

Terry taps Alonzo on the shoulder, Alonzo turns around and sees a wall like of plants (marijuana plants) with crystals on them. (The moonlight makes the crystal shine)

Terry: "No brother we not lost...we have found"!

Alonzo: "Holy shit"! Alonzo looks in shock and kind of confused "Did we just run past all this shit"?

Terry: "Man which way is the car... why it seems like it's a lot more big ass trees"?

Alonzo: "I got my watch "puts on his smart watch to locate his phone inside the car." I'm not getting a signal can't connect with my phone".

Terry: "It's like a damn swamp out here" Looks at his muddy shoes.

Alonzo: Takes out a baggie and clips some buds off a plant, gets another baggie and put some soil in it ,puts the baggie in his pocket "just in case we gotta leave with somethin".

They make their way back on to the road, but now the paved road is now a dirt gravel road.

Terry :"Is this the right way...I don't think this road was an dirt road"!?

Alonzo:"I know we must have gone further than we thought, the car should be right up ahead ".

Terry: "What's that"?

The boys look while flickering lights like lanterns appear and heading their direction, they both hide behind a huge log on the ground.

Terry: "Is that a fucking horse"?

The sound of horses and a man's voice directing their movements is getting closer. They get on the ground trying to stay out of site.

"Heyah come on heyah" they hear from the driver.

Terry:"Ah man it's probably one of those Amish people around here...we can get a ride to a gas station".

Alonzo:"I dont know bra I don't trust it"?

Terry: "Look obviously them dudes chasing us took the car towed it or something we gotta get to a phone"!

Alonzo: "Naw fool, Amish people around here ride bikes or walk,we way out here white niggas wit horses and carriage...let'em pass".

Terry:" Man Amish people cool bra they don't hurt nobody "Terry starts to get up.

Alonzo: "Wait brah...noooo...stupid "!

Terry steps into the road waving his hands "Yo ,Yo stop"!

The horse and carriage wagon slowly come to a halt and now Alonzo can see its 2 men up front and 3 men in the back riding.

(Driver): Smoking what looks to be a cigar "Boy you lost what you doing out here on this here road"? As the other riders look on.

Terry: (thinks to himself "boy"...) but knows he needs help so he looks past it)"Yes I think I am lost if you can give me a ride to the nearest gas station, I would appreciate it".

(Driver): The driver chuckles in slight confusion "And what in Jesus name is a... gas station?"(the goons in the wagon chuckle along)

Terry: "Oh you must be the comedian out the musty misfit's gang, it's a place that serves food, drinks and a phone ".

(Driver) Richard: "Well I don't know about this phone you speak of but there's a food and stay up yonder".

As Terry continue to talk to the driver Alonzo sees another carriage coming up the road.

Alonzo: "Is that a fucking stagecoach"? (Oh, hell naw)

Alonzo gets up and comes out onto the road (shirt dirty from laying on the ground) stands next to Terry.

Alonzo: "What's the move bro ".

As soon as he says that to Terry the driver (Richard Ryker) and the other guys jump out the wagon.

Richard (driver):" Is it anymore of you fugitive niggers around here show me your paper's"!

Goon: "Like it makes a difference "! (the gang chuckles)

Alonzo: "Nigga what, fuck you"!

The white men looking confused.

Goon: "No you're the nigger ...nigger "says one of the goons.

Terry: (mocking the goon)"You're the nigger, nigger... Fuck yo puss ass, dirt ass fresh outta booty mountain smellin ass nigga"! (goons smell themselves)

Alonzo:"ol goof ball, musty misfit teeth the same color as yo ass ..ol bitch made nigga "!

Goon#3:"God damn niggers crazy"he says in a trembling confused voice.

(Driver)Richard: "We don't need papers for these niggers tie 'em up, we can get something for the for'em "!

The goons start taking weapons out the wagon.

Goons: "We can get 20 maybe 50 for these niggers here..." They chatter.

Alonzo grips his hedge cutters ready for the rumble as Terry grips his knife ready for any of the goons to make a move. There all in a full-blown standoff.

Alonzo: "Fuck all you muthafukas"!

Alonzo charges right at Richard (Driver), Pow, pow 2 shots in the air stops everyone in their tracks. The stagecoach comes to a complete stop.

The driver and upfront passenger are much more militant, sporting French military uniforms, the driver keeps his gun pointed at Alonzo and Terry while the passenger reloads his musket rifle. They stare at the soldier in an awkward silence as he pulls what looks like a stick of gum out a man purse pours powder where usually bullets go into, then stands the long rifle straight up pours the rest of the powder with a metal looking ball down the barrel... then pulls an long steal rod and pushes the powder down even more takes out the rode puts it back on the side of the gun...then finally points the rifle back at Alonzo and Terry.

French soldier (driver): "You two (Alonzo, Terry) step back and put your hands out" the solider says in a French accent.

Terry: "Is that a musket"?

Alonzo and Terry slowly put their hands up in slight confusion wondering if this is real or not.

French soldier #2 (passenger): "Hands out now"!

Alonzo and Terry slowly put their hands out wide.

Alonzo: "What type of shit is this"?

Terry: "Hey funny Amish soldier man as you can see, we outnumbered, so you can point your rifle at them"!

Soldier says something smartalic in French.

Richard (driver):"Hey we got this under control "!

Rufus: "Do you"?! Shouts a man with his strong southern (Carolina) accent.

Two men step out one each side of the stagecoach. One is dressed like an 1800 senator with the wig, the other heavier set man resembles the colonel from KFC.

Alonzo: "Oh shit its George Washington and the Colonel!!(Star struck from their celebrity fame then quickly thinks about what they stand for as human beings) ...Fuuck"!

Rufus: "Your out of position Richard "As he continues to walk forward unveiling his face out the shadows into flickering lights from the lanterns from the stagecoach and the wagon.

Richard: "These two niggers came out of the woods ".

Goon#2:"Yeah fugitive runaways"!

Alonzo:"Aey man I ain't gone be no more nigg...hold on what the fuck going on."

Goon#3 pulls out a cow bell collar out the wagon grinning with his rotten teeth.

Terry: "This shit real"?

Richard: "Hell sir, you can buy these niggers right now I'll have 'em in Chestnut in 4 weeks. they've been taken care of look those fronts in that boy's mouth".

Alonzo and Terry both seal there mouth shut.

Rufus walks in front of Alonzo and Terry he looks them up and down analyzing them. He runs his two fingers down Alonzo face to his chest.

Rufus: "Where you boys coming from".

Alonzo slaps his hand down from his shirt.

Rufus: "Boy I will have you HUNG & SET FYA!!!.... Now where you comin from and where you goin Boy"?!!

Richard: "They look like one of those Nat Turner boys" Richard says in the background.

Rufus: "Hmmm...You Lukango Boy!!

(Lukango=liberty, 1rst big slave rebellion in Carolina Sept.9 1739 Led by Je'mmy , origin of slaves=Central Africa Angola Kikongo)

Rufus: Or beta yet one of those mulatto Deslondes Niggers" As he gets in Terry face.

(Creole Haitian Charles Deslondes led the most sophisticated slave revolt in U.S. history lead 200 rebels along the Mississippi river down to New Orleans January, 8th 1811)

Rufus: "Nothing but tall tales for a man of my stature yet I was just an school boy then...But that Nat Turner nigger Reverend...well let's just say he made quite a name for himself...Some of those good folks where dear friends of my family ".

James Buchanan: "Enough of the games Rufus we have higher priorities to attend ".

Rufus takes a deep breath, sucks his teeth.

Rufus: "String 'em up boys and bring their heads back to chestnut "he says arrogantly. The French soldiers gives Richard and goon #2 rifles.

Rufus and James walk back to the coach with the soldiers and proceed to take off. As the coach goes around the wagon Rufus says to Richard.

Rufus: "If you boys hurry up you might not miss the festivities tonight.

Richard: "Yes sir"!

Rufus: "Richard this your opportunity to move up in the world, there's tyrants that wants to see our way of life change. We cannot let that happen".

Richard: "Yes sir I'll see to it and meet you down yonder".

Rufus: "Good boy"!

Rufus knocks on the side of the coach telling the driver let's go in French "Allons-y"

Soldier driver: Yells "Vas-y, Vas-y (Go in French)

The stagecoach heads down the road. and now Richard and his men grab the rope and axes out the wagon.

Richard: "Put that damn cow bell up"!

Alonzo: Gives a nervous laugh "Alright man yall got us, obviously this reenactment has gone too far, I understand it's not enough Kentucky fried chicken and Insurance commercials to go around. But look playboy everybody can't be a star ya digg"!

The goons throwing rope up in the tree but can't get it to catch to the other side.

Terry: "I see what you saying bro, the George Washington dude was cultivating, fool had me like this (put his arms out) God damn boy he was serious!"

Alonzo: "Professional "

Terry: "But y'all, I don't feel it, yall don't have that... (thinking of an expression)

Alonzo: Snaps his fingers "Pizzazz "!

Terry: "No spark at all...You know like Denzel...King Kong ain't got shit on me"!

Goon#3:"Denzel"?

At this point the boys got so comfortable thinking it's still a joke they're not paying attention to the men finally getting the rope up over the branches.

Alonzo: "Sam Jackson"!

Alonzo and Terry recite together : "Blessed is he who in the name of charity & goodwill Shepherds the weak through the valley of darkness for he is truly his brother's keeper and the finder of lost children, And I will STRIKE DOWN UPON THEE WITH GREAT VENGEANCE AND FURIOUS ANGER THISE WHO ATTEMPT TO POISION AND DESTROY MY BROTHERS "!!

Richard: Shoots a tree behind them "Shut up and get on your knees"!

Goon #2 try to put them on their knees but Alonzo and Terry put up a struggle, so goon 3 & 4 jumps in wrestles them to the ground holding them to tie their hands and feet.

Alonzo head bunts one in the nose even though his hands are partially tied and Terry gets lose maneuvers to charge at Richard.

Terry:" Yeah ya out bullets now you 2 shot mafuka"!

Right when he gets up on Richard. Richard draws a big sword machete out the wagon makes Terry stop in his tracks.

Terry: "God damn what is this clown car wagon "!

Alonzo look on gassed out of breath from fighting the 2 goons when bow! Blow (punch) to the ribs and stomach.

Goon# 3: "You broke my nose" throws a couple more rabbit punches.

Richard: "Enough of this shit, Earnest(goon#2) get the other rifle "as he has the machete pointed tip at Terry's neck.

He grabs the second loaded rifle, Earnest (goon#2) and Richard wrestles Terry down next to Alonzo.

Terry: "Damn cuz I don't know if this a bad dream but know I always got yo back"!

Alonzo: "I know bro same here".

Richard: "Forget the hanging "!

Richard slides the machete against a big stone, sparks fly off the blade showing its sharpness.

Richard: "Hold 'em still "! (Terry)

He raises the blade high above his head he starts his downward motion... A knife flies into his right (hand) wrist, blood squirts out like a leaky water faucet before he can even process what happen and let out a scream, he turns slightly to his left to look behind him and another hunting knife cuts through the darkness splat into his left eye. Everybody is stunned as Richard finally let's out a terrifyingly girly scream and before the machete could hit the ground another knife fly's right between his eyes, he falls forward onto the knife pushing the knife all the way through his skull.

The gang is now in a panic, Earnest (goon#2) franticly aims the shotgun turns around to only see a big shadowy figure coming fast then BOOM hit in the face cut across his left jaw rifle taken and now getting an upper cut baseball homerun swing right under his chin with his own rifle sending him flying in the air hitting the ground hard.

The shadowy figure then swings around now to the goon holding the rope freezes as he stares down the barrel of the rifle, the shadowy figure pulls the trigger and blows the goon whole face off.

Terry: "Damn dat musket really work" he says to himself.

The last standing goon holding the lantern runs to the wagon to retrieve a weapon, when reaching into the wagon another person comes out of the shadows slices his throat from ear to ear. The two mysterious figures walk over to the goon #2 (Earnest) lying on the ground coughing up blood, the slender smaller figure lifts him by his shirt.

Minty: "Remember Me"!

The goon (Earnest) coughing choking on his own blood.

The goon (Earnest) focuses in on their faces, he whispers "it, it's you, it's too late" he tries to laugh but he's choking to bad, takes a couple of breaths then passes out so the smaller shadowy figure slowly digs a knife into his throat.

Alonzo: "Hey we ain't got nothing to do with them as you can see"!

The 2 shadowy figures walk over to Alonzo and Terry the man says, "everything going to be okay", then places a chip onto Alonzo's neck and the other shadowy figure sticks an chip onto Terry.

Just as Alonzo fades out of conscious, he catches a glimpse of the man face.

Alonzo: "Rico"? Then fades out.

END CHAPTER 1

2

*"What the F***k is going on ???"*

ERRRERR Alonzo's alarm goes off.

Alonzo jumps up in a panic, he feels his face and body checking for anything that's out of place. He goes to the bathroom splashes water on his face shaking his head.

Alonzo: Takes a deep breath "That was a crazy dream" laughs it off.

Alonzo comes out the room dressed, Terry's already eating cereal ready to go.

Alonzo: "What's up brother ".

Terry:"Yo, Hey the school must have got bought out or something they just got some major funding ".

Alonzo: "OH you read the paper now"?

Terry:"Whateva man, hey if they put those funds in the lab it's no telling what we can do".

Alonzo: "I hear that...what else going on"? As he pours his cereal.

Terry: "Not much I guess some parade this weekend...hey you going to school today right"?

Alonzo: "You can go, I still got business to handle ".

Terry: "You might as well go while you can fool".

Alonzo : "Yeah you right, well come on then".

Terry:" I'm ready" as he finishes up his breakfast.

Alonzo :"No morning joint today bra"? He says while Terry heads to his room to grab his jacket.

Terry:"Shit I'm cool "he yells from his bedroom.

Alonzo: "Yeah me too" he says to himself, quickly finishes his breakfast "Alright let's go".

The boy's walkout to see the car out front both take a secret sigh of relief to themselves. They head to the gas station on their daily routine. While driving they notice the neighborhood is the same but seems more cleaner and the run-down houses they remember are in great condition.

They pull into the gas station.

Terry :"When he upgrade the gas station"?

Alonzo: Pulls up to the pump looks at Terry "Don't worry about it I got it".

Terry: "Good look-in out ...I got the pump".

Alonzo: Walks inside the gas station, he looks around noticing the changes to the store he grabs two alkaline bottles of water and walks to the cashier.

Cashier: "Will this be all"?

Alonzo:"$15 on pump 2...Hey pops still here"?

Cashier: "Yeah, hey pop "!

Pop (gas station owner):"Hey Lonzo" as he walks from the back.

Alonzo looks in relief thinking he's losing his mind.

Alonzo: "Hey Pop...I like this retro style you did with the place".

Pop: "What you mean just like my other stores"?

Alonzo: "You got other stores"?

Pop :"Yeah my son runs the other stores but he's helping me out today but you already know this, it was your idea for me to expand"!

Alonzo :"You know, I know...ah it's like your son just grew overnight...(snaps his fingers) like boom adult...haha ".

Pop: "Hey you feeling okay"? With a look of concern...then smiles "Oh I know just what you need "reaches under the counter and grabs a small jar and hands it to Alonzo.

Alonzo :"Is this"? Looks around to make sure nobody's looking.

Pop: Smiling likes he proud to give the jar of weed to Alonzo "Sure is some of your finest..."

Alonzo:"Shhhhh...I got it, I got it" he says in a low slightly high pitch slipping the jar into his pocket smoothly.

Pop:" You don't have id band on, don't worry about it everything's on me just get better ...okay"!

Alonzo: "Okay cool thanks Pop" turns to walk out the door "okay that was some shit right there" he says to himself

Pop : "See you later"!!

While Alonzo was inside talking to Pop, Terry was out trying to pump the gas.

Terry: "What the hell wrong with this pump" The pump wouldn't slide in as normal, he looks into the gas tank it was more like a plug. Terry adjust the pump a couple times (Click) the pump snaps in. He hits the green button to start pumping but it sounds more like a charging sound (low winding sound).

Terry :"Pop done upgraddded" he says to himself.

Terry leans on the car an noticed a group of white guys on the side of the gas station hanging out. They had slick back hair and leather Jackets dressed like an old school gang from 1950's smoking joints.

Terry looking at the guys like there out of place. Alonzo gets back to the car hands Terry a water bottle.

Terry :"Man look at this shit here"!

Alonzo: "What those dudes over there".

Terry :"Naw...the other Aces of dragons around this muthafuka"!

Alonzo: "It look like they doing a photo shoot for gentrification"!

They both laugh when 4 chromed out muscle cars pull into the gas station lot right up to the group of guys, hanging out.

Terry: "All shit they jumpin out on'em"!

Alonzo:" It's going down "!

The black guys hop out their cars, they approach the white guys. Both group of guys walk towards each other and start giving each other dap and hugs showing respect.

Terry: "What the fuck is going on"?

The pump gives 3 beeps.

Alonzo: "Come on man we gotta get out".

Terry hangs up the pump.

Terry:" Pump sound like a damn microwave ".

"Alonzo, Terry" someone shouts. They look and its Will walking up to them.

Alonzo "Ah shit Will"!

Will: "Hey what's up my brother, how you livin"! Gives Alonzo and Terry dap.

Terry:"When you get out"! Terry says excited to see Will.

Will:"Ah man I've been moving and groovin since this morning "!

Terry: "Movin and groovin"?

Alonzo: "Shit man it's good to see you out"!

Will:" Well you know I was going to drop by ya pad later on tonight anyway"!

Terry : "You still got that money "?

Will: "Huh"?

While they're talking a young lady walks up wearing a black leather jacket and black pants with her hair in an afro puff.

Will: "This my cousin Yolanda, Yola this Alonzo and Terry ".

Yolanda gives Alonzo and Terry firm handshakes.

Yolanda turns to will.

Yolanda: "Let get me get jar".

Will reaches into his inside jacket pocket and pulls out weed inside a tube, hands it to Yolanda.

Will: "OH yeah I got something for y'all, if you finally want to get down with the movement" hands them a small pamphlet.

Alonzo: "What's this like some Black Panther shit"?

Will & Yolanda: "Who"?

Yolanda: "What's that"?

Terry: "Revolutionaries from the 60's & 70's"!

Will: "Don't know, brother but maybe you can put me on it next time".

Alonzo: "Yeah we can chop it up".

Terry: "Hey man you just walk around with the weed out like that"? Looking how Yolanda is just comfortably having a conversation without putting the tube of weed up.

Will: "Yeah man we came to give pop some for the store".

Terry: "Pop selling weed out the store"!?

Yolanda: "Calm down man, its legal (laughs) where ya been".

Alonzo & Terry:"School you know homework & stuff" both trying to play it off, like they know what's going on.

Alonzo:"Aey but we bout to go head and cut out, man we gone hollar at cha later".

Will: "Alright man be safe and peace to ya'll".

Will & Yolanda: "Cool, later" They all dap up then go their separate ways.

Alonzo and Terry jump into the car and starts the ride to school.

As they ride through the town, they see shops open that's been closed for years. Main Street is full of life Vendor's out front of their shops selling fresh food, next door clothes next to that furniture store.

Just a crowd of nice dressed black people shopping having lunch at the outside tables. The cars parked on the street are mostly beautiful old school cars in great original condition.

They get to the light at the corner of the block, to see some older guys enjoying their cigars and scotch outside a smoke lounge. (Group of gentlemen all wearing Tuskegee air men veteran hats and jackets) One of the men notice Alonzo & Terry looking and the gentlemen gives them a salute with a grin.

As they ride in aquert silence they hear a siren behind them.

Alonzo: "Damn not now"!

Terry: "All man we gettin pulled over ..for what".

Alonzo: "Just chill, don't make any sudden moves".

Alonzo pulls the car over to the side of the road. Two police officers walk up to the car.

Alonzo recognizes the approaching officer from the rearview mirror.

Alonzo: "Ah hell naw the security guard the made the force"!

Terry: "Oh he gone cook you wit that taser... just remember don't shit yourself until they put you in back of the car...insanity "!

Alonzo: "You know if you weren't my cousin, I probably wouldn't hang with so much".

1rst officer(Sec.Guard): "How you doing sir, I pulled you over because you're doing 10mph in an 30mph zone.

Alonzo: "Oh I'm sorry sir we're just headed to school".

1rst officer(Sec.Guard) :" It's okay I just wanted to make sure your car was running ok there's a shop right up the street here".

Alonzo: "Everything's fine we're just admiring the scenery ". Motion for Terry to get his registration out the glove.

Terry reaches in glove box SLOWLY for the paper.

2nd officer: "Oh no need you guys are fine let's just keep this traffic flowing alright kings" he says from the passenger side of the car.

The cops walk back to their car.

Alonzo: "That was weird ".

Alonzo pulls off and the confusion of the day grows even more on both their faces. They continue to ride in silence, they finally get to school and as soon as Alonzo parks both the boys yell out,

Alonzo and Terry: "Man what the FUCK IS GOIN ON"!!!

Terry: "When the hell did the outsiders start hangin wit the Black Panther's "he says hysterically.

Alonzo: "Why almost everything looks futuristically old school "!?

Terry: "Pop looking like he pops Viagra for breakfast wearing white linen to work...selling weed and shit"!

Alonzo: "The weed" He takes the weed out his pocket and analyzes it.

Terry: "Yeah roll one up, this shit crazy" Rubbing his hands together anxiously.

Alonzo: "Pop slid this to me at the store."

Terry: "Nope never mind, I'm not smoking nothing from this world..Fuuuck dat"!!

Alonzo thinks about what Terry just said about this world.

Alonzo: "Pop didn't ask me how was school going today...Hey bro I had a crazy ass dream last night".

Terry: "Dream?... Like what"?

Alonzo: "We went to the farm to get the H.T.U watermelon weed and then we ended up in some heavy wooded area".

Terry: "An then the Amish dudes wasn't Amish they were slave catchers and you called'em niggas and tried to fight 'em"!

(Terry slick lowkey blaming Alonzo).

Alonzo: "Then George Washington & Colonel Sanders pulled up talkin that weird gangsta shit"!

Terry: "Oh shit dirty dude hand damn near cut off and those knives came out of nowhere, then the shadow ninjas came out out the dark and blew dude face smooth off....(twist his face up) wit a muthafukin musket... gwaad damn...so you had dat same dream"!?

Alonzo: "Rico", he said like a light bulb just went off in his head.

Terry: "Rico what?..Ohh".

Alonzo: "Rico...Naw couldn't be ".

Terry: "Yeah Rico he defiently laced us acid, pop he got us gone off that water wata, we some zone heads (he says starting to cry) I just wanted some weed man...natural from the soil my ass, dat nigga got us "!

Alonzo just looking at Terry like he doing way too much.

Terry Rubbing his shoulders like he trying to keep warm from the cold singing New Jack city.

Terry:" Living just of enough for city of... living (he rambles on to the end)"

Alonzo slaps the shit out terry.

Terry: "A what the fuck"!

Alonzo: "I just wanted to see if its real".

Terry hits Alonzo back.

Terry: "You feel dat"!

Alonzo: "Damn bra" holds his arm.

They both start to get into a tussle in the car.

Alonzo: "Alright man Alright damn get off me"!

Alonzo: "Rico I think I saw him".

Terry: "What are you talking about...when"?

Alonzo: "last night in the woods... the dream".

Terry looks with a blank face.

Terry: "You been dreaming about Rico" he says jokingly.

Alonzo: "The shadow ninjas".

Terry: "So you think that was real"!?

Alonzo: "You was just crying 2seconds ago"!

Terry: "I thought we got laced, I don't want to be a crack head.... But you are saying all this is real and Rico is a shadow Ninja"?

Alonzo: ...Something like that".

Terry: "Then why don't you just holla at him and see what's up".

Alonzo: "What I 'am supposed to say...Hey Rico last night George Washington and Colonel Sanders told the slave catchers to cut our heads off, are you the shadow warrior that saved us"!! He says with a dumb look on his face.

Terry: "Um Shadow Ninjas "!

Alonzo: "Really..."?

Terry: "Shadow warriors was good for the context you used but its shadow Ninjas "!

Alonzo just looks at him with the come-on face but lightens up and smiles.

Alonzo: "You right Shadow ninjas kind of hard doe" He gives Terry dap. "Let's just get to class and try to think of something else for an hour and a half".

Alonzo puts the jar of weed in the arm rest.

Terry: "Yeah I feel that ".

They both get out the car to enter the school.

Chapter 2 "Wtf is goin on"

[Back to school??]

Alonzo and Terry walk up to the door to see its locked.

Terry: "Why is this door locked "he knocks on the window "Yo"!

Alonzo points at a keypad with an fingerprint pad in the middle.

Terry: "Fool I don't know the code".

Alonzo :"Try the fingerprint ".

Terry: "Nigga you do the finger print "!

Alonzo :"Why you always acting scary".

Terry :"You do it"!

Alonzo moves Terry out the way, he slowly reaches for the key print sensor.

Terry :"Damn nigga stop pump fakin"!

Alonzo: "Man shut up" he puts his thumb on the sensor.

A video picture pops on the screen with Alonzo picture wearing an lab coat and thick lens glasses smiling. A female robot voice answers "Welcome professor Alonzo (Terry laughing at the picture) a green light flash and the boys enter the building.

Terry :"Bra your picture (crackin up laughin) how they get that shit"!

Alonzo: "I have no idea, but you here that... Professor"!

Terry: "Somebody lied".

While walking through the hallway they notice things are a little different but nothing really standing out until they notice the pictures on the wall are all black influential people.

Terry :"Damn I ain't never seen these pictures before".

Alonzo:"Not even in black history month".

They pass by the administration office when one of the staff members sees Alonzo and Terry as they're coming out of the office.

Women Staff : "Oh hi Alonzo, Terry ...Glen been waiting for you guys since this morning ".

Alonzo :"Glen oh she must be new. Can you tell her I can come by Monday "?

Women Staff: "You so silly always kidding around" she says as she guides them through the staff area to the Dean of the school office. She knocks on the door peaks her head in..."Mr.Stuart and Mr.Davenport are here...ok come on in".

The guys slowly enter the office while giving the staff women a thanks alot smile.

Terry :"Just say you left the check at home "he whispers.

Alonzo:"Don't trip it is what it is" he whispers back.

Glen (School Dean): Finishes filling out some papers turns his chair around. "Hey fellas, glad you guys made it in"!

Terry:"Oh you black? with a turban? (Looks at the mantle on the wall) and a sword"?

Alonzo:"You got a crystal ball and donkey back there too"!

Glen: laughs overly hard" You guys are always cutting up, no no (goes and grabs the sword off the mantle) This was an gift I just thought it would go good in my office I mean after all this is Moore University Tech and Engineering, (He says proudly).

(Alonzo & Terry : "Moore what"?)

Glen: I'm just getting ready for the up coming festival its getting closer. But enough of my rambling I wanted to talk you Mr. Stuart about the funding ".

Alonzo:"Hey look I was going to come to y'all next week and if I got to leave then I guess that's what it's gone be"!

Glen: "Leave what? No, I wanted to thank you for the funding for the new lab the new library and you Mr.Davenport (Terry looking surprised) for only graduating 4 years ago and already a board member getting us an new kitchen and snack machines for the cafeteria".

Terry:"Well you know I do, what I do, when I can do it ahh... Mr.Dean, Glen sir "!

Alonzo just shakes his head at Terry as if he's over doing it.

Alonzo: "Well thanks Glen we appreciate that but we're going to head to our... old biology class..be..cause we enjoy to still learn"!

Terry: "Yeah cause we already graduated..Nawmean (Alonzo agreeing) give me a test (grabs a paper off the desk holds it up then drops it) Boom passed it"!!

Alonzo: "Give me a test"!

Terry:"What's 2+2"!

Alonzo:"Don't owe $12000... Bang passed dat bitch"!

Alonzo &Terry: "Thanks Dean for the good news an all but we out"!!

They both give The Dean dap and heads out the office back into the hallway.

Both chanting "Pass dat bitch, (what he say) Pass dat bitch ". They walk into the classroom that's already started. They sneak into the only two empty seats in the classroom.

Ms.Ross is already teaching the class.

Terry: "See some things are getting back to normal "!

Ms.Ross:"Alright class I'm glad to inform you that the biology department will be getting a lot of new equipment, thanks to the funding the school recently received. So future experiments and projects are going to be fun. So have fun and I'll see you all hopefully after vacation.

Ms. Ross turns the lights on and rolls up the movie screen back up into the ceiling and as the screen goes up two big posters of Alonzo and Terry standing back to back with their lab coats and taped up glasses with the words thank you alumni written across the bottom.

Alonzo sees the picture as they're walking out the class, tries to hide his face. Taps Terry on the shoulder and points to the picture.

Alonzo: "Bra look".

Terry: "Ha look at yo stupid ass... (then his side of the poster is fully revealed from the screen going up) what in the Steph-phan Ur-kal is this shit"!

After class they head to the cafeteria to grab lunch, as they take their seats at the table Yolanda walks by with her lunch tray, she notices the guys.

Yolanda :"Hey what's up y'all" She says with a smile.

Alonzo and Terry:"Yo what's up" as she takes a seat at the table.

Yolanda: "That's crazy I didn't realize that was yall in those pictures around here yall look different in person ".

Alonzo :"Pictures around the school"?

She points above the snack vending machine, Its Terry's nerdy picture giving the thumbs up.

Terry scoffs at the picture in embarrassment.

Alonzo :"Yeah we had to meet with the Dean today but we're going to head on out in a minute".

Yolanda: "Cool, well I got a class to get to, so I'll see yall later".

Alonzo and Terry :"Alright then"!

Terry :"Man she's a lot calmer than I remember".

Alonzo: "Come on, let's get outta here".

Terry:"Hell yeah I'm ready to go home go to sleep and wake up out of this shit" looking at his picture while throwing his garbage away.

Alonzo :"Hell I rather see that picture than yo mug shot"!

Terry :"I feel you on that remember you had those tiny little braids in yo mug shot back in the day" laughs.

They head back to the car walking out the building.

Alonzo :"We need to go see Rico"!

Terry: "And say what "?

Alonzo :"Nothing we just go over there kick it like we usually do maybe we can get some answers by regular conversation".

Terry: "Okay I'm wit that".

Kemitt Mirrors Chapter 2 "Wtf is going on"

[It was all a dream??]

Alonzo and Terry leave school and drives right over to Rico house. They go to knock on the door . Then Terry start knocking on the door like the police.

Terry :"Open up Rico we know you in there"!

Alonzo:"Yo chill out bra what's wrong with you "!

Rico comes from around the back of the house. The boys can tell he's been working in the yard.

Rico:" What's wrong with you".

Terry stop acting like he was going to confront Rico and calms down.

Terry: "Ah I was just hoping you had some of that famous TEA you be cooking up"!

Rico: "Knock like that again, I'll be knocking on yo forehead the same way... come around, the front is locked. "

As they walk around Terry turns to Alonzo when Rico's not looking.

Terry: "I'm telling you boy, I am let these hands go"!!

Alonzo: "Man shut up "

Walking through the backyard they see he's been growing vegetables and fruits. They go inside and the boys take a seat on the couch.

Rico: "So y'all bangin on my door for some tea"?

Terry: "Yup"

Alonzo:" Naw he just saying the tea you made was good that's all" Alonzo looks at Terry like chill out.

Rico:"The Tea yeah, I can have tomorrow"

Terry:"Yea but you can keep the hallucinations shit "

Rico walks into the kitchen opens the refrigerator

Rico:"So what are you saying "

Alonzo shakes his head

Alonzo :"The weed Tea you gave us, man that shit got us trippin, I don't know if we having this conversation or is this a dream."

Rico: walks back into the living room area "Look ya'll not hallucinating I been through this before ".

Before Rico can finish Terry hops up walking up on Rico like he's ready to do something.

Terry:(Starts talking fast and upset)" All That natural weed shit you talkin bout straight from the soil bullshit you drugged us..."!

Terry stands firm only coming to Ricos chest. Rico looking at Terry like he's one second away from an ass whooping.

Rico: "You sure you wanta cross that line" as he balls his fist up.

Terry :"Nigga I'm down fo mine"

Things are tensed, when they hear the shower cut off and a woman yells "Hey Rico can you give me a towel please ".

Rico: Still looking to break Terry in half "I'll be right there"

Terry seriously holding his ground. Alonzo steps in between them grabs Terry pushing him towards the door.

Alonzo: "Come on man T … Rico we'll talk later ".

Rico: Just nods (ok)"Later".

Alonzo and Terry leave the house and as soon as Rico shuts the front door (Araminta) Ms. Ross comes out the back room.

Ms. Ross: She looks at Rico doesn't say anything but has a look of doubt a concern on her face.

Chapter 2. "Wtf is goin on"

[The Wake Up]

Alonzo and Terry get back to their place. Alonzo goes to the refrigerator for some drinks. While Terry turns on the T.v.

Alonzo:"If everything so different why we still got the same shit in here" hands Terry a beer.

Terry:"Cuz we never got shit in that mug" they laugh.

Alonzo:"We can hit the store tomorrow, shit I'm tired ".

Terry :"Yea...damn maybe I took it too far with Rico".

Alonzo: "You think "!

Terry: "Especially now I'm starting to fill back to normal ".

Alonzo:" We both been stressed out maybe we both trippin ".

Terry :" We got cable"? Flips the channel a couple of times.

Alonzo: "Wait turn back".

Terry turns back, they both lean forward in shock to see the story coming up.

TV show narrator :(Sounds like James Earl Jones) "Malik Malcolm Shabazz along with Martin Luther king has become the Most influential leaders over the last 6 decades generating billions of dollars and spreading those earning over the United regions including the west indie islands, to South America. When we come back where going to show an 1996 interview of Mr. Shabazz about his role he plays in helping the community and maintaining the economy . Powerful leaders When we comback on Lukango news."

The boys break out of their trance from what they have just seen on tv.

Terry:"Fuck dat call Rico"!!

Doing dong (Messed up Door bell)

Terry:" When the hell did we get an doorbell "he says in frustration.

Terry goes to the door and swings the door open "WHAT"!!

Will:"Well gawd damn Maine I can comeback later".

Alonzo:"Who dat"?

Terry:"Its Will ... Naw bro you right on time , come on in".

Will: "Brought some brews "he sits a 12 pack of beer on the table.

Alonzo reads the label on the beer then analyzes the beer in his hand.

Alonzo:" Yo Will we got some questions".

Will:"What's up"?

Alonzo:"Aey but first when did Coronas become Earl Stevens?"

Later that same night Ms.Ross and Rico are on the bank of an huge lake surrounded by wooded area with an telescope reading the stars and the moon in the night sky .

Ron adjust the telescope for Ms. Ross to the north east.

Rico:"Here look" she jumps into the back of the pick up truck.

Rico:"You see it"?

Ms.ross:"Yeah there lineing up...time it".

Rico writes down coordinates and equations.

Rico:"34"

Ms.Ross : "So about 62 days here"?

Rico:" Plus 1 starting at midnight somehow they came back a day early ".

Ms.Ross: Sits on the back of the truck, lights up a joint. "Yeah I can hear the Dejavu in the conversation earlier".

Rico: "I knew when they asked for the tea you just brought that to me today I haven't even grinded it yet".

Ms.Ross: "Well lucky we caught up with'em ".

Rico: "Yeah well I hope we're doing the right thing by them their good kids".

Ms.Ross: "Its going to take some time, but they'll be right where they're supposed to be when its time, after all... we are family ".

Rico: "Alright Minty".

They look off into the distance to see another City behind an huge wall.

END OF CHAPTER 2

3

"A Different World"

[Will give'ith Game]

The night before Will filled Alonzo and Terry in on what was going on underneath the surface. How the movement has been the protectors of the regions for years.

Will told them why the movement is important and what there about. Defusing wars before a major war and keeping our treaties, and policies intact, because of the treaty agreements that where made with New Merica are now being broken, the once flight from America to Canada leaving us for dead in fear of an nuclear war with Russia was all propaganda to move in on Canada's untapped resources.

How the people of the Regions turned the old America from an wasteland from years of fossil fuel abuse, Civil wars, oil drilling, toxic produce and pollution…Into a self reliant economy.

Them seeing the progression of our communities, they're slowly illegally trying to take over what the United Regions has built.

Along with the conversation it was a night of drinking mixed with an long day. Alonzo and Terry eventually fell asleep and Will left out early in the morning.

It is now late afternoon when it sounds like an phone ringing.

(Ring,Ring,Ring)

Alonzo finds his self-waking up in his chair, while Terry passed out on the couch. Alonzo looks at the table with empty beer, and liquor bottles getting more annoyed by the phone ring. He gets up to look around to realize its coming from under Terry.

Alonzo:"Yo T move" as he tries to lift Terry head from the pillow.

Terry:" Man what you doin"? He says in a sleepy frustration.

Alonzo proceeds to reach under the pillow cushion, grabs the phone.

The caller I'd says Yola, so Alonzo answers.

Alonzo:" Hello ".

Will:"Yeah I left my phone I'm glad you found it".

Alonzo:"Yeah, Yeah, fo sho...you coming to get it"?

Will:"Give me bout 2 hours, I can be over there".

Alonzo:"Okay cool".

Will:"Hey I've been thinking about our conversation last night, I want yall to take a ride wit me".

Alonzo:"A ride?..Alright I be ready".

Will:"Right on brother I'll see you in a minute".

Hangs up the phone.

Terry:" Was that Will"?

Alonzo:"Yeah he coming by to get his phone but he want us to ride wit him".

Terry: lays back down on the couch "Man my head hurt I ain't going nowhere".

Alonzo:"Will still talking like he from the 70s".

Terry: "We still in black Mayberry"?

Alonzo:"Yup".

Terry:"Okay I'm up".

Alonzo and Terry start to clean the house and get dressed.

Meanwhile while the boys are gearing up to take an ride with Will, Ms Ross meets back up with Rico over his house. She pulls in the driveway with his truck, gets out to see Rico in the backyard planting veggies and working on the yard.

Ms.Ross (Minty):"Boy you don't take a break do you".

Rico(Mo):"This is the only thing that doesn't seem to change, life continues to go on".

Ms.Ross (Minty):"Take a break, talk to big sis"!

Rico (Mo):"Talk what, different day same problems" He tries to ignore Araminta wishes for him to stop working on the yard.

Ms.Ross:"Mo I know "trying to get a word in but Rico(Moses) cuts her off.

Rico:"What's the point of all this if we can't even go back and save the people we love!...Maybe this is hell one pitfall to another for what ,I'm tired Minty feels like we still running, where's the fuckin finish line".

He puts his tools down and sits next to Ms.Ross (Araminta) on the steps of the back porch.

Ms.Ross (Minty):"Remember what you said to me when I gave my giving up speech".

Rico: Sighs "Yeah,Yeah,Yeah" .

Ms.Ross (Minty):" You said...maybe it's not for us to keep looking back than it is for us to move forward and if we do go back its our time to get back"! They both smile .

Rico(Mo):"Well you know I can be futuristic philosophical sometimes".

Ms.Ross (Minty):"Yeah its philosophical alright cause I'm still trying to figure out what the hell you was talking about ...but you did hit an nerve with that one"!

Rico (Mo): "I feel bad about leading those boys into this situation".

Ms.Ross (Minty):"You where just following the plan".

Rico (Mo):"The plan I made"!

Ms.Ross: "Off my visions...there warriors they just got to be put in the position they'll show up".

Rico (Mo):"Alright, you right always stick to the plan".

Ms.Ross (Minty):" Speaking of this brewing situation, we got word from Tone (Uncle Tone) that we might have an mole in the movement." She hands him some documents with pictures of an building.

Rico: "Edgar (Hoover)Federal building, so the fellas kept there end up."?

(The group of guys Will and Yolanda met up with at the gas station are allies of the movement they delivered the documents to Will & Yolanda and they passed it to Uncle Tone.)

Ms.Ross(Minty):"Yup blue prints of the building, secret room compartments the whole nine".

Rico: "Good, good send word to Tone we're on our way, get everything ready we gotta move while there at minimal security for the weekend ".

Ms.Ross: "Same shit different day"!

Rico: "That might be it" he smiles.

They both get up to walk inside the house.

Rico: "Warriors Huh"? (Referring to Alonzo and Terry)

Kemitt Mirrors Chapter 3 "A different world" page. 2

A different Car ride

Alonzo hears a car honking the horn hits his knee on the coffee table.

Alonzo: "Ahh, mamma" he whines as he looks out the window. Sees Will waving out the passenger side of the suv truck.

Alonzo: "Yo T they here"!

Terry: "They who"? He yells from the back room.

Alonzo: "Yolanda and Will ...they outside... I'm heading out" Alonzo grabs his hoodie and heads out the door, jumps in the suv behind Will.

Will :"What's up brother"!

Alonzo: "What's happin ya rolling big today huh what's good Yola"!

Yolanda: "Hey".

Terry comes jogging out and jumps in behind Yola.

Terry:" What's up yall...Yolanda" he says in a deep voice messing with her.

Yolanda: She turns to Will "Yo boy got problems "she laughs .

Yolanda pulls off headed towards the highway .

Terry: "So where we going"? Handing Will his phone.

WILL: "When we was kicking the Bo,Bo last night (Terry:"Kickin the Bo,Bo"?)I let yawl in what was going down and what the movement is about, both Yawl said ya was down.

Alonzo: "We say what "? (Terry shaking his head no)

Will: "Yawl wanted to get down wit the movement to protect what we built here"!

Alonzo and Terry:" I dont recall...that...at all".

Will: "Yall kept saying...This da new movement Bitch"!

Alonzo, Terry: "Nope, no recollection "!

Will plays an video on his phone.

Video Alonzo: "Yeah fuck ass niggas yall done fucked up now nigga (Waving Will's gun around drunk.)

Terry Video: "Yea this the New Movement bitch (Blows smoke into the camera.)

Alonzo video: "What you gone do to niggas wanta test us bro"(puts the gun into the camera)

Terry video:" What I'm gone do"!! picks up an pillow and starts punching it real fast yelling (Ahhhhhh) drops the pillow does an spin move and drops an elbow on the pillow (Alonzo in the background "Yeah nigga Yeah.. New movement Bitch").

Alonzo does a couple trigger finger with his thumb ,then the Video suddenly cuts off .

Alonzo and Terry shaking their head in embarrassment.

An awkward silence goes through the car. Then Will and Yolanda bust out laughing.

Will: "The funny part is in the moment I was feeling it...they almost had me... damn so were yall fo real or bullshittin"?

Alonzo: "First of all ...was that posted"?

Terry: "Please Jesus No" he says to himself.

Yolanda: "Posted"?

Terry: "Social Media...ya'll do have that right"?

Will: "Oh social media yeah ...but it could compromise our position so we don't use it ".

Yolanda: "Yeah over last 5 years they monitor that type of stuff heavy on both sides".

(Yolanda turns on to the highway)

Alonzo: "Because of this situation with the people inside the wall"?

Will: "So you were paying attention "!

Alonzo: "Yeah its coming back to me" he sits back in his seat.

Terry: "So what's all this going to lead up to"?

Will: "MUDER!!"...Will and Yolanda laugh.

Terry: "Man I thought y'all was serious for a minute ".

Yolanda: "OH we are, what you think war is...(Looking in the rearview at Alonzo and Terry)Say around campus they say yall two took the marijuana medicine game to another level"!

Alonzo & Terry:"Ahh Yeah" they say in hesitation.

Will: "Yeah they have, I remember Alonzo working while we were partying. Even when Terry came up yawl stayed at it. "

Alonzo: "Yeah well you know...team work makes the dream work"!

Terry looks at Alonzo, like what the hell.

Yolanda: "Yeah that's some cool shit...yall defiantly not what I thought you two would be like ".

Terry: "And what's that "?

Yolanda: "You know...Kind of Nerdy...from the pictures from school".

Alonzo and Terry:(Fake laughs)"Nerdy"?

Yolanda: "Yeah you know the thick glasses, the suspenders"!

Will looking at Yolanda as she's asking these questions, thinking to himself that she's making good points.

Terry: "Those just work clothes, we players around here baby"!

Alonzo: "There you go" Agreeing with Terry.

Yolanda: "Is that right, so when did yall get to Section 9"? (Sections and Regions were code names for city and states used during the Malcom x, Martin Luther King rebellion years. The region and section codes where well known by the local people throughout the years.)

Terry: "Section 9... What the hell you talkin bout"!?

Yolanda and Will look at each other like somethings up with these two.

Yolanda pulls the car over on the side of the highway.

Yolanda: "What ya'll some coon ass spies or something"!!!

The way Yolanda said it they knew she wasn't playing.

Alonzo: "Spy"?

Terry: "Bitch who you callin a coon"!!

Yolanda pushes some buttons and a compartment opens up from the lower dashboard. Yolanda grabs the hunting knife points it at Terry and Will grabs the 357 magnum.

Alonzo: "Will.." he says applaud by Will pulling the gun on them.

Yolanda: "Who's the bitch" she looks at Terry.

Terry: "You can be anything you wanna be just be cool baby"!

Yolanda puts the knife to his neck. Terry takes her more seriously now.

Will: "Enough of the playing, now somethings up with yawl... First, I thought you're just blind to what's going on, but now I'm thinking yawl playin real dumb or to smart for your own good, Either way y'all gone have to start runnin the skinny down on something"!!

Alonzo: "Run the what"?

The whole time Will was talking Alonzo and Terry were giving signals to each other that it's more secret compartments on the back doors.

Alonzo: "Now"!

They both hit the doors, Alonzo pulls out a cigarette car lighter like it's a weapon, Terry pulls out some change and throws it towards the front. Realizing they didn't find no weapons and the doors won't open they just sit there with a stupid look on their face.

Alonzo: "That did not go the way it went in my head".

Will: "Alonzo start talkin, I'm not playin "!

Alonzo : "Man if I tell you, you gone think we crazy"!

Yolanda: "Y'all just threw a lighter and some change at us, we way past crazy"!

Terry really analyzes what Will and Yolanda have on. Yolanda all black with a big ass knife and Will all black with big ass gun.

Terry: "Shadow Ninjas"? Looks at Alonzo

Alonzo: "What"?..."Ohh"

Will points the gun at Terry.

Terry:" I ain't telling y'all shit till you get these weapons out are face".

Will cocks the gun.

Terry "Mannn...this nigga was talkin bout going to the farm to steal some plants"!

Alonzo: "Its not stealing when they shutting down the farm".

Terry: "So after he forced me to go…".

Alonzo: "OH it's my fault now, I was looking out for both of us"!

Terry: "Fool it was you who couldn't pay tuition "!

Alonzo: "You couldn't pay the light bill"!

Terry: "Because I gave this big head nigga money up front (Will looking confused "me"?) then he go to jail..plus you parked the car 20miles from the damn weed spot"!

Alonzo:" I was trying to be incognito".

Terry: "More like incompetent negro...You dizzy son of a bitch"!

Alonzo:"Yo mamma nigga"!

Terry: "My auntie bitch "!

Alonzo: "OH you want to start jabin"!

Terry:" I mean I'm not lying "!(Scooby doo voice)

Alonzo: "Wasn't it you who took yo dumb ass out and waived down the horse and carriage, that turned out to be the top goon for George Washington & the Colonel ".

(Will and Yolanda "George Washington "??)

Terry: "That ain't my fault, I thought they were Amish".

Alonzo "I thought they was Amish (mocking Terry) ...I didn't know they was slave bounty hunters! Like you never seen Roots, Django, 12 years a slave, Hidden colors, The News "!!

Terry:" I don't like slave movies".

Alonzo: "And I'm still trying to find out how we got in one"!!

Will and Yolanda looking even more confused while Alonzo and Terry argued.

Terry:" I know, when they put that rope around yo neck you start crying"!

Alonzo: "Whatever bra...that was you".

Terry: "Whispers.. it was you"!

Yolanda: "Would yall shut up...it's like two 5year olds"!

Will:" I know I really want to shoot both of 'em".

Alonzo: "You know we can hear you"!

Will: "So wait I thought yawl was just drunk, all that time lapse jive y'all talkin bout last night was true"?

Alonzo:" I don't remember everything we said but yeah it's true and we just want to get back home."

Terry: "Yes it's TRUE you owe me 2000 dollars "!

Yolanda: "So you believe this bull they talking about "?

Will: "Grandma use to tell us stories of shit like this".

Yolanda: "Old folk tales that's all they were, besides how would you know them but they don't know you"? She says to will.

Alonzo: "We do know Will he always been the homie ".

Terry: "Didn't I just said he owe me 2,000 dollars "!

Alonzo: "Look things are like the same but different like parallel universe or some shit, the Will we know was cool and a hustler from the neighborhood.

Will: "Hustler...Like what"?

Terry: "You made a lot of money sellin dope nigga...you was gone hook us up with some pounds but you got locked up after I already gave you 2000 dollars...and YOLA!... I met you...you had on booty shorts in school" he says with a smile.

Alonzo: "Matter of fact head up the road I'll take you to the spot it happened at".

Will gives the okay nod to Yolanda to go ahead and drive to the spot.

Yolanda: "Hey I want to believe y'all but if I think it's some bullshit I cuttin nuts off both yall(waving the knife at both of them) and I know you making that booty shorts shit up"!

Terry:" You aint cuttin nothin you love me girl"!

Yolanda:"Phhh...try me"? Both her and Will put their weapons up as Yolanda gets back to driving.

Alonzo: "Girl we know black girls don't cut no nuts off...yall might shoot us in the shoulder or some shit ... but yall ain't cuttin no black man's nutts off no matter how mad ya get"!

They all laugh except Yolanda, she gives the try me face.

They make it up to where the farm is. They turn on that same back road. On the right it's still farm land but not a lot of crops like it once was and to the left a big building with an security gate all around it.

Terry: "Damn...that building was not there".

Alonzo: "Yeah it was all woods over here".

They get out the car to observe the building where they wont be seen.

Yolanda: "So this is where all that nonsense happened "?

Terry:" You don't recognize this place "?(Whispers "shadow Ninja ")

Yolanda :"Yeah I do".

Terry: looks at Alonzo "What I say".

Yolanda: "This used to be the original main Water Tower resource building".

Will: "Yeah you see the giant lake out there (Alonzo and Terry :"Yeah")that was some of the most purified water around these parts, channeled through this building to keep the water rotating it helped keep the soil pure and crops healthy".

Yolanda: "Yeah back in the day everyone got their jugs of water 3 times an week from here".

Alonzo :"So what is it now"?

Will: "At first we didn't know, it was told to us they were renovating and updating the building but the only thing they did was, build a private fortress around it and it doesn't provide the water to the surrounding Communities anymore ".

Yolanda: "They been trying to do this to all our water towers across all the regions and sections".

Will: "So where exactly did this time lapse happened. "

Alonzo: "It's hard to tell now, but it's got to be right there on the edge of the lake it was just an small creek when we came through"!

Terry: "So the Water Towers getting shutdown is happening across the country?"

Yolanda: "Over the last 5 to 6 years they been trying to take over all our resources and the farmlands ".

Will: "So all that lead ya to this point right here"

Alonzo: "Sounds crazy huh".

Yolanda: "Got damn lunatic...but we gotta roll out" as she starts to get back in the car.

Terry: "Aye we can't believe it ourselves, so can we keep this quiet until we can figure something out".

Yolanda: "You think I'm gone repeat that bat crazy shit...yall secret is safe with me"!

Alonzo: "Who's the statue"?

Will: "Richard Riker he was said to be a famous general that became the president's inner circle, but in reality, he built his name on being a plantation overseer and bounty hunter for slaves escaping to the north legal or illegal.

Yolanda: "They say he stopped a slave rebellion around here but that's all was ever said."

Alonzo: "He look like the dude who caught those knives to the face the night we...entered ...the time lapse"!

Terry:" Ohh..That is dude "!

Alonzo & Terry: "The Musty Misfits Gang"!

Terry: "He got an statue, he screamed like A straight bitch before we he died"!

Will: "Fo'real"?

Yolanda: Starts the car "Do you always have to curse when you talk".

Terry: "I love you too Yola"!

Yolanda shakes her head (Yolanda: "This gone be a long trip") and drives off headed to New America.

Kemitt mirrors chapter 3 "A different world "page.3

(Ride to meet Uncle Tone)

Terry:"Aey bro wake me when we there" he says to Alonzo then puts his jacket over his head.

Alonzo:" Hey Will.. so you knew us before I guess we got here"?

Will: "Ahh yeah man".

Alonzo: "So how where we"?

Will:"Y'all where cool , a little Nerdy always talked about work and business, didn't party to much didn't curse at all".

Alonzo:" Didn't curse, what about the movement"?

Will:"Yall..they...whatever never talked about the movement, but always contributed to the city in a major way, ...everything was everythang but as things started to turn we haven't hung out in a while but I can definitely see the difference in you two"!

Alonzo: "Like what"?

Will: "Pure opposites yawl like to party, yall curse alot (Yolanda:"A lot")and y'all have more street , more edge more ,aggression in yall"!

Alonzo: "Damn you make us sound angry as shit, I see why everybody from here happy, the money recycles in the community, black businesses is thriving, nigga yall got legal weed you can get in the gas station not in the parking lot...good weed too"!

Will: "OH that weed is an energy upper, better than caffeine you also get it in drinks...We have you to thank for that ...or the other you"!?

Yolanda: "Oh yawl for surely angry about something, but are you willing to die fighting for not just for your freedom but the freedom for someone you don't even know... It took a longtime for us as a people to get to where we at today , we refuse to go back to shackles physically or mentally we've been chained to poverty for centuries, harsh prison terms because our skin color but the real truth is population control and prison is big business...We refuse to go back without an fight"!

Alonzo: "Yeah... I can dig it"!

Will: "You in...We can still take you back"?

Alonzo: "For some reason I feel like we supposed to be here...We in"!

Chapter 3 "A Different world " page.4
(Mo & Minty on a mission)

Rico (Moses) & Ms. Ross (Minty) just got word of a mole in their movement so they waste no time in putting an plan together with top ranking member Tone (Uncle Tone). They meet with Tone at an safe house early morning (Car shop) right outside the wall (New Merica=Old Canada).

They pull up to the back of the shop, greeted by some of the soldiers of the movement discreetly working security. One of the soldiers immediately opens the passenger door for Ms.Ross.

Soldier: "Tone and Professor are inside ".

Ms.Ross: "Thank you ".

They head inside, walks to the back office.

Uncle Tone:" MO ...Minty!!" Greets them with dap and a hug.

Professor does the same.

Rico : "You got any names who the mole is"?

Uncle Tone:" Nothing solid but I got my suspicions".

Professor hands them documents on a raid at one of the movement warehouses from 4 years ago.

Professor: "Remember this"?

Rico, Ms.Ross: "Yeah".

Professor: "The government of New Merica says that the Warehouse was used to illegally move goods into their country, which would break treaty trading agreements".

Uncle Tone: "Even though our original trade agreement was we will never trade with you muthafukas"!

Professor: "Yes but that was 30 years ago, Since then we made agreements from our appointed Representatives to trade with New Merica over the last 15 years".

In the documents they see propaganda of old newspaper about how the negroes of hell land (Old America)and how they live like savages compared to their New Merica heaven, to new propaganda of now moving back.

Rico: "Because of the trading they see the value of the land".

Ms.Ross: "Okay but who's the alledge informant "?

Professor drops two pictures on the table .

Rico:" Edward Robinson"?

Ms.Ross: "Ronnie Johnson" as she looks at the other picture.

Uncle Tone:" We believe these two are the ones getting their government the leads they need to seize land from the owners.

Ms.Ross: "How sure are you about this"?

Uncle Tone:"100 Percent"!

Professor: "We're not sure but they're ahead of international trading and laws are being passed that we as the people aren't privileged to knowing until its basically to late".

Uncle Tone: "So why don't we just grab'em up "he said while playing with his blow torch.

Ms.Ross: "Then we won't know who's pulling the strings "!

Uncle Tone:"Shiit" pulls out an ice pick "Plug this into an kneecap...they tell everything "!

Professor: "Here take these glasses...the blueprints of the Edgar building is loaded up...the targeted offices are highlighted...tonight it should be light security".

Rico: "Should be"? As he checking out the glasses.

Professor:" Take these (put two pistols on the table) their energy charged they can put an 500 pound bull to sleep on 3 levels "

RicoMo :"It has 5 levels on here"?

Professor: "Level 5 takes time to build and can burn the gun out quicker... Minty yours looks like your normal revolver but shoots unlimited rounds of energy projected bullets...while both guns are quite and lethal it can over heat..that can take up to 90 seconds before your able to fire again so make your shots count".

Uncle Tone: "Where my energy gun at muthafuka ...Im wit you everyday... always holdin out on me"!

Professor :" Anyways..this is an scrambler for the camera's to jam just hold the button down for 2 seconds and it gives you 10 seconds just long enough for you to do what you gotta do".

Uncle Tone: "So yall good for tonight "?

Rico: "We good ... yall make sure the shop is clear on are way back"!

Uncle Tone: "Yeah we'll be there after the party".

Ms.Ross: "Party"? As she and Rico (Moses) gear up.

Uncle Tone: "Yeah everybody going to be there, that's how we politic... and catch up what's going on".

Rico: "I don't think this is an good time for a party...wait don't tell me it's at that trap door closet for a condo you got in Feuherstadlt"?

Ms.Ross: "You having the party behind the wall..That's not a good idea "!

Uncle Tone: "First of all Mo..insults will get you nowhere, we designed that whole building (pointing at Professor), shit they want to Quietly build on are turf I'll quietly build on there's...Secondly, if yall need backup we right there"!

Rico and Ms.Ross both give him a crazy look while walking to the car.

Uncle Tone: "Look don't worry my nephew and niece are coming up I gone be on point".

Rico:" Will"?

Uncle Tone: "And Yolanda...They both been really proven their selves ".

Ms.Ross: "No room for mistakes tonight. Tone I love you but don't make us have to pull rank an shut everything down because our top guy is not being effective "!

Uncle Tone: "I got it...look the phone signals can't be traced I'm a be there every step of the way".

Ms. Ross: "I'm not worried bout us Tone..." She shuts the passenger door.

Tells the solider driving to drive, as Rico closes the slide door to the bullet proof van there taking to blend in New Merica .

Uncle Tone:" I got you ...hope you like the van" he yells as they leave out the car shop.

Uncle Tone: "Let's get to this party maine"!

Professor: "The trap closet"!! He laughs.

Uncle Tone: "Ain't he the most polite rudest dude ever "he turns to the other soldiers "Make sure yall security sweep everything before the next shift come in then make yall way up the party ...alright see yawl later"!

Uncle tone phone rings.

Uncle Tone: "Nephew "he answers.

Will:"Unc we'll be there in a couple hours".

Uncle Tone: "Ok cool I'll be there.."!

Will : "Right on".

Uncle Tone: "Right on".

Uncle Tone and professor jumps into the custom muscle car an head to the condo.

Chapter 3 "A different world " (Party@Uncle Tone)
"The truth always lies beneath the eye."

Terry wakes up from a nudge from Alonzo.

Alonzo: "Hey man we here at the border"!

Will passes out the ID bracelets.

Will: "Here you need these to get through".

Terry: "Man I thought I was gone be nervous going through the border, but that joint actually got me relaxed, feeling good".

Alonzo points to the wall, Terry Freaks out.

Terry: "What the fuck is that a Nazi Eagle"!?

Will: "They built the wall but lost their power in the 60's, early 70's'

Alonzo: “The 70’s”? Looking puzzled, but before he could ask any more questions, they pull up on the border getting ready to be checked by the guards.

Yolanda: “Just chill out let’em scan your bracelet and if they ask, your here for work”!

The guys agree but still look slightly nervous. They pull up to the line and 2 guards come up on both sides of the suv, while the others stand by with machine guns and guard dogs.

Guard#1:”What’s your visit to New Fuhrerstadt” he scans Yolanda bracelet.

Yolanda :”Here for work” the scan blinks green.

Guard#2:”What’s your visit to New Fuhrerstadt “!

Will: “Work” scans blinks green.

Guard#2:”What’s your visit to New Fuhrerstadt “he scans Alonzo bracelet.

Alonzo :”Work”.

Guard#1:”What’s your visit to New Fuhrerstadt “he scans Terry Bracelet.

Terry :”Auh yeah...work...” he says nervously looking at the guard dog sniffing around.

Guard#1looks at Terry suspiciously after beeps sound goes off after scanning his bracelet. He looks into the car more closely.

Guard#2:”And how long is your stay here”?

Will: “Three days sir”.

Guard#2 signals the other guards to bring the other dogs over.

Guard#1:”Says here you already been here for some time, can I see your bracelet once more”!

Will looks at a guard working in the booth on a computer.

Terry puts his arm back up to the window to be scanned again. Tensions are starting to brew with the two guards.

Guard#1:”Hmmm” as he scans again.

Terry :”Is there a problem “?

The guard looks at the scanner screen...finally turns green with new information.

Guard#1:”No problems “waves to the control room to let them through.

They drive through, on to a super highway to City of Fuhrerstadt.

Terry :"Man what was that... Yo bootleg wrist band almost got me fucked up"!!

Yolanda :"Do you always have to curse"!

Will: "Calm down we made it through, you alright".

Alonzo:"Yo I thought we're coming to help yall out in return yall help us figure out how we get back home...not get fucked up in the process".

Terry:"Nawmean...wait help do what I was sleep".

Will: "Naw..what..Naw mean? Look we are helping, we got friends who live here everything cool jack"!

Terry :"Yea don't start coppin Deuces now Tray" mocking Alonzo from when he was telling him before the time lapse.

Alonzo :"Okay but why we got to come all the way up here to get help back home"?

Terry: "That is true ".

Will :"Look anybody that's an somebody is going to be here tonight like Professor yawl will have a chance to talk and maybe figure something out".

Yolanda: "Besides just because yall came through some damn time warp don't mean the actual world revolves around yo asses"!

Terry: "Must you curse all the time"!

Yolanda rolls her eyes.

Alonzo :"Where exactly are we going "?

Will: "To my Uncles party".

Alonzo &Terry: "Party"!!

Alonzo: "Well shit that's all you had to say in the first place Nawmean"!!

Yolanda: "Nawmean?...Naw...Know what I mean, oh I get it"!

Terry : "That ain't all you can get it Yola"!

Yolanda: "I still got the knife ".

The guys looking out the window as they approach the city.

Terry : "Why this city looks light years ahead of our town" He said in Aww of the scenery.

Yolanda: "Yeah well the truth always lies beneath the eye".

Alonzo :"More riddles huh, I would ask for explanation but I think we gonna find out sooner than later." As they see the big sign Welcome to the City of New Fuhrerstadt .

New Fuhrerstadt City is futuristic projecting modern paradise, with big super highways tall buildings that shine miles away, the cars are curved and sleek. The high-rise apartments seem to reach the clouds in the sky. Upstate New York into old Canada has been reclaimed as New Fuhrerstadt and Canada the country is New Merica.

Yolanda takes the exit ramp off the highway they find their way to a big plain looking building.

Yolanda puts in a code to a hidden keypad inside the glove box big wall door opens, then they come to a gate she puts her thumb print in and the gate opens. They park the car in this underground garage and heads toward the elevators.

Terry : "Hey man what in the bat cave is this shit" as they get out the car.

Alonzo : "Hey yawl better not be tryna line a nigga up"!

Will : "What...come on man this my Uncles underground garage you gotta be part of the movement to get access down here, there's his cars right there".

Alonzo and Terry notice two old school muscle cars two metal black trucks and a New modern car like the ones they seen on the highway.

Alonzo: "Damn, I don't know if yo Uncle crazy or just got sauce"!

Terry : "I don't know if his Uncle a pimp or batman"!

Alonzo: "Shit that's damn near the same thing ain't it" they laugh as they get into an elevator.

Will: "Going up" Will and Yolanda smile then will push the button.

The elevator takes off fast Alonzo and Terry wasn't ready for the speed. (Ding) As the elevator doors open Alonzo and Terry holding on to the rails for dear life.

Will and Yolanda exit the elevator.

Yolanda: "Come on"!

Alonzo and Terry don't move like their feet stuck to the floor.

Will and Yolanda laughing

Will: "Yeah that first time get you ...wait till you go down...Ha let's party baby" (They can hear the funk music playing)

Yolanda: "Just looks at both of them in minor disappointment "Y'all stupid" and walks down the hall.

Terry: "So they ain't gone warn nobody ".

Alonzo: "That was some bull shit".

Alonzo and Terry get there self together to catch up with Will and Yolanda. Will knocks on the door.

Terry: "U can't just put your thumb on the knob I thought you was plugged in".

The door swings open.

Uncle Tone: "Who the fuck is it"!!!...puts Will in a choke hold followed by a bear hug. "Nephew "!! Slaps Will on back of the neck gone get in here. Then looks at Yolanda "My Niecy "gives her a nice strong hug and kiss on both cheeks "You good baby anything you want Boogie you got it okay "!

Yolanda: "Thank you Unc" she smiles an walks in sticking her tongue out at Will.

Will: "Dat don't make no damn since".

Uncle Tone: "And who the hell are you two"!

Alonzo and Terry:"Uhh well uhh".

Will: "Oh these my boys Alonzo and Terry".

Uncle Tone gives them a quick evaluation look over.

Uncle Tone:" Come on in, any friends of my nephew and niece are friends of mine."

Yolanda: "Not so quick ...Those his friends" .

Uncle Tone: "Make yourself at home there's plenty of space Will can show you to our guest rooms... wait I recognize yall"!

Alonzo: "You do"? He says out of curiosity.

Uncle Tone: "Yeah ... the goofy muthafukas that did the weed medicine shit... business is booming because of yall.. You two helped save our economy...hey but enough of that we got some hours before the get down so yall go head to the rooms...rest up shower whatever "!

Will leads them to their room.

Alonzo: "Damn bro this is a real nice thang here man"!

Will: "Yeah my Unc made a lot of good investments through the years but he's a major figure in this movement also".

Gets Alonzo to his room.

Alonzo :"Well thanks man I'm a rest up a bit".

Will:" Alright cool".

As everyone gets settled in the pen house Uncle Tone ducts off into one of his secret wall passages to a room above the pen house.

Professor is setting up the computers and communications to help guide Rico and Ms. Ross on their mission tonight.

Uncle Tone: "How's everything "?

Professor:"Ev-very-thing.. is ...good as he finishes bringing everything up on the computer monitors. Hands Uncle Tone an ear piece. "Sound is on... go ahead".

Uncle Tone: "Titty 1, Titty 2 ...come in... Titty 1, Titty 2...are you there."?

Ms. Ross :"We hear you jackass"!

Uncle Tone: "Is the eye on the sparrow...repeat is the eye... on ...the sparrow "!

Rico :"Now I remember why we don't bring him along anymore ".

Ms. Ross: "We're in position." As they watch the building from a far waiting for the right time to make there move.

Chapter 3 "A different world "
(Uncle Tone party: Truth always lies beneath the eye part 2)

Uncle Tone: "Hey I got an idea...why don't yall just drop by the pen house after you done."

Ms.Ross: "I have an idea let's have 20mins of communication silence."

The audio goes dead but the camera on their glasses are still on. They can see Ms.Ross giving the finger through Rico's glasses.

Professor laughs.

Uncle Tone: "All work ,no play...Well I'm going back down... the party starting soon".

Professor: "We got it here".

Uncle Tone: "No appreciation" as he leaves to go back down to the pen house.

Uncle Tone uses one of his emergency passages that leads to the walk in pantry into the kitchen. Terry's head first into the refrigerator, grabbing everything he can find to make an sandwich. He closes the refrigerator door to see Uncle Tone standing there staring at him eating a bag of chips.

Terry: "OH shit" fumbles the condiments and food his two arms are full of. "Gawd damn Tone ".

Uncle Tone:" I seen you googly eyeing my boogie "!

Terry: "Now hold on Unc I don't rock like..."!

Uncle Tone: "My niece fool"!!

Terry: "OH...phew..I thought... never mind that Yolanda..Yola ...oh naw she cool but I don't think she like me anyways" as he puts everything he dropped on the counter.

Uncle Tone: "Look here my niece and nephew are very dear to me so be careful especially when it comes to my boogie ". Pulls a sharp butcher knife from the side of the center island and slams the blade into the cutting board. "Fo yo sandwich" as he starts to walk out the kitchen .

Terry:" I just need a butter knife, nothing this sharp" looking at this customize knife.

Uncle Tone: Stops in his tracks turns around "This a grown man house everything sharp...just check my outfit tonight does an Morris day check in the mirror "Ooh"!

Terry: "What is it with these people and knives "dig the knife out the cutting board and proceed his sandwich making. Looks at the door slightly open next to the fridge. "Did this nigga just come out the pantry"? He looks in but doesn't see anything out the ordinary but snacks.

Will and Yolanda sitting by the bar talking, Uncle Tone walks up.

Uncle Tone: "What's up family...ya sitting at the bar, so what can I get cha"!

Will: "I'll take a beer ".

Uncle Tone grabs a couple bottles of Earl Steven's beer from the ice box.

Uncle Tone: "Earl Ste-phan fo you" slides Will an beer.

Uncle Tone:" I already know what my boogie want" grabs the Earl Stevens wine. Pours her a glass of wine.

Yolanda :"Thanks Unc"

Will: "OH lawd" referring to Uncle Tone always babying Yolanda "You know Unc you can't baby her and pour her alcohol at the same time.

Uncle Tone: “You know your problem nephew, yo head so big you never run out of thoughts...now sit on that”!

Yolanda cracking up laughing.

Terry joins in on the conversation and takes a seat at the bar with his sandwich.

Will: “So what's up for tonight “?

Uncle Tone: “Ah nothing but an get together and a little celebration “.

Terry: slides closer to Will. “Hey man I can't lie I'm enjoying this right here but who do we talk to about our situation”?

Will: “In due time man we'll get there, in the meantime enjoy yo self ...Alright”!

Terry: “Yeah, Alright “Terry sees Yolanda on the balcony by herself with her glass of wine. He easies up to her.

Terry: “Hey wassup”!

Yolanda just nods her head, enjoying the sunset.

Terry: “So this is Fur-blathf city huh” messing up the city's name.

Yolanda:”Fuhrerstadt “.

Terry: “Yea that , why didn't they just call it old York Canada “.

Yolanda: “Don't know, so what I call you?..The time traveler” she says in a sassy way.

Terry :”Oh we throwing shots”! Laughing, she smiles. “Naw you call me... you writing this down...(Yolanda:”Umhm”)2 Dimensions of a plalya”!

Yolanda: Bust out laughing “Dimensions of what”?

Terry: “You know a player from two different worlds “he says with a smile trying to clarify his joke.

Yolanda: “I am from earth I know what a player is I'm not all discombobulated like you” smiles, takes an sip of her wine.

Terry: “Discombobulated?...well through all this craziness it's good to be around beauty for a change. “

Yolanda: “What the city lights”?

Terry: Terry looks at her sincerely “No I was talking bout you”!

Yolanda quickly takes another sip from her glass trying to hide her blushing.

While having a moment they're interrupted by Uncle Tone.

Uncle Tone: “Hey what yall talking about boogie “he says with suspicion .

Yolanda: "Nothing ".

Uncle Tone: "Nothing huh"?..."Well look here people bout to start dropping by soon so yall need to get ready.

Terry: "Okay cool big homie good looking out" Terry heads inside .

Uncle Tone: "Boogie you Alright ".

Yolanda: "I'm fine Unc".

Uncle Tone: "Okay ... I need you focused tonight "

Yolanda: "Always "!

Uncle Tone: "Right on, now gone put some soap to those arm pits (Yolanda starts to head in) I came out here for the refer, it just y'all two out here puppy talking ".

Kemitt mirrors chapter 3 "A different world"
(The truth always lies beneath the eye part 3)
Mo & Minty on a mission) page.7

Professor has hacked into the camera's in & out the Edgar building. He sees what looks like the last of the working staff leaving the building.

Professor:"Alright guys the staff has left and only 20 guards remain throughout the building.

Rico:"Only 20 huh"?

Professor:"Okay yall ready"!

Ms.Ross:" No P. We like hanging around bushes all damn day"!

Professor:"We'll put the glasses on and I can see what you two see" they both put on the glasses.

Professor:"Boom we in business, ok on the count of 3 I'm going to unlock this rear door but you have to use the scrambler for the camera's...the 10second delay, shouldn't alert the guards"!

Rico:"Count it".

Professor:"3,2,1".

Rico uses the scrambler, they hear the buzz for the door and quickly make their move inside.

Professor:"Alright the yellow highlighted area is where the confidential information is. "

Rico: "But I see two rooms highlighted ".

Professor:"Well those are the rooms I narrowed down".

Ms.Ross:"Yeah but one is 6 floors up the other 4 floors down ".

Professor:"Either split up or go together but let's not be here all night"!

Rico: Turns to Ms.Ross "You go up I'll head down stairs".

Rico:"Stay on point sis".

Ms.Ross:"You know it"!

Ms.Ross heads up with caution as Rico starts down the staircase.

Professor:"The red dots are security guards I'll try to load'em as fast as I can".

Rico: "I come to a dead end but I'm only down 2 flights".

Professor:" Wait a second (typing on computer) okay here we go" he loads up more graphic blueprints from the computer to Rico glasses. "You're coming into a restricted area, I'll have to buzz that door...use the scrambler head left ".

Rico:"count it"

Professor: "3,2,1"

Rico grabs the door heads left into a dark lit hallway, he sees the camera's so he quickly moves out of their sight.

Professor:"M2 (code for Ms.Ross) you need to go through the 5th floor door and cut to the other side staircase, its three guards right in a room near the door.

Ms.Ross:"Yeah I see'em...okay I'm going through the door now".

She uses the scrambler for the camera's, she gets low passing right by the guards watching tv in the cafeteria. She makes it with ease to the other side of the building staircase and goes up.

Ms.Ross:"Okay I'm on the 6th"

Professor:"You clear... go to the right corner office" .

Ms.Ross picks the office door lock and quietly enters the room.

Rico:"I'm losing the map "as he walks with caution deeper down the hallway.

Professor:" Yeah I'm losing your visual but I can still track your moves ...turn your map off and enhance your night vision ".

Rico continues down the hallway he gets to the evidence office, the door is locked. (Sign= reads No Electronics beyond this point.)

Rico: "Can you open this door"?

Professor : Typing "I'm sure that door is Manuel"?

Rico: "Its reinforced steel ...old school".

Ms.Ross:"What's wrong bro having problems "as she finds documents in the special agent desk.

Rico:"Its like 12 bolt locks on this thing".

Professor:"Use level one on your energy gun".

Rico:"You gotta come with better names for your inventions Doc".

Ms.Ross:"Agreed" looking for more information, she comes across an file with names and pictures. "I got it I'm head back to you M1(Rico code name)".

Rico uses the energy gun to blow each lock off the door.

Rico:"I'm in" he creeps inside the evidence room blows the lock off two more security doors.

Looking through the evidence room he sees another connecting room .

Rico:"There's another room... but it's behind a vault ...the only window is blacked out".

Professor:"The room must have been renovated".

Rico:"The lock is coded so its modern unlike the other doors ".

Professor:"If I can get somehow find the codes...M2(code=Ms. Ross) can you retrieve an modem or even a computer laptop "?

Ms.Ross :"I can try" as she's headed down the staircase to the 4th floor.

Professor:" Wait a minute...I highlighted the room from lieutenant Brass, he's in charge of the evidence room.

She sees at least 5 guards monitoring this floor through the glasses.

Ms.Ross: "So much for smooth sailing "she says to herself ".

Ms.Ross stays low to the walls creeping through the hallways using the scrambler for the cameras .

She finds the office she gets close to the door ready to pick the lock but realizes the door is unlocked. She moves into the office .

Ms.Ross:"I'm in ,but the door was unlocked".

Professor:"So the lieutenant could be in the building...let's hurry this up".

Ms.Ross:"Okay I got the computer ".

Professor:"Just make sure it's on" gets to hacking.

Rico:"Can yall move this along"!

Professor:"Just.. an.. minute ...(Typing fast) Bang!! Man I'm too cold fo these suckas...okay I got'em".

Ms.Ross:"Okay M1 I'm headed back to you".

Professor:"Ready M1...its 3 different codes".

Rico:"let's go...1.9.6.9, 1.9.7.2, A.P.1.3".

Rico hears the gears in the vault door unlocking. He turns the main wheel to open the vault. He enters the vault only to see books an old movie reels pointed at an blank projector screen, he reads the labels "Moon landings" the others read "Moon Quantum sessions".

Rico:" There just a bunch books and old movie reels, from 1962 to 1982, 2002 to 2012...2022"?

Professor:"Is that it "?

Rico:"That's it "!

Professor:"Can you pack it up"?

Rico:"Uh Yeah" he goes back into the evidence room empties out an big duffle bag full of packaged drugs, then puts the reels and whatever else he can fit into bag.

Meanwhile (Minty) Ms.Ross is making her way back to Rico when two guards are patrolling the hallway, so she ducts of into an unlocked room and gets down. The guards didn't see her so they kept on their route. Once they passed she starts to sneak out of the room when she sees an board with a bunch of pictures on the wall . She takes a closer look.

Ms.Ross:"Hey P are you seeing this"?

Professor:"Yeah Im seeing it...back up to get the whole wall" Professor takes an freeze frame shot from the camera on Ms.Ross glasses.

Professor:"Okay I got it ...its time for y'all to get out of there "!

Rico:"I'm heading back up now".

The lieutenant comes back to his office sits down in his chair with his late night lunch opens up his computer laptop to see its already on...he looks suspiciously around his office but doesn't see anything out the ordinary, he logs into his computer sees a picture taken from his computer anti theft software.

Lieutenant Brass:" Shit"!! He pushes a silent alarm button.

All the guards get an intruder alert on their radio. The building starts to shut down, gates come down blocking off hallways and exits. Windows are being covered by metal shutters.

Rico leaving the evidence room hears the vault automatically close.

Rico:"Of course...it was too easy"!! He says to himself as he runs for the staircase.

Ms.Ross comes running down the staircase as Rico was coming up.

Ms.Ross:"What happened "?

Rico:"Does it matter at this point" putting on his leather gloves "P where do we exit"?

Professor:"I'm working ok ...now you got to give me some time to break down the security systems but to your advantage I got control of all camera's (typing fast on his computer base) and their radio frequency exposes their whereabouts "he loads up the new images in their glasses.

Ms.Ross:"Damn I can see through the walls"!

Rico:"Yeah I thought you said 20 guards" as he tightens up the duffle bag on his back

Professor:"That was a give or take rough estimate ".

Ms.Ross:" I see about 10 of them right above us".

Professor:"Follow the blue path to the exit point...and they called it in so you only got about 17mins".

Professor contacts the solider waiting for Rico and Ms.Ross to get back to the van.

Professor:"S1...S1 come in"!

Soldier getaway driver:"I'm here"

Professor: "Be ready for there exit".

Soldier getaway driver:"Im ready"!

Rico and Ms.Ross going up to the 3rd floor door Ms.Ross Quietly pulls on the door but its locked.

Rico:" P 3rd floor can you unlock it"?

Professor:" The security system converted back to old school tactics...but I'll get it ...give me 90seconds".

Rico "Old school tactics "looks at Ms.Ross with a grin.

All of a sudden tear gas smoke starts to fill the staircases. (Part of the security shutdown.)

Ms.Ross nods her head in agreement. They can see a guard close to the door (Guard radio: Sweep the building)

Ms.Ross takes the butt of her knife and knocks the bottom of the door.

She draws the guard attention; he comes slowly to the door with his weapon out.

The guard swings the door open but before he can make a sound Rico wraps his left arm around his neck and drives his knife into his chest, then throws him over the staircase.

Rico and Ms.Ross get out the stairwell before they get consumed by the tear gas. They hide in the doorway of the office doorway.

The lights in the hallway are bright security lights. The side hallways are blocked off the only way to go is straight through the double doors leading to the other side of the building past the administration desk with offices on both sides of the hallway.

Ms.Ross:"P is the only way to go"?

Professor:" I got the elevator's working"!

Rico :"Let me guess their through those doors with all the guards on the other side".

Professor:"Merry Christmas and Happy New year!!...I broke the security system.

Ms.Ross:"Count it "!

Professor:"In 10 seconds everything going off...I mean everythang"!

Rico:"Okay Count it fool"!! As they prepare their weapons. Rico puts the energy (Electric laser gun) on level 3

Ms.Ross loads up her pistol.

Professor:"Here we go 5.4.3.2.BOOM!!"

The lights suddenly goes dark for 3 seconds. Nothing but silence, then loud fire alarm goes off...flashing flood lights and the water system goes off.

The guards push through the door with panic. Rico steps out the doorway, hit'em with the energy gun 1-2-3 guards stunned as they fall 1-2-3 guards Brains blown out from Ms.Ross marksmanship shots.

The floor is quickly getting slick from the water system. Two more guards take cover shooting while slipping on the wet floor trying to take cover Ms.Ross hits the guard on the right in the leg he falls to an knee then dome shot to the head.

Rico and Ms.Ross move forward with caution, a guard frantically shoots the last of his shots hitting nothing...the guard reloads his machine gun but by time he looks back up Rico's fist is in his eyeball picked up by his throat and slammed into the floor splitting the back of the guard's head. Another guard hiding at the end of the hallway see that drops his gun and runs away down the hallway.

Rico and Ms.Ross just look at each other.

Ms.Ross:"You gone hit'em"?

The guard runs into a security gate, he tries to lift the gate .

Rico shoots him with the energy gun. The guard falls face first onto the wet floor.

The water system finally stops.

Ms.Ross:"Elevator's this way ".

They run right pass the passed-out guard onto the elevator.

Ms.Ross press the button to the 5th floor.

Rico:" P is this elevator safe"?

Professor: "We...got...prob.."

Ms.Ross: "P we can't hear you...P"!

They reload their weapons in the elevator.

Rico:"S1...you there"?

Soldier getaway driver: "I'm here" as he's getting back into the van.

Rico: "We'll be coming out the south west side of the building "!

Soldier getaway driver: "Got it"

Rico:"You hear from P"?

Soldier getaway driver: "lost contact about 45 seconds ago".

Rico:"Okay just be ready"!

Soldier getaway driver:"Its On"!

The elevator comes to an stop.

Ms.Ross:"You see that".

Through the glasses they see a lot of guards on the other side of the elevator's doors facing them. The doors open and nothing but gun fire flies into the elevator. They take as much cover as they can. Ms.Ross hits the button to close the door ,she pushes the 6th floor button but the elevator doesn't move the light shuts off in the elevator. The gun shots stop

Rico:"You okay "!

Ms.Ross:"I think so" .

Rico: "Okay same play I stunne'em you knock'em down.

Ms.Ross:"Yeah but what's level 5"?

Rico:"We bout to find out" he puts the energy gun on level 5 and gets low.

The elevator doors open back up... Rico shoots the gun twice hitting the guard on the left, his stomach is gone and the guard on the right leg is cut severed like slice meat.

As the other 5 guards look on in shock Ms.Ross unloads on them.

Through the glasses they see more guards coming.

They take a glance at the energy gun Rico holding and look at each other like what the fuck.

Solider getaway driver :"Yawl might want to hurry up there a lot of siren's headed this way"!

Ms.Ross :"We gotta go"!

They head for the 5th floor office room.

As they run down the wet hallway guards are coming out the stairwell with gas mask on bullet proof vest and more around the corner straight at them .

As they run towards the guards Rico holds the trigger down longer than let's go the impact takes out the first four guards with gas mask a vest damn near exploding their body parts giving them enough time for Ms. Ross to barrage the other guards with bullets. Rico kicks the door in with an running start, once inside the room they see an unfinished office with a garbage shoot for that looks like a tube hanging out the side window.

Ms. Ross :"Really Professor "she says to herself.

Rico: "Go, go" he tells Ms. Ross; he tries to shoot the energy gun but it's still recharging from the last level 5 blast.

So, Ms. Ross covers him and starts shooting at guards in the door way.

Rico:"S1 let's go" he jumps into the garbage shoot and slides down, Ms. Ross right after him, they land in a dumpster.

Soldier getaway driver: "40Seconds"!

They hop into the van and peel off.

Rico:"What happened to professor "?

They slide into the street making their getaway. Police cars are approaching the building.

Soldier getaway driver:"Wait "pulls a detonator out the glove box hits the button and all of the Federal parked cars in front of the building blows up.

The police cars stop their pursuit of the van and goes towards the building.

Soldier getaway driver:" Tone always says have an back up plan" As they make their getaway.

Soldier getaway driver: "By the way the names Sean but everybody calls me Speedy"!

Rico: "Right On"!

Chapter 3 "A Different World"
(Uncle Tone party Truth lies beneath the eye part 3) page.8

[Truth lies beneath the eye]

Will knocks on the room door as Terry comes walking towards the room him and Alonzo are sharing.

(Room looks like an 5 star hotel room double bedroom)

Alonzo opens the door to see Will and an rack of clothes.

Will: "Here's some clothes for you and Terry ".

Alonzo :"These brand new clothes "! As he sees the tags.

Terry coming up from behind.

Terry:"Damn you brought the whole rack out"!

Will:"Yeah you know the movement is self reliant, plus my Uncles owns a clothing factory".

Terry:" So this for the party"?

Will: “It’s just a lil function my Unc throws with family and friends, relax and have a good time “.

Alonzo: “Alright cool we see you in a minute “Alonzo pulls the rack of clothes into the room.

Will: “Cool”.

Terry: “Ight” he says to Will as he enters the room.

Terry: “Ah man this crib smooth ain’t it”.

Alonzo: “Yeah its good in all, but we came up here for answers and they talkin bout party”!

Terry:”Shit man what you harvern about, we need some relaxation...shit I know I do” he says while checking out the clothes “.

Alonzo: “Man I’m still trying to figure out how we even got to this point” .

Terry: “Well you worry bout that” Looks at Alonzo “Hey it’s a different world, but life goes on and I’m trying to get next to something tonight “Then gets back to looking in the mirror .

Alonzo: “What they got some hoes coming “?

Terry: “I don’t know bout all that”dancing in the mirror, while putting together an outfit.

Alonzo: “All that? Nigga who you pussy poppin fo”?

Terry: “NIGGA why you all up in mine, and another thang I’ll prefer if you wouldn’t use the N word tonight, I see folk around here dont take it to kindly “!

Alonzo: “Man you gettin way to comfortable...So you gone fake the phunk all night”!

Terry:”I’m just trying to flourish with my people...you need to tighten up my brotha” matches his outfit up on the bed “Ooohwooh I’ma breakin”em off tonight”!

Alonzo: “Man who you fronting for “?

There’s a knock at the door.

Terry: “Bro get the speedos out cha ass...lighten up damn...yeah who is it”!

Yolanda: “Willie wanted me to bring some shoes up”. She yells from the other side of the door.

Terry quickly fixes his hair and clothes, Alonzo looking at Terry in surprise and disgust, Terry goes to open the door.

Alonzo:”This nigga here”!

Terry:Opens the door “Hey Yola” he said in a smooth voice.

Yolanda:”Here you guys shoes” she said smiling.

Terry:”Thank you so much, now Ima see you in a minute right”?

Yolanda:”I guess, I’m not going anywhere “she says keeping her tough exterior but still with a smile.

Terry:”Okay see you then...Alright now” he grabs the shoes shuts the door and does a temptation spin just to see Alonzo in disgust. “What man”?

Alonzo:”Really Bruh Yolanda “!?

Terry:”Yeah man Yolanda so what”!

Alonzo:”She was just about to cut ya balls off earlier, now you trying to get wit her...boy you somethin else”.

Meanwhile people are starting to arrive. Uncle Tone got a small stage set up for the band the bar is lit up pool table turned crap table and the chief cooking in the kitchen. Uncle Tone disappears upstairs to the control room with Professor.

Uncle Tone:”How we doing “?

Professor:”They just got in”.

Uncle Tone:”Okay cool, I’ll be back up in a little bit”.

Professor:”Alright “.

Uncle Tone:”Let me know if you need something “as he heads back down to the pen house.

The party has started the music is vibrating the wall. Terry fresh out the shower, getting dressed while Alonzo is still in his aggravated man mood.

Terry:”You know jealousy don’t look too good on you Zo”.

Alonzo:”Jealous... man don’t forget why we here”.

Terry:”Look over the last couple of days to even right now, I still don’t know what the fuck is going on but right now (As he does an salsa dance while spraying a mist of cologne in the air and dances through it) T-Regional Sauce aka Two dimension shawty is still a player, so you can be an stiff ass if you want to but me...(brushing his hair in the mirror)I live by the rule Play on Playa, Play on... in any dimension I’m in...TDP I’m out this bitch “Throws the peace sign and leaves the room.

Alonzo: Gets up to look at the clothes rack. “This nigga done lost his mind... TDP. .What hell he talkin bout..(thinks about it) “Two dimensional Player... Ha! Fool done lost it”.

Alonzo finally gets dressed, comes down the stairs to see people gathering around the stage area and Terry singing with Uncle Tone and the band. Walks down to see Will at the bottom of the steps enjoying his self.

Alonzo: "Damn I didn't know yall did it like this"!

Will:"I didn't know Terry can jam like that"!

Alonzo: "Yeah...he a fool". He saids sarcastically.

Will:"My Uncle don't let anybody touch that mic"!

Alonzo:"I can't believe this shit" looking at Terry doing the Keith sweat while singing. "Ima get a drink".

Alonzo makes his way through the small crowd to the kitchen takes an bottle off the counter and pours a drink. Yolanda pops in to grab some ice and bottle of wine.

Yolanda:"Hey what's up, you know it's an bar in there right".

Alonzo shakes his head yes.

Yolanda: "The bartender makes the best drinks around here "!

Alonzo:"Round here huh? Round here...(takes his shot of liquor) Round here is what I'm still trying to figure out...I mean is this real life or a damn musical...folks out there doin the same dance moves at the same time and shit"!

Yolanda:"So in yo mind this is fake"? She takes the bottle pours shots for both of them..." Sounds like your home sick".

Alonzo:"I just want to get some info or maybe an explanation".

Yolanda:"Relax stop being so stiff and have some fun everything will come in due time you around good people "!

They cheers and take their shots.

Yolanda:"Okay I gotta get this to the bar".

As Alonzo gets hisself together, He starts to exit the kitchen when Uncle Tone walks in .

Uncle Tone: "Lonzo what's up man you need anything "?

Alonzo:"Ahh naw Ima hit the bar then chill on the balcony ".

Uncle Tone: "Alright man enjoy yourself" He takes out a phone. Checks in with the professor.

Professor: "Hurry up I'm kind of busy".

Uncle Tone: "How's it going "?

Professor:"I'm shutting down an whole goverment building how bout you "!

Uncle Tone:"I'm about to perform our hit single from 98"!

Professor:"Okay well you have fun with that" he hangs up.

Uncle Tone:"Damn I don't want Ronnie on bass".

Terry walks out to the balcony to see Alonzo and Will chillin.

Will: "What's up man I didn't know you was nice wit the mic like that"?

Terry:"Well you know I do, what I can do ,when I can do it" laughs with Will.

Alonzo:" Man you still doing those Keith sweat moves"!

Terry:"Fool you taught me".

Alonzo:"Yeah when we was kids"!

Terry:"And they still work (He does the move) so I gone keep doin it"!

Alonzo:"I can dig it bro"!

Terry: "I see you loosened up finally having fun" Will passes the joint to Terry .

Alonzo: "Ay man we here around good people, good music (Sees an attractive woman eyeing him from the other side of the balcony) on the real, tonight been pretty good ".

Yolanda: Walks over "What ya lames talking bout" as she hugs up on Terry

Will coughs as he looks in confusion, puts his drink on the table looks at Yolanda .

Will: "Wasn't you going to cut his balls off earlier "?

Terry:"Hey only if ya cool wit it I don't want to disrespect ".

Yolanda:"I m grown ya don't have to talk like I'm not standing here"!

Will:"Check dig ,no disrespect taken, hey if you cross her, she just don't got that blade, she got that man over there" points to Uncle Tone starring at Terry and Yolanda Hugging while he still performing with the band.

The song fades out Uncle Tone gets on the mic.

Tone:"I'm bout to do an song I wrote ways back but a song that always apply".

(He counts 1,2,3,4 the beat similar to Michael Jackson got me working day & night)

Uncle Tone: starts singing "I bought a shotgun for my bay bay Aey" (The song plays on)

Will Alonzo and Yolanda start laughing as Uncle Tone song plays and Terry looking in shock.

Alonzo goes to talk to young lady on the balcony that he locked eyes with a few moments ago.

A white guy approaches Will.

Frankie: “Hey man”!

Will: “You made it”! They dap hands.

Terry :”Hey man you the dude from the gas station “!

Yolanda: “He’s also one of the guys who controls the border patrols”.

Terry :”What...I almost got jammed up at the border”!

Frankie: “Yeah Tone knew his niece and nephew where bringing new faces around so he told me to make you sweat a little”.

Will :”And you did good man see we got things under control”. He says to Terry laughing.

Meanwhile Professor is in the control room and for some reason lost audio with Rico and Ms. Ross once they got into the elevator. Then the visual as well as his computer monitors went blank.

Professor: “What the...hell” he’s looking for a disconnection somewhere but doesn’t see it.

A solider from the movement comes into the control room shows him security footage from a tablet.

Professor: “Shit...mount up let’s go”.

Alonzo is in good conversation with the young lady ...All of a sudden, they see a quick flash.

Alonzo: “Who’s the pervert flying a drone looking in windows and shit”!

Will hits the drone by throwing his drink at it.

Will: “Nosey muthafukas”!

They laugh watching the drone go down they watch and follow the drone fall, to see black armored trucks and what looks like armored troops surrounding the building.

Yolanda: “Oh shit they coming “!

Kemitt mirrors chapter 3 "A Different world" (Truth lies beneath the eye) The movement vs The E.T.F.

Will: "Shit" Starts trying to get his Uncle attention but the music to loud.

Will goes to the bar, whispers to the bartender. The bartender hit the silent alarm that arms the floor in 30 seconds.

Uncle Tone sees the l-e-d light change color at the bar pays attention to his phone vibrating to see Professor message "We have to shut down Now".

Uncle Tone stops the music gets on the mic.

Uncle Tone: "Sorry everybody we have emergency to attend to so we need everyone to calmly move towards the back.

Professor and four soldiers appear from the back wall opening for emergency escape stairs and elevators.

Tone instructs the soldiers to move the crowd to safety. Professor turns all the TVs to show security footage in and out.

Professor: "It's the E.T.F (Edgar Task Force) they're trying to break through the main floor" as he controls the building from the tablet.

Alonzo and Terry are following the crowd to the escape route. Alonzo whispers to Terry as they fall in line with the crowd.

Alonzo: "This some bull shit, the ATF these niggas selling dope the whole time"!

Terry: "Yeah and got us smoking high grade reggie "!

Alonzo: "You know what I'm saying we out" they give each other dap in agreement.

Terry: "Say man can we hurry this up, This shit like the airport "!

Will: Calls out to Alonzo and Terry "Hey"!

Alonzo and Terry turn around.

Will :"Where y'all going "?

Alonzo:"Uhh where you not goin "!?

Will :"We got to stand our ground till the guest get to safety "!

Terry :"Fool we are the guest"!

Will: "We the soldiers".

Terry :"Mann we outt" Alonzo and Terry gives Will the hard peace sign.

As soon as they turn back around to get on the escape elevator the soldier locks eyes with Alonzo and Terry and still pushes the button to close the elevator doors.

Alonzo and Terry:"Awww"!!! They pound on the door and start going off cussing loud.

Terry: "You punk mutha..."!

Alonzo :"If I see yo granddaddy on the street I'm knocking the bridge out that nigga mouth...open the goddamn door"!

Terry :"Open the door "!!!

Now they're punching and kicking pulling on the doors trying to open the door while the loud threats of kicking ass start to turn into whining and crying. They suddenly realize they're the only ones making all the noise, they turn around to see everybody's looking at them in disgust. Then a loud boom sound.

Professor: "They got through the first barrier ".

Soldier bartender : "Were back with full power "!

Uncle Tone: "Everyone take your positions"!

Professor takes the tablet starts unlocking codes. First all the pictures and paintings on the wall turn to tv surveillance visuals showing in and outside the whole building . The couch moves back an control panel comes up where Uncle Tone is standing. The marble art sculpture turns around for communication panel Where Will is.

Alonzo: "Damn this shit like the got damn enterprise "he says to Terry.

Terry :"I thought that nigga was at the DJ table" referring to professor

Terry turns to Will.

Terry :"So what's your job"?

Will: "My job first level, when shit get crazy...that's when I come in"!

Alonzo & Terry:"Fo sho, fo sho ".

Professor: "We're still having problems with the power...we can't get the traps to fully work".

Uncle Tone :"The generator"?

Professor :"Its running but something is wrong "!

Will: "Just got word, All the guest made it out safely "!

Professor: "Good cause they just got through the second barrier"!

Tone: "What's the time before they reach us"?

Professor: "They'll be at the 3rd barrier in 11min, without the generator we exactly 20minutes and 20 seconds. "as he talks, he putting up analectic data, graph and bars on the TV screens as they're watching the E.T.F soldiers trying to break through the barriers with the batter ram.

Alonzo :"This shit like ESPN for police raids".

Uncle Tone: "Yolanda grab my suit I gotta get to the generator ".

Yolanda goes get the suite and gives it to Uncle Tone. (The suite resembles a Dickies suite overalls but with Professor's upgrade on it) Uncle Tone puts on his suite to only see Yolanda gearing up too.

Uncle Tone: "Where you going "?

Yolanda: "To watch your back"!

Uncle Tone: "No... this can get ugly real quick "!

Yolanda :"You been preparing me and Will for this forever...if this ain't the time to fight then when is it"?

Uncle Tone looks at Professor, Will and the other soldiers, they all nod in agreement with Yolanda.

Uncle Tone:" Okay but we need a diversion before we head out...Will we need you to do yo thang till we get the weapons "!

Will: "Yeah...uh ..you got it" puts on his headset with the microphone connected, turned some knobs looking really important.

Uncle Tone: Him and Yolanda move by the escape stairwell to the elevator's "Alright 3,2,1" makes a fist sign ".

Then through all the hidden speakers in and out the building loud.

Will:"Pow,pow,pow,bbbbbooommm,boom,boom,pap,pap,pap,pap...cushhh-h(radio static)"!!

Alonzo: "Did he just go full police academy on'em"? Looking confused

Everybody else in the room gives a smurk laughing.

Looking at the monitors it actually worked. The E.T.F soldiers inside the building take cover.

Uncle Tone laughs points to Professor then him and Yolanda dips down the staircase professor hits a couple buttons, then the bar turns around and nothing but an arsenal of guns and weapons appear.

Will:"Aint dat a blanket on the Muthafukin chicken "he saids to himself.

Alonzo & Terry looks at the arsenal.

Alonzo :"Damn that's what I'm talking about"!

Terry: Turns to Will. "So, you the ammunition vanquilques...this nigga gotta gun sock" laughing.

Alonzo: "He got a puppet Assault Rifle...name Rilfey "laughing.

Two of the soldiers passes out the guns to everyone with extra clips.

Will:"Ya'll laughing but we still gotta get outta here soon" he saids to Alonzo and Terry as he loads his gun

Alonzo & Terry gets their weapons ready.

Alonzo: "Yeah we ready"!

Professor still trying to connect back with Rico and Minty (Ms. Ross.)

Professor: "M1, M2 can you hear me, M1, M2... (no responds) Damn"!

Uncle Tone and Yolanda move through the secret passage ways heading down to the 4th floor generators. They get to the generators with ease.

The generator room is a data system that runs 70% of the building. Looks like 10 tall computers.

Once in the room Uncle Tone looks for any generator that's out, he goes to the security system generator first. He sees its running but also notice a plug on the side that's not supposed to be there. Yolanda watches his back as He unplugs the cord looks behind the generator to see an small box with two antennas blinking that the cord is connected too. He resets the generator and puts a new hard drive in. Does the same to the communication 4th generator and finds another small blinking box.

Uncle Tone: "It's going to be a while before they both reset and have the new data" he tells Yolanda.

Yolanda :"So what Now"?

Uncle Tone:"Gotta hold'em off till the security system back up...you ready"!

Yolanda nods yes pulls out her gun and reaches inside her suite and pushes a button that activates a chameleon like defense mechanism in suite to blend in changing scenery.

Uncle Tone: "Alright "he does the same to his suite and they both put their hoodie on that camouflages everything

Yolanda: looks at Uncle Tone in full camouflage "Damn Professor good"!

Uncle Tone: "Yeah but stick to your training ...you dig".

Yolanda :"Ok"!

Uncle Tone:" The generator's reloading keep me posted with the time "he says to Will.

Will: "Got it" as he looks at his tablet computer. "They've rebooted the generators 9 minutes before we're back on"!

Professor: "Okay keep the time on point Ima see what I can do in the meantime "as he gets to working on his computer.

Uncle Tone and Yolanda uses the trap passage ways to get behind the group of soldiers that's making their way through the second barrier.

Uncle tone pops out the side what looks like an solid wall pumps to bullets to side of an ETF soldier head and moves back into the walls, because of the silencer the other soldiers in front don't even notice, there to busy breaking down the 2nd barrier. The ETF soldiers finally break through the second barrier. Yolanda rolls two scrap metal grenades right in front of the front line of the ETF soldiers and disappeared back into the walls. Boom, Boom the scrap metal grenades exploded killing the front four and critically injured another three. The two soldiers in the rear back up shooting,(E.T.F soldier: "We need back up now we're hit need ba..")one falls over the dead soldier they didn't even know got hit, Uncle Tone popped back out hits the two soldiers in the face.

Uncle Tone: "Dub how we looking"!

Will: "Communication is back 100% relocating new signals now"!

Professor :"Security systems back up in 90seconds...go ahead an make your way back"!

Uncle Tone :"Got it" looks at Yolanda "let's get back to the pen house ".

Yolanda sees ETF soldiers running into the hallway behind Uncle Tone.

Yolanda :starts shooting "Watch out "!

Uncle Tone: "Oh shit, got damn" as he ducks down running towards Yolanda "I'm glad I taught you how to shoot"!

Uncle Tone and Yolanda move back into the trap walls.

The soldiers shooting while running up but stops when realizing nothing's there.

Professor: "Security systems up in 60 seconds".

Will: "Professor I got a signal coming through ".

Professor: "Can you track it"!

Will: "I'm tracking it now, and its moving fast 5miles out from us"!

Professor : "Send it through "it has to be them thinking to himself.

Will sends it through.

Ms. Ross :"P come in... (Static getting clearer) P you there"?

Professor:"M2 come in"!

Ms. Ross :"We have to get out of Feuherstadlt cut that party"!

Professor: "Yeah well the party been over, the party with ETF is still going on"!

Rico : "So we still invited "!

Professor: "The more the merrier".

Ms. Ross: "It's On"!!

As Rico and Ms. Ross make their way to Uncle Tones Trap Pen house. Yolanda and Uncle Tone make their way to the secret stairwell to the escape elevator's but once they come out the stairwell doors their Ambushed by four Elite ETF soldiers with mask on.

The 1rst soldier knocks the gun out of Yolanda hand and kicks her into the open elevator Uncle Tone tries to help.

Uncle Tone: Shoots one but doesn't slow down the Elite ETF soldier from coming at him so he shoots the soldier in the leg and foot before getting rushed by the other two soldiers.

Yolanda: Is in an all-out one on one battle with Elite soldier inside the elevator .He swings the Electric baton she dodge's the baton hits the soldier with a fast combination body, head, body,head knee to the ribs but the Elite soldier comes back with an combination, she blocks the jab and left hook but caught with a kick to the gut. She hits the wall in the elevator she sees the Elite soldier going for the their gun ,so Yolanda quickly grabs her knife drops low to one knee left jab to the stomach with the knife to only see the soldier has on body armor pull the knife back out but in one motion upper cut...the knife goes through the soldiers bottom chin the tip of the blade comes out through the middle of the soldiers nose.

Uncle Tone is fighting two Elite soldiers as one rolls on the floor in pain.

Will : "It sounds like Uncle Tone and Yolanda need backup "he says to Professor.

Professor :"Go ahead I'll take over communications and we'll hold the front "referring to the other soldiers

Will:" Come on" he says to Alonzo and Terry.

They run to the escape stairwell down the steps. They get to the same floor to see Yolanda and Uncle Tone finishing the soldiers off. Yolanda pulling her knife out one soldier forehead and Tone giving an head shot to another.

Terry: “Damn”!

Will : “Was this an ambush “?

Uncle Tone: “I think we surprised each other, either way we’ve been compromised…they were on the way up these guys are a different group from the regular task force”.

The solider shot in the leg and foot by Tone is bleeding out and what sounds like mumbling to himself on the ground, Tone goes to the badly injured soldier.

Uncle Tone: “Who sent you”! Slaps the ETF elite soldier “Who made the call” takes his mask off foam comes out of the soldier’s mouth.

Alonzo:” What the hell wrong with him”?

Will: “He must have swallowed an suicide pill…check to see if he has an ear bud”!

Uncle Tone takes an ear bud out the soldier ear and puts it up to his ear.

Unknown voice: “Mission abort block all exits demo the building”!

Uncle Tone: “Shit there going to blow the building…we gotta go”!

They get back inside the pen house.

Uncle Tone:” Everybody let’s go, we gotta get out” he goes over to his controls.

Yolanda: “If we need to go what are you doing “?

Uncle Tone : “If anybody blows this building it’s gone be me…plus this building has been compromised anyway “.

Yolanda: “It’s no way they should have known about the escape stairwell “!

Professor: “The security system is up they won’t get through the 3rd barrier… The ETF retreating out the building “!

Yolanda: “Yeah there going to blow the building “! She tells Professor.

Uncle Tone: “Alright go to the garage… (sets a couple more codes) let’s go we got 25mins “!

Boom, Boom the building shakes.

They all get to the escape stairwell.

Uncle Tone: “Forget the elevator “they take the stairs to the garage fast but cautiously.

They get to the cars Uncle Tone and Professor starts all the cars by remote.

All of a sudden, the secret garage door blows open. The E.T.F soldiers starts shooting at the same time starting to blow the building.

They all took cover as Will car is getting shot up.

Will: "My car "starts to fire back.

Then they all start to return fire on the ETF including Alonzo and Terry.

Another blast comes from them trying to blow the building.

Professor : "If we don't get outta hear the building going to collapse on us"!

Uncle Tone : "I think they know that...do you have a plan"?

Professor: "You supposed to have the plan"!

Uncle Tone: "This was the plan get to the garage nobody was supposed to know about "he says as he returns fire.

The ETF soldiers have the exit to the garage barricaded using their paddy wagon.

Speedy coming in fast right at the barricaded both side doors of the bullet proof van open Rico has the energy gun on level 5. He holds the trigger to let the power build as he hanging out the side.

Speedy: "Hope yawl got ya draws on tight"!

Speedy 180 hook slide the van Rico has a clear shot mid spin he takes his shot.

He blows up the paddy wagon killing and injuring the ETF soldiers, the barricade is destroyed.

Ms. Ross hanging out the other side of the van bustin her gun as Speedy put the van in reverse peels off backwards running over ETF soldiers then coming to an screeching stop... Rico Hops out the side.

Rico "Let's move" he shouts as he shoots at the ETF with his dessert Eagle.

Professor: "I had a plan" he says to Uncle Tone.

Terry: "Bra is that Rico"? He says to Alonzo .

Alonzo :"I guess so" he says surprised and confused.

They jump in Uncle Tone cars Will and Alonzo jumps into the 68 barracuda, Yolanda, Terry in 69 impala. Uncle Tone, Professor, the bartender and two soldiers load up in the custom armor truck .

Speedy leads the way circles back around the building heading right towards the ETF on the sides and front of the building.

Professor:M1 we only got 90 seconds before the building really blows.

Rico : "Good we only need 30 "!

They hit the corner Ms. Ross sprays her custom semi-automatic revolver taking out the soldiers, everybody else following does the same.

Alonzo firing off his weapon Terry and the soldiers with Uncle Tone follow up.

Ms. Ross : "Tone take out all their vehicles"!

Speedy hits the corner to the front of the building. The ETF soldiers start shooting, Speedy hits the gas!

Speedy: "Big Mo (Rico) you up...Last round...TKO theses muthfakas"!!

Rico hits the crowded ETF barricade trucks and ETF soldiers fly in the air from the energy blast clearing out a lane.

Will and Alonzo come right behind Alonzo shooting cleaning up, Yolanda and Terry do the same.

Uncle Tone: "Get those sticky bombs hit all the cars matter of fact hit everything ...clean up time "the soldiers start throwing all the bombs hitting cars, ETF soldier's street signs.

As they make it through of what's left of ETF barricade.

Uncle Tone: "Professor. Would you please do the honors."!

Professor: "Hell yeah"!

Professor hits the detonator button to the sticky bombs. The bombs go off taking out everything, ETF soldiers bodies exploding street signs cars and in sequence the building blows like an drum roll from the bottom up.

Ms. Ross: "Whooo"!!

Speedy: "Yeah"!!

Alonzo &Will: "Got damn"!!

Yolanda &Terry: "Oh shit"!!

Uncle Tone :"I'm mad about the penthouse but I always wanted to do that"!!

Professor: "Preparation loves victory...On to the next...let's get to the shop".

They take underground routes out of Feuherstadlt City back to the safe house.

END CHAPTER 3

4

"Minty & Mo has a story to tell"
(Vision's) Intro page

VISION'S

[Minty & Mo has a story to tell]

Intro chapter 4:

A young girl around 8years old carefully running on the side of cabins, when she slowly opens the door to a familiar wood cabin. In the cabin are 2 younger (boys)children sleeping as the mother is tucking them in for the night. The door creaks as it closes the mother looks up.

(Mother) Ritta : "Minty? "She looks concerned

Minty just stands still with a scared but still look on her face.

Mother comes over and gives her young daughter a hug.

Young Minty: "Where's daddy?"

(Mother) Ritta : "Mr. Thompson took him to the Patterson farm he'll be back soon, now I have to take you back before we all get in trouble!"

Young Minty : "No mamma please" she hugs her tight in tears.

Mother sneaks Minty back to a cabin where other children are sleeping in one room and sits her on the bed.

Mother: Whispers "Its only for a day or two okay baby then you'll be back home okay! "

Young Minty: Crying "Okay."

Her mother vanishes and a dark figure comes out of the shadows from the wall of the cabin. The young girl relaxes as the face of the figure reveals itself from the moonlight threw the window.

Haitian woman (Guardian Angel): The women softly says "Vayan Fabula." (Speaking Spanish & creole)

The young girls smiles.

Haitian woman (guardian Angel): Smiling "You been so many places...done so much." The Young girl looks away, her guardian angel (Haitian woman) guides the young girl's eyes back to her. "So much fighting... so many losses" she gently puts her hand on young Minty"s heart. "Your hurt." The young girl sheds a tear, the tear rolls down the side of her face.

The vision switches to them walking through a rain forest into a beautiful waterfall with other families playing and laughing. (Minty slowly looks around and start to smile)

Haitian woman (guardian angel):"Vengeance consumes your soul."

The young Araminta is now a teenager.

Minty:"Vengeance"!!? (She says with anger) "This is my life, everything I love is gone, I'm just returning the favor to the people who wants to continue the Genocide of my people...Lukango like what your people did"!

Haitian nurse (guardian angel):"Liberty yes, and we also paid a heavy cost because of our victory ".

Teenage Araminta: "How"?

Haitian woman (guardian angel): "After the victory they painted us as savages, no one would trade with us that lead to selling resources for cheap prices, the money goes to only an handful of people and leaves the rest in very poor conditions, people turning on each other but most of all government selling out to other countries".

Teenage Araminta: "So liberty is a myth"?

Haitian woman (guardian angel):"It is without an plan".

Teenage Araminta: "So how do I get home"? (British Troops are coming)

Haitian Woman (guardian angel):"Shhhhh quiet girl...go get your brother"! (meaning Henry)

Crackles from the wooded forest getting closer. When another tribe attacks the white solders in red coats, shooting and hollering starts a panic.

Haitian nurse (guardian angel):"Run girl".

She pushes her into the forest “Find the truth of your vengeance then you shall live”!

Sounds of gun fire and cannons leaves in the distance the tropical rainforest/ jungle turns violet dark, huge trees high grass swamp like terrain. Then falling into deep water’s feels like she’s drowning.

Ms. Ross comes too... taking a deep breath, to see Rico holding her hand. (Ms. Ross sometimes has mild seizures when she has her visions).

Ms. Ross: “I’m fine”.

(End Intro to chapter 5)

The cars race through the streets of Feuherstadlt heading towards the border.

Uncle Tone puts in the call to the control booth.

Uncle Tone: “We coming through fast “!

Control booth:” Roger that”.

As they come up on the border a border patrol guard guides them to another lane. The 4 cars speed right through the border.

Terry: “Well ain’t that some bullshit” thinking about how they harassed him the day before.

They continue to maneuver through the streets to finally making it to the (safe house) car shop. The soldiers keeping guard opens the garage to let them in. They park the cars and Uncle Tone proceeds to give a head count.

Uncle Tone: “Everybody’s here...boogie”!

Uncle Tone comes and gives Yolanda a big hug as she gets out the car.

Will: “I’m alive and well to Unc” he says getting out the car.

Uncle Tone: “I know...you came through for us nephew”.

Alonzo: “Rico”?

Terry: “Ms. Ross “?

Rico: “Alonzo “?

Ms. Ross : “Terry” she says not surprised

Ms. Ross : Turns to Rico “I told you they’ll show up when its time.

Rico : “Are you okay “?

Ms. Ross : “Vision’s getting stronger...I’ll be fine.” She heads to the meeting room with documents from the Edgar Federal building in her hand.

Alonzo: "You apart of all this"?

Uncle Tone: "Apart of it...these two leading the fight".

Rico : "Look I was going to explain to y'all why your here but right now we don't have much time" as he grabs the duffle bag and heads up the stairs to the meeting room.

Alonzo: "So that was you that night"! Following him up the stairs

Rico: "I'll explain it all to you but first we gotta figure this out" he puts the duffle bag on the table.

Everyone comes into the meeting room.

Professor gets on his computer along with Will on his.

Everyone sits down, Ms. Ross starts putting pictures on the wall.

Ms. Ross : "These files are straight out of Captain Rudolfs head of the agency desk" (on front of the folder says confidential.) She puts all the pictures up on the board. "We haven't had time to study this, but from the looks of it they are planning to move back into the regions and there starting off by purchasing our land, water sources and power supply.

Uncle Tone:" Well we figured that part, but who's selling and who's buying"?

Ms. Ross: "We still have to find that out but we do have some possibilities"

Ms. Ross puts up some more pictures.

Uncle Tone: "Ronnie? Ed?"

Ms. Ross :"These pictures are from lieutenant Russ office ...Ronald Johnson and Edward Robinson".

Rico :"Both of these men sits on the board and are representatives of the United Regions they have access to the treaties that where formed decades ago".

Professor: "And the power to change laws".

Will: "Growing up I thought these guys were heroes, they're part of the original movement...why would they fold now"?

Uncle Tone: "Power, they must have offered them something...Ronnie that no playin bass son of a bitch...and Ed he set up my... set up my securi... ty system... Damn"!

Ms. Ross throws documented paperwork from 1992 to Uncle Tone.

Ms. Ross :"Who's to say their folding now, from that document it says those two been informants for more than half of their lives".

Uncle Tone :"Damn Ronnie took the escape route that's how the task force new about it and Ed sent his team over to do the lighting earlier in the week".

Terry: "He ain't do no work in here did he"?

Uncle Tone : "No... that's why it's a safe house fool"!

Terry :"Alright man just asking, those your friends "he laughs suspiciously.

Uncle Tone: "I'm about to cut this fool"!

Rico: "Yeah he has that effect on people "!

Professor: "I can kind of see Ronnie but Ed seemed solid".

Will: "So what's the problem people been moving back to the regions for years now".

Professor: "It's about control and economics, before they saw no value and now, they see huge value...but we do have a problem lieutenant Russ computer took a picture of you (Ms. Ross)"he shows his tablet to her.

Uncle Tone: "I been telling y'all to keep your mask on at all times".

Professor: "Well Tone we also got this from Minty glasses... took this frame shot while in his office "the picture has Uncle Tone as the master mind of the movement.

Uncle Tone: "Got damn Ronnie and Ed... but on the bright side it's about time I'm respected for what I do around here...and they got my good side "looking at the picture.

Yolanda : "Only you would take pride in something like this".

Uncle Tone: "All they can do is kill me...I'm already in it".

Alonzo: "Wait a minute so yawl actually broke into a Federal agency building to get this Information"? Looking at the docs.

Ms. Ross : Nods her head yes.

Alonzo : "Then what the fuck is this"!!?

Shows a picture of Alonzo and Terry From this world in their lab coats looking real Nerdy with a big Confidential stamped across it.

Terry: lets out a low Scream "Oh hell naw"!! Passes out.

5

Minty & Mo "Has a story to tell"

(VISION'S PT.2)

Rico: "Are hero "looking at Terry passed out. Then grabs the reels from the Edgar Federal building and gives them to Professor and Will.

Alonzo leans over Terry.

Alonzo: "Wake up fool you embarrassing us"!

Yolanda: "Puts a warm rag on his face...wake up T".

Alonzo: "Ain't nothing wrong wit this boy" starts slapping him...then one good slap "Nigga stop playing (POW) "!

Terry wakes up only to see Alonzo.

Terry:"Damn..Lonzo I had a crazy dream".

Alonzo thinking oh here we go again.

Terry: "Man we went through a time warp then teamed up with a revolutionary crime fighting team and the girl I was digging ugly ass Uncle be hatin.. (Alonzo:shhh..shut up) shit was crazy "!

Uncle Tone: "What you say lil boy I kill you" walking towards Terry.

Terry jumps up realizing this still isn't a dream.

Alonzo tries to stops Uncle Tone .

Alonzo :"Man you can't kill'em in this world Unc you might put a pit-bull head on a alligator body or some shit"!

Uncle Tone: "What"!?

Terry:"Haa he talkin bout you" laughing to his self.

Uncle Tone: "Yo Mo, what he talkin bout"?

Will: Talking to Rico "Man who the hell still got movie reels, I gotta say P you stayed prepared.

Professor:" Hey I seen it all, over the years".

Uncle Tone: "MO"!

Rico stops working with Professor and Will as they put the movie reels on a machine to convert the footage to flash drive.

Rico: "What"? He says in frustration.

Uncle Tone: "What this boy talking bout this world... he one of y'all "?

Alonzo and Terry: "One of yall"?

Rico : "Got damn Tone not now "tries to get back to work.

Alonzo: "Man that was you that night"!

Rico: Raises his voice "I told you not right now, I'll get to that later "!!

Alonzo: Raises his voice back "Fuck that I want to know right now, what the fuck goin on"!

Uncle Tone: "Uh Ohh lovers quarrels, ya gotta take that shit to the lounge room, we trying to work here"!

Professor: "Don't worry about this it's gone be a little while for this load up" he says to Rico.

Rico: "You talk to damn much" he tells Terry as he heads to the lounge area.

Terry: "I was only out for 2minutes...what I say"?

Alonzo just walks past upset; they both follow Rico to the lounge area. Once they get into the room Yolanda and Ms. Ross are already in there talking and laughing.

Rico enters the room and the mood instantly change.

Rico:" Minty it's time we gotta let them know what's going on".

Ms. Ross : "Okay...Alonzo you okay "?

Alonzo: "No I'm not...why are we here?

They all take a seat. Yolanda stays in the room being nosey but Ms. Ross doesn't mind.

Ms. Ross :" First off we didn't know y'all two were going to be involved in this so soon".

Rico: "We wanted to put you on to what's going on once we got back but yall ended up here anyway ".

Terry: "Well from the looks of things, if we didn't save yall asses coming back was a slim chance "!

Rico :"You saved us". He says sarcastically.

Terry: "Boy didn't you see me hanging out the window tourchin dat iron"!

Yolanda: "We saw you scream then pass out"!

Terry :"Yola!... I was appalled of being labeled an ALLEGED confidential informant...but It can't be true BECAUSE WE AINT NEVER BEEN HERE BEFOE "!!

Rico : "We know that idiot".

Alonzo: "But why are we here"?

Rico :"Look 1rst thing yall got here on your own didn't nobody tell ya to go steal weed from the farm".

Terry: "Who did what". Turns to Alonzo "You told him that"?

Alonzo: "I didn't tell 'em...who told you that"?

Rico :"I put it out there but you made the decision to go ".

Terry: "I knew he got us some way, somehow bing bow con man "!

Alonzo: "You took advantage of my financial situation "!?

Ms.Ross :"No we put you where you're destined to be"!

Alonzo: "Is that right...I gotta hear this one" he sits back with his arms crossed.

Ms.Ross :"You two are natural fighters and very smart, but lack the discipline to focus on your goals".

Terry: "The judgement".

Ms.Ross :"The environments you come from may have prolonged those choices but you made the decision to move out of those environments, to go to school ".

Terry: "Thank you".

Alonzo nudges him with his elbow.

Alonzo: "Come on man" Alonzo's really interested in what she has to say, Terry chills out.

Ms.Ross :"Both of you had some stumbles learning to become men on your own but your fighters the key is to know who you truly are before it's too late".

Terry: "Hey I dig all dat you sayin but what does all this have to do with us being here "?

Rico: "You two are targeted, well your parallel selves are...Whatever happens in this world could butterfly effect across all dimensions... So, we got to y'all before that could happen".

Alonzo: "So what's the plan we supposed to play them or something ".

Ms.Ross: "You don't have to play them you are them, you just come from two different environments you have more warrior in you, but this time around your using that strength for the right cause".

Terry: "Okay but obviously these dudes are super smart what about that"?

Ms.Ross: "Again you are them the intelligent level is where you want it to be but the fight in your heart, and soul has to come from an certain place of self-assuredness, awareness an able to go to the darkest places mentally for it to come out physically ". She kneels down in front of Alonzo and Terry and takes both of their hands into hers "And when it comes out it's in your power to either take it to the darkest of the darkest of the abyss or take to the highest of the highest witch is the sun".

Professor, Uncle Tone and Will enter the room but just listens to the conversation.

Rico :"You saw the crystals on your body that night right"?

Alonzo and Terry: "Yes, I remember that"!

Rico :"Those were...souls attaching themselves to you, which means the universe chose you, so you were able to travel through".

Alonzo: "Neurons... souls"?

Terry :"Meaning someone died or were buried on those lands that we're connected to".

Alonzo :"Like an... ancestor maybe".

Uncle Tone :"Damn I guess Minty was right...I thought y'all was stupid ass shit... I see y'all got some sense" Eating his popcorn.

Alonzo: "Wait, wait, wait so that was y'all two that saved us from the dirty slave catchers, right"?

Rico and Ms. Ross slowly nods their heads yes.

Terry:"Yall the Shadow ninja's "!

Alonzo :" How did we end up running into George Washington look alike and the colonel, how we linked to that"?

Ms. Ross :"After so many jumps back and forth the memories gets hazier".

Ms. Ross pulls out candles out of her bag she has in the room.

Ms. Ross :"This ritual helps us to remember the details why where here doing what we're doing". She says as she's lighting the candles.

Uncle Tone:" All man right now... Professor preparing the footage from the reels I might be in the footage" still with his popcorn.

Ms. Ross :"Come on"!!

They all sit down at the table.

Terry :"Hey man this ain't no seance shit is it"?

Rico: "No this this isn't a seance".

Ms. Ross : "Everybody hold hands".

Rico: "Its Vodun".

Ms. Ross already starts to chant.

Ms. Ross :"In this tween time, darkest hours, we call upon these sacred powers, we together stand alone, command the unseen to be shown,

In innocence we search the skies, enchanted are our new found eyes".

The room is quiet, Terry opens one eye to take a peek at everyone.

Terry:" I knew this wouldn't work".

The three candles burning combine together to make one flame, the flame turns different colors then stays on blue.

Terry :"What the...".

Every one heads titles back face towards the ceiling then heads slowly drop like there in a trance.

Kemitt mirrors chapter 5.1 (Vision's pt.3)
"Minty & Mo has an story to tell "

(The vision's being projected by Ms.Ross (Araminta:Minty) are very real clear and powerful. Everyone in the trance are able to touch smell and feel exactly how Ms.Ross and Rico (Mo:Moses) did in these moments.)

The sun is at its peak in the clear blue sky. The sound of seagulls and water crashing the shores is overpowered by an thousand different conversations going on at the same time.

"Fresh fruit, best fruit in Maryland, get your fresh fruit here "!! You here from vendors on both sides of the roadway.

"Fresh meat on ice, right here,best meat around" from another vendor. On and on from apple's to wine.

An young sixteen year old Minty watches Mrs.Brodess cross the roadway in her bright white and yellow dress with an umbrella to match. Her eyes stays on Mrs.Brodess as she small talks with other people to finally making it to Mr.Brodess at the liquor stand an hooks her arm with his. He leans in to give his wife a kiss on the cheek. From Minty eyes Mr. and Mrs.Brodess were in love and one day hope that could be her.

"Hey boy!!" An man in a suit smoking an cigar says breaking Minty out of her daze.

Henry comes from the side feeding the horse.

Young Henry: "Yes sir."

Customer:" Give me an batch of that tobacco. "

Henry wraps up an batch and hands it to the man.

The customer only gives him one coin.

Minty: "That will be fifty cent sir."

The man looks down the roadway to see Mr. and Mrs.Brodess mossing down the roadway enjoying there Sunday afternoon outing. Then he looks back at Minty and Henry with an smug look, leans in slides the coin with his finger towards Minty and Henry.

Customer: "You can read?" He says in his strong Dutch accent.

Minty and Henry just put there heads down.

Customer: He leans in close" You can be hung for that "He says in an sinister undertone. He stands back straight up and throws three more coins on the table. "Give me one of those cotton shirts."

Henry grabs the shirt off the line folds it and puts it on the table unconsciously knowing not to make eye contact with the white customer.

The customer grabs the shirt flaps it out as if the new shirt was dirty than puts it over his shoulder.

Customer: "Good day" tiltes the brim of his hat and continues down the roadway.

Minty and Henry watches him as the customer walks down towards the slave auction.

Henry: "Who is he?"

Minty:" I don't know...he must be new around here?"

They see the customer stop put out his cigar fold the t-shirt over his right forearm , walks to another man bows as he hands him the shirt and tobacco then lights an match for the man's cigar he has in mouth.

Henry: "What was that?" He says confused.

Minty: "Indentured servant "Minty chuckles in disgust.

Henry:" I guess they better than us too huh?"

Minty looks at him crazy about to say something, when she sees an black woman in an beautiful purple dress walking with an black man in a golden silk suit.

Henry: "What is it? "He says as Minty looks like she's looking right through him.

She quickly grabs two shirts off the line.

Minty: "I'll be right back!" She heads in the couple's direction.

Henry: "You can't leave me here by myself ...you going to get us in trouble!"

She pays her brother Henry no mind...She makes an v line right towards the couple but as she gets closer she gets nervous thinking who are these black people walking so freely dressed like these white folks but wearing the clothes better, everything goes in slow motion for every step she takes getting closer to the couple.

She starts thinking how she might get in trouble just talking to these people. Minty thoughts ends up stopping her in her tracks...she continues to gaze at the couple in Aww. Minty catches the black beautiful woman attention (all in slow motion).

The woman looks right at Minty and gives her a huge smile and wave. Minty is star struck ,feet stuck in the ground she can't do anything but smile back. She suddenly remembers her reason for coming up to the couple, she can't talk but she starts to hold up one of the shirts as if to sale them, but she really doing it out of curiosity.

The woman turns and starts to walk towards Minty...Minty sees the woman smile quickly turns to an panic facial expression...the woman hollers something Minty tries to make it out then..BOOM.

Minty's hit in back of the head with an metal rod by an overseer, as she goes down she sees one of the slaves trying to escape from the auction . As her vision goes in and out she sees four white men on horses knock the escaping black man down, proceeding to beat him tie his feet together his hands already chained.

She can hear the man yelling something in another language as her eyes get heavy her face lays against the dirt road, from a distance her and the man lock eyes as he's getting beaten ,his bloody face smashed into the ground.

Escaping slave: Hollars "SHUJAA"!!!(Swahilli language: Shujaa=Hero, Warrior.)

Minty eye's fall shut but the words from the beaten man stays with her.

Kemitt Mirrors chapter 5.2 Visions part 4 (Mo & Minty has a story to tell) page 4

Minty finally comes to from the blow to the back of the head. Her vision is blurry , she hears an woman's voice .

Nurse: "Hey beautiful girl." she says in an Haitian accent.

Minty's vision is getting clearer, she feels rocking motion from side to side (riding in the wagon)that makes her want to jump up, but once she tries to sit up she's reminded quickly of the pain she feels from her head.

Victoria (Nurse):"Whoa slow down girl, your going to be okay but you have to save your strength. "

Minty realizes that she's back in the covered wagon, and lays back down with her head propped up on a pillow full of ice.

Minty: "Who are you?" Minty asks in a weak voice.

Mrs.Brodess: "She's an nurse honey she's going to help you out! "Mrs.Brodess looks at Victoria. "Now your not going to ask for some type of payment or anything right?!"

Victoria (Nurse):"No...she was just trying to sell me an shirt she didn't see it coming...I wish I could've grabbed her in time." She says while stroking Minty's hair with her hand.

Mrs.Brodess: "It was an God honest mistake...I mean can you believe that... Man tried to run...Like really.. You have chains on where are you going to run to...My god "as she fans herself.

Victoria: "Are we close yet ,the ice is melting fast in this heat?"

Henry: "Yes we should be there real soon." Henry holds the wet rag on his sisters head wound.

The covered wagon pulls up to the Brodess plantation, followed by Victoria's , husband Jacques horse an carriage.

The other slave workers, including the house slaves sees the carriage and start to stare wondering what's going on.

Henry sees their mother and jumps out the wagon.

Henry: "Mamma, Mamma Minty was hit in the head!"

Their mother runs towards the wagon as Mrs.Brodess and Victoria where helping her out of the wagon.

Mother: "What happened, is she okay?"

Victoria: "She's going to be okay, she just a little dazed right now".

Mrs.Brodess: "Minty happened to be in the way while an slave was trying to escape so James Lawford) (overseer) threw an metal rod trying to hit the escapee but hit Minty instead...it was an honest mistake, James is an dear friend of Edwards . "

Ritta (Mother): Hugs Minty "let's get you back to the cabin."

Mr.Brodess and Jac (Jacques Victoria husband) walk into the conversation.

Jacques: "Is there anything else we can do?"

Ritta(Mother): "No thanks...coming this far is good enough thank you." She starts to walk Minty back to their cabin.

Victoria: "If I may...I would like to show you how to properly care for her wound" she says to Minty mother.

Ritta looks at Mr.Brodess, he nods his head yes.

Ritta(Mother):" I guess that's okay...thank you".

Mr.Brodess:"Henry get some ice from the cellar for your sister!"

Henry: "Yes sir" runs to the cellar.

Victoria ,Jacques and Mr.Brodess follows them back to their cabin. Minty sits on the bed while mother keeps her cool with wet rags.

Jacques: "Here honey "hands Victoria her medicine bag.

Victoria gives Minty some erbs.

Victoria: "This shall help with the headaches...take with some water...the taste isn't so good . "

Minty takes the medicine.

Minty: "Ugh" drinks some water.

Victoria and mother laugh.

Victoria takes some other erbs and smashes them together with her hands mixes with water, then gently runs it on her wound.

Victoria: "Does that hurt?" As she rubbed the erb like ointment on the wound.

Minty: "Its okay." Her face tells an different story.

Jacques: "You gotta tough girl on ya hands here!" He says to Ritta (mother) as he laughs at the faces Minty is making.

Henry runs in with bucket of ice ,followed by Moses (Teenage Rico Mo). Sits the bucket down next to his mother.

Henry: "Is she going to be okay?"

Ritta(Mother): "She's going to be fine."

Victoria hands Ritta (mother) the medicine.

Victoria: "Give her this only if she has headaches and these for her wound ,three times a day for 2 weeks."

Ritta:" What about work?" looking at Mr.Brodess & Mrs.Brodess.

Victoria intrupts before Mr.Brodess could say anything.

Victoria: "She should be resting for at least an week."

Mrs.Brodess:"Oh okay as long as she gets better that's all that matters. "

Victoria gives Minty an wink as she packs her things up.

Victoria: "Well I guess we need to get going before sundown. "

Minty thinks of something quick to say before Victoria and her husband Jacques leaves the cabin.

Minty: "Would if I need more medicine...or something..like that?" She doesn't want to look anxious in front of her mother and Mr. & Mrs.Brodess.

Victoria: "Well I can comeback in two weeks, if it's ok with Karen...correct" as she looks at Mrs.Brodess.

Mrs.Brodess :"Um...yes that would be fine." Looks at Mr.Brodess for the okay.

Victoria:" Great I'll see you on the second Sunday from today...good!"

Minty shakes her head yes with an grin.

Mrs.Brodess:" Okay good, I'll walk you out...I'm sorry...?"

Victoria: "Victoria, my name is Victoria this is my husband Jacques!"

Ritta(Mother): "Well next time hopefully my husband Ben will be here to meet you."

Victoria: "That would be heavenly...see you soon" looks right at Minty.

Minty waves goodbye, Ritta (Mother) waits till there far enough away to laugh and pop Minty on her leg.

Minty: "Ow...what I do?"

Ritta(mother): "Where you find these fancy black folks from ,that can talk to white people any ol kind of way?"

Minty:" Today at the Eastern Shore."

Ritta(mother): "Only you can attract such souls...lord Jesus!" Laughing. "Mo, Henry set up my pots outside I'm going to start cooking super before your father gets home."

Mo & Henry: "Yes mam!"

Ritta(mother):"And Mo bring your little sisters in to get bathed."

Rico Mo: "Yes mam!" He replies as him and Henry play fight on their way out the cabin.

Kemitt mirrors chapter 5.2 (Vision pt.5)
"Minty & Mo has a story to tell "page. 5

When you build it THEY will come

Minty's vision point of view:

Victoria and Jacques came two weeks later to check on me and my family. Victoria and Jacques gained a real bond with our family as well with the other workers overtime, even the Brodess's liked them coming around. Jac got the fellas together and added rooms to each cabin for more space, taught everyone to respect the land and the land will give you life.

Victoria would teach the women about medicine using natural erbs even Mo would peak his head in those conversations.

Jacques would actually be on the porch with Mr.Brodess, my father Ben Ross and a few other men that worked on the plantation spent Sunday afternoons, talking and laughing. Once a month they'll make their visit and it was like a holiday, Mr. Brodess enjoyed their company so much they would invite them on Saturdays and stay till Sunday and on those visits, nobody had to work.

On Saturday nights my family along with Jacques and Victoria would go to the edge of the plantation near the woods and they would teach us how to read the sky and the landscape. As time went on Victoria and Jacques would tell us stories about the revolution in Haiti and how they defeated Napoleon's army. Even taught us to fight like the Haitian warriors. Victoria taught me, Mo, and Henry how to use a pistol but never shot it, the noise would be too loud but the knife and hatchet we mastered those as tools and weapons.

There where whispers throughout the nearby counties people gossip about the Brodess's and their free fancy nigger friends, but much respect to the Brodess's they paid it no mind, maybe Jacques and Victoria changed their outlook on how black people could be if given an chance in life.

[7 1/2 years later]

In my early twenties I worked more in the house than the field's. Mo (Rico) Is the main blacksmith and taking care of the livestock along with my father Ben.

My Mother ran the kitchen with my two-younger sisters, Henry worked in his shed he built with Mo. Coming up with inventions that makes work easier for everyone on the plantation. Everything I thought for those times where okay, Mr.Brodess had all the adults sign papers that would free them and their family, plus own a piece of his growing land when he retired.

Then one Tuesday evening there was an....

Knock,knock,knock at the front door of the Brodess's house on a Tuesday evening. Mrs.Brodess answers the door.

Mr.Brodess:"James Lawford, what brings you by this evening ". As they shake hands.

James Lawford: "May I." Gester's to come inside.

Mr.Brodess:"Oh by all means come on in... Ritta can you get us both a glass of scotch" Ritta goes to pour the drinks.

James seemed amazed at the likeness Mr.Brodess talks to his slaves.

Mr.Brodess: "Come take a seat." As they enter the living room.

Mrs.Brodess: "Wow how long has it been 10, 11 years."

James Lawford:"Hey don't put that age on me." Laughing.

Mr.Brodess:"So what's new!"

Ritta brings in the glasses and pours the drink.

Mr.Brodess:"Thanks Ritta, once you finish super you and the girls can go for the night."

Ritta just nods and heads to the kitchen.

Mrs.Brodess:"Well I'll let you guys catch up, I'll help Ritta with the kitchen "gives her husband a kiss on the cheek and heads out the room.

James Law Takes a sip of his drink, looks at Mr.Brodess with an smile.

James lawford:"You sure do treat your niggers nice...you ahhh" makes an face as if he's doing more with his women slaves.

Mr.Brodess:"Ahh what?"

James Lawford: "You know, getting the extras out of her duties!"

Mr.Brodess:"What No...I consider her and the Ross family great friends of mine."

James Lawford:"So I hear!" He stands up.

Mr.Brodess:"What exactly is that?" He stands up also.

James Lawford:"That you treat your slaves like family, that you wrote in your Will if you past or decide to move out of Maryland that your slaves shall be freed and OWN... LAND?!!"

Mr.Brodess :"And ...how do you know this?"

James Lawford shows a button on his jacket.("Vote for James Law")

James Lawford:"I'm going to be an Democratic senator soon and it makes me look bad to have, not just an residence of my county, but an Frat brother of mine doing business with Uppidy niggers, especially when no one else is cut in on it!"

Mr. Brodess:"Can you get to the point!" He saids getting heated a feeling disrespected.

James Law walks over to the piano, glides his hand over the fine polished blackwood.

James Lawford:"The point is either you stop doing business the way you do business or your land will be seized and all property turned over to the government."

Mr.Brodess:"You can't do that, I'm not breaking any laws!"

James Lawford:"Its funny how are names sometimes come to forwishin my last name is Law and my brother Brodess I'am the Law!"

Mr.Brodess:"No what's funny is the last time I seen you I was barely getting by. Now that I found a way for myself everybody's got something to say" (moves James law hand from his piano) "But the hell with you and anybody else who has an problem with the way I do business...you can leave now!"As he points him to the door.

James Lawford puts his drink on the piano in disrespect, Mr.Brodess picks up the drink and throws it on James Lawford suite.

Mr.Brodess:"Now you done disrespected me in my house the moment you walked through that door , now if you really got an problem we can settle this like men right here right now!" Puts down his drink and puts up his fists.

James Lawford : You'll be seeming me in November...Mr.Brodess!" Walks out the door.

Mr.Brodess slams the door shut. Me and Mrs.Brodess hears the conversation from the other room.

Mrs.Brodess:"Minty go ahead to the cabin...and don't speak of this okay."

Minty:"Okay "she heads out the back door with her mother and two younger sisters to their cabin.

Mrs.Brodess walks into to the room with Mr.Brodess.

Mrs.Brodess:"What was that about?"

Mr.Brodess:"Blood suckin leaches, that's what that's about!"

Mrs.Brodess:"I thought James was your friend."

Mr. Brodess:"Huh friend loose term...You know what's funny when I think about it...when I was in the same mind frame as everyone else nobody cared ,when I was doing bad. My twenty pluse years of knowing James not once did he reach out to help on anything. I known Jac (Jacques) for seven years done business together for six years ,made more money with him than anybody around me . Read books enlightened myself of the truth ,embraced my workers and guaranteed to reward them when I retire and now they want to push me out for it!" Pours another drink "I tell you one thing me and my shotgun gone have a meeting with that damn lawyer...telling all my business . "

Mrs.Brodess:"Just calm down ,it'll work itself out." Takes the drink out his hand and leads him to bed.

Mr.Brodess:"It'll be an cold day in hell before they take what I built."

Mrs.Brodess:"I know honey just sleep it off well figure it out in the morning."They head up stairs.

Mr.Brodess:" Then people like him wonder why that Preacher boy did what he did killing all those people, hell I'm gone do two times worst when I'm done!"

Mrs.Brodess:"I know honey just make it up the steps first okay."

I was already talking about what happened back at the cabin with my family.

Minty:" Daddy you think they were in business with Jac and Victoria?"

Ben(father):" Yeah they did some business I didn't know it was supposed to be a secret but I see why they would keep it that way around here."

Moses (Rico):"You took trips with Mr.Brodess to Louisiana."

Ben: "Florida, Georgia, and everywhere we went we where treated like royalty...some say Jacques and Victoria got ties to the royal family back in Haiti."

Ritta:"What...and you just now saying something!"

Ben:"It didn't make me none whether they were or not, all I know is Mr.Brodess was no longer a pain in the as... (looking at his children) Being gone for one week every couple months was better than being rented out to other owners 7 days a week sometimes I didn't see yall for months."

Moses: "Well I hope they come back its been good ever since Minty got hit in the head wit that pipe." laughing .

Minty throws the pillow at Moses.

Minty: "Shut up!"

Ritta:"No but they have been a blessing around here, I hope they can stay around too...but for right now it's bed time. "

Kids: "All man...okay Mommy "the two younger girls respond.

Kemitt mirrors chapter 5.4 (Vision's part 6)
"Mo & Minty has a story to tell" page 6

When days go by

Moses vision's point of view:

The next morning Mr.Brodess came back to the house just before noon. He storms into the house with his rifle in one hand Mrs.Brodess sees him and instantly approaches him at the door.

Mrs.Brodess: "What did you do?" She says very concerned.

Mr.Brodess goes straight to the kitchen and gets an glass of lemon aid, she follows him into the kitchen.

Mrs.Brodess:" What did you do?!"

Mr.Brodess:"Settle down...I didn't harm nobody...I just had an good ol conversation with my disloyal lawyer that's all" he saids calmly .

Mrs.Brodess:"Well what happened?" At this point we're all in the kitchen wondering the same thing.

Mr.Brodess:" Well I fired him as my lawyer, got all my documents...I'm done with this town!"

Mrs.Brodess:"What do you mean?"

Mr. Brodess:" It means I'm going to file my papers with an new lawyer finish these last deliveries and I'm officially retired."

Mrs.Brodess:"Okay... but what about everyone else?"

Mr.Brodess:"They'll receive everything that was signed off on?"

Ritta:"So we'll have our freedom papers? "

Mr.Brodess:"It will be done before election time." He starts to exit out the kitchen then stops an turns to my mother.

Mr.Brodess:"Oh Ritta when you get your papers you and Ben move your family to an better place, these people don't deserve to have you here... including me."

Mr.Brodess heads up stairs to his room.

Mrs.Brodess:"Hey Ritta why don't yall just come back around suppertime ok."

Ritta:"Okay."

We went back to our cabin to see my father chopping fire wood out front.

Minty: "Hey Daddy, daddy "excited about the news.

Daddy: "Hey what's up?"Continuing to chopping the wood and place in an pile.

Minty: "Mr.Brodess said our freedom papers are coming soon!"

Daddy: "Is that right." Stops what he's doing.

Ritta:"That's what he said just a bit ago."

Ben: "I thought his plan to retire wasn't for another two years?"

Ritta:"He said he's retiring before election time."

Minty:" I think its about that James Law guy."

Ben: "Well I guess we'll see."

Daddy was more on I'll believe it when I see it so we didn't go around telling everyone the news to get people excited just in case.

Later that day Mr.Brodess invited my dad to have dinner with him to let him know that there going to double the loads for all the next deliveries to finish up the year early, That meant longer trips.

So my father and Mr.Brodess heads out that weekend to make their deliveries they where gone for nearly 4 weeks, once back my father was exhausted but let us know that Jacques and Victoria where fine . Lately it was too dangerous for them to stay in Maryland with out causing people harm including the people that lived on the Brodess's plantation from retaliation.

Truth was, on one of there visits back to Maryland they came to an burned down house that they owned near the Eastern shores.

We didn't know then ,but Jacques and Victoria had the statues and power to burn the whole state of Maryland if they wanted too.

They were doing business on behalf of their country but didn't retaliate because of the love they had for the people or other different reasons I don't know. I often thought maybe they'll come rescue us but before any of us could blink Mr.Brodess became very ill.

My father took two trips without him which was very dangerous, just him and Mr.Hayden one of Mr.Brodess white business partners.

When they returned my father let us know he met an man that passed him this newsletter. The man worked with Jacques and Victoria, the man said they had to go back to Haiti to attend the needs there after a bad storm that hit the island.

As the days went by Mr.Brodess is getting terribly sick Victoria and Jacques are gone and its getting closer to November.

To make some extra money Mrs.Brodess decides to open up a stand at the Eastern shore like we did years ago taking myself and Mo.

We use to go in the summer time never fall and we can see why the weather wasn't to pleasant and the people who knew who Mrs.Brodess was , where even more harsh than the ocean dropping the temperature down what felt like twenty degrees. The slave auctions has slowed down over the years so no t-shirts were sold but we still sold some tobacco despite the mug faces of our customers.

The small talk with a smile that Mrs.Brodess has mastered was no longer working she finally sees the writing on the wall so we packed up and got back to the farm.

As soon as we got back Mrs.Brodess went to attend to Mr.Brodess as we went to unload the wagon and stable the horses in the barn.

Moses (Rico) looks around to make sure its just him and me alone in the barn.

Moses: "Hey Minty...look at this" unfolds an pamphlet size magazine.

Minty takes an look at it.

Minty: "What it's just an newspaper or something "she saids not really paying attention to it, continues to unload the wagon.

Moses: "Yeah but look at the back of the last page."

Minty: She looks "Okay what?" Still not interested in what Mo is trying to show her.

Moses: "Its the same signs that was on the newspaper dad had from his trip."

Now Minty is interested, thinking about Victoria and Jacques.

Minty:" I don't see anything but lets take it to Daddy. "

Moses: "No forget it its probably nothing "folds it up and puts it back into his pocket.

Moses continued to study that news letter night after night even taken the pamphlet dad had and comparing the two together.

It was Friday morning my mom, my two sisters an myself entered the Brodess's kitchen door to prepare breakfast as usual when we heard an scream. We ran up the stairs to see what's going on. Only to see Mrs.Brodess kneeled down crying by the bed side of Mr.Brodess holding his hand while he lays there lifeless.

I couldn't help to see even in that moment the look on Mr.Brodess face was one at piece. Better than the stress fullness man that was walking around these past months.

Later the doctor's came ,then others came to come get his body and took him somewhere I don't know we usually bury slaves in the woods it never dawned on me that people actually come to carry you out to prep you to be buried.

Mrs.Brodess left with the doctor's and everybody on the plantation was stunned not knowing what to do or what's going to happen.

Myself wandered are we free do we stay or do we go, the words of Mr.Brodess echo through my mind of leaving with my family but also about owning part of the land, I think most of us was thinking the same thing.

Later that evening Mrs.Brodess comes back, she doesn't say much to any of us she just went to her room and went to bed, I'm sure the day was long an hard for her losing her husband.

The next morning we're up again preparing breakfast when a carriage arrives. My mom Ritta answers the door.

Carriage driver: "I'm here to escort Mrs.Brodess".

Before my mother could call her down stairs Mrs.Brodess comes down stairs with two luggage bags. She gives them to the carriage driver, he takes them to the carriage.

Ritta:"Is the funeral today?"

Mrs.Brodess just give us all hugs.

Mrs.Brodess:"I had to work somethings out yesterday...it was so tedious."

Minty:"Uh,oh" I thought...Mrs.Brodess is in performance mode like when she does her small talk I've seen this all to often, somethings not right.

Mrs.Brodess:"I'm going to New York to visit my family but don't worry the lawyer is going to explain everything to all of you okay."

I haven't seen that Sunday church hat in years, I remember before Jacques and Victoria came along she tried so hard to be liked by other's...I guess she's back to her old ways.

She walks to the carriage and pulls off disappearing into the fogg. We just stood there at the porch stunned.

My mother gets us together and we head back to the cabins. Everyone's standing around when someone hollers out "we free" it doesn't sink in yet, then again "free, free, we free . "

People started dancing and singing I mean I was happy, confused, sad all at the same time . Then we see another carriage come up with three other men on horses, We gathered by the Brodess's house.

Lawyer: "People formerly of the Brodess's estate I 'am here to inform you that Mr.Brodess has been pronounced dead on arrival Friday Ten thirty am. Mr. Brodess has legal documentation that states his property of slaves shall be freed and all property of land shall be divided between the individuals who signed the deeds to the properties. Further more Mr.Brodess has issued royalties to all slaves.

Minty: "Daddy what does this mean?"

Ben: "Means Mr.Brodess kept his promises! "

Lawyer: "As of Friday 11pm the sole heir of the Brodess's estate Mrs.Brodess has sold and overturned all the properties to the Thompson family they are now the new owners of the land endorsed by Maryland state law."

Ben: "What... you can't do that we're freed people."

Lawyer: "Only if the Thompson family Grant's it by law you are now property of the Thompson estate. "

The men on the horses grin, then one climbed off his horse.

Anthony Thompson:" Thanks ...We got it from here" shakes the lawyer hand.

Lawyer: "OH Anthony remember to vote James Law is for the people!" He saids with an smile.

Anthony Thompson: "No doubt about it he got my vote!"

As the lawyer leave, more wagon's are showing up with people going inside the house moving out the old furniture, moving in new.

Anthony Thompson: "Listen up I'm Mr.Anthony Thompson, this here my brothers Absalom and Edward now this can be an easy trans...trans.."

Edward Thompson: "Transition "!

Anthony Thompson: "Boy went to college!...Now we heard there's a lot of upiddy niggers around here, but that gonna change , now my Uncle in law God rest his sole went soft somewhere but not us...if you don't follow the rules then..."

The brother Absalom let's an round off from the shotgun in the air.

Anthony Thompson:" You will be shot...Do you understand me" he says in an thick red neck accent.

Anthony Thompson: "So sense this was the most profitable plantation through out the surrounding counties it's time to get back to work!"

Every one stands around with hate in there eyes then..Boom. Absalom and Edward let off more rounds from their shotguns. Then everyone disbursed and got to work.

Anthony Thompson: "Yeah boys we gotta money maker here...go get that nigger who understood the Lawyer and bring him to the house" he says to Absalom and Edward .

Kemitt mirrors chapter 5.5 (Vision's part 7)
"Mo & Minty has an story to tell "page 7

Ben won't break

Moses point of View:

The two brothers take my father inside what was the Brodess's house. I crept around the side by the window to see what was going on.

They sit my father down on the couch in the living room. My father seem calm as ever but I can't help gripping the hatchet tighter and tighter.

Anthony Thompson: "So you the nigger overseer here?"

Ben: "No."

Anthony Thompson: "You know how to read boy" he says while putting his filthy boots up on Mr.Brodess coffee table leaning back in Mr.Brodess favorite chair.

Ben: "For what's necessary."

Absalom Thompson: "This nigger got vocabulary "he smiles showing his rotten teeth.

Edward Thompson: "You are Benjamin Ross correct. "

Moses vision's: I know my father, that look he gave that boy he wanted to tear his head off, but my father always stayed in control of his emotions.

Ben: "Correct."

Edward Thompson: "You did help Mr.Brodess grow his business correct."

Ben: "I did my job."

Anthony Thompson: "OH stop it you was his favorite nigger...I heard the stories about you and your family all in the house...this house... he treated ya'll like...like royalty... (gets up and sits on top of Mr.Brodess black wood piano. Looks Ben in the eyes)speaking of royalty...what do you know about these rich niggers from out of town."

Ben: "I don't know about anyone's riches."

The three brothers laugh.

Anthony Thompson: "This nigger smart here ain't he...I see why Brodess was fond of you...but who's the nigger Brodess got rich with?"

Ben: "Got rich with?"

Anthony Thompson: "Just give me a name...that all."

Ben: "I wasn't involved that far into the business "Ben looks at his surroundings he notices scissors on the night stand next to the chair Edward Thompson sitting in, Absalom Thompson holding the shotgun but knows he never reloaded it after the rounds he let off earlier, Anthony Thompson would be the easiest to get too but he's out numbered and the sound of men taking things in and out the house is frequent...he has to keep his cool.

Anthony Thompson: "Okay let's see.. your not the nigger overseer, your not the right hand nigger to Brodess, and you a nigger that don't know the niggers...I have no use for you...BUT...I hear that daughter of yours might know something."

Ben looks right at Anthony Thompson with fire in his eyes.

Anthony Thompson:"Uh,Oh I think he do know something...Edward "Edward gets up, hands him some documents.

Ben sees an opportunity to go for the scissors once Edward moves from his seat.

Anthony Thompson: "Says here your an free man (going through the docs) acre and an half of land...Six Thousan-dollars to the order of Benjamin Ross... But you weren't part of the business...well Brodess sure did love you." Takes the cigar lighter out his pocket an slowly put fire to the document .

Moses vision's: I can see my father brewing in anger.

Anthony Thompson: "Escort him back to his quarter's he's no use (Anthony turns his back to pour a drink), Oh an bring that daughter of his...time to have some fun!"

Before they could get to Ben, he quickly grabs the scissors slices Edward across the face ,as Anthony Thompson was turning around the scissors goes in and out his shoulder then into his left ear. Absalom comes from behind an knocks Ben down to one knee by the butt of his shotgun

Moses vision: I threw an rock through the window it stunned Absalom Thompson I had him in sight I aimed my hatchet ,began to release when I felt an pull on my arm stopping my motion.

Ritta:"Moses no!...They'll kill you."

Absalom: "They revoltin they revoltin "he screams running through the house.

Dad sees us outside and hops through the window, we take off running back to the fields.

Mo vision's: We had to hide my father in the woods that day , we can hear the Thompson men fussing and hollering the workers they brought with them rushed them out off the plantation.

News quickly spreads across the plantation to the other slaves what just happened some where scared some was ready to fight .

As time went by the plantation got more quiet the sun eventually went down. My father decided he wanted to be with the family just in case. Most of the men stayed outside the cabin keeping watch while the woman and children try to get some sleep except of course Minty.

During the night my father explained the situation to the others about the Thompsons aren't freeing anybody ,even talked about running. The group was divided some had older siblings other's small children.

The next option was to fight but only an handful was ready for that, time wasn't on our side and everyone new it. My father tried to explain he didn't want to see nobody being harmed because of his actions. He ruled that he'll take his chances escaping with his family.

We went to our cabin.

Ben:"Ritta...come on we're leaving!"

Ritta:"You sure?"

Ben:"Yes get the kids, I'll grab some things, kids come on!"

Ritta:"Where are we going to go?"

Ben:"I know some places we can camp at overnight then go north."

Ritta:"But who's going to help us...?"

My father grabs my mother face looks her in the eyes.

Ben:" I can't have nothing happen to you or the kids...I got us"! Kisses her.

Ritta:"Okay."

Moses vision: Mom stopped talking and got my sister's ready. Then we hear an scream. As soon as I poked my head out the doorway I was grabbed and beaten. Men rushed inside and grabbed everyone, they dragged us into the middle of all the cabins I seen maybe thirty men running into homes dragging everyone out. Kids crying people scared, gun shots going off until everyone was dragged outside. They cuffed and chained my whole family including my little sisters. They started to whip and beat everyone from old to young, it was just chaos.

It was hard to even know what was going on then all I heard was an muffled voice "I'm Benjamin Ross, I'm Benjamin Ross" they had some of the older men heads covered with wheat bags so they couldn't see including my father, then another voice "Hault, Hault!"

Officer Lee: "Bring that man" he says sitting high on an horse.

Moses vision: Now that the dust is starting to clear all I can see is men in uniform...soldiers. They bring my father to the front and remove the bag from his head.

The head officer leans over to Absalom Thompson and whispered something to him all I can see is Absalom on an horse next to him shaking his head yes.

Officer Lee: "Benjamin Ross I'm Officer Lee you have been charged with two attempted murders and inciting an riot."

Officer Lee: Turns to Absalom "Now this doesn't look like much of an revolt Absalom."

Absalom Thompson: "They were throwing rocks through the windows and chanting... all of'em was."

Officer lee:"I can take him but you won't gain any fearful respect from them, he would just become an martyr. "

Absalom Thompson: "Well what do I do?"

Officer Lee: "Your Daddy owe me after this...give'em all 20 lashes then lock'em in the stables."

Moses vision's : The soldier whipped my father in front of everyone, you can see the whip cutting through his skin like paper. Once he got the 20 lashes they threw him into the horse stables. Mr. Brodess didn't have torcher devices like other plantation owners, I guess this was their answer for that. They proceeded to do the same to all the adult male's , I wasn't fully grown but I made the cut. I got seven slashes and threw in the pin with the pigs. All I can hear was grunts and groans from the animals and the other beaten men , shadows of light from the sun coming up started to show but then the barn door closes...nothing but darkness.

Kemitt mirrors Chapter 5.6 (Vision's part 8)
"Mo & Minty has an story to tell" page. 8

"I see clearly now"

Vision's from Minty point of view:

Minty: They threw most of the beaten men in the barn including my father and brother. The night horrors seemed like it would never end ,the soldiers continued to beat and torcher us until the officer finally told them it was enough. They unchained us and the ones that could make it back to their cabins did the others just layed out in the dirt grass until helped up.

Half of the soldiers where I guess told they can go but the other half stayed to watch over us. I don't think nobody got sleep the pain from the beatings where agonizing both mental and physical.

Just hours after the sun was up the soldiers came to each cabin grabbing the kids, the thankfulness of them having some sort of human decency for not brutally hurting the children quickly left when they put them right to work.

I see clearly now that was part of the tactic, rule the strong with iron fist spare the weak even if that weakness is just the naive and innocence .

My brother Henry was always the smartest he look younger than he really was so he past as an young enough child plus during the may lay I seen him damn near play dead. His survival instincts actually paid off, he nursed me and my mother with the knowledge Jacques and Victoria taught us.

The soldiers didn't realize the small gardens around the cabins where also natural erbs and medicine because of Mo really taking the whole Jacques saying if you respect the land the land will give you life so serious we had the biggest garden near our cabin. Henry also snuck into the cellar for ice when he could for the swelling he gave as much as he could for everyone.

I seen him starring at the barn but they had soldiers on guard at all times. They only opened it up to feed them scraps and water, at least we knew they where still alive ,well maybe.

I seen the moon back up so I knew its been an full day, laying in this cot bed never felt this uncomfortable before I turn to see Henry concentrating hard taking notes on something.

Minty: "What you doing?" Talking to Henry .

Henry:" I think these maps are directions. "

Minty: "What are you talking about?"

Henry: "The pamphlet dad got and the magazine Moses got they both line up."

Minty: "A map?" Henry gets closer to show Minty.

Henry: "See the bear paw these are different path ways staying by streams of water. These are codes of what to say once you get to these points." Minty looking in amazement.

Henry: "Look here the one Mo got is an direct passage from these parts to the north."

Minty: "How did you figure this out?"

Henry:" I don't know Victoria said I see a lot of things in ...she said reverse... so I just start reading it backwards and circled the crossing of the words, each crossing spelled out an direction. "

Minty:" Man I would've never seen it "As she looks at the now known maps. "Keep this hidden we can't lose this.

Henry agrees and put the maps up in his hiding place under the loose boards in the floor.

Minty vision: I can hear Victoria's voice in my head.

Victoria: "Hope and faith can get you through the day but an plan can get you towards your destination."

I wish Victoria and Jac was here I hope there okay I know they wouldn't just leave us like this ,something had to happen. The thought of it just brings my heart into a rage even if not seen from the outside.

I look over to ask Henry for water but he's gone from his bed.

Kemitt mirrors chapter 5.7 (Vision's part 9)
"Mo & Minty has an story to tell "page.9

Will to live...

Moses point of view:

I been in and out of consciousness for a while now, I remember them trying to feed us , the pigs got to the food before I even knew it was there. I was to hurt to extend my arm for cup of water so the soldier took it as disrespect an just threw the water on me, called me an ungrateful nigger.

If I was laying next to hoggs I'm sure they'll be nibbling on my life less looking body.

At this point I'm ready to leave this world, I don't even know why I'm here without my family there's no point of being alive, I can't believe I thought Mr.Brodess was an good master because he was giving us our freedom but why the hell we slaves in the first place, I'm ready for peace...dying here maybe the way.

Henry: "Hey" he whispers.

Mo vision's: I opened my eyes to see "Henry?"

Henry: "Shush...the guard sleeping outside "he gives Moses bread and water, quickly rubbing erb medicine on his wounds . "I saw dad in the stables already he's hurt but he's okay...hey I gotta get to the other's here take this for the pain." Gives him more erbs, bread and fresh water. "Okay I'll see you soon."

Mo vision's: Just like that seeing my baby brother coming to my aid gave me the Will to live...and my Will for revenge...in due time I will have it!!

It must have been days or weeks before they finally opened up those barn doors. The animals weren't attended to so the stables and pens where full of pisces and my feet where covered in it.

I just heard men coming in shouting and throwing water on us.

Thompson Overseer: "Let's go get up, it's time to get back to work, let's go!"

Mo vision's: They lead us out the barn still chained up, took us over to the small lake where we swam as kids and cleaned our clothes. They stripped us out of our dirt bloody clothes and pushed us in the lake ,of course none of us liked the treatment but getting the filth off my body and water to my wounds felt a lot better. The day was gloomy but still to bright for my eyes...haven't seen the sun in a while. They brought us back to the fields where they gave us dry clothes, unchained us then put us right to work.

I realized the soldiers where gone but there where at least fifteen men overseeing us in the fields. I was glad to see my father in the distance even though we haven't had an chance to talk yet. As I looked around I saw more people working in the field than usual, even my mom and sister's are now working the fields.

Henry is by his shed trying to explain to two overseers how to use the equipment he built, but it doesn't look like its going to well for him trying to explain instructions to Neanderthal's .

I hear another guy yell something out from the barn, then the overseer on the horse start to round up some slaves and lead them to the barn. I see the slave workers carrying out a dead body, from the responds of Mary and her daughter Carrie ,I knew it was old man Lee, Mary's father. All I can think of was how long he worked on this plantation just to die in a barn but then guilt...damn is it our fault.

He was older so not eating or drinking for weeks had to take an toll on him. They took his body to the front by the Brodess house and just left him there. Mary and Carrie was made to go back to work, I felt bad my emotions didn't have anything to give but anger...I'm all cried out...only thoughts of revenge fuels me to be alive.

As time went on the Thompson Brothers were back together the bandages where gone from the two brothers but the lack of respect from the slaves and even their workers lasted especially when the incident is brought up among their own friends. We can often hear drunken arguments among the Thompson brothers and their company about what happened, who did what.

The new indenture servants who work in the house now, would tell us about the Thompsons father who really owns the plantation being embarrassed of his sons and the incident that happened.

The Thompson brothers split up the slave family's living conditions Men and women are separated now. Adult men now shared cabins, teenage boys to kids shared cabins and the same for the women and the girls.

My mother and Minty would sneak over to my cabin to attend to my wounds as well as the others. This must be the hell those white preachers be talking about all the time so if they created this hell for us what does that make them.

The Thompson brothers don't have any respect for the soil, growing too much tobacco is very harsh on the land and the way they have us working I'll be surprised if this last more than two years before the earth rejects the toxic produce.

They put my father back to the stables and care taking of the animals, he must of told them my previous job because now I'm back making horse shoes, tools, and whatever else that needed fixing.

[9 months later]

A lot of time has passed but Thompson brothers still got an guy looking over my shoulder as I worked. The Thomson's ran the plantation harsh they brought in all type of torture contraptions to keep us all in line and worst part had me make some of those contraptions. The first time I didn't even know what I was building until they used it. They called it the hot box (All Metal box), they would put a slave inside and they would nearly die from the heat or in the winter time freeze to death.

After that if they had me build something I would secretly put an escape latch somewhere in the build. We where able to sneak food or water to whoever's being tortured, Minty was the only one who used it right, one time they punished her for back talking an man indentured servant, but she snuck out the box at night time and would be in the cabin with my father then go back in the box in the morning. The overseer would think somethings wrong with her he would check on her and she would be sleeping or singing. When they let her out she came out with a smile and a "hallelujah praise Jesus!" skipping back to her cabin.

She did it just to let them know they couldn't break her... I thought it was funny but she was smart she never did anything during summer and mid winter always spring or early fall.

About two years has past and just like I predicted, the soil is drying up. Next season harvest is going to be terrible, I got to thinking how being with your family sometimes could conform you to ways you never thought would hold you.

I secretly made the sharpest blades for my hatchet and knives when I wanted my revenge now I look at those tools buried in the horse stable under the layers of hay and think that feeling has past. This is my life and at least I'm with my family, I have accepted this way of life for me because this is the way of life.

The next morning I'm helping my dad with the live stock he's upset about something but wouldn't say what it was. As the day continued the Thompson brothers had their family over for this Thanksgiving thing that was the first time, I seen the Thompson brothers' father Mr.Thompson.

My father knew Mr.Thompson from working for him back when Mr.Brodess would rent him out to other plantations way before Jac and Victoria came along. I know my father never liked the Thompsons but this time I felt he knew something was wrong. My father didn't talk much this day he just kept looking towards the house as we worked.

It was getting well into the night an the Thompsons guest are finally starting to leave. We can see Mr.Thompson(Father)carriage pull around Mr.Thompson looks at us as we cook supper by the cabins, flicks his rolled up cigarette and proceeds to leave with I believe his wife.

I can see an sigh of relief come from my father but really from my mother as she grips his hand and leans on his shoulder. I often wondered was there more to that after all my father met my mother when she worked on the Thompson plantation, Mr.Brodess bought her from the Thompsons. Mr.Thompson had an reputation about these parties and would use the slave women and slave children to entertain his guest. He's now an powerful figure threw out the counties and has close ties to the new mayor James Law. My parents never spoke of such things to us but we get older, wiser and the things left in the dark has to come to light even if it's for our own protection.

Kemitt mirrors Chapter 5.8 (Vision's part 10)
"Mo & Minty got an story to tell" page 10

Minty vision's point of view:

The next morning we're working the fields I see Mo headed towards the stables. My mother comes from the rear of the main house (Thompson house) , I can tell there's something wrong. The overseers are watching close so I don't want to bring attention I just waited for mom to take her position next to me, she sobbing and keep wiping tears from her face.

Minty: "Ma what's wrong?"

Minty vision: She trying not to show emotion.

Minty: "Ma!"

Rita: "They...(Trying to keep it together)They took..Ben...they took your father."

Minty: "What...When!"

Rita: "In the middle of the night."

Minty: "*Who* told you this?"

Rita: "Edward (Thompson) said they where just renting him out but I don't believe him...I think he's gone I think they sold him "she starts to break down crying.

Minty: "Oh mamma" as she holds her.

Overseer: "What's wrong wit her."

Minty: "She's not feeling well...can I take her back to her cabin?"

Overseer:" I see nothing wrong, get to work. "

Minty: "We'll find out what's going on mamma don't worry ok."

Ritta:"Okay baby" as she gathers herself and gets back to work.

Minty vision: Now I'm feeling scared and confused...is daddy gone or what... damn I wish we could've ran when we had our chances...Do we run now?... No maybe he's coming back. Thoughts are rushing through my head of what to do, I'm working but at the same time in a daze "Minty, Minty"...

Henry: "Minty."

Minty: "Oh hey."

Henry: "You okay?"

Minty:"Uhh..yeah."

Henry: "Well they're saying the farm no longer needs my cheap inventions so Edward taking over my work station."

Minty:" He doesn't even know how to work anything."

Henry: "Whatever...its more like he wants to take credit for years of my work...they don't even use the seeds for the soil that me and Mo took time to procreate."

Minty: "Where is Moses?"

Henry: "He's in the stables...but where's dad I haven't seen him."

Minty: "Not sure mommy thinks somethings wrong...the Thompsons said they rented him out but she don't believe it."

Henry: "So did they?"

Minty: "Don't know yet...hey here comes the overseer see if you can let Mo know what's going on."

Henry: "Okay I'll be back."

Minty Vision's: Henry walked of with his wagon full of hay he was supposed to be taking to the barn before he saw us. Henry hauling the hay kind of confirmed my mother's fear of my father being sold to me, because they took his shed away and now he's doing my father's work.

Over the years The Thompson boys really changed the feel of the plantation, we get it they want to show their dominance but all they're doing is fueling anger and working non stop constantly doesn't helped these feelings.

Later that night Mo comes by the cabin.

Moses: "Is it true Daddy's gone?"

Minty vision's: I told him what Edward Thompson said and what mom believes but it doesn't matter either way my family is hurt by this situation. Me and Mo had a short conversation before he headed back to his cabin.

Days continue to go by, one night I look to the stars and realized it's been more than a month since my father's been gone, the evil smirk I get from the overseers always let me know he's been taking away from us possibly forever.

It also showed the other families on the plantation that they could be split up at any time especially if you cause any trouble.

Then the day I dreaded most finally came.

Kemitt mirrors chapter 5.9 (Vinson's part 11)
"Mo & Minty has an story to tell "page.11

[Now I shall have mine]

Moses point of view:

Henry comes waking me up early with Minty outside my cabin.

Minty: "They taking Mama!" She saids in a panic.

We run to the driveway of the main house to see my Mother and my little sisters being loaded on to a covered wagon by French uniformed soldiers heavily armed.

The chains let us know they're being sent away for good the Thompsons could of at least let us say our goodbyes but instead held us back as they start to head out now the last vision I have of my mother and sisters are tears and frightened faces.

I make eye contact with Anthony Thompson; he just looks at me as he drinks his coffee on the porch.

I watched him smile as he heads back inside the house catching a glimpse of his scarred face and mangled ear, I guess this is part of his revenge... Now I shall have mine.

Minty vision's:

We watched the wagon taking our mom and sister away disappear into the morning dust. I turn around falling into Henry's arms when I notice Moses headed straight towards the barn. We start to walk trying to keep up with Moses but slowed down by other warm hugs from the other slave workers try to show love to us, after all we're going through the same struggle, but I can't help to keep my eyes on Moses scared for what he might do. As our people surround us trying to give Henry and me comfort animals just start to run out freely through the dust. First the chicken's, then the pigs, cow's roaming around. The noise of all the commotion catches two of the over-seer's attention.

Moses vision's point of view:

I got to the barn to retrieve my buried weapons in the horse stables, then figured fuck it...I lose my family you lose money...I let all the caged live stock out. I got to my Father's favorite horse "Goyah" an black stallion that was given to him from chief of the ChopTank Ababco Tribe , dug up my buried hatchet blade and knife out, tore my shirt to use as an holster for my weapons. Gave "Goyah" one last hug then let'em free. No more talkin! I'm ready to live... I'm willing to die...IM READY FOR WAR!!

[Rise from Darkness]

Minty vision's point of view:

The overseers start towards the barn "What the hell going on" they yell out in their hillbilly lingo. Then the horse's started to run out!! That's when I knew this was not an accident...the day has come...it's like the dawn lit fog spiraled around Mo as he walks out the barn then split in half, it's like my baby brother has transformed into this warrior Jacques & Victoria always talked about. I can hear Victoria's voice in my head describing the warriors of Port of Prince and in this moment, Moses has matched every detail. So, while everyone is stunned watching Moses rise from the darkness, I chant the warrior's prayer.

"Each scar on his body tells stories of pain and that pain Now runs through warrior's veins ,On Earth, Sky and Shiny Sea, Gracious Goddess Wand Be With Me, Come On Now The Call Is Made, Give Thy Power To My Blade" .

The two overseers are yelling threats, but Mo continues to march forward. The overseer on the horse demands the other on foot to use his whip. I'm looking into the eyes of my brother AND HE IS PISSED!!

The overseer whines up the whip, it cuts through the air hits the ground "snap" as the whip hit the ground... dirt flying up from the impact. The overseer Hollars "nigger stand down "...Mo walk starts to speed up. The overseer cracks the whip again , as the overseer pulls the whip back Mo takes off full speed pulling out an BIGG ASS BLADE he had concealed on his waste, the overseer sees Mo closing in fast so he quickly whines the whip...he thrust the whip once more cutting through the air Mo puts his left forearm up to block it...the whip hits but no snap Moses uses his forearm to block but now has the whip in his grasp...in the same motion pulls the overseer towards him takes an leap...lands and shoves the knife through the overseers right jaw takes the blade out then shoves it right through his throat.

Everybody took a deep gasp in shock what just happened including me. Moses just stood back straight up left arm bleeding from the whip...blood squirting out the overseer's neck as he whines and moans rolling on the ground. The overseer on the horse breaks out of his shock let's out an "ohhh shit" tries turning his horse around yelling "help"!..Moses quickly throws his dagger hitting the side of the horse. The horse falls landing on the overseer leg but Hop's back up leaving the overseer on the ground. Moses walks to him, blade drawn I can see revenge in his eyes.

[Wounded Prey]

Moses vision's point of view:

I approached that??.. man ready to end his life wounded prey is all I smell. Then I hear an familiar voice "stop...Moses wait." I look over to see Minty running towards me I paused and took a look around. I see everyone just looking at me, I have fresh lashes on my arm the sting from the wound fuels me. My heart is pumping iron, I look up at the window to see Absalom Thompson looking out right at me, the overseer on the ground hurt from the horse landing on his leg he's struggling trying to move.

Minty: "Wait we need him for now."

She looks at the group of people and tells them if you don't want nothing to do with this to go inside. They all head inside the cabins leaving Henry standing with us.

The Thompson brothers and four of their workers come walking up with meat cleavers and pitch forks.

Minty: "What's wrong Daddy (Mr.Thompson)took their shotguns away." She says to me.

She had a point I'll give it to Edward having some sense but almost every night the Thompson brothers get drunk with friends an often shoot guns off so their probably out of ammo anyway.

I gave Minty my knife as I picked up this sloppy piece of shit off the ground an put my hatchet blade to his neck.

Anthony Thompson: "What the hell you think you doing boy!"

Minty: "What you ain't got eyes muthafuka you keep stepping ,off wit his head!"

I thought to myself "Aarminta."

I pressed the blade on his neck, they see we not playing, they stop in their tracks.

Anthony Thompson: "You know the consequences of this, you let him go now.. you'll only do a day in the box."

Minty: "You know Anthony you never was the smartest to come out your aunties asshole...so I'll talk to Edward!"

The way Minty going I guess her revenge was little more planned out.

[Lost of power]

Minty vision's point of view:

I heard the news about the boys Daddy having health problems let's see if my observation theory is in the ball park.

Anthony Thompson:" Black bitch you'll be hung by suppertime talking to a white man like that...let alone your master!"

Minty: "Master of what...seems to me you boys lost your power months ago."

Absalom: "Lost of power" He says in disbelief. "It looks to me you out numbered nine to three."

Anthony Thompson: "Absalom you can't count the two they already got down. "

Minty: "Well Anthony you ain't to bright yourself...running the farm into a wasteland, selling off your best workers even stealing my brother's inventions and trying to sell the patent ".

Henry doesn't look surprised to hear that.

Edward Thompson: "Get to the point bitch."

Minty: "How's the old man...I haven't seen him in months...haven't seen any soldiers picking up payments in a while...Yawl having money problems and what my brother just did to the livestock...well ya Daddy ain't around to bail you out huh!"

Edward: "So this is a negotiation! "

Minty: "Yes for his life (overseer) yawl life and for the Thompson name as well as the farm not to go up in smoke and never respected for business throughout these counties again."

By this time the community of slaves has come outside to hear everything and surround the Thompson brothers taking their weapons.

Absalom: "This bitch think she knows stuff."

Edward Thompson: "Absalom shut your fucking pie whole...So what's your offer to be freed" he says sarcastically.

Minty:" I want the original documents that Mr.Brodess had for us signed off."

Anthony Thompson: "That's not an deal that's robbery."

Minty:" Livelihood or your life."

Moses: "Enough!! Either sign off the documents or yawl dead the farm dead and we still be free...you got till 100. "

Henry starts to count 1,2,3...

Absalom:" Hey he can count!"

Minty: "The servant she knows where it is".The indentured servant runs to get the Documents.

Anthony Thompson: "Bitch!"

The white European indentured servant along with the white Male indentured servant comeback with the documents.

Anthony Thompson signed off on all the documents as they were surrounded by all slaves.

Family by family they Hollard and cheered as they got their freedom and piece of the land that was promised to them.

But after signing the last documents being defeated by some slave negroes Anthony Thompson: said with an smile "That's everybody but the Ross family! "

Knowing he already burned our documents up years ago.

Anthony Thompson: "After all this.. you still nothing but an nig...."

I put my brothers custom blade through his loud talking mouth.

Mo cuts the overseer throat and the now ex slaves mobbed the rest of the brothers and their crew.

Kemitt mirrors chapter 5.10 (Vision's part 12)
"Mo & Minty has an story to tell" page 12

[Cooked before Super]

Minty vision's point of view:

The dust is settling as the dawn from the sun clears the foggy atmosphere. It's not even noon yet an we have nine bodies dead on the ground.

Henry: "What we do now?"

Mary(slave worker): "We have to burn them!"

Moses:" I say leave'em...let the message live on."

Minty:" I agree!"

Mary: "Then how will we live?"

Henry: "Yeah everybody will be fugitives."

Moses: "Fugitives in Maryland its time to leave this behind."

Minty:" Everyone here has their freedom including the servants."

Moses: "Move on start new lives."

Women servant:"Thankyou" she says to Minty. Then her and the Male servant start their journey off the Thompson plantation.

Moses: "How did yall get so close?"

Minty: "Sunday prayer."

Moses: "Church?"

Minty:" I learned the in and out about the Thompsons from her it help me put a lot of pieces together...they did a lot of evil things to her. "Watching them as they walk off.

Moses: "We need to go."

After talks about what to do everyone decided to go their separate ways. Before leaving Mary got some of the others to move the bodies inside the house then they torched the house burning it all down. I guess that was her payback for her father old man Lee .

Some went further south with family, but most went west for brand new beginnings. Me and my brothers where still considered slaves, so Henry got the maps and we headed north. We can see the flames from the burning house from the woods, bet the Thompson boys didn't know they'd be cooked before supper.

The journey to freedom is brutal, one minute your in water up to your neck the next watching out for bears to killer ants. When it rains the mud makes your feet feel 20 pounds heavier, not to mention forest mosquitoes I swear one was as big as my hand. It seemed crazy the first trip to actually run into other escapees in the middle of nowhere. We would exchange our knowledge on what to look out for in certain parts of the forest but that was about it then we went our separate ways wishing each other good luck.

Traveling through the daytime was difficult especially going through the mountains, I don't know how many times we past this one big tree. I started to see why people who ran if wasn't caught early returned anyway to surroundings they knew, the forest is beautiful but endless and dangerous even without anyone tracking your every step which we still have to look out for.

We were ready to give up we camped out near the bank of a river almost all day exhausted from the terrain kicking are asses. That night the sky was so clear we can see all the stars. Moses began to read the night sky then compare it to the map.

Moses: "Ok we out the mountains It shows here if we follow this stream north we'll be in Pennsylvania in a day or two."

Minty vision's point of view: At first I was thinking Moses was trying to motivate us to keep going but as we continued our travels I realized the sky wasn't as smoky (foggy) so he was right about being out of the mountains then we started to see the marking points that where on the maps, most of the signs where carved into trees or an patch of lilies (flowers) where they shouldn't be growing each time we past an sign we knew we're headed in the right direction but also it felt good to know we're not alone someone is on the other end waiting to help us. We traveled non stop for a day in an half, finally coming to a back road where the map ends.

Henry uses the moonlight to read his decoded message.

Henry: "Dust becomes dawn an brown in white man will come along." He says coughing while reading.

Minty: "You okay."

Henry: "Yeah this weather must have gotten to me."

Moses: "Does everything have to be a damn riddle."

Henry: "I'm sure they're just being careful."

Moses: "Well I guess we early, we got sometime before the sun starts to come up."

Moses picks a spot to rest, me and Henry do the same.

I wake up to chirping birds and galloping horses, Moses is already up watching the passing wagons.

Minty: "You see anything yet?"

Moses: "Nope, these damn riddles I hope we didn't miss'em."

We stayed hidden watching when an covered wagon is coming pass the driver is wearing an brown suit with a white shirt.

Minty: "Mo look...brown in white."

The man pulls to the side of the road as if there's a problem with an wheel.

Moses tucks his knife hands me the hatchet, comes out the woods looking just like an run away.

[Moses vision's point of view]:

"Hello sir you need help with that wheel."

The man looks at me up and down.

Warren Garrison: "Um no thankyou I got it."

I thought to myself this was all for nothing...what now?

Moses:" Im familiar with working on these wagons."

The man just keeps working on the wheel. Then hops back into the driver side ready to leave. I see an quilt hanging on the side of the driver seat it has the same symbols we decoded on the map.. I have to say something.

Moses: "Dust becomes dawn brown in white man comes along."

The man looks at me, then glances into the woods, another wagon is passing by the man just tips his hat to the passerby the two passengers in the back I can tell analyzes my dirty attire.

Warren Garrison: "Those two with you?"

I'm thinking how did he see them they supposed to be hiding.

Moses: "Yes my brother and sister."

Warren Garrison: "Well they need to hurry this road is getting more popular for fugitives." He saids cleaning his glasses.

I wave to Minty and Henry to come on.

Warren Garrison: "There's blankets in the back."

Moses: "Alright thankyou!"

We hop in the back an hide under the blankets.

We ride for a short while then come to a stop, we can hear men talking.

Jim Brown:" Are they legit?"

Warren Garrison: "Yes he used the password."

Jim Brown: "Okay, help'em out boys."

The covers are pulled from us I grip my knife not knowing what to expect. They see Minty first I see her hand clutching my hatchet, so she feels the same as me. She hesitates to move, I recognize the two younger white men trying to help us out. They were the passengers in the wagon earlier that passed by us looking me up and down.

I put my hand on Minty shoulder as to tell her to hold on. The man (Warren Garrison) comes with an smile.

Warren Garrison: "Its okay this my friend Jim Brown and his sons Watson and Owen, they watch my back when I'm out in the field...its okay come on!"

We slowly slide out the wagon. The men all have welcoming smiles but we're still worried if we had made the right decision coming here.

Jim Brown: "Its ok Mrs.Garrison has hot breakfast just waiting for us to throw down inside."

Then just as he says that an little boy comes running out the door an little black boy no more than five or six years old laughing then hearing an young lady to my surprise an young black lady "Benji...Benjermin come hear" she says laughing finally catches him as he tries to hide behind Jim Brown after all Jim stood about 6'4 about the same as me.

Jim Brown: laughs as he picks up the little boy, "hey nephew you running from that morning bath huh."

The boy shakes his head yes before getting handed back to his mother.

Sarah ODavis: "He heard you guys out here talking being nosey...now let's go wash you up!"

That was different, the energy was pure not smiling for master in fear but genuinely like I enjoy the people around me. I think that loosened all three of us up.

Warren Garrison:" Come on I'm starving."

We go inside to see an big breakfast ready at the table. I know we tried not to show it but the smell triggered our empty stomachs barely eating for months. We washed our hands and went right in on the plates Mrs.Garrison set for us.

Warren Garrison: "Usually we say prayer before eating but on this occasion hey this is a celebration...Cheers...Salute."

Everyone at the table had their glasses up where the only ones so buried into our plates we were late toasting. So, we "Cheers." It felt good never did that before. An young black man enters the room.

Louis: "Hey I see everything went well" he looks at us "Hi I'm Louis...Louis O' Davis sorry I was studying in the next room."

He joins us at the table for breakfast the little boy comes, jumps in his lap "Daddy."

Louis O' Davis: "Hey Benji" he says to his son.

His wife comes in from giving their son Benjermin a bath.

Sharah Davis: "Okay we're back ...hey everybody! "Gives Louis an kiss

Louis: "Hey this is my wife Sharah."

Warren Garrison: "And this is my wife Jo'Anna who prepared this lovely breakfast...thankyou baby."

Minty: "I'm sorry we got right to eating...I'm Aarminta, this my Brother Moses and this is Henry."

Warren Garrison: "Well I'm Warren".

Jim Brown: "I'm John but my close friends call me Jim and these are my sons Watson and Owen!"

Moses: "Glad to meet everyone!"

Jim Brown: "Now that we're all acquainted and we know we're all on the same side here, I'm an weapons man so I'm going to lay mine on the table."

He lays his pistol an knife on the table, the sons lay their knives and pistol. Sharah takes an ice pick from her waist, Joanna takes an little pistol from her back and knife from her waist.

At this time we are shocked that these people lovely people have all these weapons, but they did just risk everything helping us.

I put my Knife on the table Minty put my hatchet on the table and Henry put an sharp piece of wood on the table.

Little Benji starts laughing and points at Henry's weapon on the table...then we all start laughing.

Henry: "Hey I made mine in the woods okay "Laughing .

Warren Garrison: "Yeah we can tell."

Minty:" I can't believe all yawl got weapons."

Jim Brown: "Victory loves preparation...but what kind of blade is this?"He picks up the hatchet analyzes the precision of the cut of the blade.

Minty: "My brother Mo made this blade"My sis said proudly!

Jim Brown: "This was made with pain from the soul...look how heavy and sharp this blade is!" He hands it to Warren.

Warren Garrison: "What was the story behind these? "As he looks at the hatchet and knife.

Moses:" I started making those when they sent my father away."

Joanna Garrison: "Well since everyone is done with breakfast I'm going to need some firewood for dinner me an Sharah are going to prepare the roasted chicken in celebration of an successful journey for our new members of the family.

Sharah:" Yes collides greens, corn, yams..." Smiling!

Louis: "Hey you don't have to say no more...I'll get that fire wood myself for a dinner like that!"

Owen Brown: "When yall talkin cookin like that...anything you need Ma.. dame"! He says to Sharah as he bows his head in playful manor.

Joanna Garrison:" Well let's leave the afternoon work to these fellas I know you all are tired after your travels Sarah and I will show you to your rooms."

We follow Joanna and Sarah to a smaller house out back.

Joanna Garrison: "Now this is a four-bedroom, bathroom you have a full kitchen and living room".

Minty: "This is fine thankyou."

Sharah:"This is actually the Garrison's old house my Louis actually designed the new house you were just in."

Joanna: "Louis is going to be a great architect someday! Now you're always welcome in our home...but everyone needs their space from time to time".

Moses: "No this is...this is great thankyou. "

Henry:" I saw an empty shed back there can I use it?"

Minty: "My little brother here is an inventor."

Joanna Garrison: "Yes sir anything you need that is a blessing to have that type of skill!"

Sharah:"Yes it is!"

Joanna Garrison: "But why don't you all rest up, we'll let you know when its dinner time."

Minty & Henry: "Okay!"

Moses: "I'll help the guys out no problem."

Sharah:"You sure I know that journey believe me."

Moses:" I guess the bright side to all this is I'm used to long days of hard work."

Joanna Garrison:" Okay well here's clean clothes for you all blankets bed sheet's...go ahead freshen up and meet the boys outside." She says to Moses.

Moses: "Ok thanks."

I got dressed and met the guys outside chopping and gathering wood. As we worked, I listened to their conversation...most of it was about politics and how other countries are outlawing slavery, that the colonies must outlaw slavery, move as one nation if they want to become a powerful country.

They've talked about owner ship of land this went on an on, all the way into suppertime but I was intrigued with the conversations I never heard of nothing they were discussing, arguing, or agreeing about. All I ever knew was Dorchester county and the things Jac and Victoria taught us about Haitian culture, but I loved listening.

After supper we all ate our dessert in the dining room, I see Minty and Henry where takin back just like I was earlier this afternoon by the conversations among them and now Joanna and Sharah has joined in.

Jim Brown: "So Louis you still moving back to D.C.?"

Louis: "Hopefully within an year or so me an Yani (Sharah)here will be legally married by then" he laughs.

Sharah: "Yani's my original name, he used to make fun of my name when our tribes came together for celebrations Tata (Louis)". She plays hits him with the rag she is holding.

Henry:" So yall have two names."

Sharah :"Warren helped us get legal documents stating our freedom these where names we had to pick."

Louis: "Im from Nocotchtank, she's Piscataway where both from Ancostia teasing her was my way for her not to forget me until finally we grew up and she didn't."

Sharah :"After the many midnight slaughtering of our people our tribes combined together but ultimately they're army had more fire power and captures were forced into slavery or killed off but some of us escaped and now our childhood memories are gone and they renamed it Washington D.C!"

Minty vision: Wow their story was just as hard as ours the mood gotten a little dim but thanks to Henry's young naive mind constantly moving ahead, he lightens the room back up.

Henry: "My dad's favorite horse name was Goyah given to him from Cheif Chupuco!"

Minty :"Yeah we loved that horse!"

Warren Garrison :"What happened to the horse?"

Moses:"I set him free."

I don't think Mr. Brown misses an beat I think he saw the drawback of our faces after Moses mentions that.

Jim Brown:" So what happened to your folks? "

We all hesitate didn't realize how much it still affects all of us.

Minty:" They sold them off along with my sisters."

Warren Garrison: "Do you know where?" He says with concern.

Minty: "No just further down south I assume."

Owen:"Moses...I just remembered where I know you from...the Eastern shores in Maryland we where passing out Mr. Garrison abolitionist magazine...I took an gamble but I gave you one of the coded ones."

Moses: "Yes! That was you... that was an while ago."

Warren Garrison "How did you decode it" He says excited and curious at the same time.

Moses:" My brother the genius here did it."

Henry: "My father brought one of those pamphlets back first from the trips he did with our old owner...Mr.Brodess."

JimBrown:"Pamphlets..haha... I told you it's not an magazine!" Laughing as Warren Garrison looks at him crazy.

Warren Garrison: "He just don't know good penmanship when he sees it, proceed Henry how you decode the magazine" He says sarcastically Proud!

Henry: "Well almost an year later after my father, Moses comes back with an new one but the inside back page had some similarities the signature was the same lloyd Garrison. "

Warren Garrison:"...lloyd is my writer's name."

Joanna Garrison:"Oh my god would you let the man speak!" They all laugh.

Henry:"I read the pamph...magazine's, saw the bear claw sign in both that caught my attention, then I accidentally read the signs upside down then the words backwards an start seeing messages like directions, showed my sister and she saw it too."

Sharah:"So when they sold your mother and sisters is that why you ran?"

Henry:"Um yes but..."

Minty nudges Henry as in don't say to much.

Joanna Garrison:" What you guys can tell us we're not judging we just getting to know each other."

Jim Brown: "Well I got an funny story!"

Watson Brown: "Oh dad do we have to here this story again?" Like he's tired of the same story.

Warren Garrison: "Yes!!..Go ahead Jim!"

Jim Brown: "Well back in the day me and lloyd here start robbing boats with cargo."

Warren Garrison: "Wait...first legend had it that the Boston tea party was really about robbing the boats that smuggled gold to Britain using the tea as a front."

Jim Brown: "Correct so we hear about the French using the Mississippi and Ohio river to smuggle their gold from the gulf up to their people in Missouri ... So me and this young fool got our crew together to rob this boat at the merger of the Ohio an Mississippi ...Well we stormed on to that boat. "

Warren Garrison: "Yeah true pirates "Laughing.

Jim Brown: "These basically teenagers maybe twenty year olds ...hell we're twenty three, twenty four...anyways we storm onto their boat now they thought they were hauling just goods, food spices, things like that.. we thought they had gold which looking back their boat would've sunk if they did but what we did was intercept messages and maps to the gold."

Warren Garrison: "OH yes Ol Rufey."

Jim Brown: "So once we found out who owned these holding spots for the gold...we traveled all over these lands taking his gold and guns."

Warren Garrison: "Shoot outs with his personal army!"Chuckling...

Jim Brown: "Ever since then we been mortal enemies."

Minty: "With who?"

Jim Brown:" Rufus Devane King."

Louis: "He owns the biggest plantations in Louisiana and Alabama called Chestnut hill."

Moses:" What's the funny part?"

Jim Brown: "OH the fella boat we robbed long time ago is now our dear friend Abe Lincoln "!! Him and Warren laughs.

Moses: "Who that?"

Warren Garrison: "Abe..He's an Republican senator...he wants to run for president may be abolish slavery!"

Minty:" Really?"

Joanna Garrison:" We're still working on that Warren believes Abe will come around."

Jim Brown: " I like the Lad but he's Yellow belly."

Minty: "So the gold where does it go?"

Warren Garrison: "Well since Abe wouldn't except stolen money for his campaign he called it...we call it patriotism, but we have friends in Philadelphia that turns it to money for us so we have funded new government positions, the army and our personal finances goes towards freedom in all different ways."

Jim Brown: "Yes freedom isn't cheap everybody involved doesn't necessarily care for the fight of free slaves they just get paid for being an check point but we hold the idea of what America supposed to be so we fight until we see it come to fruition or till we die."

Warren Garrison: "That's right but in my wiser years I learned the Pen can be mightier than the sword."

Jim Brown: "Yup and I love continuing being the thron in the side of slave owners like Ol'Rufey...ain't that right boys!! Raises his glass to cheer with his sons".

Owen & Watson Brown: "That right Pop!" As they cling glasses with their father".

Sharah:"Other words Jim still wit the bullshit!!" They all laugh.

Jim Brown: "That I is..."

Louis: "Okay so what's you guys story?"

Moses:"Well we're born an raised on plantations mostly on the Brodess's farm ...it was hard then one day Minty had an accident at the Eastern shores with an overseer trying to catch an escaping slave, the lady that came to her aid was more than an nurse she was the daughter of Adbaraya Toya an original Dahomey warrior from Africa abducted an sold into slavery in Haiti. Victoria's mother Adbaraya helped the king Jean Dessalines of Haiti win the rebellion an later her daughter Victoria actually married the king's son Jacques, they became good friends to our family all the slave workers as well as the Brodess's."

Minty: "By the way we found that out after years of conversation we didn't know right off."

Henry: "Jacques and Victoria helped Mr.Brodess become an independent import, export business with my father right there the whole time growing the business."

Minty:" As slaves we actually thought we had it good the Brodess's loved Jacques and Victoria they even knew they were teaching us how to read and write".

Joanna Garrison: "So what happened?"

Minty: "This guy James Law...Lawford came and changed everything he wanted the Brodess's business but Mr. Brodess wouldn't give up his sources but I believe Mrs.Brodess did."

Moses:"Mr. Brodess was sicker than we knew and passed within months she sold the farm to James Lawford old friend Mr.Thompson my mother's old master, he let his sons run the farm and they ran it like wolves in the form of sheep that's how I always saw them ,my father did too so they sold'em."

Henry: "They ran the farm into the ground and us as their slaves they took full advantage of punishments everytime...so after selling my mom and sister's off...my brother rose up against them they couldn't stop him he was like an like an ..."

Minty: "Warrior...everything Victoria said what a warrior is... he is... and was that day... he's the reason why we're here." She says tearing up.

Minty and Henry made me not so embarrassed about talking about it...I'm mean the Thompsons deserved everything they got but I was afraid of being looked at as an monster like Jacques said the French made the Hatian people look after winning their independence.

Owen: "So what happened to the...Thompson sons?"

Henry: "Well Minty made them sign off everyone's freedom papers except ours of course because they've already burned our papers years before."

Watson: "Okay we get why you here...what happened to the masters?"

Minty looked at me with assuredness then says.

Minty "We sliced there fucking throats!"

There was an pause in the room, then...

Sharah:"Well hell I'll drink to that...salute!"

Then everyone else "Cheers!"

I knew then we are truly free well almost.

Kemitt mirrors chapter 5.11 (vision's pt.13)
"Iron sharpens iron" page.13

Minty vision's point of view:

It's been four months and these four months, I've had the most rest I ever had in my entire life, even between helping out around the house.

Moses started gardening around the house the Garrison's let us stay in. Joanna liked what he was doing so much she ask if he could farm their land and she would pay him and whoever he wants to help.

The land wasn't as big as an traditional farm but it was good enough for us to start making an living doing what we knew how to do. Jim would teach us how to really shoot the shotguns and pistols while we taught him and the others on hand to hand combat plus the art of knife throwing.

Jim, Warren, Owen,Watson are all very confident men, but what surprised me was Louis . He was so much into reading and studying I didn't think he'd payed any attention when where sharpening our combat skills.

For some reason after lunch time Jim would like to have combat activities. We would have five minute fights with each other, shooting and knife throwing contest then one afternoon we finally got Louis to join us.

When I say he won every contest I mean he won with ease no contest, now him and Sharah where the youngest out of all of us besides Henry, an come to find out they grew up learning how to fight, hunt and also medicine which was great me an Sharah exchanged our knowledge on medicine an different meditations for channeling different spirits.

Louis and Warren really got us into books, Henry really took to it strong we would find him studying books like Louis, and Warren did often. Louis being an architect really helped Henry with his ideas on inventions.

While Warren was helping us with our freedom documentation, we learned Louis and Sharah where born free, the army moving in on their tribal territory eliminated the unity among the neighboring tribes. Turning tribes against each other by offering one tribe guns and the other tribe drugs one tribe would feel superior to the other then they would war amongst there selves. The tribe that lost the battle, the American government would play devils advocate by punishing the top warrior's and Chiefs by death and the rest forced into slavery sometime by there own people but different tribe, they considered it prisoners of war. The other tribe would think the Union was on their side until they did the same to them…eventually.

Either way the aboriginal people where conforming to American lifestyle wealth meaning power , slowly losing their own principles and beliefs. Louis and Sharah met Warren Garrison in Virginia speaking against the slave trade and the present government they've been with him ever since.

On the documents Moses thought it was best for us to have new identities not linking us to Maryland at all.

So Moses chose Rico Greene, I chose my mother first name Harriet Green, Henry chose Robert Benjermin Green.

We got more involved in helping escaping slaves, through Warren's magazines setting up more check points for safe houses, planting vegetables and fruits along the trails we code in our maps. But the more we build the secret society the more money is spent so close to an year of doing this Jim came back from setting up safe houses (for escaping slaves) in the west (present day midwest) with an plan.

On a Sunday Morning Jim comes into the Garrison's home with Owen and Watson each carrying big bags on their shoulders. They lead us into the Library room.

Warren Garrison: "Jim what is it?"

Jim smiling from ear to ear, then empties his bag onto the table, fills the table with money and gold coins.

We all looked in shocked, especially us we never seen money like this before.

Then Watson empties his bag more money, more gold coins.

Warren Garrison: "What you do?" He says with concern.

Then Owen takes an metal case out his bag opens it...brand new pistols an boxes on top of boxes of ammunition .

Warren Garrison :analyzes the gold coins with the French stamps on them "Ol Rufey?"

Jim Brown: "That's right my friend but that's old Rufus, follow me"!

We walk outside to Jim's wagon's he has bags full of more stuff.

Louis:" More money?"

Watson jumps in the wagon opens up an bag hands Jim an package. Jim's shows Warren the package.

Warren Garrison: "What's this?"

Jim Brown: "That's pure powdered opium...Ol Rufey gotta brand new bag... and we gonna take it down!!"

Kemitt mirrors chapter 5.12 (vision's pt 14)
"New war old enemy"page.14

Moses point of view:

So what I get from all this is Jim has found an new war with an old enemy. He seems excited but Warren seems more cautious about this. We head back into the library room to discuss this situation.

Warren Garrison: "We have enough on our plate as it is...why focus on this?"

Jim Brown: "Did you not see the drugs?...He's flooding the drugs into the flat lands going west past the Mississippi."

Warren Garrison :"What does that even mean?"

Louis:" He's going to weaken any form of resistance that might come in the expansion of the nation." Jim agrees.

Warren Garrison :"We're not opposed expansion."

Jim Brown: "Its not just about expansion its about him taking the Louisiana purchase back and taking the slavery market out west to build New France."

Warren Garrison: "I'm not convinced this is our fight." He says firmly.

Jim getting frustrated Warren not seeing the big picture.

Jim Brown: "Owen the book... get the book!"

Owen: "Right pop!"

Owen runs out the room comes back with an slightly rusty box. Owen opens the box takes out a book, hands the book to Jim.

Jim's puts the book on the table opens it to the beginning page.

Jim Brown: Points" What does that say" he says to Warren.

Warren Garrison: Huffs then reads carefully "The Prometheus of William Rufus Devane King...What?"

Warren reads the first page to himself.

Warren Garrison: "Where did you get this?"

Jim Brown: "Long story short, one of our safe houses for escaping slaves in St. Louis was made ,so after moving the house sitter's to an new location we.. somehow ...found or ran into the crew responsible for the harassment...but instead of rushing them we followed the suit man."

Moses: "The Suite man?"

Jim Brown: "Yes the suite man that's congregating with these low life's in an place (An rough saloon bar /brothel) he looked not to belong too."

Warren Garrison: "An whore house." He knows his good friend Jim down to the Teeth.

JimBrown:"Entertainment...Potato, pota-to...anyways we watch him for two weeks, he turns out to be an trustee to the bank, across from the Pony Express mail office ,across from the Governor mansion, across from the local newspaper factory."

Warren Garrison: "So you see the crew meet with the banker at the bank." He says sarcastically.

Jim Brown: "No but we see them in and out the newspaper factory all week."

Minty: "So there using the newspaper factory to cover up drug deliveries."

Owen: "Well we know that now but didn't know that at the time."

Warren Garrison: "So you catch and torture the banker to give you information."

Jim Brown:" Ha!!! You remember fall of 39(1839)...Savannah Georgia, Butler plantation...hey we freed 100 slaves that day but no."

Warren Garrison: "You stumbled on to Rufus gold smuggling which you still can't let go of...so what the banker say?"

Jim Brown: "We didn't catch the banker...We kidnapped the Governor!"

Warren Garrison: "You did what!!...I told you one day you'll go too far and you done did it...then you come back here putting us all in danger!"

Jim Brown: "Well can I finish my long ass short story Warren...please!"

Warren Garrison: "Fine...what else."

Jim Brown: "So after knocking out the Governor's knee cap."

Warren Garrison: "Dear lord."

Jim Brown: "He takes us to the basement, we moved an false wall to see an tunnel...that tunnel intersected all the businesses on that block...the Governor was nothing but an appointed lieutenant in Rufeys organization."

Warren Garrison: "How did you figure that out?"

Jim Brown:" He kept saying (Mocking the Gov. whining voice) do you know who your fucking with... this Rufus King, money."

Owen: "That's Rufus King gold" also mocking the Governor.

Watson: "That's Rufus Kang drugs "mocking the Governor.

We all kind of laughed at the story...it was funny.

Moses: "What about the guns?"

Jim Brown: "OH yeah..That's.."

We all joined in even Warren "That's Rufus Kangs guns!!"

Warren Garrison: "So what do we do now?"

Jim Brown:" You in?"

Warren Garrison:" I do believe the pen is mightier than the sword...but sometimes you gotta get in blood...I'm with you brother!"

Jim Brown: "Thanks Warren I can't do this with out you...without yawl...I know there's a lot at stake we got families...you see my boys with me, but we cannot let this take over happen, beyond the drugs and money if this book makes it out it can shift dictatorship to new levels… everything America is not supposed to be!"

Warren Garrison: "Nobody here has to join this fight... Jim and I been friends and comrades going on twenty plus years but everyone in this room I know I can trust with my life so if your in... Cheers!" He holds his glass up.

One by one we joined the cheer ,but Louis walks out the room...he comes back in to toast his glass.

Louis:" I didn't have an glass."

We had an laugh and a drink it was still early all we had was water or milk...I look towards the left to see Joanna smile but walks away with concern written on her face, Warren goes to talk to her.

Jim Brown:" Hey Louis, I need you and Warren to plan these moves out, we gotta be tight with this."

Louis: "You got it."

We all left out the library room into the dining room living room area, Warren and Joanna comes back down to join everyone.

Joanna seemed to be in better spirits, it seemed crazy when I thought about it...just a little more than a year ago we're slaves not knowing nothing but the surrounding counties in Maryland, now where entering an war maybe before an war, I thought maybe this is what I was meant to do I finally have purpose... I'm ready!

Kemitt mirrors chapter 5.13 (Vision's part 15)
"Stay in the Shadows" page.15

Stay in the Shadows

Minty vision's point of view:

We went weeks mapping out different routes Rufus may be using to move his drugs and money but the guesses where endless. Warren's library basically has turned into a war room, I was impressed how far Warren and Jim name went as far as the underworld goes. I guess over the years they gained a lot of friends themselves.

The information on certain spots came right to us ,I thought we were going to be kidnapping and torturing people every time like Jim's story...I learned money can get you far when you pay the right people.

Warren and Jim went to Philadelphia for a couple days came back with updated maps and information that Rufus King was using Lake Michigan as an import, export check point.

I thought to myself...if Rufus Devane had enemies in high places to know his business, than I wondered who his friends are ...they must be even higher than his enemies.

We all geared up to hit the road, Henry wanted to come but he was young, and we needed someone to watch over Joanna and Sharah while we were gone, yeah, he was mad, but he understood.

We started out headed towards Illinois Jim and Warren had alot of friends there. We knocked over an couple of Duvane small drug and money runners in the rural areas we had information on their routes coming and going.

Louis and Warren had a gift of mapping out and pinpointing locations like war generals...I see why Jim said he really needed them. We eventually worked our way up to Chicago. Chicago is a beautiful modern city but rugged, everybody that was somebody had their hand in something we had to be careful.

We layed low during the daytime and went to work at night. We quietly pushed our way around town gaining names and leads to our next targets. We were quickly learning that the name Jim Brown definitely rang bells...To the younger guys he was an myth but to the older guys that stood on the opposing side, his name meant your darkest nightmare just came true. Most Information was freely given once they saw it was Jim and his crew pressing, but they still left the situation with an eye missing or an elbow blown out, if they're the boss of that operation their throat was slit, that was mandatory from Jim and Warren. With the help of local old friends that Jim an Warren knew we were able to shut down two of Rufus Devane's factory fronts for his drugs, but we needed to find how he was getting the drugs in.

Louis and Warren broke down the landscape and narrowed down every lead we got. We know the main docks weren't being used by Devane but his organization fingerprints are all over place here.

So after we scoped out every dock along lake Michigan, we find an small dock on the east side of Chicago. This dock was heavily armed with security I don't know if this was the normal precaution or our presence was being felt but either way, we gettin up in there.

We plan our attack back at the safe house. Louis felt we needed two diversions if we wanted to get inside the docks. The first diversion will have to be near one of the boats at the rear of the docks, the other near the front gate.

Owen: "How we get to the boats first?"

Warren: "The building closest is the fish factory...we need you Minty and Louis to get around the back then sneak into the water to get to the boats."

Warren: "Watson and I will post on the left side...Jim and Mo your on the right side of the building, once we see the signal we move in."

Louis: "We can only carry so much so we have to use these wisely and try not to get water inside the jar."

Louis has six jars of kerosene.

Warren Garrison: "We have different caps...the close one you can throw and break but you'll have to light it for it to be effective, if you need instant damage switch the cap with the wick you got ten seconds when lit, before it explodes or you can throw it to cause more damage."

Jim Brown: "The goal is to shut down this hub but also get Duncan Berwick , one of Rufeys top generals he's supposed to be there."

Warren Garrison : "Are time is limited if word got back about the other factories, we shutdown. So tonight, we go...we go in smart do what we came to do an get out!" We all agreed.

As we prepared for the night, I was trying to figure out how many weapons I could carry without weighing me down especially through the water. I liked the guns Jim gave us the new Colt 45 was light an water resistant.

We waited till early morning to ride out, before we left the safe house Jim asked me to do the warrior's prayer...the same one I did for Moses back on the plantation. So we huddled up, we did the prayer, then headed out to the docks.

Moses was driving the wagon we got to the fish factory, like clockwork me, Louis ,and Owen hopped out the wagon and headed towards the side of the building.

The factory was closed but we still played it cautious. Climbing these high fences and landing without an sound I see another tatic from Louis and Warren...us three are smaller an lighter than Mo,Jim and Watson their big guys and Warren just too old to be jumping fences.

We get to the edge of the building; we can see the boats at the dock straight across and even these hours in the morning security is tight over on that side.

We follow Louis, we get as close as we could before entering the water, Louis goes in the water first.

Louis: "Shit it's cold "He says quietly.

Owen Brown: Goes in "It feels good, come on Minty!"

I jump in ,I don't say it but "shit it's cold."

We stay close to the dock walls to not be seen but the water was deep for me I actually had to swim while Louis and Owen where shoulders above water. I could of easily grabbed Owen's shoulder but for some reason I had to show myself and them I'm not an weak link.

If Mo was here I've would have jumped on his back with no problem...for about three seconds I realized how much I miss my brothers but quickly got my mind back in the mission. The closer we got we can hear the men talking, some was talking English others French that's how I knew there working together but separated at the same time hell we could of sent Owen and Watson for decoys but never mind their faces are getting the same recognition as Jim's and Warren's..."Minty stick to the plan" I tell myself.

We get right next to the first boat, Louis start doing signs we didn't discuss, pointing to his eyeballs then pointing out that it's two guards right above us. Were so much in synch me and Owen actually understood this black Indian muthfaka and if Owen said what I just thought I'll punch"em in the throat... naw the chest that's my brother...Louis had little bottles of kerosene, he squirted the liquid all over the side of the boat and the railing. Then throws more signs to follow him, so we go underwater under the boat...Louis put the kerosene to the second boat. We gather at the ladder that leads to main ground...now the plan was to put the boat on fire but because it's more guards than we thought it would be... we had to improvise.

Louis:"Owen go back and take the other ladder, it's one guard above us it's two over there I'll take the guard above us yall take the two from both sides, don't give them time to think...count to twenty then we strike...shadows!" We took the play.

Shadows meant staying in the lines of the darkness before striking in all remaining silent.

Owen swam back to the other side of the first boat, to the ladder. We started the count at the same time...5,...10...15.

Louis propelled his body off that second ladder so fast, I thought well at least the man won't feel it...I was two seconds behind him and when I glanced at the guard Louis already had an knife in his temple, at the same time I stayed low struck upward...put my brothers made blade (Moses custom knife) through the other guards chin the point came out the middle of his nose... then drew it out as easy as slicing bread, Owen straight knocked the other guard unconscious. We slowly put the bodies in the water.

Louis threw another sign...there's guards up on the left and right tier of the building patrolling.

He took off up the left stairs, we took off to the right stairs but in my own competition I wanted to get my kill before Louis.

I race up the flight of stairs...I get low on the side of the building, Owen catches up and gets behind me. I'm looking at Louis, from across...this fool climbs on top of the roof of the entrance to the top tier, waits an gets behind the patrolling guard jumps down and drives his knife into the guards throat from behind then quietly pulls his body into the dark corner.

The guard patrolling my tier disappeared from the other end, I see Louis giving us signals to look out. I thought maybe the guard went in one entrance and came back out the other end near us. (The guard went inside to get his cigarettes talks to another guard then proceeds back out the other end).

I hear footsteps getting closer than a shadow suddenly appears then stops ... I hear an flick then smoke comes across my face. I pop out fast hitting the guard in his stomach and his side, I started to pull the guard into the dark corner the guard tries to yell "Intrus" (Intruder=French language)...then Owen punches him in the face. The guard is quickly dazed the force from Owen's punch makes the guard fall into the rails I try to regain my grip on the guard's jacket to pull him in, once again the guard hollars "Intrus!" Owen now gets a clean hit, knocking the guard out but over the railing... The guard falls into a pile of crates and boxes creating a lot of noise from below the tier.

Minty: "What are you doing "I whispered to Owen!

Owen Brown:" I didn't even hit'em that hard...he got a soft face."

Minty: "What?" A soft face, I thought.

Then men start to come from the lower main level to investigate the noise.

Guards: "What is he drunk "A man says in English, to another guard.

Guard# 2:"His face is busted up" as they roll him over an see the blood from the stab wounds.

French Guard#3:"Retourne travailler" (get back to work=French) walks up.

Guard: "Hey you not the boss of me frenchie" they argue.

By time I noticed the lit cigarette balancing on the tier, the wind catches it and it falls off the ledge...It was like slow motion.

Me and Owen watch then step back into the dark corner.

I thought maybe they didn't see it.

Owen Brown:" Maybe they didn't see it" he whispers.

Guard: "He's dead" the guards analyzing the wounded man.... when the lit cigarette lands right on the layed out French guards' body."

Guard# 2: looks up" left teir, the left tier he yells!"

The French guard starts blowing a whistle.

French guard:"Inturs!!! INTRUS!!" He yells.

Owen Brown:" I think that's Intruder "he saids to me .

Minty: "Yeah I got that" As I prepared my guns.

Men start to pour into the main driveway below...some are starting to cautiously make their way to the steps of both tiers.

I look over to where Louis was... All I can see was a flame launched from the dark corner flying through the air.

Minty: "Shit the kerosene bombs "I thought! "Owen give me your bomb switch your cap."

Louis bottle hits bullseye center of the boat on the right side of the dock.

All you heard was "Fleww" the fire was instant.

The now crowd of workers and guard's attention was stunned watching the boat on fire. The first guard that was running up the stairs directly to us got to the top of the stairs and was greeted by my Colt 45 to his face.

"Pow" I let my pistol ring off into his face...he falls backwards down the steps dropping his rifle.

Owen lights the bottle of kerosene hands it to me...I launched it towards the other boat like Louis did...mine was a little short an little off target but it still caught fire so I'll take it. While my boat slowly caught fire, Louis's boat explodes from the barrels that where onboard. I look over to Louis for some reason he's laughing...I think he saw my throw...so I pointed at him to say okay watch this...(at the same time the boats on fire where the signals for

Mo,Jim,Warren, and Watson to come in through the entrance. As I accept Louis challenge...I slide down the railing as kerosene bombs land in the middle of the drive entrance hitting multiple guards lighting them on fire.

I reach the bottom of the stairs taking out three guards with my pistol...I look up to see Louis watching me an started shooting an throwing guards coming out the doors on the upper tier...he throws me an thumbs up an disappeared inside the building. I look around Owen goes inside the building from the top also. There's an connecting covered bridge merging both sides together and threw the windows I can see Louis chopping and shooting his way through the guards. He's going for the checkmate I gotta get to the boss first to win this secret competition but it's an crowd of men coming right at me and some are actually on fire.

So now it's time to go to work. I empty two bullets into an guard head tuck my now empty weapon spun to my left whipping my other pistol out, staying low taking three other guards out, two of them were on fire...so I did them an favor really. Bodies are dropping and now I can see my brother Moses an everybody else fighting the guards... which half of the guards are on fire. The number of guards dwindled to the only five standing is us.

Jim: "Where's Lou and Owen"!!

BOOM,BOOM,BOOM ...Explosion goes off inside the factory.

Minty: "They're inside. "

We go inside to smoke, flames, men yelling, more people on fire, and constant gunfire ...I look up to see Louis and Owen on the top tier shooting it out with the guards.

The factory turns out to be a wine and brewery that has a lot of barrel's of alcohol.

I can see Louis an Owen are both headed towards an corner office up top that's being guarded heavily.

I get Warren's attention through all the chaos and points to the racks of barrel's next to at least fifteen men running out from the back. He gets the message, throws his bottle of kerosene against a wall of barrel's and starts to shoot at barrels but has to return fighting the guard's. So once I got an chance I'd shoot the barrels...Boom,Boom... the explosion took out more guards , I picked up a rifle from an dead guard and shoot towards the men guarding the office.

I fire..pow that's one down...pow that's two down. The rifle is out but there's four more guards outside the office. I get Moses attention he shoots at the guards taking two more out.

The guards Moses takes out are the remaining armed guards on the top tier Louis an Owen are now able to close in on the office. Once inside the office a guard gets thrown out the window landing below where the fighting was. Once the remaining guards and workers saw that we got to the office they either surrendered or ran.

That's when I knew we got to the boss of this operation. Louis walks out the beaten man holds his face up to verify his identity.

I thought to myself well played Louis...well played.

Jim Brown: Yells "Its nice to meet you Mr. Ducan Berwick."

Ducan Berwick: "Your dead Brown "he struggles to say.

Owen comes out with an book.

Owen: "We got everything!" Pointing to the book.

Jim Brown: "It was nice meeting you!"

Warren Garrison: "Wait!" It was too late to get information out of him.

Louis slices his throat, tosses him over the tier.

Warren grabs one of the surrendering guards.

Warren: "Where's the next shipment of drugs!"

The man points to the burning barrels.

Warren Garrison: "Where's the rest of it?"

Guard: "Its already gone!" He says afraid.

Jim Brown: "Where to?"

Guard:" I...I..all I know it goes to Indiana then loaded to an train."

Jim Brown: "Train? What train."

BOOM,BOOM,...more explosions.

Watson Brown: "We don't have time for this!"

Warren Garrison: Puts gun to the guards head "Where too!!"

Guard: "Mississippi..that's all I know!"

Jim let the guard go and we got out of there. We got back to our wagon and rolled off, we watched the building burn in the distance .

Kemitt mirrors chapter 5.14 (Vision's part 16)
"Track the tracks "page.16

Moses vision's point of view:

We got back to the safe house, didn't stay long just packed up and left for Indiana. On the way to Indiana we compared the maps we had to the maps we got from Ducan Berwick's office at the brewery factory.

If it's true that Devane is using Railroads, they are not on the current map Warren got from his connects in Philadelphia... So, our plan is to get to the Ohio river and follow that route to Mississippi.

So we rerouted our travels we didn't see no sign of a train but as we got closer to the Mississippi, Ohio river connection we did see small bridges but to faraway to tell it had train tracks.

So we end up stopping in a town called Cairo... we pulled into a hotel to lay overnight.

The people here where very friendly I was surprised of the welcoming especially to me and Minty. Warren got us in, he paid the woman at the front a little extra so we all wouldn't have to check our names in. He told her he was a writer and he and his entourage where rating the best hotels going west.

At this time the gold rush was still happing. People traveling far west to get rich, Jim and Warren always said the gold rush really was propaganda for American's to move west but it worked.

We all had our own rooms on the same floor, we sleep in good. The next evening, Watson along with his brother Owen came to my room to get me to go to the saloon across the street. I wanted to rest and keep a low profile but figured what the hell, I never been to a saloon before.

So I told them I'll meet up with them once I freshened up. I got fresh tucked my blade and walked across the street, it was already nighttime and I'm walking in public by myself even though its only across the street "This what freedom feels like."

I turn around to the look up to the hotel window to see Minty given me the mamma Minty... watch yourself eye, I wave to her, she just waved back. I proceed to walk into the saloon bar, this wasn't like I expected most of the men just stared at me when I walked in. I just slowly walked to the bar but then I hear "Rico"... it was Watson.

Watson Brown: "Rico!"

Watson calls me over to the table. I forgot Rico was my new legal name, I'm glad Watson remembered, Watson an Owen have already start drinking, Owen pours a glass and slides it to me .

Owen Brown: "CHEERS TO MY TRU BROTHERS AND TRU WARRIOR'S!"

We took shots...I tried to keep it together, but I almost died.

Moses: "What the hell is this?" I never drunk alcohol before, but I didn't tell them that.

Watson: "Somebody give this man some milk please "He says as we laugh.

Moses: "Hey this taste horrible. "

Owen: "Don't worry about it, you'll get the hang of it" Pours more in everybody's cup.

Then two I guess locals come over.

Tarvis Brown:" Hey I heard someone say warrior, how bout some poker!" He says while his dirty mouth friend chuckles at every word this guy speaks.

Owen: "What's your name partner!?"

Tarvis goon:" The names Tarvis...Tarvis Brown!"

Owen: "Brown huh..well Mr.Brown no disrespect but we're just trying to unwind and have a good night no poker for us but thank you."

Tarvis Brown: "Ok... but we got two grown fellas here, I'm sure they can speak for themselves!"

I can see the brewing aggravation coming from Owen as he leans back in his chair and takes sip of his drink.

Watson Brown: "Like my brother said we just trying to have an good night but thank you anyways! "

Tarvis Brown: "Well we still got one left now..Let me guest these your brothers and you just want to have an goodnight . "His friend chuckles again.

I just nodded Yes because he got two seconds before I put my fist through his face.

Tarvis Brown: "Ok you gals...um fellas have a goodnight ya hear."

Him and his friend get up from the table like they're about to leave, then he turns back to us.

Tarvis Brown: "But one thang , how is a nigger your brother!"

Owen got up before I did.

Moses: "You wanna say that again Boy!"

I see half of the saloon is on these dudes side but it doesn't matter .

Tarvis Brown: "That's what I'm talking about...gone get'em boys!"

Half the bar starts to corner us in, so I draw my knife and the bar draw their guns.

Okay this might not go the way I had it in my head, I thought...but fuck it.

Jim Brown: "TARVIS PUSSY BOY BROWN...DIDN'T I TELL YOU TO CHANGE YO LAST NAME 15 YEARS AGO!!" Jim and Warren walks in just in time.

Tarvis Brown: "John?...Jim is that you?"

Jim Brown: "It ain't yo no balls havin ass papi!"

Warren Garrison:" I can't believe you still around here...(looks around) and your the leader (laughs in disgust) let me guest you shake down out of towners for a living...still!"

Tarvis Brown: "Wild Lloyd?!...come, come take a seat...Everybody stand down!... Go back to what you was doing...play the damn music Sam!!...First round on me!"

We went from bout to tear this place up to sitting at the same table.

Tarvis Brown: "So these yall boys?" He says with a nervous smile.

Moses: "We already introduced ourselves."

Jim Brown: "So Tarvis you still around here."

Tarvis Brown: "Yeah I've done quite well for myself."

Warren Garrison:" I remember you saying if we let you go we will never see your face again...but here we are. "

Jim Brown: "Why are you still around here?"

Tarvis Brown: "I'm working here, I run the import, export business for Cario."

Warren Garrison: "You run the business or it's your business?"

Tarvis Brown: "Come on I'm legit now?"

Jim Brown: "It looks to me like you have goons, do they know about your true conniving back stabbing past."

Tarvis Brown: "Hey you guys got that gold back right...I thought we were square?"

Warren Garrison: "You want to be square?"

Tarvis Brown: "Of course?"

Warren Garrison: "Who uses the Railroads?"

Tarvis Brown: "The Railroads are new maybe an year old we just unload what we supposed to unload and then take it out west, then it continues down to Mississippi, Louisiana. "

Jim Brown: "What exactly are you unloading."

Tarvis Brown: "Fresh fish, whiskey, wine, newspaper."

Jim Brown: "Who you working for!"

Tarvis Brown:" I work for me."

I tapped Warren to look at the table in the corner the men at the table where smoking and snorting a substance.

Moses: "You work for you huh."

I walked over to the table of men some looked half sleep but they woke up when I grab the plate off the table... One jumped up but quickly sat back down once he saw I wasn't playing.

I walked back to our table and put the plate down in the middle of the table.

Warren Garrison: "So this is what your exporting!"

Tarvis Brown: "What this... its nothing its harmless!"

Jim Brown: "Then here ,show me its harmless."

Tarvis Brown: "No man I was warned not to do it."

Jim Brown:" I knew these men aren't following you because they just like you...you feeding them this poison!"

Warren Garrison: "You haven't changed a bit!"

Jim Brown: "Where's your shipment."

Tarvis Brown: "My shipment?...Listen here Jim I ain't gotta answer to you or him I'm the boss around here, in fact I want you out my town...Now how you feel bout that!"

Jim Brown: "How I feel "he says sarcastically.

Warren Garrison: "How you feel!"

Watson Brown: "He da boss!"

Owen Brown: "He is the boss of the operation!"

Moses: "And we know what happens to the boss of the operation!"

Tarvis Brown: Gives an whistle all the men stand up "Naw what happens to the boss of the operation nigger "Laughing!

Moses: "By the way the names Moses!!" I stuck my knife through Tarvis Chuckling friends throat then Tarvis hand nailing it to the table.

Jim Brown: "Whooo!! He fast ain't he!" Smiling at Tarvis.

Warren Garrison sees Louis outside the window ready to shoot.

Warren Garrison: Turns to the crowd "Now before you all terminate your life ...we just want ol Tarvis here... the rest of yall can enjoy your night!"

Tarvis:"5,000 to who brings his head!" He says crying while pointing at Moses.

The doped-up goons start towards our table. ("Kill'em")

Warren Garrison start pointing...pow,pow, two men drop from Louis shooting through the window. Minty comes busting in with her two colt 45's ...

Minty:" I know yall ain't think it was gone be that easy!"

Tarvis Brown: "Get'em" Still crying hand stuck to the table.

Minty start shooting taking out who ever has a gun.

Jim Brown: "Always take the bartender first" He yells to me.

I see the bartender duck down then comes up with a rifle shooting towards the window where Louis was. So I pick up and throw Tarvis Chuckling friends half dead body at the bartender then charge to get the rifle from him.

Owen and Watson doing what they do best knocking people out taking there (goons) guns and using them against them. Louis is outside still shooting, Minty must have ran out of bullets cause she went to work with my hatchet master blade...I'm so proud.

After the fighting was over Tarvis was whimpering with my knife still in his hand...he reaches for a gun on the floor, Watson sees him and punches him in the jaw.

Tarvis Brown: "Fuck you Jim "he says spitting out blood whimpering.

Jim Brown: "No fuck you...Now where's that stash!"

We walked Tarvis outside to his stash spot. To a barn that stabled horses with the same barrels that was back in Chicago on the docks.

Louis: "Hey come look at this!"

We walk to the back of the barn.

Warren Garrison: "Train tracks...I'll be damn."

Jim Brown: "So Rufey really got an train...well it looks like we got fresh horses we better get going if we want to catch up."

Tarvis Brown: "Alright you got what you wanted ...so we square?"

Jim Brown: "Yeah we square...even though you did just try to kill us...but forget all that, we're square."

Warren Garrison: "But Jim he is the boss of this operation "he says sarcastically .

Jim Brown: "OH that's right."

Tarvis Brown: "Wait I got money..."

Owen slits his throat.

Warren Garrison: "Alright everybody get your things let's mount up!"

We got our things from the hotel put the stash on fire and rode horse back following the train tracks.

Kemitt mirrors Chapter 5.15 (Vision's part 17)
"Old new friends" page 17

Minty vision's point of view:

We followed the railroad all the way to Mississippi, we already had our plans for Mississippians own Stephan Duncan. He wasn't just the wealthiest slave owner in Mississippi according to Ducan Berwick bookkeeping he ran the banks for Rufus Devane king.

After knocking some heads around Jackson (Mississippi) we got information on Rufus Devane new banks along this route and the banks is how he moves his money now.

We also found out this person Stephen Ducan who's in charge of all the banks means he's an integral part of the organization but only the hubs are where you can possibly find money and drugs at the same time.

We know Tarvis Brown was small time but if Rufus gets people like Tarvis all over the country he will succeed in getting the drugs deep into the west.

We got more information from workers from the banks to beaten overseers in the cotton fields, but all we got was Stephan Ducan wasn't here in Jackson (Mississippi) but we did know the next hub was in New Orleans.

Hope Stephan Ducan didn't mind us burning more than half of his plantation and freeing his slaves...he'll get the message.

Traveling through Mississippi was very dangerous slave labor drives this state this far down south I don't think people would care if you got freedom papers or not.

The Railroad must have been very thought out it was very discreet but going across people land I wondered if these were drop spots like Cario was.

After a long ride we arrive in New Orleans and finally see two trains at a small station. Nobody seems to be working, and what do you know a bank is right next to the train station. Its early morning the birds are chirping.

Watson: "Where are we going...I'm tired."

Warren Garrison: "Where almost there."

We go through the city...it's beautiful, the buildings are a different structure build from anything I've seen in these travels more like artwork.

We go straight through to a big village of houses lined up. It's obvious this is a sectioned off side of town...but I'm not used to seeing black kids playing out front, women and men gathered together talking and laughing...there's no master house around here. We stop and Warren jumps off his horse and knocks on a door, I usually don't have to question Warren but...

Minty: "What are you doing?"

Warren Garrison: "I got it" He continues to knock.

Then I see a group man walking up the side road. "I hope you know where you at white man" He said in his New Orleans accent.

Warren Garrison: "I know where I'm supposed to be!"

Jim Brown: "Hand for hand!"

The man: "Eye for Eye"

All three together: "May this iron protect me!"

Jim jumps off his horse to greet the men along with Warren.

Leaving the rest of us confused but excited at the same time.

They all shake hands and hug.

Whesile Madville:"So you brought friends huh...come on in please."

The other men helped us with our horse's as we all headed inside the house.

Inside the house was nice, it had so much culture I've never seen before I just heard from my mother, father, then Jac and Victoria.

We sat down at the kitchen table.

Minty: "You have a nice home here."

Whesile Madville: "Thank you we built them ourselves, this was nothing but the slums ten years ago."

Moses: "All yall free here in Louisiana?"

Whesile Madville:"No... we're a small percentage of free blacks but more of our people are coming from the Caribbean free."

Louis: "An a lot of us where already here."

Whesile Madville:"That is true...but let's not get into politics right now its Mardi gras, we celebrate...So you finally made it I was getting worried...going through Mississippi is not a game."

Jim Brown: "Unless somethings changed Louisiana is just as harsh. "

Whesile Madville:"It is but we managed to carve out an little piece for ourselves here."

Minty: "So yall own this land?"

Whesile Madville :"This small area yes outside of this you have to be careful even with freedom papers. "

A woman walks in through the back door with bags of food.

Maria Madville:"Unless your Whesile his face is known all over Louisiana." She says as she gives him a kiss.

Whesile Madville:"This is my wife Maria."

Warren Garrison: "Wife! Well it's an pleasure to meet you I'm Warren, Warren Garrison!"

Maria Madville:"It's a pleasure, I heard so much about you two ...so if your Wild Lloyd, you must be crazy Jim."

Jim Brown: "That is I Mrs.Madville!" Jim says in humble arrogance taking his hat off in respect towards his chest.

Moses: "Hi I'm Moses. "

Watson Brown: "I'm Watson. "

Minty: "Minty."

Owen: "Owen."

Maria Madville: "Nice to meet yall ...now I know yall hungry so let me get this food burning "She says smiling.

Whesile Madville: "Wait Little Owen...No... man you were a baby...Watson was a baby last I seen "He says so excited.

Jim Brown: "They go everywhere I go."

Whesile Madville :"Oh yeah soldiers too huh...well I'm not gone bore you all on old times at least not yet ,I'm sure yawl wanna eat and sleep so when ya done I'll show you where ya stayin...seen (yes)."

We finished our meal, then Whesile and some of his guys took us just a couple houses down from his. He had four new houses on the block, and he gave us three of them. Of course, Mo and I stayed together, Owen and Watson had their own, then Warren, Jim and Louis took the three bedroom next door to Whesile.

Once again when I finally get some good rest, I'm awakened by something, but this time it was by good energy. This Madi Gras thing got the people up in spirits, the beating of drums and singing automatically put me in a good mood as I looked out the window.

Moses is outside talking with Whesile and the fellas from the neighborhood, so I sat out on the front steps to take it all in. Kids playing without a care in the world, people dancing in the middle of the road makes me wish my mother, father and sisters where here to see this even Henry.

Maria comes to me while I'm sitting on the steps.

Maria Madville:"Hey Minty...Come with me" We go over to another house on the block.

An older beautiful woman opens the door, she waves us to come in. I see beautiful dresses on manicures lined up around the house. The older lady is busy with a needle in her mouth finishing up a ballroom gown type dress.

Maria Madville:"Minty this here we call mamma she's the tailor around here along with her daughter."

Mamma :"Now who you tellin my got damn business too...I ain't got time for late ordered dresses seen."

A young lady comes through the door with suite jackets over her shoulders.

Tiny: "Mommy I got the jacket's done...Whesile said he needed four more."

Mamma: "Well he better pick something out the back or learn how to sew... all of these are going out tonight and where's Keith at?"

Tiny trying to get situated with the clothes.

Tiny: "He coming I just saw him...hey Maria you picking up your dress?"

Maria: "Yes but do you have any extra for my friend Minty?"

Maria looks me up and down.

Tiny: "You look about my size."

She goes into a bedroom and comes out with an black and gold dress, she gives it to me to hold.

Tiny: "You in luck, I changed my colors, so I have a gown ready to go...You like it?"

I just shook my head yes.

Mamma: "It ain't free baby."

Maria: "Momma she avyon de libete (haitian=Freedom Fighter) taught by Adbaraya Toya daughter Victoria and Prince Jacques. "

Minty vision's: I just understood the last part.

Mamma: "Oh is that so...How did you meet them?" She says without a care in the world.

Minty: "She nursed me back to health, Victoria and Jacques was with us for six, seven years...taught us a lot." My nonchalant answer must have hit a truth for her.

Mamma took a pause from her sewing.

Mamma: "The N'Nonmiton!" (means=Our Mother) She knows anybody can talk what they have heard but Minty saying Victoria nursed her back to health is the underline definition of N'Nonmiton.

Maria: Don't worry Whesile gonna take care everything Mamma."

Mamma: "She good for this one dress but anything else got to pay."

A young man walks into the house at the end of their conversation, Minty catches his eye instantly.

Keith: "But the man who wishes to take an lady out for an extravagant evening should extend himself for all attentions needed." He says smiling right at me.

Maria: "Try it on in here" she pushes me into a bedroom. "

I put the dress on ...looking into the mirror reminded me when I first saw Victoria...I can't believe this image is me standing here... I walk out the bedroom to show the dress.

Maria: "Your gorgeous!"

Tiny: "It fits you so good. "

Keith:" I'll love it if I could escort you to the ball tonight "! He says while gently holding my hand.

Minty: "Ok... yes I would love to go." She says humbly.

Keith insisted to pay for my dress, then Maria and I went back to the house to get ready.

I freshened up then put the gown back on along with the black and gold pearls tiny gave me.

I step into the living room to see Moses putting on the finishing touches to his suite with a derby hat.

Minty: "Is that my brother looking all handsome!"

Moses: "Is that my sister so... beautiful...the queen herself!"

We both hug each other laughing.

Moses: "Can you believe we're going to a ball dressed down like this."

Minty: "I know...I'd never thought a day like this would ever come...and guess what?"

Moses: "What" As he checks himself out in the mirror.

Minty: "I have a date for tonight."

Moses: "An what?" He looks at me crazy.

Minty: "Keith, Tiny's brother he asked me out for tonight."

Moses: "Ok that's cool sis but he better not cross that line."

Minty: "He's a true gentlemen. "

We hear a knock on the door, it was Keith with a nice suit on. We stepped outside to see a line of silky black Clydesdale horses different colored carriages out lined in gold for everyone that's going.

It was like half the neighborhood is dressed and ready to go.

Moses: "Oh we gone have a good time tonight!"

We all get to our carriages, me Keith, Moses and Tiny rode together. The carriages started to pull out, it was funny to see Warren and Jim around all black people usually it's the other way around. We ride through the town getting stares from everyone, some smile some frowned, but they all starred.

Keith: "My mom really took a likening to you, what ya'll talk about?"

Minty: "We just found out that we got a lot in common. "

Tiny: "I told mamma about their freedom fighting!"

Keith: "Oh really that's what yall do?!"

Moses: "If you want to call it that, we just want equality for all people."

Keith: "Well we all want that; we fight everyday down here just for the little we have...you see the look on them faces (white people starring) they looking at us like we're from a different planet "! He saids smiling.

Moses: "Yeah we fighting to live life."

Tiny: "Oh we gone live tonight, there's the French quarter's."

We look to the sea of people enjoying themselves, live music it was great. We stop not too far from the French quarters. We arrived at these buildings with a courtyard yard, we stop and we all pour into the courtyard headed inside the building.

Inside there was band playing, people dancing I never seen this before. Whesile led everyone to our tables, then him and Maria hit the dance floor. Keith pulled me to the dance floor just like Tiny did Moses, I thought I couldn't dance until I saw Warren, he literally tearing the dance floor.

Who would've thought the most fun I ever had up to this point would be in the deep south.

The night was great we partied to the early morning by time we got back the sun was coming up. Keith was a complete gentleman the whole night and we all got back safe and sound.

Kemitt mirrors chapter 5.16 (Vision's part.18)
"Dogg Day Afternoon "page 18

Moses vision's point of view:

I woke up to Minty and Tiny talking and singing, I go into the living room wondering how did they have the energy.

Tiny: "Well good afternoon!"

Minty: "Hey brother...last night was fun right!"

Moses: "Yeah it was different for sure."

I go into the kitchen for a drink of water.

There's a knock at the front door Minty opens the door to let Louis in.

Louis: "We're all getting together to prep tonight...I just came to relay the message."

Minty: "Okay...well me and Tiny wanted to go to the French Quarter's!"

Louis: "For what Sunday Mardi Gras is over any underline boundaries are reset."

Minty: "Oh Louis you worry too much, we just going for a nice early evening lunch, enjoy the weather and be right back."

Tiny: "It'll be fine, we'll be back before dark and Moses coming right."

I was thinking no I'm resting but saw the smile on my sister face.

Moses: "Yeah but I'll need a suite." Trying to out of going.

Tiny: "Don't worry about that."

Louis: "Okay I'll let the fellas know."

Minty: "You welcome to come Louis, we all family...I just wanta enjoy this before we leave!"

Louis: "I know sis...I'll see yall in a little bit." Louis heads out the house.

Tiny: "I'll go and get Keith an bring something for you two to wear."

Minty: "Ok! "

Tiny leaves out.

I can see my sister is living a dream, I can't take that from her by not letting her go out.

Moses: "Ima go freshened up."

Minty:" I think Tiny likes you!"

Moses: "You think, or you know?"

Minty: "I can tell"?

Moses: "Well it doesn't matter I don't have time to be daydreaming about some fairy tale with bullets passing my face" He says while brushing his teeth.

Minty: "Yeah... I feel you. But you're going to be nice to her right?"

Moses: "I don't have a reason not to... besides, I have major respect for the way she carries herself."

Minty: "Okay I got you...now I'm ready to have some fun!"

We got freshened up, Keith and Tiny got us some nice clothes to wear out, Keith got one of the guys to pull his nice horse and carriage around. I wave to the fellas outside playing chess others playing cards, Jim gestor's that I have my pistol I gave him the thumbs up.

We jump into the carriage and head to French Quarter's.

The ride in the daytime was just as interesting than the night before, Keith's carriage was really nice we ride through the Italian section of the slums, I see an woman flip us off at the corner I guess seeing black people dressed nice riding nice really rubs people the wrong way.

I remember driving Mr. Brodess wagon with my dirty t-shirt, dirty sandals or no shoes at all...I got a lot more smiles. Was my appearance of going nowhere in life reason for others to smile...hum that's something I'll have to figure out.

I do understand my sister, it feels good to dress nice, ride nice and finally have fun whether people like it or not, I'm glad I came.

It's crazy how the poverty and wealthy neighborhoods where literally next to each other, not like the farm areas where everything is spread out.

We finally get to the French quarter's; Keith takes us to the only shop that would serve us lunch. We sit out front of the shop to enjoy our food and drinks all the activities and partying is still going on, so I try to loosen up, plus Minty is really having fun. We get to walking down the street Minty hooks my arm.

Minty: "Can you believe this...we're walking freely this is exactly what Jacques and Victoria must've felt like on the eastern shore that day!"

Moses: "Yeah I wish everyone could feel like this!"

I look over to see a young girl being treated wrong by a woman while just trying to sale goods I'm sure for their master.

For a quick second I thought she could be my little sister ("Sophie?") but quickly remembered Sophie would be a young adult by now.

Minty: "Do you think people look at us like somebodies...hey?"

I hear Minty talking, but I must intervene on this altercation... I see a white woman smack one of the girls across the face and proceeds to yell at her as the girl tries to pick up the fruit off the ground. I can tell the woman is about to strike the child again I sped up to catch her arm I start to reach out when...

Minty: Catches her arm "No need to strike the child, she understands!"

In that instance I can see the little girl with that same glare in her eyes that Minty had every time she saw Victoria and Jacques when we were kids. I always got it but now I'm living it, she's just like us when we were kids you never saw black people in this light before.

I bend down to help with the dropped fruit on the ground.

Moses: "There you go pretty lady" I said with a smile.

We can see the scariness in the woman's face when Minty caught her arm, but the woman looks around sees people are watching then mustard up some courage.

By this time Keith and Tiny has caught up with us.

Woman slave owner Catharine Ducan: "Get your nigger hands off me" she says in her Mississippi accent.

Minty let's her arm go.

Moses:" No need to hit her she's just a child."

Woman slave owner Catharine Ducan: "You niggers need to learn how to talk to a white woman...Thomas...Thomas!"

A black man comes out the shop we're in front of.

Thomas (slave):"Yes ma'am."

Woman slave owner Catharine Ducan: "Escort these Uppity niggers out my face!"

I can see she's now performing for the crowd. I look at the black man she called to her aid he looks at us I can tell he's embarrassed to even say anything to us.

Keith: "Come on yawl."

Keith gets us walking back down the road site seeing.

Keith: "Damn ya"ll really bout that huh, grabbing that white woman up like dat" he says laughing.

Keith and Tiny found that to be really funny they laughed so much it made us laugh.

Within minutes I had already put the situation in the back of my mind plus any harm to that woman those girls would have got the repercussion from it.

Keith: "Yawl ever had a reading before?"

We stopped in front of this dark door front.

Moses: "A reading?"

Keith: "Yeah come on!"

Tiny: "Yeah come on yawl!"

We walked through the door to be greeted by a creole woman with long loc dreads.

Banita: "How can I help you?"

Keith: "We would like a reading."

Banita: "All of you?"

Tiny: "Yes".

Banita: "Okay but it'll cost you...each!"

Keith and I gave her the money for everyone.

Moses: "So white folks let you run a business here in French quarter's?"

Banita:" When you know people darkest secrets you can work things out."

Tiny: "Banita runs the whore house in 9th ward."

Banita: "I told you bout talkin my business in my business. "

Minty: "So yall know each other? "

Banita: "Yeah we know each other but Tiny talking scandal secrets. I'm do soul reading, when you know the truth of a person... (laying out her cards) past journeys, strength, fears, and Future "She's takes a long pause looking at me and Minty then back at her cards.

Banita: "That can't be right!? "She mumbles to herself.

I look at the lady shuffling her cards around, I want to laugh at the host then I look at Minty still face like she's concentrating. The woman stops shuffling and lays out the cards on the table.

Banita: "The way you read people is how dim or vibrant their soul projects... Aarminta N'Nonmiton(Our Mothers) in Bon Dieu (The Good god) I'm with you this is not a challenge."

I can see Minty relax, I'm amazed she knows Minty name.

Banita: Sees dark souls behind Aarminta and Moses but are defeated by the light.

"Your souls are fueled by dark, but the sun always overtakes the darkness... you live many lives many worlds...you can't fight every battle you just have to win the Ones!"

Then she comes out of her trance, looks right at Minty and me.

Banita: "You've been searching for her...I'm sorry...but she's been... protecting you...protecting your family.

Minty: "Victoria" Minty grips my hand as she holds back tears.

Banita:"Your travels are beyond here...you have to leave in order to return... balance is in the hands of the be holder."

Moses: "Minty I saw it; I saw the vision's...how did I see it" I turned to Banita.

Banita: "If family has tru bond, it's easy to transfer vision's that perhaps others won't see unless their bond is also true with yours... But you can also create a hateful or unwanted bond if souls are strong enough to intertwine."

Tiny: "This is getting too deep for me."

Moses: "So what do we do?"

Banita: "You have to answer when she calls on to you...you might not have her forever."

Tiny:" We got to get going it's getting well into the evening."

Banita:" You have another brother. "

Minty: "Yes...Henry!"

Banita: "Keep him close he's..."

Tiny starts to heads for the door I had a couple more questions when the door fly's open and Tiny is grabbed up. We rush outside to see what's going on, only to be surrounded by men with weapons.

Cassandra Ducan: "Those the Uppity niggers ...tell'em Thomas" Pointing them out.

Thomas the slave: "Yes sir ...Master Ducan sir ... that's them" he says with shame in his voice.

A tall slender man comes forth out the crowd.

Stephen Ducan:" Which one of you niggers put your dirty hands on my wife!"

Keith: "The lady here was whippin on a defenseless child "Keith steps up.

Stephen Ducan: "So it was you!"

Keith: "Yeah it was me, so you gone hold court here!"

Stephen Ducan:" I rather shall...men aim!" Four men with Ducan raise their guns and the Sherrif just stands next to him not saying a word.

Catharine Ducan: "It was the girl Stephen!"

Stephen Ducan: "Bitch shut your trap, when a man's talking, Thomas get her out of here "Thomas escorts her away.

Stephen Ducan :"Now aim" puts his hand in the air.

I reach for my pistol when...Boom...Stephen Ducan brains are splattered all over the sheriff, I hit the two men on my right, Keith takes out the remaining men on the left... As the crowd scatters I see Louis with his gun smoking.

Louis: "Let's go!"

The same spectators that said nothing when we were lined up about to be death squadded right in the French Quarters are now trying to fight us as we try to get back to Keith's horse and carriage and I feel obliged to give out ass whooping's...man charging side step.. right hook crack jaw (man fall into crowd of people) big man straight ahead tough guy, he swings hard wide... step in... duck uppercut (he stumbles back)..straight left, straight right, kidney body shot (man holds his side)..side step left, fist throat.. connects (man chocking) ..pick man up full power slam, brick road head fracture... man coming blind side has knife,back step...man swings knife ...counter block with left, quick right right jab nose (crack broke), take knife, shove in stomach...next man Sherriff reaching for gun...I reach for mine...his eyes glances off...I cover ground lead with right shoulder, boom right to his chest, follow up, left, right ,dip, power left hook (crack)..his body does an 180 degree spin into the fresh pile of horse manure...he's out cold.

Minty, Louis and Keith clean up all the other runner uppers.

I can see the slave girls from earlier watching with a smile. We get to the carriage while Louis was on horseback.

Moses: "Damn Louis you right on time!"

Louis: "It was getting dark, so I came to check on ya'll."

Pow, pow gun shots come our way.

Louis: "Lead the way" he says to Keith!"

Keith gives Minty his extra gun.

Keith: "Hope you know how to put that to use (he winks)...Heyah...yah!" He gets his Clydesdale horses fired up and we took off racing through the streets.

There're three wagons on our trail shooting at us, so we shoot back. Minty rips out of the gown with her all black shirt and pants remaining.

Minty: "That's more like it...sorry Tiny."

Tiny: "It's okay...you paid for it."

Moses: "Always stay ready "I also remove my jacket for more flexibility.

We're moving fast through the streets, going back through the Italian section we just missed a man and woman crossing the street but the wagon behind us runs the couple over.

The horses trample the bodies, and the wagon runs right over them.

I shoot the driver of that wagon and they're blinder eye covered horses veer off crashing into a building.

The next wagon is closing in, Keith is hitting corners fast making it hard to aim. We hit a straight away, we're slowly leaving them behind, but they have a clear shot, I shoot the last of my ammunition and Minty six shooter is done.

Minty: "I'm out!"

We get Louis attention that we're out of bullets, he slows up and turns off. We got shots going pass our heads.

Keith: "Get down we almost there!" Back to the Whesile neighborhood

We get down but still watching the other wagons.

Tiny: "What happened to your friend?"

We look back to see Louis coming up behind the second wagon chasing us.

He gets beside the wagon leaps onto the wagon, takes a gun laying in the wagon in a bag of bullets shoots the passenger, drops him from the wagon then hits the driver in the shoulder and throws one of his kerosene bomb onto the wagon.

The fire quickly spread through the wagon, Louis leaps back onto his horse from the wagon (Minty:" Show off" she says with a smile), we can hear the extra ammo popping off due to the fire...the driver actually jumps before the wagon crashed landing very awkwardly on his head.

There's only one wagon left, Louis catches up to them, the driver sees Louis coming and just turns off giving up the pursuit.

We finally reach the neighborhood; everyone can tell something has happened by the way Keith was running them Clydesdales horses. Once we stopped Whesile and Warren came right up to us.

Whesile Madville:"What's happened to ya?"

Keith: "That's a long story, I need to put my horses up, I'll be back."

We got out the carriage, as Louis come right behind us.

Warren Garrison :"What happened!"

Moses: "Stephen Ducan is what happened."

Jim and everyone else are coming out to see what's going on.

Warren Garrison: "Stephen Ducan we missed in Mississippi?"

Minty: "Tall slender guy northern accent...yeah he was going to fire squad us right in the French Quarter's and even the Sherrif, Marshall whatever was going to let it happen."

Moses: "All because we stopped this woman from beating on a child.... If it wasn't for Louis, we wouldn't have made it back!"

Whesile Madville:"Okay everybody off the street meet behind my house!"

Whesile Madville:"If yawl took out Stephen Ducan there going to come here we got to prepare!"

Kemitt mirrors chapter 5.17 (vision's part 19)
"Leaving Ain't Easy" page. 19

Minty vision's point of view:

We all gathered behind Whesile and Maria house. We ran down the details of what happened all the way till we got back to the neighborhood, nobody gave the I told you not to go speech made me feel a little better. Besides it's way too late for that now we need a plan.

Whesile Madville:"Listen up Stephen Ducan was part of an organization that is not only trying to take the piece of land that we own in this city but is putting opium into all poor neighborhoods to weaken the people. In this organization Ducan has a major role in planning to build railroads heading west from the docks, they already have railroads running alongside the Mississippi river to the north and we have found info on railroads heading east.

Putting our information together with Warren and Jim it's plain to see they want our land because were in the heart of the loading docks."

Neighbor Chancey : "What does this have to do with us?"

Whesile Madville:"Stephen Ducan was killed in self-defense earlier today, I'm sure they're going to link us to that, so we must get the woman and children out.

Neighbor Chancey :"Is it safe to stay in the city?

Whesile Madville:"Get the word out for everyone to pack what they need then get back to me."

Neighbor Chancey: "Okay "He leaves out from the group.

Maria Madville:"He has a point should we stay in New Orleans?"

Whesile Madville:"I can't give a yes or no right now, but we definitely need to stay on guard for the rest of the night."

Jim Brown: "Perhaps we can use this to an advantage...anyone know how to drive a train?"

We sent everyone home to pack up except the ones that's going to help fight they needed to hear the plan.

Jim comes up with a strategy using the maps Louis and Warren had outlined for the secret railroads that Rufus Devane had constructed.

Our original plan was to take down the bank and destroy the drugs but now Jim has a plan to use the trains to get everyone out of town.

Whesile had his men keep guard in shifts while we stayed up planning all night.

Warren Garrison: "Its two trains that will be moving in the early morning, so we have to move fast."

Jim Brown: "If anybody has a direction, they want to go in let it be known, the faster we can board the trains the less chance of anyone getting hurt."

Whesile Madville:"Okay let's do it."

It's now 3am and we're ready to put the plan in motion, Chancey been gone for hours but finally returns.

Neighbor Chauncey : "I got the word out to everyone."

Whesile Madville:" I'm a need you to gather everybody and get the wagons loaded and meet us at the trains."

Neighbor Chancey: "Alright "He goes to get everyone ready to leave.

Whesile Madville:"Maria please make sure everyone shows up at least thirty minutes behind us."

Maria: "Got it."

We gathered our things and headed out, some of Whesile men stayed behind to escort the people to the trains.

Keith has the guys pull his wagon around and another wagon for us to drive, we load up an make our way to Devane's bank.

As we ride it starts to storm then heavy rain comes pouring down, there is no one on the streets at these hours of the morning, we stop across from the bank.

Louis and Owen break inside, it only took them about ten minutes before they come running back out.

Jim Brown: "Where's the money?"

Owen: "There is none, the vault wasn't even shut but nothing inside. "

Jim Brown: "Alright let's go."

Warren Garrison: "Well the drop was supposed to be for this morning maybe we're too early."

Jim Brown :"Yeah but nothing inside that seem more strange then coincidence!"

Whesile:"Keith I need you to look out for Maria and the others!"

Keith :"You sure?"

Whesile:"Yeah we'll be fine...hurry back."

Keith turns his wagon around to go check on the others.

We continued down to the trains; we jump out the wagon quietly moving towards the trains but there's nobody in site.

Watson: "There's nobody here" He jumps onto an empty train. "How you get this thing moving?"

Moses: "Yall hear that?"

It was hard to tell the difference between the harsh stormy weather or a train coming.

Warren Garrison: "TRAIN take positions."

The train is starting to slow down, were in the shadows laying low ready to pounce on our prey.

When a man looks to be beaten with hands tied together running out in the open from behind us.

He's yelling out something but the gag around his mouth muffled his words, as he gets closer, we can see its...

Whesile Madville:"Chauncey?"

Whesile runs out to get him.

Jim Brown: "No Whesile..."

Gun shot rang out hitting Chauncey in the back, Whesile catches him takes the gag from around his mouth. At the same time about twenty-five men come out from the direction Chauncey was running from.

Neighbor Chancey :"Sorry...Whes, I thought... I was saving us."

As the train comes to a stop two car doors opens...it's full of armed French soldiers, it's clear we've been compromised and now we're boxed in from both sides.

Officer: "Whesile Madville you are under arrest for murder!" He says revealing his face.

Officer: "We couldn't wait for you to slip up...toss your weapon (Whesile tosses his pistol) but to kill an man like Stephen Ducan, well I personally never liked that yankee cock sucker, always criticizing our southern customs but yet he made an fortune in Mississippi can you believe that...(he gets closer to Whesile)but none the least he is an white man an on top of that an top trustee to the Order ...and with that being said where's Brown I hear he's in town Jim Brown please come to the front "The officer yells out.

No body moves from their position as the officer looks around and Whesile stands firm in front of him.

Officer: "No Jim Brown...well I can't call ol Chauncey boy here an liar... we're all here ain't we!" He puts his pistol in Whesile face "Jim Brown come on down Jim Brown...huhh" He hits Whesile with his revolver then cocks his hammer back "1..2.."

Jim Brown: "Your little young to be (tosses his gun) yelling my name like your disgusted...let me guess your mamma said I was the papa or better yet ya papa met my left hook back in the good ol days!"He says while coming out of the darkness.

Officer: "You're a little too old to be running your mouth ain't cha" He replies with a smurk.

The rain finally slows up making everyone more visible.

Jim Brown:" Why don't you put that pistol down and show me how old I 'am "!

Two of the officer's men walks up like they're willing to fight.

Officer: "You sure you want to do that old timer!"

So, Watson comes out of the shadows.

Jim Brown: "See I can tell ya daddy must have been a jack rabbit of some sort but see Ima lion and lions raise lions!"

Moses walks out to Jim and Watson.

Jim Brown: "Oh another tip young man lions run in pride's...we don't need thirty men to do our dirty work!"

Officer: "Enough of shittin around old man... Devane got a bounty on your head dead or alive! "

Jim Brown: "Rufus?...What I tell yall...jack rabbits (he says amused) So you taken orders from little Rufey (laughing) how much the bounty "He says smiling.

Officer: "How much...fuckin lunatic two fifty dead five hundred alive...put these cuffs on and nobody gets hurt" He throws the cuffs hitting Jim feet.

Jim Brown: "Two fifty..five hundred...TWO FIFTY, FIVE HUNDRED!" Jim getting upset.

I know Jim very well he's taking this low bounty as an insult he's about to blow, I catch eye contact with Louis, and Warren I get my kerosene bomb ready I show to Warren...

Jim Brown: "TWO FIFTY, FIVE..!"

Jim quickly spins to his left taking the pistol out of Moses back waist band, Moses quickly gets low throws two daggers knives hitting the officer in the chest and throat , Watson gets low shooting the goons on the left beside the officer while Jim shoots the goon on the right then shoots the face off the officer point blank range.

Shit goes haywire quick everyone starts shooting I throw my kerosene bottle, Warren shoots the bottle right before it lands into the crowd of men sparking a burst of fire right in front of their faces.

Louis throws a lit kerosene bomb into the train car hitting a crowd of French soldiers.

Owen jumps from the parked train where he was laying low onto the train car of French soldiers shooting them while most of them on fire...I'm starting to think that's our signature move, hell it works...Jim takes one in the shoulder from the crowd of men now charging...me, louis and Warren cover Watson and Moses as they pull Jim and Whesile to safety. Now we're in an all-out shoot out even though Jim runs out of ammo he's throwing rocks, mud anything he can get a hand on while be pulled to the side...he has anger issues... with all the damage we've done fighting we're out numbered .

The soldiers are jumping out the train car their closing in on us from both sides.

I work my way to Moses and the guys, I give them more ammo.

Whesile Madville:"We gotta do something the others will be here soon.

Minty:"I have one kerosene bomb left."

Louis:"I got one left."

Moses:"look yall help Owen take the train me and Minty will help Warren hold the men off!"

Watson:"You ok pop."

Jim Brown:"Its just an scratch...let's go."

I light my last kerosene bomb throwing it into the remaining crowd of men, then me an Moses just unload on the crowd, but still to many of them , I can see Warren going to the knife I know he's out of ammo damn something needs to happen or we're going to lose this battle the men are moving in closer.

I take cover to reload, I close my eyes to call on Victoria's strength and a quick warrior's prayer..I get back to shooting emptying my last twelve rounds from my two Colt 45 revolvers. I can see Warren and the others gaining control of the train, but the men out here are still too many, I look at Moses.

Minty:"We gotta get to the train."

Moses:"Go I'll cover you. "

Moses fires a couple more shots.

Then more shots start to ring off but from another direction hitting the goons from the side direction, then Two huge black Clydesdale horses come busting through the crowd of men, the horses stump through the fire like it was nothing, trampling over falling men heads.

As soon as I seen the Clydesdales, I knew it was Keith and he got the guys with him, Moses pulls out the hatchet master blade throws me the big blade knife.

Moses:"Time to go the work"!

Keith and the guys just made it an even playing field we're no longer boxed in the middle from the mobb of goons and the soldiers by the trains.

Moses runs towards the crowd, I run to the trains towards the French soldiers. I get to twisting an turning this blade cutting through limbs like stacks of cloth, I get an glimpse of Moses doing the same but he loves to show off ,like slamming people to the ground by the throat with one hand ,then driving his master blade through their face, throat, arm anyway to make the next runner up to think about it.

I guess I do the same but I got finesse with brutal power like Louis taking out these soldiers gives me nothing but fuel, before I knew it we had taken out the remaining soldiers the mob of men lay dead or severely injured burning in the flames from the Kerosene bombs... Keith and the guys really came through.

Maria comes around with the other's from the neighborhood I'm sorry the kids had to see this mess but if they don't see it on this end they could see experience on the other end, the losing end and don't nobody wanna feel that pain.

We got the people aboard the remaining train the other two trains where to damage for anybody to travel in.

Owen and Warren found the driver, conductor hiding on the train, so in the middle of night we proceeded to leave the great city of New Orleans...I hope Devane gets the message!!

Kemitt mirrors chapter 5.18 (vision's part 20) "Q & P's "page.20

The engineer was alright with me this was just a job for him. It's been an couple hours now we made it out of Louisiana the sun is now up and I see nothing but land up ahead with no one in sight so it's an good time to see how's everyone's in the back is doing especially the kids and the older folks on board.

Moses: "Stop the train here."

Conductor:"We never stop the train."

Moses:"At this moment you work for us and I'm telling you to stop the train!"

The engineer brings the train to a stop me and Owen make sure he doesn't leave our sight, we had him walk to the back with us, we step back onto the first car.

Moses: "Is everyone okay?"

Everyone on board seemed fine some already sleeping. I'm just noticing how nice this trailer car is, comfortable long bench seats, it held up to at least thirty people.

Moses:" Was this for the soldiers?"

Engineer:"Yes this trailer and the next three are to hold many people."

Moses:"Everyone go stretch your legs, if you're not sitting with your siblings, they might be in a different part of the train so go walk around but we get back rolling in fifteen minutes alright!"

The people:"Alright "They start to move around.

Owen:"This train is different from the others."

Engineer:"Oh yes the others where for hauling more cargo...this is for traveling."

Moses:"Please walk us through."

The engineer walks us through the trailers showing us how their all connected.

Seeing everyone safe in each trailer was good to see, we get to the fifth trailer and it gets really nice the six trailer even nicer.

Engineer: "This is the executive car still holds around thirty guest but usually only up to fifteen people occupies this car."

Owen:" Well its filled today and they deserve this."

We get to the last car.

Moses: "Let me guess...the executive suite."

Owen: "So this is where the party at"!

Jim Brown: "Hey Mo guess who seat I'm in...I don't know but they got good taste!"

He says laughing shoulder all bandaged up.

Minty: "Brother" Minty gives me a big hug.

Owen: "How's the shoulder pop?"

Jim Brown: "It'll be better with some shine or wine!"

Engineer: "OH right here" he turns a table around and it's a full bar.

Warren Garrison: "There it is!"

Minty: "Any food around here?"

Engineer: "Everything is fresh...here's the ice box". He pulls out different compartments containing food drinks water.

Warren Garrison: "So who exactly owns this train?"

Engineer:"Mr.Devane gifted it to Stephen Ducan for contributions to his campaign from what I understand."

Whesile Madville:"Campaign?"

Engineer: "Yes Mr.Devane king is going to be vice president...you haven't read the papers?"

Warren Garrison: "We been on the road for months." The engineer reaches into an compartment then hands Warren the newspaper.

Warren Garrison: "This is for today's news!"

Engineer: "Yes well Mr. Ducan was to board this train to Philadelphia this evening, like I said everything is freshly loaded."

Minty: "Is there enough food for everyone?"

Engineer: "Each car has an ice box aboard so yes."

Minty: "Can you show me so we can feed the passengers."

Engineer: "Not a problem."

Maria & Watson: "I'll help!"

We start to walk back out.

Jim Brown: "Wait...you don't seem to apprehensive about this situation...do you know Devane?"

Engineer:" I assisted in driving this train for him for a while, seen him but never met him personally."

Jim Brown:"Devane only puts his own people in positions so how did you end up driving brand new trains for him?"

Engineer: "Believe it or not I lost an card game to an associate of his, but they said it was an paying job so I was trained to drive his cargo trains then this train and when he gave this train to Mr. Ducan I became conductor of this train."

Warren Garrison: "So you have an seedy past yourself."

Engineer: "You only meet associates in seedy places."

Jim Brown: "So why take the job you don't sound like the work for you type?"

Engineer:" I was known as an gambling man...I hear people say I married my wife because she inherited 500 dollars from her father...now I have daughters and two growing sons...I couldn't come home empty handed...again."

Warren Garrison: "Well seeing that once Devane hears about this trip you'll be out of an job, so if you get us to Pennsylvania in a timely manner safe and sound we can pay you an nice service package for your services."

Engineer: "Will do, I'm going back to Ohio myself so thank you". The engineer tips his hat in appreciation.

Jim Brown: "So what's your name conductor?"

Engineer: "William...William Rockefeller Sr."

Jim Brown: "Well alright William"! He raises his glass in salute.

The engineer "William" went back to the front we loaded up and got back moving.

Owen went with him I can tell he enjoyed learning how to work the train. I do to but that fruit tray and cold glass of water is calling my name.

Minty, Maria and Watson finally came back from making sure everyone ate.

Watson: "Do you know it's a toilet in every trailer car...where does it go?"

Mint: "You just stay out of this one understand "She says laughing.

Watson: "Whatever!"

Warren Garrison:" It says right here that William R Devane king will be vice president to Franklin Pierce. "He gives Jim the newspaper .

Jim Brown:" This gotta be rigged...(he turns to front page) The Alabamanian newspaper hell he probably owns this too."

Minty: "Well that explains who his friends in high places are."

As we get moving again, looking out the window noticing the Landscape it feels different from physically traveling through it...it's actually beautiful its really relaxing for an change, then I get to thinking about the runway slaves and how hard it was for us and we were way closer to an free state, down here where can you go even if you can read the sky how long would it take before the bounty hunters catch up with you and now out west past the Mississippi there is no law...I almost feel guilty not doing more, then I think about my own family...where are they, are they okay...did I walk right pass my sisters it's been years will I still recognize them, will they recognize me...last time any of my family seen me I didn't have an spec of hair on my face...

My wandering thinking was broken by Minty...I think she can read my mind sometimes.

Minty: she sits next to me smiling "Hey!"

Uh oh she knows I can't resist her smile she's about to grill me. I just try to smile back I can't show weakness with everyone around they might be watching.

Minty: "You thinking bout mom and dad" She puts her head on my shoulder.

Moses: "A little bit."

Got damn it... she got me.

Minty: "Its okay you can talk to me...you know I used to change your..

Moses:" Birches, I know "Laughing.

Minty:" I know I think about them too a lot but that's why we fight so hard maybe one day we'll be able to see them again were fighting for their freedom too."

Moses: "Yeah but would if were fighting wrong I mean this Devane guy seems to be 10 steps ahead we're knocking his buildings down but he continues to build...he's about to be vice president of the country even though he's one of the biggest criminals ..he's playing an different game then us!"

Warren was passing through but must have overheard us talking.

Warren Garrison: "Sorry I couldn't help to hear what you just said and I understand believe me, that's why I stopped fighting and losing air protesting and started writing that turned into an underground newspaper that led me to meeting some of the most incredible human beings including Louis and his family.

I ride with Jim because his heart is pure and maybe the writing wasn't as effective if my target audience are not allowed to read or write...(chuckles) do you know at one point Jim was going to school to be an Priest.

Minty and I laugh in surprise.

When I met Jim I was in my darkness, he rode with me through thick and thin...Back when we first laid our eyes on that stolen gold it triggered something in him...not the gold but who was smuggling the gold."

Minty: "Rufus Devane father we know that part."

Warren Garrison: "Let's go to the back and let him tell it."

Moses: "Its no need to bother we finally get to relax its ok."

Warren Garrison: "Believe me if it's a story to tell, Jim won't mind telling it ... come on."

We start to head back to the sixth car.

Jim from day one amazed me, his fight for justice I never questioned it...in fact I believe in it, but I guess I do have questions... are we going in the right direction.

We get to the back to see Jim, Louis and Whesile looking at maps. While Watson and Maria relaxing in their chairs.

Warren Garrison: "Hey Jim, Moses, Minty and I were just talking, and Moses got some questions for you."

Jim brown: leans back into his chair "Oh go ahead Lion."

Moses: "This thing with Devane I wonder if chasing him is blinding us from a different path to fight."

Jim Brown: "So you're wondering if this is an obsession or the right path... correct."

Moses: "Yeah that's correct."

Jim Brown: "Well it's both "He says with a stern face.

I gotta give it to Jim he doesn't beat around the bush.

Minty: "Okay but why?"

Jim Brown: "OH you want the story...by all means no problem!"

He pours another shot of wine, crosses one leg I can tell he's in the mood for a story.

Jim Brown: "When I was an boy we moved around a lot my family was very religious, my father wasn't a certified preacher but he held a lot of sermons in different cities and small towns. Back in Michigan we stayed for an long while, I had become close friends with a boy named Marcus and his sister... we were all around 11,12 years old...I knew they were slaves but never thought much about it."

Minty: "Wait there was slaves in the north?"

Jim Brown: "OH yes...it was normal at least to me at the time... even though I knew it was wrong because my father spoke against anyone being held against their free will...anyway we lived in an cabin right next to the big farm, as kids we worked on our own little farm and when we got the chance to play we would go over there and play...well after maybe an year and an half I remember we were moving again so my father did an sermon on a Saturday morning so later that evening I go to see my friends to say goodbye...the Master of that farm son had guest over when looking back maybe some college school buddies, when I spoke to Marcus he was angry he express how he didn't like these guys and how they kept pressing up on the women including his mother and sisters...he said no one would say anything to these guys he said "that Rufus King guy is telling the adults what to do like their afraid to say something to him"...I told him ol don't worry about it they'll leave soon...first time I sugar coated trying to protect someone's feelings, I should have told someone but I didn't...I thought he took my advice to let it blow over...so we finally loaded up our wagon and started down the road passing the front of the masters house I can see an young black boy arguing with young but grown men just when I made the boy out to be Marcus he was hit from behind with an shovel to the head...his sister running to him, her bloody lip shirt torn holding his lifeless body...I remembered shouting to my father to stop but he act as if he couldn't hear my screams to stop...I left from there with that vision in my head with my friend Marcus hit with that shovel ,his sister crying over his body, Rufus King name ringing in my head and my father doing nothing but preaching about freedom...I never hated my father he was an good...great man...I even followed his footsteps and tried to be an ordained minister but no matter how much I believed in the word I never got over that image...then I met this teenage misfit here (Warren smiles) I knew I found an great friend but he got into a lot of mischief and the god fearing servant in me thought at the time I can save my friends soul... we traveled together I would be holding service and can you believe Warren and a couple of our friends would rob my congregation homes when they're at my sermons!"

Warren Garrison: "OH god please forgive me...we were broke hungry and he wouldn't collect money from his sermons, so you know"... Chuckles.

Jim Brown:" I didn't know at first until he almost got caught in Missouri...this fool comes running into the middle of service with men chasing him yelling we got to go...we got to go...so I run with him we hop into our wagon and hog tail it out of there...that's when he came clean about what he was doing and that's when we found the information about the gold once he emptied out his sack full of stolen items.... I saw that named Rufus King connected to this gold smuggling operation...I just had to see it for myself, so once we did the heist and I saw the gold I felt something... I felt this was a way to hurt Devane...and fight back...even though Marcus was an boy he died fighting for his family...it sparked something I couldn't shake it...I mean I would try to live a normal life but I couldn't stay still...hell at one point he was coming after us...so we got back on his tail and we almost had him in Carolina...what 32 (1832)."

Warren Garrison: "up 32."

Jim Brown: "We where going around taking his men down freeing slaves then Nat Turner happened in Virginia...and that scared the shit out of all them slave masters on top of that, this time it was wrote about, the news made it to New York and Philadelphia newspapers...times where starting to change at least Mind wise...so when we caught up to him face to face he had an small militia that we knocked into the dirt but he escaped next thing we hear he done went back to France."

Moses: "So what happened after that?"

Warren Garrison: "We had this same conversation about maybe this is the wrong way to go about it, that people are starting to speak more against slavery."

Jim Brown: "We decided to go live our lives I had an young growing family Warren started writing met his wife Jo."

Minty: "So when did you get back into it."

Warren Garrison: "For me ever since I started writing and going to speaking events up and down the colonies."

Jim Brown: "ME 47, (1847) I read about an 8-year-old girl tied to a tree and whipped to death in St. Louis I got my boys and got back to the fight then picked up on news that Rufey was back stronger than ever and so was I!"

Moses: "So when did yall get back together."

Warren Garrison: "Well in 47 Jim got back to knocking heads off but in general we never left each other we always kept in touch the routes hidden in my magazines mostly came from Jim then enhanced by escaped slaves then Louis, he grew up within generations of indigenous tribes he knew the land at 15 years old better than anybody and Jim guarded the routes when he could."

Moses: "Okay I get the whole thing with Devane what's the difference between then and now?"

Jim Brown: "Back then… Rufey to the masses was just an unknown overly privileged little cunt that ran under his Daddy criminal enterprise!"

Warren Garrison: "Now Rufeys an publicly known cunt that runs his own criminal enterprise and the biggest slave owner in Alabama. "

Minty: "But slavery's not illegal."

Louis: "Yes but a senator now soon to be vice president... has a slave rebellion that's big news."

Jim Brown: "It shows weakness, he can't keep his own house in order."

Minty: "It could make it easy for his high-powered friends to turn on him from the backlash and the abolitionist more fire power to outlaw slavery!"

Moses: "Especially when they follow the trail of his burned down warehouses , a top contributor to his campaign shot dead."

Minty: "Using French soldiers to help move his money and British gold stolen from the Islands he'll be looked as an turn coat...by helping putting England back in power in America but wait...(She notice the patterns of new financial Banks on the map) he's not only trying to get territory back to the French he going for a full takeover."

Warren Garrison: "And guess who goes from president to Dictator…Jim you where right from the beginning." Looking at the maps and all the documents they have of the moves that Devane has been making.

Jim Brown: Jim pours an drink for everybody "The difference between then and Now we Got my boys, Louis, Queen Aarminta and a Lion named Moses cracking codes(everyone toast their drinks) we know your endgame Rufey and we coming but first we got to make an stop...Chestnut hill time to make some noise...Lukango!!

Everyone: “Lukango”!!

Whesile Madville & Maria :”Sante! ”

Kemitt mirrors chapter 5.19 (vision's part 21)
"Chestnut Hill "page 21

Minty vision's point of view:

So its settled we decided to make a route to Chestnut Hill, Rufus Devane Kings biggest plantation in Alabama. Moses went to the front to tell William the engineer our new route towards Chestnut hill and what do you know! Rufus has a secret railroad that can take us right to the rear of the plantation according to William the engineer.

The plan is to take out his men, set the slaves free, burn the main house down it's simple but the big picture is hurting Rufeys reputation amongst his colleagues.

Being that we're only a couple hours away we informed the passengers of our route change. Even though half the guys are soldiers under Whesile Madville we understand we could be putting the families in danger, but this is going to be in and out we can't pass this opportunity up...they were all for it. I love our Louisiana family they're compassionate but not afraid of nothing.

Louis and Watson prepared more kerosene bombs, amongst other little gadgets we can use even gave me an vest he found on the train and Mamma made little sleeves for my dagger knives. Tiny took leather from the seat cover and made Moses new holsters for his hatchet master blade. Keith took the metal plates out the seats and had Mamma and Tiny make bulletproof vest for everybody.

We also found more ammunition and more rifles inside the train compartments where the French soldiers usually sat at. We need everything we can get being our ammunition is limited. We went over our planned attack then rested up for night to fall.

The slowing down of the train wakes me out of my light sleep. I can see an huge house in the near distance, a tall fence separates parts of this huge plantation.

I can hear Jim's voice "Alright let's mount up!"

I get myself to together putting on my bullet proof vest with my daggers, kerosene bombs and my two-colt 45's. I'm in my all black head to toe, so is everyone else.

This time Whesile, Keith and the guys are joining us just like back in New Orleans.

Maria, Tiny and the others staying back will watch over the passengers and keep an close eye on William the engineer.

If in an emergency Warren told them to blow the air whistle from the train to warn us.

We make our way off the train we can clearly see two sets of Railroad tracks that leads right to the rear of the plantation.

Whesile Madville:"He has his own loading docks!"

Warren Garrison: "This the headquarters, stick to the plan Alright."

We all agreed, we creep inside the train docking center inside the rear fence.

Two overseers relaxing talking I assume their guarding the plantation.

Louis and I quickly take them out slitting their throats taking their guns.

Minty: "They have the same 45 I got "I say to Jim.

Jim Brown: "It makes since I got'em from Devane" he whispers back.

Jim waves for Whesile, Keith and the guys to come on.

Looking around we quickly realized this isn't a normal plantation, it's an full on factory.

You can see loads of cotton and sugar bundled up ready for shipment, the fields where far and wide neatly divided by skinny dirt roads with of course the big white mansion out front, from here it seems so far away.

Moses, Louis, Watson, myself and some of the guys from New Orleans took the left side, while Warren, Jim, Owen Whesile, and Keith took the right side of the fields.

Phase 1 of the plan is to take out all the overseers or guards then meet at the slave quarters.

So we split up...we stayed low moving through the fields. We spotted a guard patrolling the fields. He stops trying to lite his rolled cigarette, I quickly jump out in front of him by time he seen me...my knife was in his throat, we pulled his body into the fields took his gun and kept moving forward. As we got closer to the slave cabins, we crept passed all type of contraptions for punishments even an row of containment (jail) cells.

Moses:"Shhh."

We all stop in our tracks.

Moses: "You heard that?"

Slave:"Hey,hey"

There was somebody in one of the hot boxes, at this time it was getting cold at night so more like an ice box.

Moses motions the slave to stay quiet, Louis picks the lock and lets the slave out quietly.

Moses: "Stay down and stay quiet "He said to the young boy.

We got close to an cabin we see three other slaves out smoking and talking by the fire. We start to move towards them when the slave stopped us.

Slave boy: "There overseers."

Minty: "Who them?"Looking at the group of black men up ahead.

Slave boy: "Are yall here to help us?"

Minty: "Yes."

Slave boy:" They will alarm the guards."

Moses: "Where are the guards?"

Slave boy: "There mostly near masters house, they take turns walking around the fields making sure were inside our sleeping quarters."

Minty: "Ok but we need you to go inside and wait for us to come and get you all out."

Slave:" I can help."

Moses: "Wait for us."

The boy sneaks his way back into one of the cabins.

Moses gets next to a cabin and crouches down, he throws a pebble against the cabin gaining the attention of one of the black overseers.

Slave Overseer: "I'll check it out."

We can hear them joking around

Slave overseer: "If that's Johnny boy again I'm whippin the ghost out the boy if he thinks master bad wait till I get my hands on.."

The slave overseer turns that corner right into the hands of God...Moses chokes him so hard the man passes out.

The other two got suspicious not hearing any response from their friend.

Slave overseer #2: "Toedy..Toedy what you doing" he calls out walking towards Moses.

Before he could see the passed out body Louis whistles causing the slave overseer to turn his attention Moses quickly chokes him out from behind dragging him to the side of the cabin.

The third slave overseer tosses the last of his smoke and pulls out a whip.

Slave overseer #3: "Toedy...Dillard..!?...lil John this better not be you boy...I'm not afraid of you boy" He says cautiously approaching where the other two overseers disappeared.

I look around to see if anyone is looking all I can see is Warren and the guys coming from the other side, no guards around I have to do something quick if he sees the two bodies lying there he could run and alarm the guards.

So I get away from the group and pop out into the open. I walk towards him like I wasn't just hiding bringing his attention to me.

Minty: "Hey."

Slave overseer #3: "What you doing out of quarter's "He grips his whip.

I lift my head up so he can see my face, look him in his eyes.

Minty:" I hear you masters boy." He looks in confusion right before Moses knocks him out from behind.

Another young man sticks his head out the cabin, I signaled him to be quiet.

Minty: "Can you tie these men up."

Slave (young man):"Yes mam "He says with a smile.

I think tying them up would give him much pleasure from the look on his face.

We met up with Warren, Jim and the others.

Warren Garrison:" We took out two guards on the other side and I see ya'll covered this side also" Looking at the knocked-out men.

Jim Brown:" The guards we took out where smoking opium in cigarette, it has to be here."

Moses: "Okay let's take the house."

Louis: "There's more guards up front."

Warren Garrison: "Ok yall take the front well take the back door well meet inside."

Minty: "We need guys outside just in case."

Whesile Madville:"Hey fellas yall stay out here just in case someone tries to run up on us inside!"

Whesile Soldiers :"Alright, got chu." Four of the soldiers keep watch outside the house.

We proceed to once again split up, we can see more guards towards the front but this time it's a couple French uniformed soldiers but their so relaxed they're doing more hanging out than guarding.

We move quietly alongside the house, we can hear the men conversation as they speak broken English with French accents.

Moses: "What they saying?"

Minty:" I don't know...what they saying "I said to Louis.

Louis just shrugs his shoulders while me and Moses looking at him. Louis and Watson give us a blank stare, I can feel there's a guard right behind us.

Watson Brown: "What you black bastards doing out here!" He switches sides maneuvers his way next to the Drunken guard that was just as surprised to see us.

The guard looks at Watson in confusion then Watson punches him before he can break out of his shock knocking him to the ground with his bottle still in his hand . The soldier had his pants unbuttoned when he hit the ground.

Watson Brown: "I think he was taking an piss."

We can hear laughing from men and women around the corner to the front of the house. Watson peeks around the corner, it's about four guards five women.

Watson Brown: "I got this" He takes the French soldier jacket and hat puts it on.

Louis: "No ,you can't speak French. "

Watson Brown:" I can speak drunk."

All of us said ..."Nooo" as quiet as we could but he pulled away from us. He spun out of our grasp, starts singing some French drinking song while walking backwards.

The French soldiers joined in on the song not paying attention that it's not their comrade that's singing. The girls continue to laugh as Watson edges his way on to the porch.

Girl: "Wow you seem taller than before" She laughs drinking her wine.

Watson drops the bottle turns around with two guns pointing at the soldiers and the girls.

Watson Brown: "Why thank you darlin now would you all mind moving the party inside."

Minty: "He is his father's child."

French soldier: "Boy I hope you got an army, you know where you at."

Watson Brown: "OH I know where I'm at."

We all came around the corner with guns drawn.

Watson Brown: "Oh got an army too ...get ya ass in there."

The soldier's rifles where inside the doorway, we get inside and locked the door... Watson puts up his guns an take their rifles.

Watson Brown:"Thank ya kindly...now go in there" Gesturing to the first room on the left.

Jim, Warren, and everyone else comes in through the back shoving a couple of overseers through the hallway.

Whesile Madville:"Well take upstairs. "Whesile , Keith and few guys go to clear upstairs.

Owen: "The kitchens clear...who jacket you got on" He saids to Watson eating a piece of bread from the kitchen.

Warren Garrison: "Are these all the guards?"

Moses: "Minus the ones left in the field."

Jim Brown: "Alright put them all together, tie'em up...let's find whatever evidence we can get."

Owen Brown: "We'll check the basement "Referring to him and Watson.

Watson Brown: "Why you volunteer me...(looks at Jim Brown) man I don't know what's down there" He complains while they make their way to the basement.

Warren goes to the room straight across he realizes its Devane office. He goes thru his desk, library books then come across a sealed box, he opens the box to see a bunch of packages.

Warren Garrison: "Jim."

Jim Brown: "What you find?"

Warren pulls out a package.

Jim Brown: "Opium!"

Warren Garrison:"Feels like an...(cuts it open) book."

Jim Brown: "Book?" Warren tosses him the book; he quickly flips through it.

Jim Brown: "He wrote a memoir?"

Watson Brown: "Dad , dad" he yells running up the stairs from the basement.

Watson Brown: "Look what we found!"

Owen Carrie's up a barrel.

Owen Brown: "Yeah thanks for the help". He takes the lid off.

Jim reaches in pulls out a fist full of money.

Jim Brown: "The whole barrel!!... Warren man we hit this time!

Warren Garrison: "Jim we didn't come for money we trying to prove Devane is going to turn on the country."

Owen Brown: "OH no there's barrels on top of barrel's down there, With all types of money!"

Watson Brown: "And wine."

Whesile comes down from upstairs.

Whesile Madville:"Upstairs is clear but we found this in his study."

Warren Garrison: "An list of names...okay Owen get the barrels."

They bring up five more barrels with help from the guys, we look into each one.

Warren Garrison:"There's French money, American money, British money, Portuguese and Haiti gold and silver?"

Minty: "The money has his bank name on them, so he had to cut an deal with the British."

Warren Garrison:" The British navy still rules the ocean him cleaning their dirty money only puts him in favor with the British."

Louis: "Makes it easy for his own ships to move around with no problem but no opium here only what we found on the soldiers" Takes out a little bag of drugs hanging out the tied up solders pocket.

Jim Brown: "The money and gold will do it's still smuggling. "

Warren Garrison: Shakes his head in agreement "Load the barrels onto the train here take the books too. "

Keith: "There's wagons out back...let's make this quick."

Keith, Owen and Watson made sure the barrels got to the train.

Moses:" So what now. "

Jim Brown: "Check the place one more time make sure we didn't miss anything...then we burn this bitch down."

We searched all over the place, even tortured the soldiers but got nothing retaining to drugs, the house was so big we don't have enough time to be here all night.

Keith, Owen and Watson made it back with the fellas.

Keith: "Everything's loaded up."

Jim Brown: "Alright let's torch it."

We start pouring wine and kerosene from the lanterns out along the walls preparing torch the place when...

Whoo..whooo... we hear the warning sign from the train. We all stop in our tracks, I look out the front window I'm seeing wagons of soldiers pulling up.

Minty: "Hey we got an problem!"

Jim Brown: "The train... they leaving us?"

Whesile Madville: Yells from top of the stairs "It's another train coming from the opposite direction!"

Keith:" It's a cargo train like back in New Orleans!"

Minty: "Whes you and Keith take the guys and go protect the train, we can handle this!"

Jim Brown: "Well Alright Rufey throwing us an party!... Now have an little gratitude...this was getting easy(cocks his rifle)Let's show'em how we get down!"

I'm thinking this was supposed to be easy, oh well let's do it!!

Kemitt mirrors chapter 5.20 (vision's part 22)
"Battle at Chestnut" page 22

Minty vision's point of view:

The soldiers in the front are coming midway down the driveway and formed two lines with soldiers kneeling in front then a line of men standing up behind them with their weapons drawn.

Jim Brown :"Ok look this is how it goes I shout something they call my name out more words exchange then we fight!" He arrogantly says to us.

We all look at Jim like okay, whatever.

Jim Brown :"Soldiers put down your weapons and I'll let you live!"

Jim gives us the thumbs up smiling.

Pow,pow,pow,pop,pop they just start shooting.

Warren Garrison :"I guess there not fans of yours Jim" He saids while we all take cover.

Jim Brown: "Oh they will be...Louis you ready!"

Louis :"Yup!"

Louis put bags on the solders heads we had tied up, then drenched in kerosene and wine.

Jim Brown :"Wait we have hostages we're willing to let them go if you stop shooting!"

The soldiers stop there shooting, Jim pushes the first two tied together out the door.

Once they're embraced by the soldiers Jim throws a lit kerosene bomb hitting the tied up soldiers, fire spreads to the other soldiers.

Jim then pushes the women out, knowing they won't shoot while their in the cross fire ,waited till they got half way to the soldiers outside then pushed the other soldiers we had hostage out without the bags on their heads, he lit them on fire going out the door.

I thought Jim done officially lost it...

They ran around like crazy beheaded chickens they headed right for the soldiers outside, the soldiers that weren't already on fire started to run around trying not to catch fire from the burning human chicken heads.

Jim Brown :"Now fire!"

We all start shooting, taking them out like fish in a barrel. Jim craziness worked we take out an good portion of soldiers but they regroup an start to fire back with consistency I can also hear a gun battle out back of the house.

French soldiers from the cargo train must be making there way up.

Warren Garrison: "Where going to need more ammunition!"

Jim Brown: "They are too...seize fire!"

Watson :"What are you crazy" keeps taking his shots.

Jim Brown: "They have to be running low stay down...wait for the reload."

They get to tearing the house apart with gun shots then the shooting stops.

Jim Brown :"Now!"

We let off a barrage of shots killing or wounding the remaining soldiers the ones still standing ran for cover.

Watson :"Alright let's get'em!"

As soon as we start to charge outside, a cover is pulled off an wagon some of the soldiers where using for cover.

Jim Brown :"What the fu...get back,get back inside!"

We fall back inside trying to duck for cover. They start to fire off this big machine type gun one soldier winds an lever making the bullets run through the chamber while the other soldier aims.

The house is getting torn to pieces, then catches fire and they're not running out of bullets it seems nonstop.

We get back inside trying to find any cover we can find. I see Louis crawl his way out a window, the soldiers finally have to reload this massive weaponry, the smoke is getting thicker from the fire.

Warren Garrison: "We gotta get out of here" Covering his face with his shirt from the smoke.

Jim breaks one of the windows he jumps out yelling" come on" I see everyone making it out the window, from the room across from me... behind me the room is goth in flames.

The smoke is thick, the shooting starts back from the soldier's big machine gun, I'm trapped between the fire and the unlimited bullets cutting through the house. I can't see through the smoke I'm choking... I can hear Moses yelling for me I'm starting to fade out from the smoke.

I fight to stay conscious my mind starts to race I fight it off... not now I can't zone out...I'll die here...the words from Banita from New Orleans ring in my head "She's with you don't ignore when she calls!" VICTORIA?...I catch an glimpse of her face...I feel my body being pulled...

Victoria: "You have an spirt here." Flashes of my little sister Linah fill my head.

My watery eyes open I'm being pulled by the boy from the Hot box.

After about 10 maybe 15 seconds I stopped, I'm suddenly picked up and ended up on the front porch Moses handed me to Keith. (Moses shoots into the fields at soldiers)

I'm choking and coughing I see Louis made it to the soldiers shooting the machine gun the three soldiers lie dead on the ground next to the wagon.

Keith :"Minty come on breath, breath "while he holds my head up... I start to catch my breath.

Keith :"You ok?"

Minty : "You made it back "I'm still coughing and spitting up.

Keith :"Their fighting with us (slaves)!"

I'm coming back to my senses, I step off the porch the whole field is in battle, the true warrior's has risen.

Keith :"They kept the soldiers from moving in on us!"

Minty: "Mo (he turns to me) the boy from the hot box!! (He gives me the What?... Face as he shoots into the field) Linah our sister is here the boy is her's!!"I gain his full attention.

Moses: "How do you know?"

Minty :"Victoria showed me."

Warren Garrison :"Moses a little help!"

More French soldiers are charging the side entrances into the fields.

Moses and Keith help pull the wagon into position Warren winds the machine gun Louis gets to shooting hitting the soldiers running into the field.

I get back into the thick of the battle with Jim, Whesile, and everyone else the fight is going our way, the soldiers where good but the hand to hand combat couldn't match up.

The firing from the machine gun stopped as Louis and Warren cheer in victory ...I look around we did it we took all the French Soldiers out. The whole field lights up in excitement. We cheer in victory as the people start to jump up and down while chanting songs, I look for the kid from the hot box and my sister but can't seem to find them.

I yell her name "Linah...Linah...LINAH"...Nothing.

A man comes up to me.

ExSlave: "Sheeja (Sheeja=Gift of god) it is you I knew we would meet again someday... true Shujaa" he says to me in broken but good English.

It took me an second but I recognize the man...he was the escaping slave from the auction many years ago on the Eastern Shore. His use of languages I can see he's one that has traveled his current enslavement darkens his true self.

Beyond the cheering I can hear more rumbling, I look around to see a hostile crowd moving through the Dawn misty fog straight at us in the fields no French solider uniforms from what I can see. They're coming from all sides and there coming fast with men on horses leading the charge.

The man I was just talking to walks to the front and start to yell out commands in his native language, the crowd fall into battle formation.

The energy from the people (slaves) is now getting electric as the cheering in victory turns into war chants, as the recognized opposition is getting closer.

The angry mob start to fire there weapons into the air none of us budge in fear, in fact the jumping up and down is now in a militant form preparing for battle, the only remaining ammo is from picked up guns left in the field from the dead soldiers.

The angry mob continue to charge...So Now...We Rush!!

Kemitt mirrors chapter 5.21 (vision's part 23)
"Battle at Chestnut" pt 2 page 23

From the Abyss to the light

Moses vision's point of view:

We run full speed clashing with the mob , shots are being fired sounds of blades clinging but I'm not here for an one on one sword battle.

NO I'm here to chop down anyone that's in front of me and in the time of me thinking this I ran through about 5 and a half people, just chopped an man's arm trying to get Jim from behind...oh yeah his head went with it, who needs an gun when I got my knife and hatchet master blade with the silver wrist cuffs that Louis made me nobody in this field can see me .... uhhhh I suddenly flying backwards, damn my arm stings...my side too....did I just get shot, who the fu...k... just shot me!

Ohhh this shit burn...I got to get up, I'm getting up now ...got damn I can't get up ...take your shirt off tie around your wound...okay my left arm isn't moving shitt!

Ok you got this the metal plate caught most of the damage... just crawl a little get some motion going...fuck is that mud in my face...okay maybe one of the guys will see me.(A body drops beside Moses face) Okay I got to concentrate, what would Minty do.

I calmed down to meditate, I repeat the soldiers prayer in my head with one eye open...Okay seriously Mo you have to meditate, I repeat the soldiers prayer and then the unseen to be seen prayer...its not working... wait ok good I'm standing up where is everyone?

I see a young boy (Alamo/Johnny) standing in the middle of darkness he waved for me to follow him. I recognize the boy from the hot box as I catch up with him, color fades in like an painting I've lost sight of the youngin and ...I'm back at the Brodess farm how?

It's dark but I see men escorting a slave out an cabin, some words are exchanged then a struggle ensues. The slave is outnumbered 3 to 1, I run towards the altercation..Dad?...DAD!! The men beat him then put a bag on his head tie and shackled him.

It's the Thompson Brothers, I throw punches, but nothing happens as if they don't even see me or feel me, Dad is thrown onto a wagon then driven off.

I catch an reflection from the window it's younger me...I hear sounds coming from the house I run through the front door to see Mrs.Brodess in an office taking money from James Law , run through the living room Thompson brothers are signing papers (Purchase of Sale)for my mom and sister's the house goes up in flames I run through the back door, the whole farm is on fire an wagon with my mom an sister's roll past I see my sisters crying then they disappeared into the wind, I hear cries for help inside the barn I run past the vision of me and others being whipped by the Thompson overseers. I run inside the barn and fall onto a ship in the middle of the ocean.

People are fighting on this ship...Boom...an cannonball rocks the boat, pieces of the boat go flying...I look out to the ocean to see men climbing aboard the ship being fought off by black sailors.

Then I see Jacques throwing a guy overboard, I turn to see Victoria driving her sword though an man's chest. I look at the other ships I recognize the Two Headed Serpent with horns symbol but can't think of where from. Jacques and Victoria meet in the middle of the sinking ship their men continue to shoot at the other ships...they motion for me to come over they all hug me they're all here. The little boy, my mom dad ,my sisters Jacques and Victoria we all hug each other...BOOM...another blast the ship is torn apart Jacques and Victoria are underwater some how I'm standing on the water reaching down for them they grab my hand...Now I'm face to face with the biggest Lion I ever seen...I don't blink I'm not Afraid…the lion sizes me up... let's out the biggest ROAR...shooting flames, then leaps inside of me I can feel his spirt inside my soul.

My eyes open I'm back on this dirt ground the Sun is a Quarter up in the sky and a blade is in my face attached to an rifle.

I stop the blade from going into my face wrestles the gun from the man's grip, kick him in the gut he stumbles backward I grab my blades jump to my feet in a swift motion slice the man's stomach open, he falls to the ground I see the battlefield different now it's like looking through the eyes of the lion , the energy from the sun powers me the dark part of my soul from pain causes my relentless savagery to defeat any who oppose what I stand for and for this reason alone THEY ALL MUST DIE!!

My mind body and soul are all in line my blades are an extension of me. Everything is in slow motion; every move is quickly calculated from my head to my feet. I can see my blades cut through 3 strains of wind before it even goes through an arm, leg, head, throat, stomach I didn't see who shot me but I'm sure I got'em when I looked back at the trail of bodies.

I hear fast rounds of ammunition being fired off, similar to the machine gun from earlier. I turn to see the gun being fired from the other side of the field, so I start my hunt towards the wagon with the machine gun.

I look into the fields I see an path inform of an sideways U. So I move inside the pathway destroying anyone on the opposing side in the way.

My blood is boiling my senses is at an all-time high my energy is at blue flame levels I chop and slice my way through enemies the look on their faces let's me know they had planned for an different outcome to only have my blade go through their skulls, eyeballs, ears, chest even chopped an man's foot off, hands , fingers they all got it.

The machine gun is starting to do damage I make my way to the left side of the gun...I stay low where they can't spot me...they sway the gun to the right side... I take off full speed I can see them getting ready for the reload I leap onto the wagon cutting the shooters head clean off before the second man could look up, I stuck my Hatchet master blade between his eyes.

I can feel the sun at my back I see the mansion in full flames the angry mob numbers has dwindled to only maybe two dozen, so I raised my Hatchet Master Blade and shout "LUKANGO!!!"

Once the remaining men saw their biggest weapon was overtaken, they surrendered some try to run but got shot down.

Then the whole sea of fist goes up "LUKANGO!!!"

Kemitt mirrors chapter 5.22 (Vision's part 24)
"Aftermath of Chestnut "page.24

Minty vision's point of view:

I look up to see my brother with his Hatchet Tomahawk master blade raised to the sun his voice ROARED LUKANGO!!

Even in victory I see all pain in his face like he just beat his own demons, in another situation my brother would be King for the people... he is King!

The people crowd around my brother giving him praises, I can tell he was a little taken back from the response. Warren and Jim look on proudly we all smile at each other.

The familiar man again walks up to me.

ExSlave:"Sheeja ...Thankyou." As he helps the people board the train.

I'm still in Aww it's the escaping slave from the Eastern shores when I was a teenager...the same day I met Victoria and Jacques...I was happy to see him but busy guiding the people towards boarding the train and looking for Linah.

I look around to see all the dead bodies in the field, on both sides I look to see family's finding their dead relatives, I look around for Linah I still don't see her.

The men have already beheaded remaining members of the angry mob, I guess we really didn't need their information anyway.

Warren Garrison: "People everyone...you all fought for your freedom here, I'm sorry for the losses but they went down fighting for justice an new opportunities for everyone here if you want to give proper send offs please do, but we have to move quickly. "

Louis: "What are we going to do we don't have room for everyone?"

Watson: "We have to take them where they won't be returned to slavery!"

Minty: "Pennsylvania?"

Jim Brown: "We didn't get Devane, with his political ties in Pennsylvania doesn't mean their safe from being found?"

Owen: "Then where?"

Warren Garrison: "Chicago, Cincinnati, Cleveland?"

Jim Brown: "Jersey we have strong ties there!"

Louis: "We don't have room."

Owen:" We got another train right there."

Louis: "Who's going to drive it?"

Owen: "Me!"

Jim Brown & Warren : "You?"

Owen : "Yeah it's really not that hard."

Jim Brown: "It's not that easy!"

Minty: "What's the alternative?"

Nobody has nothing to say.

Jim Brown: "Okay let's go!"

As we board the trains up I finally caught the attention of an woman I asked about Linah she said she was sold and moved weeks ago after her oldest son was beaten then put in the hot box for weeks till his death.

I thank the woman for her information, but I don't know what is worse knowing or not knowing what happened.

Owen and Watson got the cargo train going, our train followed behind then we headed towards Ohio.

As we're leaving, I see the boy waving smiling running I hollar "Wait" the boy runs into the corn fields then fades out. That was the spirt of my nephew, he was waving goodbye... I hope we freed his soul.

I sat next to Mo on the train... Put my head on his shoulder.

Minty: "I saw Linah and our nephew. "

Moses: "Yeah me too."

Minty: "You did!"

Moses: "I take it you already know about Jacques and Victoria!"

Minty: "Yeah I saw it in New Orleans. "

Moses: "Well I'am looking forward to a home cooked meal (grunts)."

Minty: "Mo...you hurt?"

I look over his body for wounds and I see two.

Minty: "Come to the back...Now!"

I get Tiny and Maria to help me clean Moses wounds and bandage him up... luckily, he will be fine. I make him rest up.

We spend the hours singing and playing around with the kids I can't help but wonder what's next, so I go to the back with Jim ,Warren and Louis.

I see Warren reading some skinny loose piece of paper, so I get nosey thinking he's planning something.

Minty: "What's that you reading?"

Warren Garrison: "Tiny found this while keeping an eye on William."

Jim Brown: "It seems William notified the mayor's office back in Alabama that we have arrived."

Minty: "How is that possible, he was on the train the whole time."

Warren opens up another compartment out the seating and pulls out an telegraph, well since Tiny or Maria never mentioned him being back here, I assume there's one in the front also.

Louis: "A mobile telegraph? "

Jim Brown: "Make since if your way back here to communicate with the engineer, or arrived in town, yeah Rufey pulled no punches with this iron horse here."

Minty: "So what we gonna do about William?"

Jim Brown: "We're going to get the closest we can to Pennsylvania than we'll go from there."

Whesile Madville:"The closest?"

Louis: "According to the map train tracks run out right between Ohio and Pennsylvania."

Jim Brown: "Yup so I advise everyone rest up look like we'll be taken the rest of the trip by foot" He says covering his eyes with his hat leaning back in his chair.

I check to see Moses is fine then find me a cozy spot for me to rest in. Keith comes an sit next to me, at first, I'm like man I'm trying to rest but Keith gets to talking with his Louisiana accent makes me laugh we end up talking for a while, I guess.

I wake up to an stopped train in the middle of nowhere. I thought I was just dreaming but I hear Jim's voice fussing outside the train.

I step off the train to see the cargo train stopped behind us I start to walk towards Owen, Watson and Warren at the front to see William the engineer thrown off the train hitting the ground hard. "Oh shit" then It all comes back to me about the telegraph thing. Jim tosses the telegraph to Owen ,then jumps off the train.

Owen: "I thought this was a compass" Looking at the mobile telegraph transmitter.

Warren Garrison: "What you gotta say for yourself now...Devil Bill" Puts the pistol in his face.

William the engineer: "So you know my name huh" as he wipes blood from his lip.

Warren Garrison:"I knew who you where when you said your name...you ain't the only one who frequent seedy places!"

William the engineer: "You know my reputation..I told you I changed!"

Jim Brown: "You changed?!...You notified the enemy we where coming!"

William the engineer: "What was I supposed to do...taking the original route straight to Pennsylvania I could explain being held hostage but going to Chestnut hill it looks like I'm in on it ...Ima dead man once that got back to Devane...besides I thought it was going to be in and out...we should've been gone before reinforcement showed up."

Jim Brown: "That doesn't excuse nothing we could of died out there!"

William the engineer:" You could've died in New Orleans...I didn't run off the train once I saw it was Jim Brown fighting...and Wild lloyd" he saids slowly getting off the ground.

Jim Brown: "What's that supposed to mean!"

William the engineer:"1826 I was with my father Hells Kitchen New York city an known gang was beating up on an man talking against slavery amongst other things.

I guest the gang leader was tired of hearing the continuous preaching so they jumped on the older guy then two younger guys with an couple of their own guys jumped in and beat the snot...piss out of the harassing gang members.

On our ride back home my Pa told me the guys coming to that Preacher's rescue was his son John Jimmy Brown, and his tyrant friend Wild Lloyd Garrison...in my eyes those young guys where the toughest thing around..

heroes to an 15 year old boy, I mean Hell's Kitchen till this day is nothing to play with...but I see you go by just Warren now."

Warren Garrison: Warren lifts the pistol back up to his face "So we supposed to believe an con man you could've heard that tell anywhere!"

William the engineer: "Its the truth...that's all I got" he saids like he's at the end of his rope.

Jim Brown: "Did you marry your wife for the money?"

William the engineer: "What?"

Jim Brown: "Did you marry your wife for the 500 dollars?!"

William the engineer: "..Yes...but I do love my family!"

Jim Brown: Thinks about it "You mentioned Cleveland. "

William the engineer: "Yes sir!"

Jim Brown cocks the gun doesn't trust William, I had to step in.

Minty: "We pay you and you guide these people the rest of the way North!"

William the engineer: "I can do that."

Jim Brown: "Pay the man...we gotta get moving "he says to Watson.

William the engineer: "Thank you sir I'll be sure to instill these lessons into my boys!"

Jim Brown: "Just make sure they become productive for all of society...they don't' want to see my face for repercussions of their father!"

Watson comes back and pays William the engineer Rockefeller along with the families that chose to head that way the rest of the people came with us which mostly was our New Orleans people.

It was an far journey but not as treacherous now being more advanced on direction and just knowing how to travel through rough terrain.

We still had to be careful not to be spotted by bounty hunters but we made it back to Warren's hall where he holds his meetings and writes his news letters.

Warren and Jim let the people know we can help them with living situations and money but its going to take an couple weeks some would have to stay here some at the house till then.

We made it back to Warren's house only to greet them with an extra 9 people.

They didn't even care we all where so happy to see each other, I hugged Henry so tight I swear he grew an extra 3 inches hell its been about an year since we left. We went to the library room, Warren showed them we didn't come back empty handed, he explained we had enough to help get everyone an place to live and us to maintain.

I can see the excitement and concern on their faces, I know explanations and dinner table stories where in the near future but we're all happy to be back Im glade we actually can call this place home.

Kemitt mirrors chapter 5.23 (Vision's part 25)
"Back Home" page. 25

Moses vision's point of view:

The next afternoon I rode with Warren and Sharon in to town for food. Warren made some contact with some friends of his about buying land ,property and freedom papers I'm sure it's the same guy who helped get us our new identities.

We got back to the house Joanna, Sharah with the help of Maria and Tiny cooked for us and prepared food to take over to the hall.

Maria and Tiny was excited they had the ingredients to make huge pots of gumbo for the everybody.

We acknowledge all the new gadgets Henry made around the house ,Warren showed Henry two new telegraph's for the house and the hall, Henry was taken back of the new mobile telegraph.

Once we got over to the hall Minty , Sahara got to teaching children and adults how to read and write we brought clothes blankets wash rags for everyone. We set up food stations as the day went on Sharah, Joanna and Henry heard about all the funny stories to the real war stories from the people, Joanna popped Wild Lloyd upside the head maybe 10 times...now that was funny.

The people shared their experience about Chestnut hill, the usual horrific stories about slave life but I noticed Devane definitely ran his plantation like an factory.

Minty and I learned a little about my sister from the few people from Alabama that came with us Linah came there by herself as an child grew to get married had an child.

His name was Alamo but went by Johnny. By time he was 9 both Linah and her husband Big Alamo was sold ...He was an good child but gave the overseers hell he never respected them then one day they went to far and whipped him surverly then left him in that hot box for days where he died from his wounds. They said when an full moon was clear in the sky they often heard Alamo's voice around the plantation late at night.

All type of stories where traded that night songs...people backgrounds... ,orginal Tribe stories that battled against Spain, England then America before getting caught up in the slave trade.

A lot of the stories blew my mind...before then Louis and Sharah where the only ones that talked about the tribes that where here before any settlers.

The night went on and on it was like this for two weeks till Warren got everything situated for the people with freedom papers new names and money.

Warren also arranged drivers to take everyone further north to Jersey where him and Jim had strong ties to just like Ohio and Illinois.

It's sad to see Whesile and everybody go I seen Minty an Keith was building an bond but he went with his people he has an strong status within there community, I hope we all can meet up again sometime.

Over the next few weeks things are getting back to normal at least like before we hit the road.

Warren and Jim has been making connections about the stolen Devane gold and smuggled money we but no one is really up to taking on Rufus Devane right now.

The news on Chestnut hill made its way to the papers it has all the politicians arguing with each other again about slave revolts and the country's financial future but Rufus Devane name wasn't named in the big papers only in the small or underground abolitionist papers like Warren's.

One night after dinner I expressed maybe it's not the right time, Devane will be in office in a few months it's to late for an power change it's still a lot of white northerners who agree with keeping negroes underneath the white race and the Southern economy is to strong, who's going to go against that.

Maybe it's time to either go our own ways and live our lives or continue the fight but with smarter strategies getting slaves to freedom.

We all discuss our opinions I think we all knew we wanted to continue the fight some type of way.

Joanna comes into the kitchen with an telegraph note and hands it to Warren. Warren reads the note then takes an deep breath, Joanna just stands there smiling with her hand on his shoulder.

Warren Garrison: "Abe is coming!"

Louis: "Abe..who?"

Jim Brown: "Abe is coming here?"

Warren Garrison:" Yes" showing the telegraph note. "I been writing him letters about having an sit down and he answered."

Joanna Garrison: "Well he answered the telegraph he probably get hundreds of letters being a senator!"

Jim Brown:" An Republican not to mention an mediocre lawyer I hear he's not to well respected in Congress."

Warren Garrison: "So you know what's going on in the Capital now!?"

Jim Brown:" I know George Washington chose to be in Virginia, Maryland so his slaves won't be so persuaded to escape so easily in New York or rebel n Philadelphia."

Sharah O'Davis:" I thought Abe was your friend?"

Jim Brown: "I consider him an friend but why would he suddenly want to meet after all these years?"

Warren Garrison: "He's beginning his road for president."

Jim Brown: "President..?! So what he needs our vote (he says jokingly)or something."

Warren Garrison: "And a little... contribution to his campaign."

Jim Brown: "Contribution?"

Warren Garrison: "Just an enough that can be spread out during his campaign."

Jim Brown: "Throwing money at his campaign, we might as well just throw it all into the lake."

Warren Garrison: "Jim we have to start playing the game different, we can't kill every slave master or free every slave, if we can get an man in office with the same views as ours than we really have won one."

Minty: "Well what about the underground passages for escaping slaves are we still doing that?"

Warren Garrison: "Of course that will not only help those who seek freedom but continue to put pressure on the Capital on the abolishment of slavery."

Jim Brown: "You sound like an politician, why don't we just put the money behind you "Jim saids sarcastically.

Sharah O'Davis: "Who's to say your friend Abe is in the same fight as us?"

Jim Brown: "Thank you!"

Warren Garrison: "We can decide that once he's here in front of us."

Moses: "Okay I'm in."

Jim Brown: "MO?"

Louis: "I'm in too."

Jim Scoffs as he sips his whiskey.

Minty:" I think everyone is in...at least see what he has to say."

Jim Brown: "Boys...(Looking at Owen and Watson ,they agree with the others)..Okay then, we meet" Slams is cup down as he finishes his drink.

Kemitt mirrors chapter 5.24 (Vision's part 26)
"To be or not ... "

Minty vision's point of view:

It's been almost a month an Abe Lincoln has arrived for the meet tonight at Warren's hall. We have prepared everything from food to the security...which is us.

Warren is in a pleasant mood while Jim is still skeptical but knows this meeting is worth the discussion.

It's now evening and we're waiting on the arrival of Abe Lincoln, Owen comes inside to tell us he spotted Lincoln coming up the road.

Warren Garrison: "Good, good secure the perimeter."

Jim Brown: "Secure the perimeter ...Ha ...I believe we already agreed for him to take our money."

Obviously, Jim still has his doubts about this whole thing, or he just like to argue either way this meeting is happening.

Abe Lincoln enters the hall with two other people with him.

He was very polite greeting everyone, he introduced his driver and campaign manager then we sat down to start the meeting.

Jim cuts right in.

Jim Brown: "So Abe what's your plan if you make it to presidency."

Abe Lincoln: "First thing is to continue to build the economy for the American people."

Jim Brown: "Does this plan include every American or just white Americans?"

Abe Lincoln: "Well Jim god willing I want the best for everyone that represents the American flag."

Warren Garrison: "What about the ones the flag doesn't represent but in fact takes advantage of free labor and inhumane treatment?"

Abe Lincoln: "Well if you're implying the slave trade in this country...It can't just be one president that can change the law it has to be a vote amongst the people and the Senate."

Jim Brown: "Ahh cut the bullshit Abe you don't care about freedom for the real people who helped build this country because it doesn't affect you, in this room alone you have ex slaves and aboriginals who people has been here generations before any settlers came upon this land but yet they are condemned to the same so called reason we broke away from England or any other background Americans come from, so how are going to change that!"

Abe Lincoln:" I understand that but to be truthful the majority of white Americans wouldn't want to change the status that they have here in America whether they're rich or poor."

Minty: "Have you lost any family close to you?"

Abe Lincoln: "Why yes I have just recently matter of fact."

Minty: "Well have you lost family where health was not an issue that disease or old age wasn't the reason they died but because of being beaten for an disagreement or an look, your father and mother being sold to an place you have no idea where to, leaving children to masters and overseers who don't give an damn about you and if they do show you any attention it's not the kind you want."

Moses: "Older white men rape black women and children consistently with no consequences but will kill a black girl in a blink of an eye...make their offspring house niggers or disowned them even their wives will stick by their husband side through it all, hell at least there not lower than a nigger but they call us uncontrollable beast."

Louis:" A rebellion happens out of pain then it's those wild savages that's why we have to control them...it's all dishonorable!"

Abe Lincoln: "That is a hard thing to hear but it's a chain of command that has to happen before a Law can change."

Warren Garrison: "Those aren't just thoughts told to you those are real life situations they've lived through, this is a terrifying time ,place and mindset to be in especially when the moniker of the country is Land of the free."

Jim Brown: "So if you can't change the law for the better of the people, what the hell you running for president for or you just here for the money?"

Abe Lincoln:" I want to make a positive contribution to my country and to go after what you ask would possibly mean war."

Jim Brown: "Now you're talking my language...a legitimate war will put these racist slave owners out of business."

Warren Garrison: "That's every President of America so far."

Jim Brown: "So be it, off with their heads let me call it!"

Abe Lincoln: "The Country at war with itself can be detrimental it could collapse the economy."

Jim Brown: "Being that the southern states are carrying the load with free labor an little to none taxation it leaves the Northerners fearful of war the south has the economic power and who ever got the money has the power but the north has the big military that can outweigh any militia the powers that be in the south could ever put together."

Abe Lincoln: "It's an interesting scenario, war isn't cheap, and the south has multiple millionaires who money can reach far."

Moses: "Reach to who, they have no allies cause if they did, they would have to give up territory for those allies and we all know that's not what these rich slave owners are willing to do."

Abe Lincoln: "Agreed."

Louis: "That's right it has to be one of their own to blindside them while turning on the union at the same time, by time anyone realizes it'll be too late."

Abe Lincoln: "That sounds very difficult and preposterous! "

Minty: "But would if there is a man that has the money, the allies and soon more power to actually pull that plan off."

Warren Garrison: "Matter of fact the plan is already in motion as we speak."

Abe Lincoln: "Are you going to tell me or dribble on all night!"

Jim Brown: "Finally getting to the point no more pussy footing but first if you had cause for action and the power to do something about this what's your suggestion. "

Abe Lincoln: "Normally I would say a trial would take place but in this scenario case with supreme evidence... HUNG by noon for treason."

Warren gives Owen and Watson a signal to bring the evidence. Warren slams British money, French money, and stolen gold on the table.

Warren Garrison: "This is your evidence! "

Abe Lincoln: "And What I'm I looking at?"

Warren Garrison :"Stolen gold that Spain steals from South America, Spain hands it off to the French the French smuggles the gold from the gulf particularly Louisiana all the way up to lake Erie particularly Chicago melts the gold to coins which is smuggled threw Canada to the Atlantic ocean ruled by British Navy, money is exchanged also drugs pure opium is coming in from France and once its unloaded back in Illinois the majority of drugs go to these hubs set up in the south then out west.

Abe Lincoln: "Why out west?"

Warren Garrison: "Because smallpox doesn't really work anymore so if you get powerful tribes into a drugged-out state, they ultimately destroy themselves making it easy to be defeated, taking their land would be a lot easier."

Abe Lincoln: "So your saying France and Britain are secretly allying lead by an American?"

Warren Garrison: "Two countries that lost land to America by war or..."

Abe Lincoln: "Louisiana Purchase … I get it...So who's leading this takeover?"

We all looked at each other in caution how is Abe going to take this information but not Jim.

Jim Brown: "William Rufus Devane King!"

Abe paused for a minute, then starts to chuckle in laughter.

Abe Lincoln: "You all are mad you believe the soon to be vice president is a turn coat smuggling gold and by the way legal Drugs...you're going to have to come better than that."

Owen puts Rufus Devane memoir book on the table.

Owen: "His book is basically a guide to dictatorship."

Abe Lincoln campaign manager: "How did you obtain all of this?"

Warren Garrison: "We took down a couple of Devane operations."

Abe Lincoln: "You did what! ... You two still up to your old tricks...You know what I don't need or will accept anything from you and don't think I don't see an piece of this puzzle missing like stolen American money so it's been entertaining but I will be on my way!"

He starts putting on his coat and hat, looking at his campaign manager scanning the book pages.

Jim Brown: "Well go ahead then I hope your coat turns yellow too!"

Campaign manager: "Chicago, Mississippi, New Orleans, (he takes a good look around the room at us) You guys...you're the Shadow Bragade!"

Everyone: "The what!?"

Campaign manager:" Illinois paper had an article talking about months of terror banks was robbed an torched along with other small business then east docks went up in flames, men shot and wounded everywhere...the months following was more banks being robbed and burned, all new banks all owned by Rufus king except the one in New Orleans that was owned by Stephen Ducan an top contributor and influencer for Rufus king shot in the head in the middle of the French quarters who just had an slave rebellion on his Mississippi plantation weeks prior before his death."

Abe Lincoln: "Are you serious?"

Campaign manager: "It's my job to find out all background including dirt on all opposing sides and if we go against the rich Democrats, we're going to need every dirty deed on the competition...I mean these are horrible greedy men in my eyes senator were in the presence of heroes because of them you can't lose we have all the ammunition to win!"

Abe Lincoln and his driver just stand by the door in ahh of what was being said from his own campaign manager.

Campaign manager reading the intro page to Rufus Devane king book.

Campaign manager: "This book was written from Chestnut Hill, Alabama 1851 released date1853...it's not even out yet ...oh my god the recent slave revolt at Chestnut hill that was you guys the Shadow Bragade!!!"

Minty: "Can you please stop saying that."

Jim Brown : "Yeah where did you get that name from?"

Campaign manager: "From the Philadelphia Readers a few weeks back rumors has it that the owner of the paper was kidnapped and been missing ever since he published the story...(Pulls out the article) can I get an autograph?"

Jim smiling enjoying the fan out this guy is having bout to sign it, when Warren stops him by cutting in to read the article.

Warren Garrison: "Sounds like the writer is not fond of Devane basically making fun of him the whole article."

Jim Brown: "Ha he calls him Rufey too!"

Abe Lincoln: "So all this is true?"

Warren Garrison: "Ah what part."

Abe Lincoln:" Britain regaining power in America...the gold, the money the plan for France, to take the west."

Warren Garrison: "It's all here "Pointing at the maps and evidence on the table."

Abe Lincoln: "I'm on my way to Washington I won't speak a word of this.. when I come back we will put together an strategic campaign and end Devane kings plan along with the slave trade... with the country United we'll be stronger than ever...I want to thank you for the fight I myself will do my job in helping to clean up what's not just on top but what's underneath the surface."

Warren Garrison: "So we on the side?"

Abe Lincoln: "Through these next couple years we're going to be fighting side by side an political war I don't need your money I need you to have my front and my back it going to get ugly "He goes around the room shaking every one's hand.

Campaign manager: "One thing Stephen Ducan French quarter's in the middle of Madi Gras...How?"

Minty:" I hear it was Pure coincidence and self-defense."

Campaign manager: "Well save that for me later please...Shadow Bragade I can't believe it." He says putting on his coat.

Everyone is in good spirits after the meeting but before Abe can open the door, we hear a man yelling outside "John Brown, William Garrison you are summoned to come out with your hands out!"

Jim Brown: "Who is that?"

Abe takes an peak out the window with Watson looking from the other side.

They both turn around to us.

Watson : "Don't know but it's about four out front!"

Louis: "The backdoor is barricaded, where trapped!"

Kemitt mirrors chapter 5.25(Vision's part 27)
"Crossing Paths pt1" SB vs Rufus K. Page 27

Moses vision's point of view:

We hear the man again "Jim Brown and Warren Garrison is wanted by the United states of America they are here to be taken dead or alive."

Abe Lincoln: "Your wanted?"

Warren Garrison: "First I heard of it."

Minty:" Somebody say something keep them talking" She gets on the telegraph.

Abe Lincoln: "There's no wanted men here, your business here is misguided!"

The man hollers back "And who is this speaking?"

Abe Lincoln: "Abraham Lincoln, lawyer and Whig party representative!"

Watson Brown: "Pop I see'em!"

Jim Brown: "Who?"

Watson Brown: "The guy calling the shots, he's in the couch to the right "

Jim moves by Watson to get a better look.

Jim Brown: "No it can't be...(sees Rufus king face) Rufey crooked Devane!"

Warren Garrison: "Rufus...Your fucking with me (peeps out the window) it's really him..!"

Louis : "Look like we have to shoot our way out."

We got to pulling guns from everywhere. Abe wasn't fazed he opened his coat had an revolver of his own .

Abe Lincoln: "That's Rufus Devane, we can't fight him he's a top level senator vice president for Christ sake!"

Jim Brown:" He's an crook, thief an manipulative puppet master he makes you see what he wants you to see, but us here...we seen the truth people like Devane preach they walk with god but plays by the devils hand. (Steps in Lincoln face) and I love playing with the devil...no remorse, anything goes... so what side you on! Jim cocks his rifle.

Abe Lincoln:" I Demand to see Prudential's before anyone comes out!"He yells out to Devane's men.

Richard Riker: "I'm appointed goverment Deputy Richard Riker by the way of New York city, Jim Brown, Warren Garrison and company is declared by

Williard Rufus Devane King to surrender or be taken by force you have ten seconds to come out!"

Ricard Riker:"9.8.7.6.5"

Were all ready for battle but it seems Devane blindsided us with this...how did we let him get up on us like this.

Beyond any of our wishes Abe's campaign manager walks out showing his hands.

Campaign manager: "In regard to Mr. Brown he has constitution rights.."

Bang, bang two shots instantly rips through the man's hat and chest killing him on the spot.

Abe quickly grabs the axe next to coat hanger and launches it through the doorway hitting the shooter right in the chest...then they all got to shooting inside the hall.

Watson and Jim returned fire out the front window while Abe shoot from the doorway. Louis and I worked on breaking down the backdoor before my third shoulder strike to the door could make contact, I heard scuffling outside the door then it opened to see Henry, Joanna and Sharah and a man lying dead .

Sharah : "Come on" she whispers with her bloody knife in her hand.

Henry: "There's two men on the left side of the building." I catch Warren's attention to come to the back.

I signal for Minty, Louis and Owen to take the right side.

We can hear the shoot out from the front, I creep around the left side of the building I shoot the two men down realizing they're more than four to five men out here.

Moses: "You ready to use that" I tell Henry as he stays close behind me with his pistol.

We must take pressure off them shooting up the front. We pop out shooting at the so called Deputy but from the looks of him and his crew they carry themselves like slave bounty hunters.... at the same time Minty and others get to shooting from the right side of the building.

I catch an good look at Rufus and his position being guarded by more French soldiers, I mean how many of these soldiers does he have I see Rufey must enjoy being up close to the action so I'ma show him something up close and personal.

I lay low waiting for the reloads I tell Henry to go protect Sharah and Joanna. The wagon with the bounty hunters where right in my sights ...I see'em going for the reload I stay inside the shadows I quickly move in for the kill catching one with my blade shooting the other point blank I see Minty and Louis moving in as well shooting down the unequipped lower level henchmen I see why he keeps soldiers with him.

We take the pressure off Jim, Warren and Abe. Rufus must have start to feel the pressure himself he steps back in his carriage with his passengers, says something to his soldiers and starts to ride off.

Damn I wanted that kill we shoot it out with the soldiers that stood between us and Rufus helping his escape taking them out swiftly.

We take control of the battle; I see Warren and Owen shoot the Richard Riker guy then take out a couple more soldiers.

Jim and Abe shoot at Rufus's carriage from the road of a shot from the woods takes Abe down Watson and Jim goes to pick Abe up pulling him back near front of the building for cover

Warren Garrison: "Jim, get out of there!"

I look to see where the shot came from, just to see a ...Dynamite stick fly through the air right towards the building.

Just as I thought we fended off the soldiers I heard a blast then saw an chunk of the hall building has been blown apart with Jim, Abe and Watson caught in the blast.

Warren runs to the half dead Richard Riker and shoots him in both shoulders and legs.

Warren Garrison: "Here you bleed out like the pig you are!"

We run to the building trying to find any life of Jim, Watson and Abe.

Abe driver comes out of hiding.

Abe driver: "Look!"

He points in the direction Rufus went I see Minty is on his trail.

Louis: "Go Mo...Go!! As they remove rubble from the blast.

I run as fast as I can to my sister and brother.

Kemitt mirrors chapter 5.26 (Vision's part 28)
"Crossing Paths "End of the Beginning page 28

End of The Beginning

Minty vision's point of view:

I see Rufus making his escape as we take out the rest of his soldiers, I look up to see gun fire coming from up the road where Joanna, Sharah and Henry went for their escape back to the house.

I unleashed a horse from a destroyed wagon and gave chase.

I'm catching up... I see Henry telling Joanna and Sharah to run up the hill as he shoots back at the three soldiers on the carriage the one on the back is aiming right at Henry I take'em out with two shots , I can see Rufus and his passenger look back at me I aim for their heads but miss, Henry cuts across the road to take the attention off Joanna and Sharah.

As he runs across, he lets a shot off at the two soldiers upfront driving as Henry reaches the other side of the road, he's hit from the soldier's revolver.

I get to the side of the carriage dumping my last two slugs into the passenger side soldier. I throw my dagger knife into the window carriage hitting Rufus in the stomach that's when I saw another solider riding inside with Rufus and another passenger.

The soldier slides his pistol out the carriage window shoots the horse I'm riding throwing me off onto the grassy area.

Henry: "Minty!!" he calls for me.

Minty: "I'm here"! I find the strength to say, the fall took the wind from me, my hand is num but burns I feel its broke. Henry comes to me with a bloody shirt I see his shoulder is wounded.

Henry: "Come on, there coming!" He tries to help me to my feet.

The carriage has stopped on the road, the soldiers and the passenger attend to a wounded Rufus, his passenger friend points our way I catch eye contact with Rufus Devane and smile I knew I got'em.

All of an sudden someone just lifts me to my feet.

Moses: "Keep moving!"

The soldiers start to give chase letting off shots at us as we run deeper into the woods.

Henry is grazed in the leg he struggles to keep his strength.

We look up and see two brown men head less bodies hanging from a tree, that was even more motivation to keep moving.

We pick him up to keep going, the soldiers are getting closer I can hear their broken English accents getting clearer.

French soldier: "Leur tier dessus!"(shoot them)

French soldier: "Surrender or die!"

It starts to thunderstorm rain coming down instantly turning the soil into what felt like quicksand. We can only see the path from the moonlight ... Boom from the soldier's shotgun knocking bark off the tree, boom another I can hear the shotgun pellets wiz by my ears, we get to the edge of a lake.

Moses: "We gotta cross!"

We had no choice but to try to escape by crossing the lake.

Minty: "Come on Henry you can make it!"

Henry was hesitant once Moses and I started to go in the water.

Minty: "Come on!"

He starts to jump in we grab his arms but felt a tug holding him back, one of the soldiers has caught up and has an hold on Henry's leg. The soldier pulls out his pistol , Moses pulls out his hatchet blade and puts it through the soldiers wrist as I throw my last knife into his shoulder the rain was falling so hard l lost my grip from Henry I felt the floor just open beneath my feet falling into crystals, Rays of light more than deep waters.

6

"This is real"!

[Who the Hell are you!!]

Minty and Moses visions walked everyone at the table through there life and how they ended up where they are today. The visions come to an end pulling everyone out of the trance.

Alonzo:"Yo what the hell was that... felt like I was there"!

Terry: "OH so yall not fuckin around...I thought yawl was together my bad". Looking at everyone frowned up faces at his comment.

Uncle Tone: "The ignorance...hey that was deep"! He says humbled and amazed.

Will: "So that really was yall story...your life... I salute both of you"!

Yolanda:" Ms.Ross I didn't know you got down like that I applaud both of your strengths"!

Alonzo: "Yea Rico or Moses...WHO DA HELL ARE YOU a damn assassin"!

Rico (Mo):"I'm the same person you known for years.

Terry: "And where were you before...Huh... hitching booty from the pirates ship".

The lights flick on Professor comes down to tell us he's got the footage cued up.

They all start to head upstairs to see what was found on these footage reels.

Professor: "It was hard piecing these together most parts have no audio...but let's see what we got...What's with the long faces did I miss something"?

Uncle Tone: "I fill you in later P. go ahead".

Professor: "The footage starts off in the 1700's but start to get more documented in the 1820s it shows secret pictures of an group of white guys in an fraternity type of environment it shows men holding British flags, French

Flags, Spanish Flags...Then a picture of Rufus Devane King is shown being appointed minister to France. Other Pictures of him shaking people hands inside the White House by this time it's clear he's head man of the group.

Alonzo: "Hey that's dude we seen before we went through the time lapse that's the man yall went to war with from the vision's".

Rico (Mo): "Yeah that's him".

Professor: More pictures of him with his fraternity this time notice Spain reps aren't in the picture and the two headed serpent sign is clearly visible in these pictures taken in 1846. James Buchanan begins to be in a lot more of the pictures as well as personal pictures with just the two. William Rufus Devane king mysteriously dies around 1852 and the group goes underground. James Buchanan becomes president a few years after, he dies in the late 1860's.

Decades go past before the two headed serpent sign pops up again but in the form of a book. This picture was taken in Cuba 1932 Adolf Hitler with the book on the bookshelf behind him. In1962 J Edgar Hoover has the book in hand seen here.

Ms.Ross (Minty):"So they're connected".

Professor: "My guess is this book is really exclusive, you have to be somehow connected to this fraternity for it to be available ".

Rico (Mo):"So Hitler and Edgar are connected "?

Alonzo: "If we're in a different dimension how do we have the same oppressors"?

Professor: "Other than both having this book a personal connection isn't clear but their views where clearly the same. Fast forward 1972 the government puts a division together to track quantum continuum time lapse throughout the world believing people could travel through parallel worlds.

Will: "So how did they figure out it was time warps"?

Professor: "Not sure but there's more...2002 they record an successful jump through a time continuum that was pinpointed".

Uncle Tone: "So they're able to jump too".

Professor: "Obviously Yes but There isn't an reference saying the program was successful or not I assume to keep it secret, but 2012 another jump was recorded, and the last jump recorded in section 9 aka Pennsylvania was marked.

Rico (Mo) and Ms.Ross (Minty)just looked at each other.

Terry: "Did I miss something I thought we were going futuristic NOT hindsight 20/20".

Uncle Tone:"Uhoh young boy bout to get his issue "! He says referring to the dark stare Rico is giving Terry.

Alonzo just shakes his head.

Alonzo: "Look yall really can't take everything T saids to heart...but he does have a point, can we get an explanation why are we here "!

Terry:"Thank you"!

Professor: "It seemed New Merica has all the information in these files here .In 2009 an young professor perfects medical marijuana treatments that cured and prevented cancerous diseases helps the United Regions economy due to cannabis could be home grown later 2012 the same professor perfects the PhD balanced alkaline water systems throughout the Sections bringing back farming and natural foods into its height no longer having to trade with other countries, New Merica also has this documented...2016 the young professor along with his new partner develops an lithium battery that can light an whole town for two years cutting electricity cost by 60 percent".

Terry: "Now that's what I'm talkin bout fuck bills"!

Professor:"2019 the two professor's perfect this battery to run solar powered generated from the sun and can operate nonstop for 5 years at an time also making the Regions the strongest independent economy in the world, eliminating poverty by 90 percent among the Regions ".

Uncle Tone: "That's the enemy taking notes".

Terry: "Do they know Will owe me 2,000 dollars or is that classified ".

Professor: "New Merica now wants to move back to the once prophesized ruined lands but they also want the two professors for reasons unknown".

Alonzo: "No please don't tell me"!

Professor pulls up the next picture of the nerdy picture of Alonzo and Terry.

Uncle Tone:"Ha,ha so these two are the key"!

Yolanda: "So they want Terry and Lonzo to build them a battery or something ".

Will: "Probably a weapon ".

Uncle Tone: "These fools here can't even change batteries in the remote control ".

Terry: "The hate" he says shaking his head.

Alonzo: "So if they can track jumps can they track us "?

Professor: "Its possible"!

Will: "How did you learn to jump"?

Ms.Ross (Minty):"The first time was an accident but after reading the sky we began to see patterns that was taught to us since childhood Mo mastered that skill ".

Yolanda: "But if yall from way back how are yall still here and young looking".

Rico (Mo):"Every time we have jumped we went back before jumping again and going forward every time it's like the first time all over again".

Ms.Ross (Minty):"But older memories can fade after so long".

Alonzo: "So those meditation trances help keep the memories"!

Terry: "Stronger the energy stronger the vision's ".

Will: "Right on, you mentioned before stronger the family bloodline or bond makes a stronger connection enabling you to reach deeper into meditation... besides Mo who else is the bond "?

Movement soldier: "Minty, Mo, Tone the vehicles are here and we need to move if we want to make time"!

Ms.Ross : "Alright let's move ".

Professor packs up the footage he transferred onto flash drives destroys the reels and joins everyone in the garage.

Escorted by the soldiers and Uncle Tone instructions they all jump into the armor vehicles.

Will jumps into the passenger side of the truck while Alonzo and Terry Pile into the back. Uncle Tone follows the soldiers' truck as they head out.

Terry: "Damn this thang topline boy"!

Will: "I told ya Unc don't spare no expense when it comes to the movement "!

Alonzo: "Where the hell is Yola they gone leave us".

Will: "Yolanda with Minty and Tone".

A young soldier jumps into the driver seat while Rico Mo jumps in the seat right next to Terry.

Rico Mo: "Let's go"!

The driver pulls out fast catching up with the others.

Alonzo: "Got damn nigga what you think this is a Honda Civic ".

Speedy: "If that means fast then hell yeah".

Alonzo: "No nigga it means slow this bitch down...you got playas aboard this contraption".

The solider lowers his face mask.

Will :"Speedy man what's happnen "!.

Speedy :"You know Bragade business, it's good seeing you too, I saw yall gettin down back in New Feuherstadlt".

Will: "Sho nuff... you were the one drivin Mo & Minty "!

Speedy: "That's what I do"!

Will: "Right on"!

Rico Mo is busy pushing buttons setting up the communications between the other vehicles.

Rico Mo:"M2 come in M2".

Ms.Ross (Minty):"M1 I can hear you".

Professor: "Okay we'll be approaching the Mags within 20mins".

Rico MO: "Got it". He turns on the camera's outside the vehicle.

Alonzo: "Damn this like the A team van 3,000"!

Terry: "So I recon Minty is M2".

Rico Mo:"umhm" agreeing.

Terry:"Sooo... about this tea you gave us". (Alonzo:" here we go")

Rico MO: "The tea that you took not given...no it's not an hallucinate...you haven't processed that by now".

Terry: "No I have not...I have been in the 1800s twice in 3 days, my cousins boss slash OG is a Shadow warrior master killer that can jump between dimension and Will still talking like he from the gawd damn 70s"!

Alonzo: "Shadow Ninja...we agreed on that".

Will: "Shadow Bragade is the name, we're the known unknown ".

Speedy agreeing with Will, while Rico Mo just shakes his head.

Rico MO: "The tea actually helps you stay focus after the jump...everything that transpired over the last couple days for you two is real".

Alonzo: "So yall need us for access but for what "!

Professor comes over the radio: "Engage for railing".

Speedy: "Got it" as he hit switches.

They feel a slight bump as the truck connects with the railing built in the highway.

Professor: "Increasing speeds to 300,320,330". He says over the radio.

Professor: "Got it".

The increase in speed presses them to their seats.

Alonzo: "OH shit now in a damn time machine "?

Terry: "Rico where the tea at mannn.."!!

Alonzo and Terry shaking in their chair like they're on a Jet taking off.

Alonzo: "Where we going now 3,048"!

Speedy, Will and Rico Mo look at them like they're crazy.

Speedy: "We're going to section 10".

Terry: "Where dat"?

Will: "Alabama man"! He says laughing.

Alonzo and Terry calm down.

Alonzo: "Then how the hell we going so fast".

Will: "These trucks are made for the magnetic railing system allowing us to travel at high speeds...elite status ".

Alonzo: "OH...Now that's some innovative shit"!

The trucks speed down the highway through the early morning Alonzo and Terry became more observant of the landscape outside and the modern look of the Cities they quickly past through cities and small towns to finally reach section 10 Tuskegee Alabama.

They pull to a high-rise building that looks like it belongs in an art museum surrounded by streams of water and waterfalls all over the landscape with trees and bright colored flowers everywhere.

They see professional looking people walking around also modern cars, bikes all kinds of transportation devices.

They exit the vehicles they follow Rico over to Uncle Tone Minty and everyone else.

Alonzo : "So Tuskegee is the big city now"?

Will: "Its the capital of the Region's ".

Terry : "What?...Oh yeah this different ".

Uncle Tone:" Alright we need to get to the 11th floor its ya"ll time now! He reaches into a tub like box and pulls out lab coats.

Alonzo : "Time for what"?

Uncle Tone : "Time for yawl to be professor's".

Terry: "How we supposed to act like people we don't know "?

Yolanda : "Just act like you know what you're talking about".

Ms.Ross (Minty):"Speak only when spoken too".

Ms.Ross (Minty) and Yolanda dress Alonzo and Terry as they talk, professor puts the glasses on them.

Terry: "OH hell Naw suspenders ".

Alonzo: "We don't even know where to go".

Will: "The 11th floor is what I heard".

Professor turns on the glass's maps.

Alonzo and Terry what the hell.

Professor: "I'll be guiding you the whole way".

Rico, Uncle Tone and Will dressed like personal bodyguards.

Terry: "Hey Yola you look nice".

Yolanda: "And you look smart" she said smiling fixing his collar to look like the pictures.

Terry: "Okay I'm ready"! He says with boosted confidence.

Alonzo:" I swear ta god..you sumthin else".

Professor: "Ok the fellas are your bodyguards, and the women are your business advisors ".

Terry: "You mean personal secretary "! He gives Yolanda an look.

Yolanda: "He knows how to kill a mood" she says to Minty.

Professor: "Mission is to find documents on who's communicating with New Merica government ".

Alonzo: "Okay but I need a gun".

Professor: "That's what you have bodyguards for now go before people realize your almost an hour late".

Alonzo tries to say something but Minty starts to push him along towards the entrance.

7

The time lapse "S.B. at the Water Electric Tower

Professor: "OH yeah remember you guys are still like ass holes just Nerdy ass holes".

Alonzo: "So the glasses double as a radio "!

Ms.Ross: "We're all linked in".

They walk towards the building entrance they get a lot of hello professor along the way.

Terry: "This like being on campus". Enjoying the attention.

They get inside to walk through the metal detectors.

Ms.Ross and Yolanda go through no problem.

Security: "Hey Mr.Alonzo, Mr.Terry good morning to you"!

The metal detectors turn red when Will goes through.

Security: "Sir can you come to the side "!

Yolanda: "Hey ...(Reads name tag)Thomas we have very important meetings to attend you think we have time to explain to the board that you personally held us up to search the security that's provided by W-E-T Corp. "!

Security: "Ah no mam sorry, please proceed". He lets everyone through.

They Graciously walk on to the elevator.

Yolanda: "Business advisor "!

Terry: "That's right baby tell me what to do, advise me got damn it"!

Professor: "Good you're in"!

Rico Mo hits the scrambler then passes weapons to Ms. Ross (Minty) and Yolanda.

Alonzo: "Okay we're on the 11th ".

Professor: "Follow the path on the map".

Will:" I guess nobody's going to touch the fact this building name is WET Corp ..huh ...to easy...I get it"!

They walk pass conference rooms and co-workers; they continue down the hallway to a secured door.

Alonzo: "T put your print up there".

Terry: "You do it"!

Alonzo:" I did it last time".

Terry: "So what, do it again "!

Ms.Ross (Minty) grabs Terry's shoulder puts his hand on the security pad, the door unlocks.

Alonzo laughing as they get on to another elevator.

Will: "It's only one button in here"!

He pushes the button it does nothing

Yolanda: "Its another security pad"!

Terry: "Yo turn bra "!

Alonzo starts to argue with Terry again but looks at Ms. Ross (Minty) and puts his hand to the security pad.

More buttons suddenly appear. Alonzo reads the map in the glasses .

Alonzo:" I thought we had to get to the 11th floor...97th flo it is "!

The elevator launches off going up, they hold on to the railings, then the door opens.

Ding...they keep their composer getting off the elevator.

Alonzo:" Oh that's why they call it WET...damn near piss myself ".

Terry: "What the hell is going on here"?

They step on to a floor of many different lab experiments going on at the same time. They continue walking down the hallway amazed at the work that's going on.

A scientist is coming down the hallway with an creepy gas mask on dressed in all black toxic suit. As they continue to walk it seemed the creepy man is headed right towards them, they all are on high alert. The man comes right in front of Alonzo, Minty steps in front ready to take him out.

Scientist: "So you finally decided to make it"! He saids in a dark aggressive tone.

Alonzo: "Say what"! He responded back aggressively.

Scientist: "Oh..(Takes off the mask) So you finally decided to make it" he saids in a nasally chipper voice.

Alonzo: "Oh, yeah".

Scientist: "You guys are like Rockstar's around here I mean the cover of Jet Setters Digital ...Legendary "! Shows them the photo from his tablet.

Magazine cover title "The Two Men Who Shocked The World...Literally "!

Ms.Ross (Minty) and Rico Mo can't hide their smiles from seeing the cover.

Scientist: "We wanted to throw you guys a party, but you disappeared on us".

Terry: "Well you know these last couple days it's been like living in a different dimension "!

The scientist laughs awkwardly hard with a snort.

Alonzo: "So....Lester why don't you run down the particulars of the projects in progress for us".

Lester scientist: "OH for sure"!

Terry: "Bars cousin "he whispers to Alonzo.

They follow the scientist Lester down the hallway.

Lester: "Well first of all we're glad you guys kept it home grown with battery".

Terry: "Why wouldn't we"?

They walk into an lab with a model of the batteries and how much power they generate throughout the United Sections.

Lester scientist:" Hey I'm just saying either way you guys were going be rich beyond belief but keeping true to the soil made you Legendary status. Other scientists start to gather around.

Ms. Ross (Minty):"But you insinuate there were other offers".

Lester scientist: "Offer.. more like threats...hey you tell me, it's better than hear say".

While Alonzo and Terry freestyle their tall tell, Moses is breaking down the demo model that's showing the placement of the batteries throughout the Sections.

Moses secretly take pictures of the demo model he whispers to Minty as she quickly analyzes the demo model herself. After Rico Mo and Minty do their own scanning the premises Professor saids he has enough that we can get out of there but first they gotta get Alonzo, Terry and Will from entertaining the next room full of scientists.

Alonzo: "So after we put the horse head in the bed ".

Terry: “The movie producers greenlit the movie”. All the scientists laugh and cheer as they tell their stories.

Rico Mo gives sign it’s time to go.

Will: “Alright ladies and gentlemen we have to get the fellas to their next engagement but thank you, god bless and goodnight “!

They all head back the executive elevator’s, Ready to get back to the trucks.

“Hey Antonio, Tone”!

Uncle Tone turns around to see Ronnie Johnson... greets his teeth, puts on a grin smile.

Uncle Tone: “Ronnie (bitch made) Johnson how’s it going BROTHA!?!?!

Ronnie Johnson: “Yeah sorry we had to skate so soon from your Ching dig but you know when the wife calls you gotta pause so you won’t fall”!

Uncle Tone: “Yeah whatever so what are you doing up here”!

Ronnie Johnson: “We moved our offices down here”.

Uncle Tone:” Is that before or after you realized the boys wasn’t selling out”!

Ronnie Johnson happens to see who Alonzo and Terry is with and decides to let the conversation go.

Ronnie Johnson: “We’re just doing our best for the United Regions, but it’s back to work for me, so I’ll be seeing you later”.

Uncle Tone: “I can’t wait”!

Uncle Tone joins everyone on the elevator.

Uncle Tone: “Man I wanted to slap the grease outta that bitch”!

Ms.Ross (Minty):”Looks like Ronnie got a promotion at least we know who was trying to get the boys to New Merica”.

Will: “Wasn’t he at the party”? He asks as they walk out the building back to the trucks.

Uncle Tone: “Yeah and ironically our security was compromised “.

Alonzo: “So what’s the move now”?

Rico Mo: “We get back to section 9 dissect these current events somethings brewing, we gotta get ahead of it”.

Meanwhile Ronnie Johnson has placed a call involving his recent encounter with Uncle Tone and the others.

Uncle Tone jumps in the truck passenger seat with Ms. Ross and Yolanda with a movement soldier driving. They hit the highway and engaged the Magnet speed railing.

Yolanda: "Hey Minty, you and Mo really proud of the boys huh".

Minty: "Yeah they made tremendous progress for the people "she says proudly.

Yolanda: "Is it deeper than that"?

Ms. Ross (Minty):"I guess your gonna tell me" Cutting to the chase.

Yolanda: "The Vision's...your vision's where deep seeing you and Mo face after the trance I can tell even you two weren't ready for some of those dark places"!

Ms. Ross (Minty) relaxes leaning back in her seat listening to Yolanda.

Yolanda: "I saw you and Mo look on proudly while talking to the other scientists like proud parents, made me realize we're the bond for the energy but their the bloodline that connects your family enabling you to go deeper even if you weren't prepared for it".

Ms. Ross (Minty):"And you got all that from a smile"!

Yolanda: "Only my cousin Will and Uncle Tone give me those smiles, so I know when its genuine ".

Ms. Ross (Minty) smiles: "You know we met Tone 18 years ago being chased by New Fuhrerstadt police... talking about fireworks...as crazy Tone can be, he inspired us to look for the family we have in the present...for a long time ...years we were fighting to get back to the past not the future".

Yolanda: "So Terry and Zo are your grand...kids..."?

Ms. Ross (Ross):"Nephew's my sisters Linah and Sophie...I found it amazing Alonzo and Terry where able to know each other as well as grow up together".

Yolanda: "The time lapse... you two where the guardian angels much like Victoria & Jacques where to you"!

Ms. Ross (Minty):"Something like that" never thought about it in that way.

Yolanda:" So why the switch"?

Ms. Ross (Minty):"In my experience cognitive behavioral is also developed from environmental circumstances, in this dimension there are more influential successful groups of people directly involved in the development of what you see today among the neighborhoods of the Sections , Alonzo and Terry from both dimension have the same attributes but wear they come from influential people are the ones who made an bad situation work for them but once their government finds that they have become successful from the same thing they put out to destroy them those individuals are Harshly punished for it or even worse people turn on each other for what they think is advancement in lifestyle .

Yolanda: "Looking at Ronnie that still exists ".

Ms. Ross (Minty):"Yeah the unpredictable actions of people will never change ".

Yolanda: "So in other words Nerdy Alonzo and Terry from here where able to focus on being innovators but little survival skills while knuckleheads Alonzo and Terry came from survival first then trying to adjust you chose to switch for their survival skills in time of brewing war".

Ms.Ross (Minty):"I learned to trust and believe in my visions when sent to me I'm just following directions".

Yolanda: "And maybe just maybe avoiding a situation where the boys could have been persuaded to turn on the Regions destroying their legacy"!

Ms. Ross (Minty) just gives her an look that Yolanda theory is correct.

In the middle of their conversation rapid gun fire ricocheting across the truck bullet proof windows. Then more continuous gun fire, Professor comes over the radio to arm the trucks as they race down the magnetic railing at 330mph.

[The trucks linked together forms a train like vehicle increases the speed and is armed to the Teeth]

They see drones flying around firing off weapons, a voice comes through a drone to" stop the vehicle's and surrender", Uncle Tone quickly shoots them down, more drones come shooting up the highway.

Uncle Tone: "I know this got to be Ronnie on this sucka shit "he says to himself.

The military type drones start to blow the streets up disabled the magnetic railing.

Professor: "We have to disengage magnetic railing, or the trucks are going to flip ".

They disengage and control their individual truck's, they shoot down the drones, but now enemy vehicles are able to catch up due to their reduced speed.

As they fight off the enemy soldiers by firing back war drones come firing upon the trucks.

Uncle Tone: "The armor won't last much longer "referring to the drone military bullets piercing the armor off the trucks.

Rico (Mo):"Prepare the choppas"! He says over the radio.

Alonzo: "What the hell"? His seat raises up to the top protected in a clear shield, controls to the machine gun appears right in front of him.

Rico Mo:"Just aim and shoot"! As he prepares the side weapons.

Alonzo looks ahead to see Yolanda already shooting off the weapons from their truck.

Alonzo:"Okay ,aim and shoot "! He presses the trigger button feels the recoil from the gunfire. "WHOO that feel good...okay let's get busy "! He lets the machine gun cannon reign off knocking the other military drones out the sky along with Yolanda from the truck ahead.

More Enemy trucks quickly approaching firing off machine gun weapons.

Professor: "Assume formation "!

The trucks aline side by side taking up all lanes of the highway. The backseats become battle stations sliding out sideways protected by bullet proof glass all around.

Terry: "Hey man what the hell" as his seat start to slide out a helmet covers his head"!

Rico Mo and Will: "Aim and shoot"!

Terry start shooting at the trucks taking out the whole front of the enemy causing the trucks to blow up.

Terry: "Oh yeah Ima enjoy this here"! Continues to let off rounds at the enemy military vehicles.

Alonzo: "Yeah boy that's how you shoot!" He yells over the communication line.

Everyone yells "hell yea", pumped over the victory.

Speedy: "Oh shit we not done yet!" he says looking at the backup rear-view camera.

A big Armored military truck the size of a two story building is coming full throttle blasts through the fire scrap metal of the blown-up trucks.

Will : "What the hell is that a tank or a building"?!

Professor: "Whatever it is it's coming fast…Shoot"!

They all let the cannons go full blast from all vehicles.

Alonzo: "Aey this big muthafuca NOT slowin down"!

Rico Mo: "Reload ammunition!"

The enemy truck has green energy force forming bigger as it bullies its way up the highway then fires a dark green energy blast with gun fire behind it.

Will: "We're hit"!

The power in their truck goes out for a few seconds but quickly returns to full power, the Huge truck rams their bumper.

Moses and Will try loading the ammunition into the cannon slots when... again their hit and once again their truck lose power falling behind.

Minty: "Okay I'm going in" She snatched off the headphones grabs the automatic machine guns with hollow point ammo goes to the emergency button.

Uncle Tone: "Minty You can't go by yourself "!

Yolanda: "I'm going too!

Minty: "Just maintain the speed "! She says to Uncle Tone.

As Minty put on her gloves with the metal magnet hand grips, the custom black and silver dirt motorcycle is ready for take-off.

Yolanda: "I drive you shoot"!

Uncle Tone sighs but understands his comrades are under fire.

Uncle Tone: "Alright I'ma fire you off in 5seconds".

The rear door of the truck is fully open Yolanda rives the engine while Minty gets on the back.

Uncle Tone: "5.4.3.2.1 "!

He releases the bike like an sling shot, Yolanda comes out truck in full wheelimode rear tire smoking Minty puts her right hand down to keep the bike balanced scraping the metal glove across the concrete causing sparks to fly as they fly pass Moses and others truck.

Terry: "Dat right go got'em Baby"!!

Terry remembers Uncle Tone still on the communication line.

Uncle Tone & Will: "Baby"?!

Terry:" I mean Boogie…Go get'em Boogie"!

Yolanda lands the front wheel, Minty pulls out the machine guns from her holsters and starts to shoot the enemy truck front windshield.

The high-quality hollow points start to pierce the glass, Minty can see the driver and passenger take cover.

Will : "You gotta dig'em from the from the inside "!

Yolanda get close to the side of the truck, but the truck has guns firing out a slot from the side of the huge tank.

As Yolanda hits the gas to avoid the gun fire, Minty throw a sticky bomb on the side and the front passenger tires.

Yolanda hangs a hook slide as the Enemy truck is starting to regain its momentum.

Yolanda: "Unc blow dat bitch"!

Uncle Tone: "Mamma say mamma saw who ma ca sa"! Pushes the detonator button.

The two bombs go off damaging the front wheels and side of the huge Armed vehicle.

Yolanda hits the gas catches back up with to the Enemy's vehicle.

Minty: "Get me to that ladder "!

Yolanda pulls the bike as close as she can.

Minty: "Alright Louis I am pulling one of your moves I need your spirit with me". She prays to herself.

Minty holds on to Yolanda shoulder as she positions herself.

Minty leaps from the bike onto the ladder. The fast paste almost makes her loose her grip, she's swung from the strong wind but gets a firm grip once she gets her left hand onto the ladder.

Minty works her way to the top of the high speeding vehicle.

A man hops out the tank like entry door into his fighting stands.

Minty not even thinking twice puts two hollows in his face then watches the heavy wind snatch his body away like an autumn leaf.

Minty : "Stupid "!

They're quickly approaching a tunnel, this monstrous of machinery is so tall Minty has no choice but to jump inside.

Minty ducts in right before the tunnel could take her out. She lands inside automatically disarming an enemy soldier knocking his head into the metal wall.

Yolanda :"M2 you good "?

Minty : "Just be ready for me "!

Minty heads for the cockpit, when a soldier blindside her knocking her against the wall , she responds with a hard hitting combo, while the man is knock out on his feet she takes her knife drives it into the enemies chest then kicks him through the cockpit door.

The driver is surprised by his wounded comrade falling on him making him swerve the huge battle machine into the wall as they exit the tunnel.

Alonzo : "I can see her"! As he looks through the windshield of the Battle vehicle.

Will: "Is she ok "?

The passenger of the battle vehicle is thrown through bullet riddled front windshield.

Moses doesn't say anything but any doubt in his face was replaced with a grin.

Minty puts a bullet into the driver head…tosses a belt full of grenades from the dead soldier, then climbs out the broken front windshield.

She sees Yolanda on the bike. Yolanda holds it steady while Minty takes a calculated leap onto the back of the bike.

Just as Yolanda hits the gas the Monstrous battle machine starts to blow up from the inside out.

They all cheer them on as they make their way back to the truck with Uncle Tone.

Alonzo: "Now that's how you do it"!

After destroying the drones and enemy soldiers the road becomes clear.

Will:" Radar showing enemy bougies 2 miles ahead"!

Uncle Tone:"How it look on your end Professor"?

Professor: "I'm getting the same reading but visually looks clear from here".

They feel a hard bump.

Terry: "What was that turbulence, don't tell me this thing fly too"!

Speedy: "No we slowin down "as he presses the gas pedal to the floor.

Professor: "They place some type of electrical wall up...look there's another up ahead, looks at the devices on the side of the highway".

The enemy soldiers put up an electric field fence unlike roadblocks or stop sticks the Electric field fence when passed through can shut down an whole vehicle along with any electronics.

They pass through the second Electric field fence the electronics and communication start to malfunction.

Minty: "Cut all electronics "!

Uncle Tone cuts off everything.

Soldier driver: "We still got power...there they go" He hits the gas speeding up while the other trucks are falling behind.

Uncle Tone spots the man controlling the fields then looks at the road sees little red lights.

Uncle Tone: "Wait STOP THE TRUCK!!

They roll through another Electric field fence.

The soldier tries to stop the truck.

Soldier driver: "No brakes"!!

Uncle Tone :"Minty, Boogie hold on"!!

They roll over the blinking lights, fast beeping went off then boom,boom,-boom the armored truck jumps in the air from the blast but so heavy lands back on all six tires.

The blast rocks everyone inside, the others see what's going on from a distance their truck has been disabled stopping them miles back.

They enemy soldiers come out from their post pulling them out of the truck and toss them into their trucks. Rico Mo hollers for his sister "Aarminta" he fires his weapon but to faraway. The enemy soldier controlling the Electric fields stares Rico Mo and the crew down from the distance then jumps into his vehicle and they disappear up the road.

Terry :"FUCK"!!

Alonzo walks over to the device that generated the fence, brings it to the professor.

Professor takes it apart instantly.

Professor :"This came from water towers they use these electrical fence fields to keep any toxicants out of the water it's part of the filter process, but they weaponized it".

Will: "So New Merica government is behind this"!

Professor: "No doubt about that but this device from section 9".

Speedy gets the truck started back up.

Alonzo: "Well shit what we waitin for let's move"! Grabs Rico Mo to get back into the truck.

They head to section 9 in a hurry.

8

"F...k Riker Tower"

Once back to Section 9 (Pennsylvania) they pull into an safe house garage.

Rico MO: "Will get everything we need ...hey I need you to step up Alright you trained for this, we're gonna get them back".

They all get geared up bullet proof gear strapped to the T.

Rico Mo:" Professor what you got"!

Alonzo:"Yo I thought they wanted us, why would they take them"?

Professor going through his computer files.

Professor: "Has to be the picture from the ETF building, I pulled it out their file and erased it but maybe they caught it before I got to it".

Rico MO: "At this point it doesn't matter why or what... they took my sister, my crew they die"!

Terry: "Damn...Ah Rico forget any bad thing I ever said alright"!

Rico MO: "If you wasn't my nephew I would of been pop that pimple you call a head a longtime ago"!

Terry: "Oh now you got jokes...wait nephew "? Looks at Alonzo confused.

Alonzo: "Nephew "!?

Rico Mo:" Yeah and Aarminta's your Aunt...if you haven't put it together by now I ain't got time to explain.. let's roll"!

Professor: "Tone got new trucks in the back garages" He saids to speedy.

Speedy takes the other movement soldiers to get the trucks.

Will: "So how are we going to get in the building undetected "?

Professor: "Damn this Minty thing". Looking at the blueprints of the Water Tower on his computer, Professor thinks how would Minty enter the building... looks at Alonzo and Terry then at his computer then Alonzo and Terry.

Alonzo: "OH hell Naw I'm already suited".

Terry: "Yeah yawl got me fucked up I'm not doing dat shit again "!

The next thing Alonzo and Terry know they're at the front gate dressed Nerdy getting buzzed in through the front gate of the Section 9 Water Tower taken over by New Merica government surrounded by enemy soldiers.

They walk through the gate to the front door.

Alonzo: "P. You better be ready".

Professor :"Just make sure you face the security pad directly".

Professor has an device to intercept codes disguised as Alonzo and Terry pen protectors in the lab coat pocket.

Merica Soldier: "What's your business here"!

Alonzo: "If it was your business you'll be out an Fucking job"! Puts his handprint to the security pad, The door unlocks .

Terry pushes his glasses up looks the soldier up and down Scoffs at him shaking his head.

They both walk through the metal detectors with no problem.

Alonzo: "Alright P where we going"?

Professor: "I'm putting your heat seaking visual on now".

Terry: "OH shit...I can see through the walls".

Rico MO: "Can you locate where they're holding them". He says to Professor as they watch the visuals .

Alonzo: "They deep in here man...wait,wait". A guy is walking towards them.

Merica scientist: "So you guys finally took the invite"!

Terry: "Yes... why don't you include us on the particulars on the project...".

Merica scientist: "Oh..certainly "!

Alonzo: "Bars"! He whispers to Terry.

They head to the elevator.

Merica scientist: "Finally get to meet you guys...so you finally decided to join the big leads"! He says with an smile.

Terry:" The big leagues"?

Merica scientist: "Yes it's not as big as the New Fuhrerstadt building but the previous owners of the building didn't know what they had".

Alonzo: "You referring to the black owner's "!

Merica scientist: "No offense but yes , just to have this as an water purifier plant is crazy the energy that flows through here is off the scales "!

Alonzo: "But the natural energy is what purified the soil".

Merica scientist: "Yes brung back the farmers economy blah ,blah,blah but combine all the water towers with all the resources the world can change "!

They walk through the hallways past laboratories but unlike the main water towers in (Alabama) section 10 where they experimented on enhancing and maintaining the organic energy for produce.

Here there experimenting on animals in one lab and what looks to be controlled weather in other lab.

Alonzo and Terry see an controlled thunderstorm being generated.

Alonzo: "How are you guys doing that"?

Merica scientist: "I can take you to Dr.Cox for that".

While following the scientist to the end of the hallway Terry sees an room with an black man looks to be experimented on, he taps Alonzo to look over at the room. The scientist puts his hand to the security pad the door opens ,they enter an hollow oval shape room with an huge metal rod coming from the ground where the water passes through all the way through the roof with a big looking metal ball at the tip of the rod.

Alonzo: "An conductor rod"?

They walk over to a man very indulged into his work recording notes at an control panel.

From the looks of Dr.Cox it's easy to tell he doesn't get out much his long silver knotted hair dry skin partially tells his life story. The scientist introduces Alonzo and Terry to Dr.Cox.

Dr.Cox:" Can I help you"? He continues to work barley recognizing their presence.

Merica scientist: "These are the two scientists that developed the battery"!

Dr.Cox adjuste his glasses to get an goodlook at the two.

Dr.Cox:"Humm they never informed me you where negroes... shouldn't you be in New Fuhrerstadt "! He returns working brushing them off.

Alonzo: "We like to be where the real work is being conducted ".

Dr.Cox lightens up ,from his response the boys can tell he doesn't get enough appreciation from his dedicated work.

Dr.Cox: "Is the that right, I would think new guys like your selves would want all the fancy gadgets working in the big facilities".

Terry: "As long as we got everything we need to work productively we're good"!

Dr.Cox:"Ahh that's refreshing ,you don't know how many times an scientist makes an simple break through then wants to move up to New Fuhrerstadt an month goes by and their right back here ,it's pathetic "! He looks at the other scientist. The scientist avoids eye contact with Dr.Cox as he makes his way out the room.

They follow Dr.Cox back into the hallway.

Dr.Cox: "So you two are the inventors of the solar powered energy coils".

Alonzo: "Coils yes"?

They enter an room to look through the window of an lab experiment.

Dr.Cox: "Oh yes...see we made an replica minture battery discovering your sophisticated coils can maneuver and manipulate condensation for long periods of time ".

Terry : "Oh Yall discovered it after we built it".

They watch as scientists use the miniature battery energy to form an small cloud using water causing an small thunderstorm.

Alonzo: "This isn't the purpose the battery was built for".

Merica scientist: "Yes but it opens up an whole new wave for science... to control"!

Terry: "To control the weather...I think its genius Dr.Cox" Terry saids to keep them thinking their interested in working with them.

Professor: "We're in, we have located where they are holding them keep them busy".

Terry: "So what's the big project we can help with"! He says with an smile.

Dr.Cox is happy to show his work.

Dr.Cox: "Follow me"!

Kemitt mirrors chapter 8.2 "F..k Riker Tower part 2

Rico Mo, Professor, Will, and Speedy watch Alonzo and Terry make their way into the building from a distance.

Professor keeps tabs on them as they enter the building.

Professor: "The building is protected from outside frequencies from infiltration ,we built that years ago".

Speedy: "Maybe that's why they chose this water tower to take over first".

Rico MO: "That's one of the reasons ".

Professor: "I'm downloading the heat seeker vision to you now! He radio's to Alonzo and Terry.

Will :"What are we waiting for?

Professor: "I built an transmitter into there pen holders now with them inside I can get the layout of the building, the heat seeker visual helps see all around...even below...bang that's our entrance"!

Will :"Under the building ...How the hell we do that"!?

Rico Mo: "Can you can swim "!

Will: "Yeah I can swim, they refer to me as the shark "!

Speedy points at the water that runs through the bottom of the tower.

Will: "OH shit...do doggy paddle count".

Professor gets the diving gear suits out the truck.

Will: "You just stay ready, huh professor ". He says sarcastically.

Professor: "Yup I got that way from my Pops and your Uncle"!

Will: "Oh you just gone throw Unc into it, well Unc like to blow shit up too what about that part...let just go and blow shit up". He says putting on the gear. "Are these scuba jump suits...what are we working on cars or fishing in style"!

Rico MO: "You sure are talking a lot ,if you scared you can stay here"!

Will: "I'm not scared I just like running through doors, windows things of that nature "!

Professor: "Alright Speedy warn us if things get crazy out here...let's go"!

They make there way into the water without being seen. An automatic door opens and closes allowing an limited amount of water to pass through every couple minutes.

Professor and Rico Mo had no problem making it through but Will almost got caught by the door with his advanced doggie paddling.

Professor: "We're in keep them busy"! He communicates to Alonzo and Terry.

Rico Mo: "Everything looks solid...we have to climb up".

Professor: "Put your glasses on...now you see".

They can see hidden passageways through the building.

Will:"Ahh...could be an emergency exit we don't want to trip any alarms".

They get to the hidden door, professor hits an scrambler disabling any alarm or cameras that could go off once through the doors.

They enter an long dark hallway using the heat seeking glasses they can see enemy guards making their rounds.

Rico Mo leads them down the intersecting hallway and guard comes walking down, once close Rico Mo snatches the guard slicing his throat.

Professor takes the id badge off the guard, then they proceed down the hallway to see 4 guards standing around talking.

Rico Mo takes his energy gun out.

Rico MO: "When I hit'em we rush'em".

Rico Mo makes sure no one else is coming then zip,zip,zip...hits the 3 guards they rush the guards driving their knives through stomach, chest,throat.

Professor uses the guards badge to open the next door.

They quietly creep through the door coming onto an floor full of holding cells.

Rico Mo leads them into the control room...they sneak up on the guards slicing their throats. Professor goes through the security camera's inside the cells its only an couple people they see being held then finally see Uncle Tone, but no Yolanda or Minty.

Uncle Tone is yelling at the camera...then the visual goes blank.

Will: "What is he doing"?

Professor: "Go, I'll unlock the cells when you get to Tone".

Rico Mo and Will go down the hall through the doors .

Uncle Tone: "Hey I hear you muthafukas either yawl kill me or bring me some got damn toilet paper...and a plunger...Damn...hey"!

Uncle Tone cell door opens, toilet water comes spraying out. Rico Mo and Will peak their heads around the door covering their nose.

Will:"Unc that's disgusting "!

Uncle Tone: "OH shit Nephew, Moses...oh that's what I'm talking bout let's go"!

Will: "You gone take the shirt from around yo face and wash yo hands first"!

Uncle Tone: “My bad nephew this jail life when you a born rebel you always ready for war “! He gets his self together.”Hope you never go through that”.

Will: “Its been less than 24 hours”!

Rico MO: “Where’s Minty, Yolanda “!?

Uncle Tone: “They been taking people upstairs all day but they don’t come back down”.

Rico Mo:”Okay let’s go”!

They run back to Professor waves for him to come on. Professor unlocks the rest of the cells and joins his team.

Will: “Here’s the elevator “.

Rico MO: “No we take the stairs”!

They continue using the guards badge to get through the doors taking out guards along the way. They get to the staircase and head upward.

Kemitt mirrors chapter 8.3 "F..k Riker Tower part 3

(Blow this Bi..h)

Dr.Cox is really enjoying Alonzo and Terry’s company he shows them room after room giving them an true tour of his appointed work.

Terry: “The tour has been nothing but amazing but what’s that room”?

Dr.Cox: “Sorry fellas but I would actually have to get consent from New Fuhrerstadt to bring anybody in that room”.

Alonzo: “What!!! Consent it looks to me like you run the show here “!

Terry: “That’s right when we come to work we’re coming because of you...You the man...you the man”!

Dr.Cox thinks about it.

Dr.Cox: “Okay come on this is my Legacy experiment”!

Dr.Cox goes through the security face scan to open the doors gives them oxygen mask before entering, they walk through an decontamination booth then enter the laboratory room.

Alonzo and Terry see an older black woman hooked up to an machine looking like she being drained of life.

Alonzo: "What exactly are we looking at Doc"?

Dr.Cox: "You are looking at time travel"!

Alonzo: "Time travel come on that's just flabbergasting" he saids as if he's in disbelief.

Dr.Cox: "For centuries time travel has been nothing but myth but there is evidence that we have time travelers among us".

Terry: "So what's the evidence "?

Dr.Cox: "Follow me...I have an inside plug from the higher ups in New Fuhrerstadt after all this is illegal there but here nobody has an clue what's going on".

He shows them an picture from his tablet.

Dr.Cox: "This group was known as the Shadow Bragade in the 1850s...they where known for fighting for human rights and taking out numerous slave masters, but one night after an gun battle some of the members disappeared right here in Pennsylvania, Richard Riker got his name to fame and the Great William Rufus Devane King took an poisoned knife to the gut he died six months later in Cuba after becoming Vice President of the old United states of America.

Alonzo and Terry looks at the picture seeing Aarminta and (Rico) Moses with the whole group they saw from the Vision's.

Alonzo: "So how you get time travel "?

Dr.Cox "Sorry for rambling Devane king is an legend to me (Shows his ring with the two headed serpents with horns symbol)but here's an picture of the two from that picture in 1962 as mug shots, then recently this picture of the woman inside the Edgar Federal building in New Fuhrerstadt ".

Terry: "Come on Doc these photos could be photo shopped these days"!

Dr.Cox: "Oh Yeah"!

He walks over to the next curtain, pulls it back and there's Minty passed out with tubes hooked all on her".

Alonzo and Terry keep their composure.

Dr.Cox: "If we can drain their DNA maybe we can see how they're able to travel all the way through".

Terry: "But this older woman is...dead".

Dr.Cox: "Well sometimes you hit and miss part of science "!

Alarms start to go off guards running around in a panic.

Alonzo: "Well Doc your Legacy is definitely sealed maybe you'll get an building named after you too"!

Alonzo Takes the razor pen out his pocket protector and shoves it into Dr.Cox neck.

Terry chase's the other scientist cutting him in the throat too.

Alonzo starts unhooking Minty, Terry goes to the next bed pulls back the curtain to see it is Yolanda so he began unhooking her also.

The beeping began getting faster.

Terry: "What we do Zo"!?

Alonzo sees an Epi pen on the table he sticks her in the leg...she lefts right up taking a deep breath.

Terry: "Come on baby I can't loose you now"! Terry does the same to Yolanda using an Epidural pen.

Yolanda wakes up...then slaps Terry.

Yolanda :"That's for taking so damn long"! Then gives him an passionate kiss.

Alonzo throws them some clothes, Terry looking at a way to hook the tubes back up to Yolanda.

Alonzo: "What's are you doin"?

Terry: "I'm bout to kill her then wake her up again "!

Minty: "Guards coming hand me that scalpel ".

Alonzo: "Yes mam"!

Minty looks at him suspenseful .

Terry: "Yeah Uncle Rico told us auntie Minty "! He says in the little kid voice that gets on every one nerve.

She looks at them with an smile then back at Alonzo.

Minty: "Don't make me cut him"!

Guards trying to open the security door, then one by one start getting took out. They see Rico Mo looking through the window.

Alonzo and Terry lead the way out the Laboratory.

Yolanda: "How we get out of here"?

Alonzo:" I know "! He goes back and grabs Dr.Cox body drags him to the security face pad puts his face up to the scanner the door opens .

Rico Mo hugs Minty, Uncle Tone hugs Yolanda and Will.

Speedy: "Let's go I see people escaping?... guards out front lock and loaded"!

Will: "Must be the people from the cells"!

Professor: "Ok we have to leave the way we came"!

Speedy: "Make it quick I gotta plan"!

Professor: "Twelve minutes top"!

They head back through the basement an couple guards see them but run the other way.

They make it back to the water. Professor has more underwater oxygen mouth pieces for the girls and Alonzo and Terry.

They make it out from the building to bank of the water stream, They see guards all around.

Professor: "Speedy you up".

Speedy: "Yes sir"!

He jumps into one of the two trucks he already loaded up with explosives.

He mashes the gas the truck comes flying over the hill aimed right for the front.

Professor: "Run Now"!! They run towards the other truck while they have the diversion.

Speedy jumps out to watch the truck mash through the gate running over guards crashing into the front building.

Speedy hits the detonator...BOOM,BOOM, BOOM, the explosion takes out the whole front of the building including the statue of Richard Riker.

Speedy: "Yeah Fuck Richard Riker"!!

Uncle Tone:" I taught that boy well"!

Will: "Now that's the way you blow that Bitch "!

They all meet at the other truck, jump in and peel out. They make it to one of Uncle Tone Condo safe houses in Section 9.

9

"Dajavu"

Once inside the penthouse they finally get a chance to relax and exchange what they learned from the Riker Water Tower.

Terry: "So wait what Uncle Tone do"? Laughing

Will: "He almost sprayed us wit toilet water man mojo and all chief "!

Alonzo: "He was geared up"!?

Uncle Tone: "Hey they brought us there on some bull I wasn't going out without an fight but seeing these two faces man it went from ready to kill and die to ready to kill ...to live that quick, man love yall fo that one"!

Alonzo: "Yola done smacked this fool then kissed'em after he hit her with the epi pen "!

Uncle Tone: "Kiss...at this point I'm not even trippin you gotta worry about her more than me"! They laugh.

Rico MO: "So what yawl see in there"?

Alonzo: "Man first of all the picture Professor was talking bout, they got it along with some old photos of yall with the original Shadow Bragade then some picture of yall like an mug shot or something in the 60s"!

Terry: "Also they've been experimenting on people looking for DNA connected to time jumpers but he also said experiments conducted on people was illegal in New Fuhrerstadt that's one of the reasons they took over that water tower".

Alonzo: "Honestly I think they owned that tower longer than what people know I mean they had an giant energy conductor from the bottom to the top".

Will: "For what"?

Alonzo: "To control the weather using the batteries".

Rico MO:" I knew they wanted the learn the inner workings of that battery... it all makes sense now...the battery has been upgraded to be solar powered which is constant power if you can use that energy to control the weather you can possibly open time portals all over the world but at the same time every one isn't built to jump".

Minty: "So the DNA turned into some kind of elixir could help anyone to jump".

Alonzo: "Damn... but to control the weather could offset natural habitats, to move an hurricane from hitting civilization is one thing but to constantly use energy for personal gain".

Professor: "It could soak up all natural resources killing the earth".

Yolanda: "After taking it over... imagine sending troops anywhere at any given time".

Will: "You right the batteries in the wrong hands is now an weapon "!

Terry: "Rico Tea"!!

Minty: "What's Rico Tea"?

Rico Mo: "Oh god here we go".

Terry: "Rico or Uncle Moses drugged us, I mean we thought he drugged us but it was watermelon weed in the drink it was delicious but what I'm trying to say is Rico Tea turned out to help focus after the jump, we create an fake elixir like with real poison and present it to the powers that be in New Fuhrerstadt ".

Uncle Tone:"The Mojo"!

Alonzo:"Hey it makes since, their extracting not just DNA but melanin ".

Minty: "Because of the Ray's from the light "!

Yolanda: "Okay What "?

Terry: "When you travel through it's like swimming in a sea of light...it's real quick bright and hot".

Rico Mo: "So if you are not chosen by the universe to travel through but make a man made contraption to travel ".

Alonzo: "You wouldn't make it through the light rays "!

Will: "So you would need an elixir or some type of solution to that … like a special suit...speaking of solution's, we can just blow the building up and call it a day"! (Speedy agrees)

Minty: "Look we'll figure this out later the adrenaline rush is officially wind down so I'm going to get some rest".

Yolanda: "Me too"!

Terry: "Yeah me too I'll join you ". He yawns like he's tired.

Uncle Tone: "I'm not that passed it". Puts his hand on Terry shoulder not letting him stand up.

Minty and Yolanda calls it a night and make their way to bed.

Alonzo: "Rico in the vision's you were looking for Linah... as in my great, great grandmother Linah Ross"?

Rico Mo : "Yes and Sophie's your great, great grandmother … our other sister". He says to Terry.

Terry:"Yo that's crazy, so the family house up here was you and Minty looking out for us "!

Rico Mo: "We try, all you had to do was keep the water & lights on". He said with a smile.

Terry:"Touché Uncle Mo Touché "!

Alonzo:" I see why you never whooped this boy ass".

Rico Mo: "Now that's still a test I'm trying to pass"!

Uncle Tone gets off the phone walks back into the conversation.

Uncle Tone:" Hey look everybody rest up we go see the old man tomorrow "!

Terry: "Who's that"?

Uncle Tone: "You find out tomorrow...I'm out"! He heads to his room.

Kemitt mirrors chapter 9 "Dajavu" part 2
"Plan with the Old Man"

[Plan with the Old Man]

Minty and Yolanda wakes everyone up with the smell of breakfast, one by one the fellas come into the kitchen.

They joke around but Uncle Tone reminds them about going to see the old man this afternoon.

They all got dressed and headed to the garage .

Alonzo: "Uncle Tone your taste in cars is impeccable "! Referring to Uncle Tone car collection.

Uncle Tone: "Look at you and yo vocabulary but thank you, take your pick"!

Everybody jumps in the drop top muscle cars.

Uncle Tone: "OH no bullet proof trucks today...okay cool we home, I haven't drove my favorite in a while"! Uncovers his hard drop top 1,000 horsepower luxury sport Cadillac.

Professor: "I'm taking the truck I stay ready"! Speedy jumps in driver seat riding with Professor.

Uncle Tone: "Mo, Minty let's ride".

They pull out the garage riding through the streets of Section 9. The sunny day has main street full of people from the parade a few blocks away, as they hit the corners people smile and wave.

Uncle Tone pulls over in front of the cigar shop on the corner.

Alonzo, Terry and the others follow Rico, Minty and Uncle Tone lead as they greet the older guys out front with much respect, the older gentlemen show much respect back.

They head inside greeting everyone while heading to the back of the cigar lounge. An older gentleman sees them coming his way he raises his glass in salute and happy to see them.

Rico Mo: "Ben I see you still in fighting shape"!

Ben O'Davis : "At least my mind is (laughing)...Minty it's been months (gives her hug) ...Tone I see you still enjoying those cars".

Uncle Tone: "Yes sir...This my Nephew Will and niece Yolanda "Ben greets them.

Ben O'Davis:"Alonzo and Terry it's good seeing you again ".

Alonzo: "Its good seeing you too"!? He saids happily and wondering the importance of this guy getting so much respect.

Ben O'Davis :"Sit down, pull up a chair youngins...so what's new "!

Minty : "Were going to take down the dictatorship of New Merica "!

Ben O'Davis :"Well you always aimed high (sips his drink) ...do you know who you're going after".

Nobody responds to the question.

Ben O'Davis: "Exactly you haven't seen who's really pulling the strings they've been smart on that part, when you look behind that wall you think of an entity as identity not just one face as representation"!

Uncle Tone: "But that's an play out our book ".

Ben O'davis: "Isn't it always"!

Rico MO: "So what do you suggest "?

Ben O'Davis : "Controlling… the weather...Hum"!

Terry: "How does he know that"?

Ben O'Davis: "You gotta blow that mother fucker up (Laughing)no, no.. (looks at Professor) Do you believe this way is preventing a major war"?

Professor:" I do"!

Ben O'davis :"...Okay then...whatever you need"!

A woman walks in dressed beautifully head to toe".

Minty : "Mrs.O'Davis hi"!

Mrs. O'Davis : Comes in greeting everyone "I got the files baby ".

Ben O'Davis : "You got the floor babe lay it out"!

Mrs. O'Davis :" I'm sure you all know about the shipment that was intercepted headed to our Caribbean sections containing solar batteries".

Terry: Raises his hand "Um No Mrs. O'Davis all of us wasn't aware but it all makes sense now thank you Mrs. Davis "!

Mrs. O'Davis : "Terry shut up"!

Everybody tries not to laugh.

Terry: "How does she know me"!?

Mrs. O'davis:" The batteries has been tracked down, everything is here". Hands Professor an package with all the information.

Minty :"Thank you "! Minty glances at the picture of her old comrade Louis on the wall, then they all proceed to leave from the meeting.

Ben O'Davis : "Benjamin"! He said as everyone else steps out to the street.

Professor stops in his tracks but doesn't turn around.

Mrs.O'Davis : "The business part is over you show some respect"!

Professor returns back to the table. The look on his face shows he's slightly annoyed.

Ben O'Davis : "How are you doing"?

Professor shows little emotion.

Mrs.O'Davis : "I'll leave you two to talk". Gives Professor a kiss on the cheek.

Professor:" I love you too mom".

Mrs.O'Davis leaves the room.

Ben O'Davis: "So is there a reason you only communicate with your mom and not me"!

Professor: "She overstands what I'm doing "!

Ben O'Davis :"I know I was hesitant about you, becoming an mercenary for the movement I just wanted you to enjoy the life we fought for you...raise an family but I come to realize you're doing what comes naturally, fighting runs through our veins...I'm proud of you son "!

Professor:"Thank you"!

Ben O'Davis:"My son an member of S.B. you'll forever be legend in your own right "!

Ben O'Davis gives his son a hug as they start to head out the store.

Ben O'Davis : "I have something for you...I was going to leave it for you once I've left to glory but I think you deserve it now". He pulls out an small box hands it to Professor, Professor opens the box.

Professor: "Your Shadow Bragade ring and necklace "!?

Ben O'Davis : "It's your time son and you earned it on your own"!

Professor: "Its funny, Minty still hates that name but yet embodies it the most"!

Ben O'Davis :"Well they learned from your..."

Professor:" Grandpappa Louis.." They both smile proudly looking at Louis picture on the wall.

Ben O'Davis fixes his son Professor collar in the doorway of the store looking him in the eye.

Ben O'Davis :"Not too many people can say they have walked with real guardians we have been blessed son"!

Professor: "Yes sir"!

They join the others outside the store the older gentlemen sitting out front of the store where finishing up their funny war stories.

Alonzo:"Yo P. you ready Mo wants to go grab some things from the house".

Professor :"I'm ready". He gives his mother a kiss and hug then jumps in the truck with Speedy".

Mrs. O'Davis :"Oh yeah don't worry about Ronnie Johnson"!

Ben and Mrs.O'Davis smile as they pull off, the older gentlemen sitting outside salutes as they sip their drink.

They get back to rolling through the streets full of people on every block.

Alonzo: "What's going on today "?

Will: "The Independence parade"!

Alonzo and Terry observed in amazement.

They arrive at Rico Mo house they wait outside enjoying the weather while he runs in. Uncle Tone sparks a joint while leaning on the car and is suddenly joined by everyone else.

Uncle Tone: "Well got damn, should have stayed in the car".

Alonzo: "So who's the old man besides P's pops".

Uncle Tone: "He's Chief Mansa"!

Terry: "Man what"?

Uncle Tone: "Mansa, sultan, king, emperor".

Alonzo :"Like Mansa Musa"?

Terry: "What...he runs the Sections out an cigar shop"?

Uncle Tone: "Where you expecting the big house built by slaves".

Will: "Everything he needs is on that block besides our government doesn't have a face".

Alonzo: "Who's secretary of defense the men out front"! He says sarcastically.

Uncle Tone just gives him an look like yeah.

Minty: "Just put it like this...something happens to him then people like us are on yo ass"!

Alonzo: "Well put".

Inside Rico Mo pulls up his floorboards unlocking his hidden safe he pulls out his Hatchet master blade, knife, Minty vest, and a few other items".

He comes out with a duffle bag puts it in the trunk.

Rico Mo: "Alright let's go "!

They head back to the Penthouse. Once inside Rico takes the items out the duffle bag. Carefully places an laced tied container on the table.

Terry:"Aey you ain't bout to pull no fancy draws out are you"?

Yolanda: "You can't help yourself can you".

Rico Mo unwraps the cover pulls out his hatchet master blade and the sharpest knife they ever seen.

Will: "Is this the original blade"?

Alonzo: "Got damn look how sharp the blade is".

Professor: "The craftsmanship "!

Minty puts on her vest that holds her daggers.

Terry: "Yeah auntie you can still fit that thang"!

Minty: "Shut up...but thank you ". She laughs.

Uncle Tone:"Ya'll not the only one wit weapon's now"! Grabs his remote.

Tables get to flipping and turning laced with weapons, the Electric fireplace turned around for more weapons than a hidden wall door opens. A blue lit room appears, all you see is artillery from a 6-inch ice picks to 100 round shotgun machine guns .

They walk into the room amazed at the weapons then start picking out weapons for themselves.

Minty: "Alright let's get to the game plan "!

10

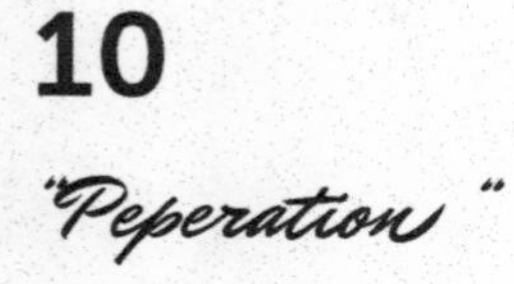

Terry walks into the kitchen the next morning to see Rico Mo cooking up, while looking over plans.

Terry:"Yo Unc, what's up ".

Rico Mo: "This Unc..Uncle thing is an little too soon ain't it"?

Terry:" To soon… man you like174 years old what you think I don't mean it"!

Rico Mo gives Terry a look basically saying no.

Terry :"I know I say the first thing that's on my mind its rude hell sometimes wrong... in timing but I see what I see, before all this I saw something in you...it wasn't bad I just felt it wasn't the whole truth... dig what I sayin".

Rico Mo: "How was I supposed to explain all this to you".

Terry :"I can dig it… fo sho but you know right before I came to join Zo and go back to school I had an dream from all the bad things I was into...one night I was caught slippin some dudes from the other side popped out on me ...I took off through an cut then hit the alley I remember it being dark.. cold ...they cut me off had me surrounded I made my peace with god or death or something I had an long two second blink confirming my understanding of this might be it, when my eyes opened the guys were severely injured all I heard was weak breathing from the dudes on the ground I caught an glimpse of shadows disappearing into the night I didn't know what just happened... just took off running".

Rico Mo looks on.

Terry: "The next morning I saw the news, the day after Zo and Will was at my door telling me to pack my stuff...as I spent time with Zo I felt like I had more of an purpose in life, like for once someone had my back on the positive side".

Rico Mo: "Shadow ninjas huh".

Terry: "Yeah...(laughs) thanks"!

Rico Mo: "You ready for this...nephew".

Terry: Laughs "I'm more ready than it could ever be"!

Ms. Ross Minty comes walking in.

Ms. Ross (Minty):"Should those knives be out like that with you two alone"?

Terry: "Auntie you crazy"!

Rico Mo and Terry laughs.

Minty: "What kind of kumbaya shit is this"!?

Terry: "Whatever do you mean auntie".

Minty :"I'll slap the shit out of you boy"! She says jokingly.

Alonzo: "What's happinin...what the hell you fixin up Unc"!

Rico Mo goes to his duffle bag throws a bag on the counter.

Alonzo: "My smart watch…is this (smells it) H.T.U watermelon weed"!

Minty: "Is that what yall call it"!

Terry: "This from when we jumped...damn I forgot about that"! Smells the bag.

Alonzo: "Yeah man which one of yawl changed me that night cuz Rico I love you, but I don't need yo man paws touching my man parts"!

Terry: "Minty must of changed me because I smelled like baby powder when I woke up"! He said smiling, Alonzo calculated what Terry just said and responded with a frown on his face. Rico Mo got back to the subject.

Rico MO:" I made some tea...Rico Tea for everybody it gives us focus and endurance".

Minty: "And what's this potion you got going on here"?

Rico MO: "This is rare mushrooms brings anything you fear to life...what you call it"?

Terry: "OH the elixir ".

Alonzo: "You actually listen to this crazy fool"?

Rico MO: "This can be drunken, but Professor is going make these into gas bombs too ".

Minty: "Like tear gas ".

Rico MO: "Yes but anybody who digest this here if not in control of their own fears are liable to turn on each other...you can't breathe this in ".

Alonzo: "Damn that's crazy how did you learn this"?

Rico Mo:" It's all in the soil, you respect the soil with seed it will grow anything you desire"!

Terry: "That's the kind of talk that gets me on yo ass"!

Uncle Tone, Will, Professor and Yolanda comes walking into the penthouse.

Uncle Tone: "Alright man we got everything yawl asked fo".

Rico Mo: "Good, good P. You up I got everything ready".

Professor: "Alright we are taking all this to the lab yall leave us alone for a while"!

Professor and Will head to the lab.

Alonzo: "Damn Uncle Tone you like the black batman, labs and trap doors and shit"!

Terry: "In every crib tho you ballin for real "!

Uncle Tone: "Hey all due to Moe and Minty without them it probably wouldn't be possible ".

Minty: "Alright I'll see the rest of yall in the rec room ".

Terry: "Rec room, I'm trying to fire this up"!

Minty: "In 20 mins let's go"!

Rico Mo:"Aey she ain't playin"!

While Professor and Will work in the lab everyone else goes to the rec room not knowing Minty and Rico was going to be given out hand to hand combat lessons.

Rico Mo finally got a little payback with hard sharp body shots on Terry from all the shit talking but overall, they were impressed how good Alonzo and Terry hands where.

They continued the sparring session's and work outs, then hit the in house gun range. The training and preparation remained while waiting for the time to go.

It's been a few weeks everyone was enjoying sitting around having dinner conversations.

Alonzo: "Okay wait Nazi Germany actually made it to Canada and built that wall"?

Terry: "So how did it become New Merica without war"?

Professor: "That Nazi regime didn't last too long at least in plain sight. My theory is that this, Circle Order organization was working the whole time. Parts of Canada was already secretly controlled by this group...it was easy to use propaganda to move majority whites to this so-called Northern utopia to finance their secret agendas…especially when the media said let the niggers, spics, kiks, and wop goombahs, have the wasteland".

Uncle Tone: "Don't forget they sabotaged every alliance relationship we had for trading, after a while the people who could pass or accepted as white folk they were gone".

Will : "I believe the goal was let us build, bankrupt us then grab the land back".

Rico MO: "Like Haiti".

Alonzo: "Like Tulsa ".

Yolanda: "Our people fought together but once all of us where together, together we just steadily kept thriving the purified water system through the Sections just took it to the next level of independence ".

Will: "And we got an army that can match there's "!

An yellow light starts to blink, Uncle Tone opens the hidden door to the artillery room and grabs the phone from out the emergency glass.

Alonzo: "This nigga got an bat phone "?

Terry: "Hell yeah it got an cord an everythang"!

Uncle Tone hands the phone to Professor. They can hear Professor trying to whisper .

Professor: "I'm fine okay...love you too"! (Hangs up)

He turns to see everybody looking, then they all start laughing.

Yolanda: "What's the word"!?

Uncle Tone: "OH we move tomorrow night... that was his mamma"! Laughing

Professor gives them the middle finger.

Professor: "Time to mount up"!

11

"Dajavu to Mayhem "

[Dajavu To Mayhem]

The next day everyone mounted up heads down to the garage ready to go.

Yolanda:"Uhh... where not taking these cars are, we"?

Uncle Tone: "Boogie come on now...(Hits the walkie talkie radio) Speedy"!

The secret security door opens three new trucks enter the garage.

Speedy Hops out the truck.

Speedy: "You rang muthfaka "!

Rico MO: "The Old man never fails "!

Will: "Damn new trucks"!

Professor: "Not just new trucks, stealth mode can't be detected or tracked by any system... Vanablack paint absorbs light making it damn near invisible at night"!

Speedy: "Not to mention all proof, bullet proof, bomb proof, Electric... fence...field proof"!

Professor: "That's right, a bomb can land directly under the truck it won't budge"!

Alonzo: "Well does it turn to a fifty-foot robot"!

Terry: "Does it spit out 2,000 dollars "!

Looking at Will, (Laughs)Will just shakes his head.

Professor: "Instead of the glasses through these contact lens I can see what you see"! He haves them take out one each out the case and ear bud for communication.

Rico Mo: "Alright let's go"!

They all hop into the trucks taking an senic routed highway to New Merica ".

Will: "Okay Speedy what else can this truck do"?

Speedy: “We can lock together for speed without using the magnetic railing “!

Will: “So we’re able to respond faster in case of attack “.

Speedy: “Right on but watch this...P ready to engage”?

Professor: “Ready”! He responds on the radio.

The trucks like before linked but this time the rear truck cockpit opens up when connected.

Will looks behind him to see Uncle Tone Mo and Minty.

Terry: “This thang done turned to an whole train “!

Alonzo : “Oh this live”!

Speedy : “That’s the old Man”!

They speed through backways and upgraded tunnels making it to New Fuhrerstadt undetected.

Professor comes over the radio telling everyone to turn there tv screens on to New Fuhrerstadt news.

Alonzo, Terry, Will, and Yolanda move to the rear truck to join Mo, Minty & Uncle Tone.

Alonzo: “Well, Well, Well I see who got the executive suite”!

Minty: “Boy come sit down “.

Moses: Leaning back in his chair “Hey Minty who’em I “...Moses crosses his leg right to left has an drink in his hand “Let me tell you an story “!

Minty: Laughs “Oh that’s Jim all the way he hated Devane but he enjoyed that train almost more than telling stories... look how far we’ve come”!

Moses: “Yeah Jim ,The boys ,Warren and Louis would’ve loved this.. Madville”!

Minty: “Keith”...she reminisces thinking what could of been if things played out differently.

They watch the news as an protest is going on through the streets about taxes being raised in New Merica.

Will:” There making there move to get people to start moving back”.

Minty: “People moving back isn’t the problem they’re going to use those people for their own personal gain for power”.

New Fuhrerstadt News Caster:” The people are taking to the street in protest of increase taxes in New Fuhrerstadt while at the same time the “Global Spectrum” Announced the news of United Regions becoming the most powerful independent Country this fast in history. From technology all the way down to old fashioned farming their economy is reminiscent of the Ancient Kemet lands of Africa".

New Fuhrerstadt News Caster# 2:"Are you saying Ancient Egypt were black people "? He disagrees.

New Fuhrerstadt News Caster 1:"If you want to be truthful...yes...its time to start telling truth, the people of Africa are the original people (News caster#2 interrupts, disagreeing as security raids the news studio)okay well people go get this book...hey, hey get back"!

Suddenly there's scuffling an even what sounded like an gun shot before The broadcast cuts off and the technical difficulties sign comes across.

Terry: "Damn did they just spill dude on air"!?

Alonzo: "That's what it sounds like to me"!

Will: "Yeah they not playin ".

They make their way up into the hills looking over into the city. They hop out the trucks to peep out the scenery.

Will: "That's the building "? Referring to the pyramid like building.

Yolanda: "How do we get through, its people everywhere "?

Minty: "Yeah nothing goes according to plan "!

Professor takes out the drone and flies it over the building.

Professor: "Security is tight "!

Rico MO: "What 10,20"?

Professor:" I count 25 outside so maybe 20 to 25 inside ".

Rico MO: "Either we're on their radar or there prepared for an riot"!

Alonzo: "It might be an long night but they not gone riot".

Professor has his radio on loud the news resumes after the technical difficulties.

Sports reporter:" And the New Feuherstadlt Eagles has won the Cup"!!! (Crowd going crazy in the background)

Terry: "Is that hockey"?

Professor: "Yeah".

Alonzo: "OH they gone riot tonight "!

Professor "Okay I see a side entry, an company truck is going in now...and one coming out"!

Uncle Tone: “Keep us on track with that truck...come on”! He jumps in the truck with Alonzo and Terry.

Uncle Tone races down the hill.

Professor: “Make an right at the next street”.

Terry: “Its to many people out here”!

Uncle Tone: “Shit I’m the one drivin the truck they better move”!

Professor: “Left now “!

Uncle Tone makes a swift turn into an tight alley running through garbage cans scraping the fence.

Professor: “He’s going to be right on you coming out the alleyway”!

Uncle Tone presses the gas even more, Alonzo and Terry gear up. Uncle Tone slides out the alley right in front of the unmarked hauling truck making the truck come to a slamming stop.

Alonzo and Terry quickly move on the driver and passenger before they had time to think, as Uncle Tone aims the semi-automatic shotgun right at the driver.

Terry and Alonzo put them in back of the unmarked truck, Alonzo jumps in the driver seat and they peel out.

They make their way back to the lookout spot. They open up the back-trailer door with caution, the two men are in the back scared for their life.

They get the men out the truck.

Rico MO: “What are you hauling “?

Driver:” I don’t know “!

Will: “Tell us what you moving before we put the cut on you jive turkeys”! Pullin out his switch blade.

Alonzo and Terry: “OH my god”.

Terry: “Its like nobody notices this shit” he whispers to Alonzo. Referring to Will’s 1970’s slang.

Alonzo: “Nothin nobody saids nothing bout it”!

Driver: “We Know Nothing “!

Minty and Yolanda steps up!

All the fellas step back mumbling at the same time “Ooh you done fucked up now we tried to be cool “!

Minty: “One more time...what’s in the truck”!

Driver: “We Don’t Kn...”

Yolanda strikes the driver twice with her pistol. He stumbles back into the truck holding his nose then spits out blood and a tooth.

Driver: “You broke my nose you black bi...”

Yolanda lands one more blow knocking the man out.

Uncle Tone gives Terry an smile. Minty and Yolanda turns towards the passenger.

Professor and Speedy is in the truck throws back the cover.

Professor:” Whatever It is its sealed tight”.

There’re 3 big metal boxes, locked inside a cage.

Passenger: “We don’t know, all we do is pick up and drop off that’s it”!

Yolanda starts to raise her fist.

Passenger: “But, we been transporting to this same disclosed location for months now”!

Professor goes inside the cab and transfers all the GPS data onto his tablet.

The passenger is breathing hard sweating.

Uncle Tone comes back over from his truck.

Uncle Tone: “Here man you done good, cool off an bit” . He hands the man the elixir drink. The man gulps it down then Minty knocks him out.

Uncle Tone: “Damn Minty I wanted to see if it worked “!

Minty: “We’re wasting time let’s move”!

Alonzo: “The two dudes that can get us in are knocked out”.

Minty: “Well wake ‘em up and clean his face”.

Moses: “Professor get the uniforms ready”!

They woke the driver and the passenger up and cleaned them off. They explained to the workers that there going back to the loading docks of the building .

Speedy and Professor will hang back to watch every move.

Everyone put on maintenance workers uniforms and jumped in back of the truck.

Professor: “Remember we’re every step of the way so don’t get special “! The driver agreed.

They head right to the building to the side gate; the driver slides his key card and continues through the gate.

He pulls into the second security check.

Security guard: “Hey Marv” he says while looking down at his tablet “.

Driver: “Hey Stan they got you working late tonight”!

Security guard: “Yeah man...hey your back kinda early aren’t you “?

Driver: “Yeah Dave here forgot his key cards in his locker”! He tries to give the security guard signals somethings wrong. The security guard finally looks up.

Security guard: “Goddamn Marv either you got in another bar fight or you got another woman bigger than you...again...Jesus Christ, hiet Hitler Marv go ahead”!

Driver: “Ha,ha you with the jokes”!

He drives inside to the loading docks; the driver knows he actually has to sneak them in now because he’ll look like he’s in on it if he gets caught. He sees the coast is clear and lets them out.

Alonzo: Looks at the passenger “He alright “?

The passenger is sitting very still with his eyes wide opened, his lips moving very fast in silence.

Driver: “He’s fine”!

Passenger:” I... have...to...go...to...bathroom”.

Driver: “No we have to go...fuck my nose bleeding...alright come on Dave”!

The driver opens up the passenger door, the passenger takes off running full speed into the locker room.

They all look at the passenger crazy.

Terry: “Come on Zo”!

Professor: “Ok you have to split up there’s a boiler room on the east side the other on the North part of the building.

Rico MO: “You guys take the east Minty, Uncle Tone and I take the north”.

Alonzo, Terry Yolanda and Will make their way to the east boiler room.

Will picks the lock to get in they begin pumping the ventilation system with the gas.

Professor: “Remember to take the Rico tea chews to repeal the gas but it only lasts a couple hours so be mined full”!

They exit the boiler room continuing to follow the path to the others on the Northside of the building.

Making their way down the hall passing employees a guard informed them the building is closing in 20mins.

Then the guard noticed there continuing to walk in the opposite direction of the exit, he walks back towards them.

Security guard: "The exit is this way"! He says getting suspicious.

Alonzo: "We have to fix the water heater on the North side of the building"!

Security guard: "Hum...it takes four niggers to fix a water heater I don't know why they keep lettin you people through the borders". Then gets on his radio.

Yolanda: "Damn that was just blatant".

Half the Lights in the hallway are starting to blink".

Terry: "You see it's a lot of work we have to do"!

Security guard radio: "Where having an little scrumish in the west hall if your close please respond "!

Security guard: "Okay you can...go"!

The passenger truck driver runs up out of nowhere with nothing but tighty whiteys on and takes a chunk out the security guards' neck.

Everyone: "What the fuck"!

The look in his eyes where gone his pupil's all black.

Terry: "Is that the gas doing this"!?

Terry: "He had elixir drink remember "!

The passenger truck driver drops the security guards body and starts walking towards them...then lunges at them.

They all light him up at the same time the shotgun bullets close range rips the man apart.

Once they're shooting stopped, they heard more shooting throughout the building.

Alonzo: "Minty are yall okay "!

Minty taking a knife out a guards face.

Minty: "Oh where fine but the gas spread a little faster than we thought it would".

Uncle Tone: "We have to get the goose, don't let the goose fly with the golden egg"! He shouts over the communication

Terry: "What the hell"?

Moses: "P if he keeps it up, cut his feed"!

Professor: "My finger is on the button...and sorry about the gas we didn't have time for proper test"!

Uncle Tone:" I can hear yall"! He said while shooting running up guards.

Professor:" I set an randavu spot your only 3 minutes apart from each other"!

Rico MO: "Okay let's go"!

They all continue to fight guards as they head towards the meeting spot.

Alonzo, Terry, Yolanda and Will fight their way through the hallway to see Minty, MO, and Uncle Tone at the meeting spot in the center lobby of the building.

They form an circle facing the guards in battle position.

Terry: "They done turned zombies "!

Alonzo: "Zombies are dead and not real".

Moses: "Your right there operating off of fear...Minty give them something to fear"!

Minty: "What I can't just get inside their head"!

Rico MO: "There state of mind is beyond human form you have the energy and bond right here.. show them their worst nightmare in front of them"! He said as they continue shooting to hold off the guards that's surrounding them.

Minty goes into meditation...repeating the 9's prayer the guards keep coming then slowly start to back away.

They're human nightmare beliefs come to true vision the guards see an circle of African warrior's standing tall.

Egyptian monumental protectors come to life standing in blue flame.

The guards start to turn on each other rather than fight the extraordinary beings.

Not only does the guards see the inner souls of Minty and the crew . The Shadow Bragade crew can feel the energy themselves.

Will:" I thought P said 50 guards tops"!

Moses: "Minus the others, that's about right"!

Will: "Then what about them"!

They look up and there's guards standing firm in the middle of the huge spiral staircase with gas mask on.

Uncle Tone:"Got Damn ETF soldiers "!

Moses takes out his hatchet master blade coming out his matinence suit, Minty drops her uniform as well into her all black with vest full of blades and pistols on the side.

The rest of the crew follow suite coming out of the uniform into their battle gear.

In the standoff they can hear total chaos throughout the building as well as the guards fighting each other right next to them.

Professor: "The guards are protecting the top floor...the goose is through those doors...go get'em"!

Uncle Tone: "OH it's cool when he say it". Looking at Mo and Minty"!

The ETF soldiers start to march forward down the steps with their stun sticks.

Moses an Minty lead the charge up the steps.

Once the battle started the guards on the ground stop fighting each other and once again start attacking them.

Alonzo, Terry, Will unloaded their weapons onto the out of mind guards.

The guards up front can't handle the pressure lead by Moses and Minty as they slash, cut and throw guards off the staircase, into the walls, through closed doors.

They continue to move forward to the second level a whole new wave of heavy armored guards are coming from everywhere.

Alonzo: "Get down"! He yells to Minty, Moses, and Uncle Tone as the make up the front.

They take cover as Alonzo, Terry, Yolanda and Will unload their semi-automatic shotgun 100 rounds each RIP through the armor of the guards.

As soon as the gun fire ends Minty, Moses, Uncle Tone gets to work charging the remaining guards fast and swiftly taking them out.

Uncle Tone: "That's for my Pent house muthafukas "! He yells after throwing a guard off the huge staircase.

Making their way to the next floor up, Moses throws a guard through a blacked-out glass door they enter the room to see three masked men in kung fu stance.

The three masked men charges them... Minty quickly throws her daggers hitting one in the face, Uncle Tone shoots the other in midair,

Moses catches the last masked ninja like man leaping kick raises the man all the way up... then slams the man's body to the ground three times fast full force, breaking the man's back.

Alonzo walking past the broken back man.

Alonzo: "Got damn nigga can ya whoo, whoo, whoo "!

Terry: Comes right behind him singing"Whoo,whooo, whooo".

Uncle Tone kicks in the next door ready for the runner up, everyone enters the room ready to rumble only to see a huge empty room.

Alonzo: "What the hell...Is that it"!

Everyone looks puzzled, the room is plain no pictures, no furniture nothing.

Will: "We fought to get to a dead end"!?

Yolanda: "This can't be right ". She feels the walls looking for an opening.

Minty: "What happened P. We're at the room"?

Professor:" I don't know, that should be the room". He tries to figure it out on his computer.

Terry:" I know exactly what happened...we won got damn it...you see what happens when you fuck wit the Bragade we take out all you cockaroachs "! He yells in his best Scarface voice.

The kicked in door suddenly closed off by a big metal door, the other three walls starts to open.

Professor: "There's another room behind the wall"!

Rico Mo: "Yeah we got that"!

The whole room is now revealed, and the Shadow Bragade find their selves surrounded by soldiers.

Professor: "I'm reading a room full of people "!

Minty :"P. Unless you have an plan stop being two seconds too late"!

12

"Who Ya Wit" (Night of the Long knives)

The Shadow Bragade is surrounded by soldiers with nowhere to go.

Soldier: "Drop your weapons "!

Uncle Tone: "Drop yours first"!

Soldier: "We have you surrounded "!

Minty: "Looks bout even to me"!

Everybody trigger fingers are getting itchy, the position in this scenario doesn't look good.

The huge glass window turns to footage showing the Shadow Bragade causing havoc from the time they snuck out the company truck into the building.

A man enters the room from the side rear of the room clapping his hands "Wow, y'all haven't lost an step...I always hoped we would meet back up... didn't know it would be like this".

Uncle Tone: "Edward is that yo treason ass"? (Edward Robinson along with Ronnie Johnson been informants for New America government for years)

The soldiers start to part as the man walks through. "Eddie...Robinson, oh no his value ran out for us just like Ronnie ran out for y'all...I guess there on vacation together sort of speak"!

The man reveals his self once he makes it through the crowd.

Minty: "No"! She starts to tear up but frozen where she stands.

Moses takes a hard look but doesn't show emotion.

Terry: "Damn bruh you black how you over there"!

Alonzo: "Yo timing is terrible "!

Henry: "What's wrong Mo, no hugs for your little brother "!

Moses is confused he carried the burden of letting his little brother die spent years manipulating time trying to get back to that exact period to undo that scenario but now Henry is here no longer an teenager, he's grown and on the opposing side.

Henry: "Well"!?

Moses: "You been here this whole time"!

Henry: "You mean after you two left me for dead"!

Minty: "We didn't leave you Henry "!

Henry: "And that's what I kept telling myself for years ..my brother and sister would never leave me, there not just my own blood there bigger than life itself...the mighty Moses and Minty mercenary injustice fighters, Shadow Bragade"! (mocking the name)

Moses: "We spent years trying to get back to you"! He says intensely but firm.

Henry: "Is that right...well it pleases me to hear that...in your defense after years of studying and mastering Quantum time continuum I've learned that split second landed us in the same time but in two different places... to my offense I've learned your recent activities has been destroying everything I've built here"!

Minty: "You built?...putting your own people back into oppression is your idea"!?

Pat Buchanan :"Not entirely"! A man says as he turns around in a chair behind the desk.

Terry: "Damn the colonel remix done made it through the time lapse"!

Alonzo: "He was in the chair the whole time "?

Alonzo and Terry: "Pizazz"!

Pat Buchanan: "We provided the tools Henry needed...He has given us inventions and technology that for years put us light years ahead of any country".

Alonzo: "He couldn't make the battery tho".

Henry: "So you turned scientist into fighters ...you two still amazes me"!

Terry: "Naw it's the other way around fighters turned scientist patna"!

Minty: "They're aren't just any scientist Henry...there your nephews"!

Henry: Laughs in disbelief "So these are your kids?...Ya'll done took, take your kids to work day to far "?

Uncle Tone: "Now that was funny"!

Yolanda: "The untimely humor does explain a lot "! She whispers to Will, they both look at Alonzo and Terry.

Minty: "Sophie, Linah"!

Moses: "Your great, great nephew's, we have a family a big family ".

Henry:" This can't be true"?

Moses: "Name me a time we ever lied to you"!

Henry: Henry analyzes Alonzo and Terry "How could this be"?

Minty : "Time"!

Henry mind is shuffling, for years...decades he's been on his own, the two scientist they've been trying to lure this whole time was his own family.

He always felt as the outcast for wanting to invent out of this world things but yet his own nephews just revolutionized the world… something he couldn't do.

Minty: "Can't you see it... evolution but the mind comes from the same seed"!

Henry's quietly taking it all in.

Henry: "Then join me we can be great together all of us"!

Moses and Minty gives him a puzzling look, like he doesn't understand that he's on the wrong side.

Pat Buchanan: "The irony of family values...My great, great Uncle James Buchanan stood with the tremendous Rufus Devane king ".

Alonzo: "Yeah they stood together all right ".

Pat Buchanan: "After Devane's death my uncle continued Devane legacy co creating The Circle Order (shows his necklace of the two headed dragon in a circle) we're taught personal value in life...how long does one value last, is it short term, is it long term...in history the greatest most powerful Nations have all fallen in due time but if an person combined the Powerful with forever then there value isn't measured in time...they'll rule the world forever...and live to see it".

Professor has snuck into the building planting more gas bombs along with c4 bombs.

Professor: "I'm in the building, you'll hear my signal in ten minutes, get to the randevu spot"!

Moses: "Your a follower of Devane and I'm guessing you know who we are"!

Pat Buchanan:" I work with Henry My Uncle and Devane has actually spoken highly of you, I'm giving you a chance to be on the right side of history "!

Alonzo: "So we build you the battery in return we live in a dictatorship paradise "!

Pat Buchanan: "An since of humor in a scientist...hard to come by...so what do you say"!

There's a pause in the room all eyes are on Alonzo and Terry.

Terry:" Come work for you"?

Alonzo: "How much we talking"?

Pat Buchanan: "Anything you ever dreamed of at your fingertips Endless wealth for all of you"!

Terry:" Now that's an offer"!

Alonzo: "Its an offer...I wanta use the time machine and get all the Luke dancers from 92"!

Terry: "OH that's good now you talkin national treasures...but ahh I guess we have agreed to say"!

Alonzo, Terry, Will : "Fuck naw"!

Terry: "Puss ass boi"!

Alonzo: "Ol Chump ass nigga"!

Will: "You ol jive chicken tender foot ass bitch"!

Everybody in the room looks down at Buchanan's long Brown buckled pleather shoes.

Pat Buchanan: "Kill'em, kill'em all"!

Henry jumps in front of Moses and Minty.

Henry: "Wait you can't do this; it's got to be another way"!

Pat Buchanan: "This is what happens when the value is none and void "! He pulls out a gun and shoots Minty in the chest.

Minty going down was like slow motion choosing to die rather than selling out was an easy choice in this situation but to see Minty go first was shocking to all of them.

Before Minty could hit the floor, Henry had a knife in the side of Pat Buchanan head.

Explosions suddenly start going off inside the building rocking the whole room.

In a blink of an eye Henry has taken out a solider took his weapon and start shooting the other soldiers.

The heavy vibration from the explosion was the diversion the Shadow Bragade needed to go to work.

Minty pops up next to Henry as the Mayhem in the room proceeds. She takes out two guards.

Minty: "Stay dangerous "!

The numbers on the guard's side are subtracting fast. Explosions are going off the building is on fire.

Uncle Tone:" I can smell the gas let's get out of here"!

Henry hits the button to open the metal door closed behind them.

They fight their way back out the room, Uncle Tone throws an extra gas smoke grenade into the room before Henry locks the door.

The guards bang on the door, then start to fight each other.

Yolanda : "Where's Professor "? She says as they're running back into the crazy guards' direction, going down the staircase as the building is in flames.

BOOM a truck slams right through the heavy glass into the building running over guards and trampling everything else in it's way. Professor and Speedy shoot crazy guards attacking the truck.

Minty : "Are rides here"! She saids to Henry.

Henry: "Same shit different dimension"!

They make their way inside the truck, Speedy pills out the building "!

Professor grabs the detonator "3,2,1"

BOOM,BOOM,BOOM the building goes up as they escape through the streets.

13

"Deadjavu "

They get back to the lookout spot and to the other truck. Everyone Hop's out the truck.

Professor:" I know it was a lot going on back there but who you bring with you"? He asks Moses and Minty as he attends to Minty wound taking her bullet proof vest off, Minty calls Henry over.

Minty :"Professor this is our brother Henry, Henry Professor". She says with a smile.

Professor: "Brother...nice to meet you...how this happen"?

Moses: "Its a long short story but he had our back in the end ". Mo is still skeptical where Henry loyalty lies with.

Will: "So what now we got more than we came for"?

Yolanda: "Yeah P we took the man behind it all out"!

Moses: "Did we"? Looking at Henry.

Minty: "What...spit it out"?

Moses: "The man talked like Devane and Buchanan was still alive...they spoke highly of you".

Alonzo: "He did say that".

They all rally around to hear what Henry had to say.

Henry: "Hum.. we broke a lot of ground with our experiments while I was up there".

Professor :"Like pinpointing time lapse "!

Henry:"I see you been watching us too but yes that's one part of the program the other part was weather changing and ...well spirit channeling"!

Minty: "Spirts, that can be dangerous"?

Henry: “First of all The Circle Order is nothing to play with they’re an global secret society and because of the book Devane wrote before his death he’s seen as the martyr of the group”.

Alonzo: “So you part of a cult”?

Henry: “No I’m not but I guess I did buy into what they were selling me, the power to oversee all projects and get the credit I deserve “.

Terry: “Part of an cult mufuka”!

Will: “So what about the batteries”!

Henry: “We where able to duplicate the battery to an certain extent”.

Moses looks to the sky, notices the weather changing.

Moses: “So where exactly is this place”?

Henry:” I couldn’t tell you where at, we get picked up in a blacked-out van blind folded, but I have been inside I know my way around a little”.

Professor: “OH I got directions, right here”!

Alonzo: “What we waitin fo we didn’t come this far to not finish the job”!

Everyone agrees.

Minty: “Okay, Henry you can give us the rundown on the way...let’s ride”!

They load up into the trucks headed to The Circle Order secret headquarters.

Will: “Henry how the jive junkie drivers got the skinny on the pad and you don’t”?

Henry: “Come again “?

Terry: “OH god nobody says nothing...he’s saying how the wacked out workers get the directions and you... the executive coon master don’t have this information”?

Henry: “Some of the workers, or drivers are actually members and others come up missing every couple months and I’m nobody’s coon”!! Henry saids with aggression.

Everybody in the truck mumbles under their breath: “Well I mean you was kind of on some bullsh...”.

Uncle Tone: “Well who fried the tomato on yo lettuce chief “!

Will and Yolanda: “For real doe, exactly”!

Terry: “What”!?

Alonzo:”That’s why nobody says nothing It makes perfect sense now”. (Uncle Tone talks this way)

Minty: “Don’t mind them, you’re with family now”!

Terry: “That’s right Uncle Henry you wit fam now”!

Henry: “Uncle “! He looks at Minty with a smile.

Moses:” I thought Devane was writing his memoirs about his life”?

Henry: “He did but after his death Buchanan made the book exclusive becoming...an cult like bible”!

They continue discussing what Henry knows about the Circle Order, then finally start to come up on the headquarters “!

Terry:” I thought we were going to a building... Man what kind of haunted mansion shit is this “!?

Alonzo: “It better not be some giant turtle dragon inside this bitch”!

Going up to the house its only one long driveway. They see clouds slowly starting to rotate above and around the mansion.

Yolanda: “What the hell are we walking into”?

Terry: “Got damn house of Frankenstein “.

Speedy finds a spot to hide the trucks in the dark. They see big bolts of lightning.

Professor: “OH I got something for that”!

He gives everyone special suits to wear”.

Will: “Are these bullet proof too”?

Professor: “It’s bullet proof not as heavy as our vest so be careful, but its light in weight, waterproof, increase of strength and in this case shock proof “.

Uncle Tone: “You know you could’ve been gave us these”!

Yolanda: “Let me guess they haven’t been tested”!

Minty:” I just got shot close range...it’s been tested “!

Rico MO: “Good enough for me”!

Professor suits up his self.

Speedy: “Alright I’m here if ya’ll need me”! He saids sarcastically, really wanting to go.

Professor: “We need you to keep the communications clear I’m sure it’s a lot of dead spots in there”!

Speedy: “You got it P.”!

They start their way Crossing the road into the fields. The huge mansion sits on the bank of a huge lake surrounded by nothing but land and forest in the distance.

The wind gets stronger as they get closer to the house. Henry leads them into a side door his key card works.

They enter a huge room with antiques and old paintings all around.

A loud ZOOM sound and vibration goes through the house.

Henry : "This way"!

They stop at the corner of the hallway to see two men dressed in uniform as Circle Order members with hoods on.

Henry waves everyone to follow him as he follows the men, the two men go inside an study room.

By time Henry and everyone enters the study room the men are gone.

Yolanda:" Where they go"?

Moses: "Another hidden wall, Tone where would you put the wall"?

Zoom again shaking the house.

Minty: "What are they doing here Henry "?

Henry:" I haven't been here in months and only in the labs not up here"!

Alonzo: "So we gotta go down "?

Zoom!! The lights go in and out.

Will: "Look at this"!

They walk over to the window Will looking out of. The window overlooks the courtyard in the middle surrounded by the house.

Will: "This not just a mansion it's a whole damn castle in form of a circle"!

Alonzo: "They have a conductor rod just like the water tower"!

Minty:" The base of it must be underground".

Yolanda: "Yeah but look"!

Men start to crowd inside the courtyard with hoods on gathering around the conductor rod chanting.

Alonzo: "There holding an ritual"!?

Yolanda: "Who they praying to is the question "!

Uncle Tone : "Found it "! Uncle Tone found a book on the shelf that's an lever to the secret door.

Henry: "The batteries are down here".

They look down the slightly lit dark cave staircase. They creep down the stairs into a futuristic lab, with different lab stations throughout the floor.

Henry: "This way"!

Minty: "Wait they can see us".

Henry: "Its reverse mirrors, scientist can't see out, that's how they watch them".

As they walk down the aisle, they see people getting worked on inside the labs.

Professor: "What's going on here"?

Henry: "I'm not sure, it's not my station ".

Minty: "If it's like the water tower they're extracting DNA "!

Moses: "Let's keep moving "!

Henry: "Extracting DNA...oh no they finished the project..let's go quickly "!

They head down another pathway to an elevator.

Moses: "No elevators, we'll take the stairs "!

Henry: "The place is like a maze; we don't have time to figure out which way to go"!

Moses hesitates but steps onto the elevator.

Will: "This thing is old can it hold all of us"?

Henry: "We bout to find out"!

Henry closes the door, presses the button and start going down.

Alonzo: "So what's wit the anti-elevator thing"?

Minty: "Because the greating on the other end usually isn't so friendly ".

Uncle Tone: "You ever shot fish inside a sardine can"!

Alonzo: "Yeah we have..target practice".

Minty, MO, Uncle Tone:"Exactly "!

Terry: "Uh oh I understood him, its rubbing off Zo ".

They come to an stop Henry lifts the old elevator door, to see no one.

Alonzo: "Everyone must be at the ritual".

A change of different color light reflects off the walls coming from around the corner.

They creep around the corner to see an lit up globe like structure floating, glowing with energy... (Zooom), an power surge is channeled from the floating energy structure to the huge conductor rod base that sits right above it... the vibration this close is much stronger.

Professor: "Its like a pulse.. a heartbeat ".

Henry:" Pearl"! He looks in amazement.

Terry: "You named it"?

Henry: "Pearl...the world of worlds"!

Scientist Porsche: "Its beautiful isn't it"! He says coming out from the darkness.

Everybody ups their weapons in Porsche's direction.

Scientists Porsche: "Yes we finally did it, thanks to your theory Henry "! He says calmly.

Henry: "Mr. Ferdinand, but how... it's impossible without the battery "!?

Scientists Porsche: "Your right we couldn't figure out that god forsaken battery but anything...is...possible "! He gives an sinister chuckle.

They follow the eyes of Porsche to see two men working in the area.

Zooom the bright flicker of light illuminates the room they see half dead versions of Alonzo and Terry in lab coats working on the batteries behind an glass enclosure.

Alonzo and Terry: "Man what the fuck"!?

Scientists Porsche: "Since you couldn't deliver, we did the next best thing, oh don't worry about their looks we just needed their brains, you bringing them here now is a little too late...that is.. what you were doing...right Henry"!?

Speedy: "Hey can yall hear me...this storm is gettin crazy out here"! The communication is staticky.

Alonzo: "You know bootleg products ,get you bootleg results ". Referring to the clones.

Zoom another flicker of light shows the room full of armed soldiers.

Scientists Porsche: "It looks like you took a side Henry...Kill'em all"!

Terry: "Wait...just wait a got damn minute now...okay ya'll cloned us ,I'm flattered an disgusted at the same time but you taking all those people DNA tryna jump worlds...when we have the last piece to your puzzle right here"!

Terry signals Moses to show him the elixir. Rico Mo pulls it out shows him the crystal bottle with the drink inside.

Scientists Porsche: "And it supposed to do what"? He saids not amused.

Alonzo: "Obviously the melanin you all have won't protect you going through an Quantum time continuum because of the Ray's of lights, excuse my French without this you'll come out the other end lookin like a bowl of shit"!

Scientists Porsche: "Does it look like I play games "! He yells in frustration.

Alonzo:" Why you think you or anybody couldn't find us...because we weren't here, we traveled back to this world".

Terry: "You might have the fakes in the room but we the real deal holmes so what you want a believe "!

Porsche smells the elixir rubs his finger along the rim then tastes it, then puts the cap back on.

Porsche: "And you will make this for me"!

Alonzo: "Let my people go we'll whip a whole ton of it"!

Porsche looks into the eyes of Alonzo and Terry, stares at everyone else assessing the proposal. He looks into the eyes of Minty, then Mo.

Zoom the lighting hits near their feet as Porsche stands in front of Minty and Moses. Porsche sees the energy is gravitating towards them.

Porsche: "Benjerman Henry Greene...better yet...Henry Ross (Henry surprised he knows his real name)...No it can't be (Speaking German) Take their weapons now"!

The soldiers take only the weapons they see.

Porsche sees the Hatchet master blade and the daggers from Mo and Minty. He admires their weapon's.

Scientists Porsche: "The legend is true, you are here to the date...take them to the courtyard "!

The cult soldiers guide them towards the courtyard, going up through the passageways, into the hallways there's old oil paintings of prominent Circle order members from the 1800s up till now. Devane's picture is huge centered amongst the others, Buchanan's under his.

They're led by the soldiers into the courtyard in the middle of the ritual, the cult crowd part as Mr. Porsche leads them through backed by the soldiers. Three open caskets are in the middle near the metal conductor rod.

Terry: "It's a got damn sausage fest, where the women at"?

The leader heading the ritual looks down from the steps recognize the interruption of the ceremony holds his hand up...the cult followers stop chanting.

Cult Leader: “Who is this you bring to our circle of worship “!

Scientist Porsche: “I’m bringing you the completion of the prophecy”!

Cult Leader: “Completion by what scripture “!

Scientists Porsche: “Exert 20:22 Our Devane king will be brought back by the same spirits that sealed his fate”.

The leader comes down the steps to get a better look at them.

Cult Leader: “Sacrifices”? He says only revealing his beady red eyes under his hoody.

Scientists Porsche: “Better than that my lord, they’re world jumpers...these are the spirts that took Lord Devane king “! He has the soldiers push Moses and Minty to the front.

The occult members gasped in amazement.

Cult leader: “Ahh I see it”! Looking into their eyes.

He shows the cult leader the weapons, the hatchet blade, the daggers.

The cult leader goes back up the stairs, pulls back his hood, revealing his goat head the cult members do the same wearing different type of animal heads.

Yolanda: “These people wacked out they mind”!

The Cult leader goes back to leading the ritual, the wind starts to get stronger the lighting gets stronger. The castle has conductor ball points on 5 points of the roof, the bolt of lightning starts to combine with the energy surges coming from the pearl transferred by the conducted rod.

Professor: “They’re seeing things we can’t”!

Moses: “Minty you have to use your gifts”!

The three metal open caskets start to rattle charged by the energy and lighting. Minty tries to concentrate when her and Mo gets hit with the energy lighting. The energy lighting reflecting off of them back to the caskets.

Alonzo: “Well we know the shock proof test failed”.

Dust begins to rise from the caskets, forming into human like form from Skelton bone.

Scientists Porsche: “Its working “! He saids to himself teary eyed, pupils are black from the elixir.

Alonzo: “Go to the darkest of the dark “!

Moses: “Deep as the Abyss “!

Terry: “Face your fears to get back to light”!

They reiterate what Minty had told them before. Minty continues to meditate, the energy is draining her and Moses, the dark energy is slowly taking part of them into this wall of energy that's forming.

The three separate fragments of dust become James Buchanan, Devane king and Stephen Ducan.

Uncle Tone: "Face your fears "He whispers to Professor . Showing he has his gas bomb.

Will catches Uncle Tone gesture to go for their weapon's, while everyone's distracted.

Cult leader: "Lord Devane we call upon you to lead us to the New World Order"!

The half spirt half man looks around with his glowing eyes as he floats above.

Devane looks at the cult leader, Devane extends his hand to him. The cult leader reaches out in praise. Devane grabs his hand then drains the energy from the cult leaders' body till the leader was no more than a rubbery skin suit.

Will: "Eww"!

Devane adds a little more power to himself.

The way the cult members are responding Devane's communicating something only they can hear.

The members drop to their knees praising their god. The energy is steady pulling from Minty and Moses.

Devane motions along with Buchanan and Stephen Ducan, the cult members raise to their feet, start aggressively close in on them.

Uncle Tone: "Shadow Bragade mudafukas "! Signals Professor they both throw the fear gas grenades.

Uncle Tone throws his in the crowd, while Professor throws his in the air, the bombs explode... The mist of the bombs falls over the crowd ...Will and Yolanda attack the solders to get their guns back from the soldiers.

The wind carries the mist of gas across the whole courtyard, everyone gets in gulfed with the gas.

Alonzo and Terry see Yolanda and Will tussle with the guards they immediately jump in. They get a hold of their weapons an proceed into a gun battle with the soldiers.

The cult members start to scatter all over the courtyard some running back inside.

The fear gas starts to kick in, the cult members with the animal heads start to look like real vicious creatures.

Everything is alive now they can see the castle was filled with satanic souls crawling on the walls coming in through the portal.

The energy lighting striking the ground all around the castle anything that was buried on those lands is coming up out the ground.

Dark light is coming out of Devane eyes and mouth as he's gaining power Minty starts to levitate toward Devane, Buchanan and Ducan. As they continue to take Minty and Moses energy.

Moses: "Dig Minty, Dig deep"! He holds her arm to keep her from going into the hands of Devane while she's in deep meditation, but he's getting pulled in his self.

All type of old souls coming through the portal Moses recognize a couple he put down himself. Then he sees Richard Riker and his goons come through the portal.

Henry: "No it can't be"! Looking at Richard.

The rest of the Shadow Bragade continue fighting, Terry and Will start to fight each other.

Will:"Ahey man it's me, it's me fool"!

Terry: "OH my bad bra, yo head was growing like a clown balloon "!

Will: "Control your fears...you scared of clowns"!?

Terry: Screams then shoots "Ahh its was bear behind you "!

A man with a bear head lies dead on the ground with a knife in his hand.

Will: "Thanks"!

The spirit of Buchanan, Devane, Ducan are becoming more powerful and more human like by the minute.

The wind along with the light rain is getting stronger.

Moses: "Minty wake up, I can't hang on much longer"!

Henry grabs on to Moses:" I got you"!

Minty reaching deep she tries to find her old comrades Warren Garrison, Jim Brown, Owen, Watson, Louis...she finds Jacques and Victoria boat as its sinking on fire.

Minty: "VICTORIA, VICTORIA, JACQUES "!! She yells for them as she walks on top of the bloody ocean dark waters, she finds them together hanging on to a piece of the boat as cannons from the enemy ship continue to fire off.

Victoria :"Ahh you came"! She says so calmly.

Minty: "We need your help...I need your help"!

Jacques: "It looks like we need you"!

Minty disappears from the courtyard.

Moses and Henry: "Minty, Araminta...Aarmintatataaaa"!?

Henry pulls Moses down falling back once Minty disappears.

The Shadow Bragade crew looks on in hurt and confusion... Buchanan, Devane and Ducan are strong enough to move around, while old soldiers continue to come through the portal.

Yolanda: "Its too many of them" as she fires shots".

Alonzo: "We gotta destroy the pearl"! He yells .

Terry: "We can't leave them out here"!

A Bright golden light appears in the middle of the portal. The light blinds everything in the courtyard.

Araminta appears floating in the wind, in golden armor the lighting and rain surround her. The gold light shines through her eyes and mouth.

Yolanda: "Minty "!

Buchanan, Devane and Ducan shoots their dark light at Aarminta but it doesn't faze her. She returns fire shooting her golden light from her palm knocking Buchanan, Devane and Ducan back .

Minty: "This is what happens when you take what's not given...You want to play in my world...then let's play"!! Her voictress voice is in spirt mode she is one with the gods.

Terry: "OH she big mad"!

The guards try shooting at her it doesn't work.

Her golden light turns dark purple along with her armor, the energy lighting is going crazy she puts her light on her love ones giving them the light that represents their souls as warrior's.

Minty(Aarminta):"Now it's time to face your fears...YOU SOW, SO SHALL YOU REAP "!!

Spirits start to jump out the portal, the original Shadow Bragade, Whesile Madville, Keith the whole New Orleans crew and the ex slaves Alabama tribe, then Jacques and Victoria in Haitian warrior armor.

Jim Brown: "Moses, the lion, like old times Aey ". Picks up Moses hatchet master blade.

Moses looks in amazement but can't help to give a grin.

Warren Garrison: "Henry my boy well you a man now (takes a deep breath) I can't smell shit, but I feel good...let's go"!

The runaway ex slave Minty connected with as a child has his traditional warrior gear on yells "Shujaa"!

Everyone charges then clashes, the courtyard has turned into a full-blown battlefield.

14

"You Sow, So Shall You Reap"

Moses: "We got this handled, go close the portal "! He yells to Alonzo.

Alonzo gets Professor, Terry, Will and Yolanda.

They enter back into the castle.

Will: "You remember the way"?

Alonzo: "Yeah, down ".

Yolanda: "Yo Professor what's up with the communication"? As they make their way through the hallways.

Professor: "Don't know can't get through to Speedy...the frequency gotta be thrown off.

Will: "Yeah nothings working in here". Tries his heat seeking glasses once more.

The hallways all look the same as they creep through cautiously.

Terry: "Hey Professor I can't lie I want to bust you in back of the head but I'm keeping it together "!

Professor: "What I scare you"!?

Terry :"No yo fade fucked up I'll be doing you a favor "!

Alonzo: "Yeah after this we gone hunt down your barber and clapped his ass"!

Professor:" I think the gas just got yall high"!

Will: "Shush".

They hear fighting in the next room. Will kicks in the door, two cult members scuffling freeze backing up frighten to death.

In the two cult members eyes they see upset warrior gods coming for revenge.

Yolanda hits them with the custom long nose 357.

Alonzo: "What the hell does a squirrel and a moose got to do wit anything dark"?

Professor: "This whole castle is like a library".

Looking at the wall full of books. Professor looks at a mantle with a clear box outlined in 24k gold.

Zooom the room shakes.

Will: "Maybe there's a hidden door in here too".

Professor takes the book out the case a whole bookshelf wall opens to another secret passage way .

Will: Professor you did it"!

It's a crowd of cult members with animal heads rushing the room.

Yolanda: "OR maybe they did it"!

They clash with cult members. Alonzo and Terry unload on the crowd with automatic machine shotgun, killing the cult members.

Terry: "Damn I'm out".

Alonzo: "Me too"!

Yolanda tosses Terry her big hunting knife, Alonzo takes the machete off the wall.

Before they can get down the secret passageway a group of men attack from the hallway rushing into the room. Yolanda and Will take out the first four but they continuously keep coming...all of a sudden the cult members go down by Electric shock.

A man with an gas mask walks in pointing his weapon, the guys are surprised, then the man takes off the mask.

Will: "Speedy "!?

Professor: "You supposed to be doing communication ...from the truck"!

Speedy: "Your Welcome...if you can't tell the frequency reception isn't good around here is like it has a block or something "!

Yolanda: "Why are you here"!

Speedy :"I was planting our just in case getaway "! Shows his detonator.

Will: "How we supposed to getaway when our getaway driver is in here"!

Speedy: "Obviously yall haven't seen the front yard, full of dead creatures, I got trapped in but I stay ready". Opens his backpack full of gadgets and ammunition.

Terry: "My Man"! Everyone got to reload their weapon's.

Alonzo: "I'm keeping this machete tho"!

They move forward into the passageway.

They come into a room with bench pupils and an round stage with the Circle Order symbol in the middle.

Terry: "This a church "?

Will: "That's what it looks like"!

They walk on the stage.

Terry: "They got a camera, a microphone".

Alonzo:" I betchu they music suck"!

Terry grabs the mic starts singing "Rollin down the highway wit the devil all within meee"!

Alonzo: "Yo P. you right he just high now".

Yolanda: "And stupid "!

Sounds of creaking doors, startles them they quietly take cover ready for whatever.

Creepy half dead deformed creatures charge the stage.

They began shooting quickly learning these creatures are elusive climbing the walls and ceilings very fast.

Alonzo: "Got damn can we get some light in here"! He saids while shooting.

Professor: "Speedy hold the trigger before releasing "!

Speedy: "Hold the trigger "? He holds the trigger for a couple more seconds than releases.

The energy gun not only lights up the room but takes out the whole left side killing a bunch of the creatures.

Speedy: "OH shit that got some kick"!

Alonzo: "Will...don't...move"! Looking real concern.

Now everybody faces turns real serious. Will feels a sudden brush of coldness, then a growl next to his face.

Alonzo: "Kill it Speedy"!

Speedy hesitates to pull the trigger he doesn't want to hit Will by mistake.

Yolanda positions herself for a clean shot then pow,pow, she takes the shot, once the creature was blown backwards Speedy hits it with the energy gun killing the creature.

Will shoots it three more times making sure it's dead.

Will: "What the hell are these things"?

Alonzo and Terry unloaded on the rest of the creatures, Speedy cleaned them up with the energy gun.

Guey type dark slime from the demonic creatures cover the walls ceiling and floor.

Alonzo: "First flying spirits now evil people creatures what else"!

Professor: "It look like they perform sacrifices in here too"! Looking at the marble stone flat with restraints on all four corners and dried up blood.

Terry: "What's behind these curtains"! He pulls the rope the floor opens up dropping everyone down an slippery slope landing them in a pile of dead body parts.

Terry :"AEY"! He shouts down the open floor shoot.

Alonzo: "Man fuck this house"!

Terry: "My bad"!

They look around to see a giant room with a huge furnace.

Yolanda: "Get yo ass down here"!

Terry: "I'ma find the stairs"!

Everybody: "Now "!

Terry taken back by the response: "Alright damn" He slides down the shoot landing in the dead body parts... He comes up spitting.

Will: "This must be where people disappear every couple months"?

Professor looks at the writing and drawing on the wall.

Professor: "It shows the hate for the black race, keep them down from reaching their eternal selves of becoming who they truly are the original people, the first architects, astronomers, Doctors, Emperors. Keep the Jews and Muslims fighting against their own brothers over gods we will remain The Superior... dismantle their truth is our Will for supremacy ".

Alonzo: "That's what they say in their fake hieroglyphics "!

Yolanda: "These people are really Waco's ".

ZOOM the vibration once again rocks the castle.

Will:" Dig we gotta keep movin "!

They enter the next room full of jail cells and torture chambers.

Alonzo: "These folks got a dungeon "!

Speedy: "At least no prisoners"! As they look at the empty cells.

Speedy: "OH the furnace ".

Alonzo peeps through the window of the sliding doors .

Alonzo: "Alright there it is"!

Speedy: "There what is "? He peaks in the door window to see Pearl, looks in amazement.

They sneak through the doors, making their way to the control room. Four Armed soldiers patrol the room .

Alonzo: "Stay in the shadows"!

They creep along the walls...Alonzo takes out a guard quietly with the machete.

They split up to cover both sides of the control room Laboratory.

The three soldiers are in a conversation with the Scientists Porsche. They see an opportunity to move on them, as they run up on them Speedy hits the three soldiers with the energy gun, they swiftly surrounded them taking out the guards.

Scientists Porsche: "Wait, wait to be fair because of me your still alive "! His back against the control panel as he slides his hand across a red button.

Professor: "Close the portal "!

Scientists Porsche: "Whatever you want...let me see here"! Fakes working on the control panel.

Terry Looks at the blinking red button then sees backup coming into the control room.

Terry:"You fucked up Doc"! Blows Porsche face off close range with the automatic shotgun machine gun.

Alonzo starts working on the control panel himself.

Will:" You know what you doing"?

Alonzo: "Computer science was my first love"!

Terry: "Yeah Zo been crackin codes since a git"!

Will: "Ya work on that we'll hold back... the clones"?!

The Scientist Porsche had released the half dead clones from the labs.

Alonzo, Terry and Professor work the panel as Will, Yolanda and Speedy fight the half dead clones.

Alonzo: "Okay there running negative c ++ language".

Terry: "Got damn amateurs no wonder they couldn't crack the battery code"!

Professor: "Okay I'm in the energy scripts logs".

Alonzo: "Okay let's shutdown down on a simultaneous countdown ".

Terry: "Shutdown to quickly can cause an atomic bomb effect we have to set it at least thirty minutes and that's pushing it"!

Professor: "Confirm thirty"!

Alonzo and Terry: "Thirty confirmed "!

They each pull down the levers to their left at the same time.

Computer: "Thirty minutes to shutdown "!

Terry: "Alright let's get back to the other's...Henry we done here let's go...why yo shirt off "?

Henry grabs Terry arm knocks his gun out his hand slams him against the control panel.

Terry: "What the hell wrong wit you"!

Terry punches Henry then kicks him in the stomach to escape his grip. Henry stumbles back.

Terry:"Zo"!!

Alonzo turns from shooting the last of the attacking clones to helping Terry. Alonzo doesn't want to shoot Henry, so he hits Henry in back of the head with his gun.

Henry doesn't budge he grabs Alonzo and tosses him across the room.

Henry turns back towards Terry, Speedy hits Henry with the energy gun, Henry falls to one knee but fights it off getting back up Henry takes off running towards Speedy when Boom closed lined by...

Terry: "Henry "!??

Henry picks up the clone throws him into a glass booth headfirst. The clone regains his footing his facial structure is cut to the bone.

Henry: "Get back"! Henry's gets in fighting stands.

Clone Henry charges Henry, Henry charges with an flying knee connecting with Clone Henry's chin, clone Henry slides backwards across the ground but quickly jumps to his feet rushes Henry, Henry throws an uppercut, clone Henry side steps it grabbing Henry suplexes him on to the ground.

Alonzo:"Ohhh...get up Unc "!

Henry: "OH you wanta suplex huh"!

Henry gets up, clone Henry throws a left,right, ,body,body Henry blocks the combo, the clone jumps for kick, Henry slides under Clone Henry leaps catches him mid air super suplexes the clone breaking his back and neck.

Everyone :"DAMN"!!

Henry : Takes a breath "We gotta get to the courtyard".

15

"You Sow .So Shall You Reap " part. 2 (Aarminta Reign Supreme)

The courtyard is up in smoke the cult members are all dead, but the portal keeps evil creatures coming through.

(Aarminta)Minty is still in full inner soul spirit mode she uses her hand, blasting the evil creatures with her light beam, while still fighting Buchanan, Devane and Ducan.

The original Shadow Bragade is in an endless battle.

Alonzo, Terry, Will, Yolanda, Henry and Speedy are making their way back to the courtyard.

Alonzo:" So you didn't know you were being cloned"?

Henry: "No, but it confirms a lot thoughts for me"?

Alonzo: "But to clone you they have to get some form of DNA correct ".

Henry: "Yes...So what's your question"?

Alonzo: "Forget about it, this night confirmed a lot for me too"!

Alonzo thinks about the conversations he had with Minty and Moses at different times, he realizes what they meant about being here is where he and Terry was destined to be to realize who they truly are.

The new Shadow Bragade joins the battle in the courtyard.

Devane sees he can't defeat Aarminta she's too strong.

So Devane pulls the energy from Buchanan and Ducan killing them to absorb their power.

Rufus Devane grows with power and in size.

Speedy: "Is that..Minty"? He sees Minty and Devane fighting in the sky.

Alonzo: "Yeah and that's Professor great grandfather and those are demon creatures"!

Speedy: “And yawl want me in the car fuck that”! Starts shooting the energy gun but realizes the energy from the gun gets sucked up into the huge wall of energy so he pulls out a knife and goes to work.

Devane powers has massively increased glowing an firey Hades (Greek god of the underworld) green but with the power he's also more vulnerable becoming more whole none the less he displays his powers against Aarminta knocking her to the ground, she fires back knocking him backwards but not phasing him. He raises to the sky taking more energy from his followers gaining more power.

Rufus Devane:”DIE!!! ONE BY ONE I WILL TAKE YOU..DO OR DIE... DIE”!!

His voice vibrates the soil as well as the castle.

The dead cult members are risen as demonic demons becoming half animal half demon.

Terry: “OH hell naw...Speedy”!

Speedy tosses Terry and Alonzo 100 round drums.

One of the demons jump onto Speedy he stops it from biting him by wedging his blade between him and the drowling mouth of a demonic rabbit.

All of an sudden the demonic rabbit man has an knife through the back of its head out his eyeball...Speedy sees Louis standing there. Louis gives a nodd then gets back to the fight.

Aarminta is throwing everything she has at Devane but he's not being phased.

Aarminta and Devane lights up the sky while fighting.

Jim Brown: “Minty needs more power “!

Warren Garrison: “How”?

Victoria:”Aarminta use my energy “!

Aarminta hears her but ignores her wishes. She continues to fight Devane but he's too strong now nothings phasing him.

Devane is starting to dominate the fight against Aarminta armor is beginning to chip away, she's struggling to keep him at bay and Devane knows it.

Devane let's off a powerful green firestorm onto Aarminta knocking her into the ground like an falling meteor her crash to ground earthquakes the ground creating a huge hole .

She gathers herself quickly and skyrockets herself back into the sky throws everything she has her rapid-fire purple light hits Devane to the point he couldn't defend himself she releases a bomb like light beam against Devane...

BOOM!! The rays light up the sky like fireworks Devane has disappeared in purple sky even with his size being so massive it's like he disappeared out the sky.

Devane looks to be defeated nothing but royal purple smoke fills the atmosphere. Some start to cheer in Devane's defeat.

The energy from the conductors on the roof of the castle is suddenly all directed towards one spot in the sky fire green beam cuts through the purple clouds of smoke like an laser hitting the ground killing a lot of the spirit tribal warrior's .

Then the beam knocks Aarminta out the sky into to side of the castle wall.

A demonic laughter comes from Devane as he glides through the smoke-filled sky.

Jacques :" Minty no matter what you do you can't change what already happened...we're here for you and Moses if you want to avenge us, then use us"!

Victoria: "Its Okay you're not taking we're giving...It is your time... AARMINTA REIGN SUPREME"!!!

The ground battle is starting to take a turn in the demonic creature's favor.

Aarminta looks at her brother's, then Jacques and Victoria she sheds a tear, then absorbs Victoria and Jacques energy.

Aarminta's powers grows her glowing crown turns blue flame, she sprouts wings with the mystic colors of red, gold, and green.

Speedy hears beeping coming from his backpack he checks to see what it is.

Speedy: "OH shit "The detonator auto timer has been pushed.

Speedy fights his way to Moses.

Speedy: "We gotta get out of here everything's about to blow"! He saids to Moses.

Devane uses his dark light against Aarminta she doesn't budge, he throws everything he has at her...nothing.

Explosions start to go off inside the castle.

Devane realizes Aarminta has become more powerful, so he looks down from the sky, he spots Moses and dives toward him.

He rather take out someone she loves before facing defeat by her...again!

Moses cuts the head off Richard Riker turns around from fighting to see Devane flying right towards him.

Right before Devane can reach out and touch him Aarminta is there in front of Moses.

She throws him against the wall with a flick of the wrist, quickly picks him up goes up above the castle then throws him to the ground.

Devane feels every bit of the pain that's being wrecked upon him. Aarminta picks him up throws him against the castle then like an tru lioness roars golden fire into his face, peeling his skin back.

Araminta Reign Supreme:" Even in afterlife you been busy, oh you been busy, stealing people scratch, stabbing them in the back and we don't think it fair"!

She makes and spear that glows red, gold, green then shoves it in his chest shooting red, gold, green light into his body.

William Rufus Devane King screams as his powers are draining from his body.

The power to the portal is shutting down the portal is starting to close.

Demons still jumping out the portal but are landing as globbs of mush when they land.

Henry: "We have to get to the rooftop "!

Explosions start to burst around them and beneath them through the ground.

Aarminta throws Devane around plenty more times its clear Devane is defeated.

Devane throws his hardest barrage of dark light at Aarminta Reign...but she glides right through continuing forward towards him.

Aarminta grabs him by the throat slams him one last time in the middle of the courtyard.

The demons are defeated the portal is closed.

The whole Shadow Bragade meets in the middle of the courtyard looking at a defeated Devane king.

Moses hands Jim Brown his hatchet master blade.

Jim Brown: "When we found you, you where nothing now you a hard nothing is there room for unrest...now you will Die"!

He drives his knife into his chest.

Dark light spills out (Devane screams) the light dems out as his body crumbles.

The ground shakes from explosions.

William Garrison: "Thank you "! He saids to the new Shadow Bragade and especially to Aarminta and Moses!

Louis: "Shakes his great grandson hand (Professor)...Now go"!

Jim Brown: "Its been fun"!

Araminta Reign puts her golden light on her friends as their physical spirits fade to particles blowing into the wind.

The castle is in flames trapping them in the courtyard.

Henry: "Minty get us to the rooftop "!

Aarminta still in spirit mode uses her powers to get everyone to the rooftop. She lands on to the rooftop herself joining the others.

The powers slowly fade she's clearly exhausted. Henry guides them to the rear edge of the castle.

Henry: "We have to jump"!

Alonzo: "Jump...that's like 50 feet"!

Moses: "It looks like we don't have a choice "!

The middle of the castle explodes.

Terry: "Got damn Speedy"!

Speedy: "Hey all of that ain't me"!

Then a big explosion comes from underground causing the metal rod conductor to lean.

Will: "If we don't jump this thing gonna fall on us"!

Terry: "I'm not jumping I'm making my way to the truck"!

Boom, Boom explosions caused the rod to start falling their way.

Terry runs past everyone jumping off the building into the lake.

Minty: "That's your nephew "! She says to Moses tired but smiling.

Everyone leaps off the rooftop into the huge lake.

The building fully explodes the energy from Pearl world of worlds exploded like an atomic bomb.

16

"When the dust clears"

Terry wakes up, wearing gray shirt, gray pants. He notices other cotts in the same room are empty.

Terry: "What the fu.."?

Hears men shouting "Lets go, time to work let's go"! A man Hollers in the doorway.

He steps out the cabin, finds himself in line with other black men.

Covered wagons with horses are lined up the men are piled onto the wagons overseen by white men with guns.

Terry :"Hell Naw"! He turns around looking to escape.

An rifle ends up in his face.

Guard overseers: "On the wagon boy"!

Terry eases onto the wagon ,he looks for Alonzo or anybody he recognizes.

Terry:" Man this is not home, I'm really a slave ". He thinks to himself.

Terry spends the long afternoon, in the middle of nowhere chopping Concrete blocks ankle chained with an heavy metal ball.

Terry over hears two white men talking...

Overseer#1:"So he's the fugitive "?

Overseer #2:"Yup don't know where he came from, but the nigger had crazy weapons on him...I don't think he's from here look at the mark's on his arm"!

Terry looks at his tattoos.

Overseer #1:"He's gotta be from around here somewhere ".

Overseer #2:"No I mean here ..as in this planet"!

Overseer #1:"Aw man I told you about that damn picture tube you been watching too much its warping your young brain...now gone on get the water bucket I'm boiling out here"!

The whispers continued not just among the overseers but the other chained workers in the field.

After the long hours late into the evening they get back to the compound for supper. People try to speak to him but he just stays quiet to himself...Food trays are filled with one spoon full of slop then passed down to the other men until everyone has an tray.

Guard: "Maybe he a Russian spy who else makes that type of weaponry"?

Guard#2:"A nigger spy from Russia that'll be the day that's like saying one day we'll have an Russian for a President...he'll over my shotgun and my dead body"! The guard said as he lights up a cigarette.

Terry analyzes the mashed-up slop covered with flies. He walks outside the food hall pissed about the food, pissed about being there.

Terry:"Aey man what the fuck is this "! He says to the guard.

Guard overseer: "Shut the fuck up nigger... eat or don't eat"! He responds to Terry with his discolored teeth chewing tobacco.

Terry: "Okay... ". Bang Terry hits him with the tray in the face then commits to whooping on the guard .

The crowd of black men cheer on.

Other guards race out shooting in the air. They grab Terry, dragging him into a separate shelter with 6 cells.

They throw him into a cell.

Guard: "You want to fight fugitive then fight him"!

Terry: "Fuck you, Fuck you"!

Cell Mate :"All that hollering is going to get you nowhere ". Holds out an cup of water.

Terry takes an breather...thinks about receiving anything from a stranger but it's hot and he's thirsty.

Terry takes the cup.

Terry finds him an place to sit, his mind races for the next couple hours.

Night has fallen and its finally cool enough to think straight.

Terry: "Where are we"? He asks the man.

Cell mate: "Where are we...Alabama ". He looks at Terry puzzled.

Terry: "Alabama...No I'm supposed to be back home"! Jumps up, talking to himself out loud.

Cell mate: "Where you from "?

Terry: "What you a fake ass lawyer or something , what's wit the suite"!

Cell mate: "I'm just the man of the people ,they say I would rowel up the other prisoners ,so they put me in here".

Terry: "Prisoners?...So this not an plantation "?

Cell mate: "Technically... yes it is an plantation "!

Terry: "Nigga are we slaves or is this jail"! Getting frustrated with the mans slow answers.

Cell mate: "Yes you are a slave, this is prison and don't call me nigger"!

Terry: "Whatever Holmes.. where you from"?

Cell mate: "Georgia "!

Terry: "OH yeah ..."! Terry hears commotion going down outside the cells, he's busy trying to get an good look.

Cell mate: "And you"?

Terry: "OH me...I'm from the sun chief "! Terry said with an smile.

The cell mate is taken back by his answer. An guard opens up the cell, then Yolanda shoots the guard in the face.

Alonzo: "What's up brother, you wasn't in here too long was you"!

Terry: "Way to long...You coming chief"? He says to his cell mate, the cell mate is hesitant. Minty, Will and Moses come walking down the hallway.

Minty: "Let's move"!

Moses: "Martin right"! He saids to the man.

Cell mate: "Who are you"!?

Alonzo and Terry look at each other.

Alonzo and Terry: "We The muthafukin Shadow Bragade "!!!

The end of Kemitt Mirrors vol.1 Feat :Visions "

Got an story to tell"

Kemitt mirrors Alonzo's Letter

If you're reading this text it means my world still exists and my boy TwinStreez got this letter to you.

I don't know how but he's the only person who can receive my messages.

Ever since me and T went through the time lapse our lives been turned inside out...first we had to realize the world we ended up in wasn't ours I mean a lot of things looked the same but different at the same time.

For instance, my homeboy Will in my world we know him as an all-around street hustler and his cousin Yola...well I know she was always smart and kind of wild...but in this parallel world they're soldiers climbing the ranks inside an secret team of mercenaries fighting an underground war against injustice, somehow me and my cousin Terry fell right in the middle of it.

In this world we been up against the most evil of beings I ever seen in my life that's including scary movies... maybe pieces of Lucifer himself but hey that's not for us to judge it's our job to stop'em before they cross worlds ...besides you wouldn't believe it unless you see it for yourself.

Terry and I main goal was to get back to our ordinary lives but the whole team just jumped again and we're still not home, I think I'm supposed to be sad but I'm not ...I actually feel this is where I'm supposed to be.

I walk with my family true guardians underground myth S.B. , Hand for an hand ,Eye for an Eye , may this Iron protect me!

P.s.

So now you and Twin the only ones that has our story... just in case...make sure its told the right way. Remember Living is life... on our way to bust Terry out of prison...once your read it you'll get it...see you in the next quadratum.

Yo Boy Lonzo
Muthf@#kin SHADOW BRAGADE!!
Derrik "Twin" Stro 513-815-7044

END OF KEMITT MIRRORS VOL.1 FEAT VISION'S

"Got A Story To Tell"